M000311856

THE OPPOSITE OF FALLING

jillian liota

This book is a work of fiction. While reference might be made to actual historical events or existing locations, the names, characters, places and incidents are either the product of the author's imagination or are used fictitiously, and any resemblance to any actual persons, living or dead, business establishments, events, or locales is entirely coincidental.

Copyright © 2020 by Jillian Liota

All rights reserved. In accordance with the U.S. Copyright Act of 1976, the scanning, uplo¬ading, and electronic sharing of any part of this book without the permission from the author is unlawful piracy and theft of the author's intellectual property. Thank you for your support of the author's rights.

Love Is A Verb Books

Book Cover Design and Layout by Jillian Liota

Editing by C. Marie

Formatting by Jillian Liota

Cover Photo © PeopleImages

Chapter Graphic © Freepik.com

ISBN 978-1-952549-06-9 (paperback)
ISBN 978-1-952549-07-6 (eBook)
ISBN 978-1-952549-08-3 (kindle)

to Cam and Marylou
for constantly demonstrating
just how badass women can be

CHAPTER ONE

Briar

I stare at the three available jobs advertised in the weekly paper with slumped shoulders, realizing with a staggering clarity just how bleak my prospects are.

I don't even think most newspapers have jobs in them anymore, but when you're looking for employment in a small town like Cedar Point, an online job system just seems superfluous. So, businesses like the craft store and the coffee shop and the grocery store advertise their open positions on flyers in their front windows—generally horribly designed, usually with fonts like Comic Sans or Papyrus—or in ads in the *Cedar Reader*.

Full-time nanny.

Weekend barista.

Grocery store cashier.

Those are my options.

If I'd moved home at the start of the summer, maybe I could have found something else. The tourist season in Cedar Point always tends to provide employment opportunities that at least sound enjoyable.

Lifeguard at South Bank Resort.
Counselor at Cedar Lake Summer Camp.
Bartender at Dock 7.

Back in high school, I worked a catch-all job at the community library, shelving returned books and cataloguing new ones, ordering supplies, leading a weekly class on basic computer skills for seniors. But the little spot at the end of Main Street that served as my haven was torn down a few years ago and replaced with a row of shops that are, admittedly, very cute and probably do good things for locals. A bakery. A cute little art gallery. A rustic home goods store with hand-painted signs and quilts and little tchotchkes that say things like *Life is better on the lake.*

I'm sure if I talked to my dad, he'd have some sort of insider knowledge of a job I could find that isn't listed in the *Reader*, but asking either of my parents for help kind of defeats the point of, well, not asking for any more help. They've already allowed me to move back into my childhood bedroom—a shame I never thought I'd have to face—in the wake of my recent breakup and decision to leave behind the life I'd created down the mountain. I can't *also* expect them to find me a job, too.

I'm back in Cedar Point. Single. Broke. Unemployed. And, if I'm honest, a little lonely and a lot lost. Moving home with my tail between my legs definitely wasn't something I ever could have envisioned, but that's just life. I need to accept the circumstances I'm faced with, no matter how distasteful they might be, and that includes working whatever job will pay me, even if it doesn't sound like my cup of tea.

I cross out the nanny job I'm not qualified for and mark an X through the barista position that won't be enough hours, circling the full-time cashier job at One Stop Shop with a bold red pen.

Truthfully, it's the only choice if I'm going to get some serious hours under my belt, even if it *is* minimum wage.

A job is a job, and money is money. The last thing I want—even less than having to move home—is to leech off of my parents for any longer than I absolutely have to. My mom and dad are two of the most generous and loving people out there, and it wouldn't feel right to take advantage of the fact that they'd be more than happy to take care of me. They usually manage a pretty good balance between nudging us kids out of the nest to face the world and providing a safe space to come home to when that world is as cruel as can be.

Even so, that doesn't mean I shouldn't still pull on my big-girl panties and get my butt to work.

Besides, my younger sister lives at home, too, and Bellamy manages a part-time waitressing job along with a full load of college classes online; she'd never let me live it down if I chose to laze around the house all day for months.

Speaking of my sister…

"Can I borrow your car?"

Bellamy pauses, a tortilla chip with an aggressive amount of salsa hovering in midair as she looks over to me and lifts a brow.

"Where are you going?"

I nibble on the inside of my cheek as I decide what to say.

My younger sister gives off the vibe of a totally rambunctious ball-busting 21-year-old, but she's a lot more observant than she lets on. She's been watching me wander almost aimlessly around the house since I moved home about a month ago, and I'm sure it hasn't gone unnoticed that I haven't gone anywhere in town even once.

Nowhere requiring a car, at least. I don't need to drive if I'm running the trails, which has been my primary method of relieving stress since I was in junior high. Other than that, I've stuck close to the house, preferring to avoid any unwanted run-ins with curious townies who are likely to have questions about why the eldest Mitchell daughter has suddenly moved home.

Regardless, it makes sense for my sister to be curious if I'm wanting to borrow her wheels.

"One Stop. Need anything?"

I know I could tell her I'm applying for a job, but I'm not in the mood for the trail of questions that will come in the wake of revealing the fact that I'm planning on sticking around for a while. Telling my sister I left my ex and my old life behind with basically nothing to my name is a conversation for another day.

Or never.

"Nah, I'm good," she says, stuffing another chip into her mouth and returning her eyes to her computer.

"Okay. I'll be back soon."

She waves a hand but doesn't look in my direction again, her eyes already scanning whatever she's staring at on her screen. "Don't worry about it. I've got my first test tomorrow so I'm not going anywhere. Take your time."

I head out of the kitchen and through the living room, stopping in the entry to nab the last pair of car keys on the little table by the door.

Realistically, I could take the one-mile stretch of road between our house and town and walk to One Stop in about twenty minutes. I don't *need* a car to get there, and since I've never owned my own car—my ex and I used to share his—I'm used to having to walk or bike to get places I need to be.

But as I pull out of the front drive and head in the opposite direction of town, opting to take the longer route around Cedar

Lake with the windows down and the country CD Bellamy likes to keep in her stereo on blast, I decide I need to do this more often. Instantly, I feel like I can breathe deeper, and I take my time enjoying the sun on my face and the wind in my hair.

I don't know why, but visiting my hometown has always made me feel a little itchy, like I'm being shoved into an old flannel shirt that's too small. It makes me feel shitty, especially because I really do love my family, and I know my mom works hard to make my childhood home feel warm and welcoming.

My sister loves living here and never wanted to leave, and I'd bet money that my three other siblings will return at some point, even if they're off exploring and doing other things right now. Me? I've always known living in a small town just isn't something I'm interested in.

Sure, there's something whimsical and wonderful about the small, lakeside town where I grew up. Cedar Point is tucked away in the Tahoe National Forest, a pass-through between the much larger cities of Sacramento and Lake Tahoe. It's a beautiful place to live if you enjoy having to drive an hour to go to the movies, are happy with only having two options for places to go out to eat, and don't mind shitty cell service.

Okay, that's not fair.

There are lots of wonderful things about my hometown. It's a friendly community filled with locals who are legitimately invested in where they live. There's the obvious benefit of living on a beautiful lake, the calming scent of pine and cedar trees, and the fantastic hiking trails and outdoorsy activities you can only find in the mountains.

But there's something about small-town life that's just always felt…well, small, I guess. So the *second* I was able to move away, I was out of here like a shot, off to the bright lights of San

Francisco as fast as my long legs could carry me.

My parents were sad to see me go, but they were much happier with my choice to live three hours away than with my brother Boyd's cross-country move to Boston. Thankfully, he took the brunt of their frustration, and by the time I turned 18 a year after he did, mom and dad pretty much gave me a thumbs-up as I drove out of town to go to college down the mountain.

I just knew getting outside of Cedar Point would finally make me happy. I didn't know who I was or what I wanted to do, but I had lots of ideas. Big ideas and big plans for the big life I was going to live in the big city.

Yeah.

Pretty much nothing has gone according to plan.

As I round the farthest point of the lake and begin to move closer to town, I breathe in the crispness of the late summer air. The first official day of fall is next week, and I can already feel the weather starting to change, which is one of the few things I really do miss about living in Cedar Point.

Seasons.

California is a desert. Everything on TV and in the movies makes it seem like all Californians live at the beach and enjoy sunny weather year-round.

All. Lies.

The summers are dry and hot, with temperatures rising up to 115 degrees on the really bad days, and there's hardly any wind if you live inland and away from the beach cities.

And then there are the crazy dips in temperature during winter, though only at night. During the day, it still cranks up into the 80s and 90s, making it necessary to constantly carry around a backup sweatshirt in case the weather suddenly changes.

Ultimately, California's seasons can be summed up in just a

few words.

Summer. Fire season. False winter. And spring—oh wait, just kidding, it's already summer again.

Living in Cedar Point is unlike any other part of California. It's like a completely different world, which means I get to experience my favorite season.

Autumn.

I love when the foliage begins to change. Even though the majority of trees around the lake and in Tahoe National Forest are evergreens, there are still enough deciduous trees sprinkled in, the ones that get the orange, red, and yellow leaves, to make it really feel like fall.

If I'm going to be back at home for a while, at least I get to enjoy the best time of year. It means I'll get to wear sweaters and scarves and the temperature will dip enough to enjoy coffee on the back patio in the morning. Mom and I can go get warm apple cinnamon donuts like we used to do when I was in high school.

As I pull up in front of One Stop Shop, I admire the way the sugar maple trees lining Main Street are starting to show just the barest hints of orange and red. I take a deep breath, trying to remember that life could be crazier. Things could be worse. I made a choice to leave my old life behind. It's only natural for it to take a while to figure out what's next.

You're not stuck here forever, I remind myself. *Just until you figure things out.*

When I see Andrew Marshall walking toward me from the back, I'm unsurprised by the little shiver that rolls through me when he sends a charming smile my way. Though he's always been an attractive guy, I don't remember him being quite so… muscly. Or tall. Like a slightly younger Henry Cavill.

It's been a while since I've seen the grocery owner's son. He was in the athletic crowd with my brother Boyd, which meant he came over to our house for dinner a lot and ruffled the top of my head like I was a puppy instead of a teenage girl with hearts in her eyes.

Mostly I remember Boyd and all his friends as a group of guys who liked to spend their time in pointless competition with each other over *everything*. Physical activities. Major league sports. Drinking challenges. Even dating was practically a sport, and I can remember quite a few nights when I'd sit at the top of the stairs and listen to Boyd's friends talk about the girls from school like they were playing tug of war.

Andy, though…he was different. Charming, sure, but genuine in a way the rest of their friends—sans Boyd—never were. He always had that kind of warmth to him that was incredibly disarming, and I looked at him like he'd hung the damn moon.

It's hard *not* to notice a guy like Andy Marshall.

6'2" with a swimmer's build and a smile that sends a bowling ball through my stomach. The thing I found most attractive was when he studied at our house and wore a pair of glasses as he read from his textbooks. On days like those, I might have made several trips to the bathroom or kitchen or who the hell cared, just so I could make extra passes by Boyd's bedroom to see Andy hunched over a book with those black rims on—not that I ever let *him* catch on to my observations.

The way I felt about Andy back in high school was this frustrating dichotomy I could never seem to manage. Wishing I had his attention yet fleeing the room any time he came over. Day-dreaming about the day he'd notice me then just staring at him blankly when he'd actually ask me a question.

Though it wouldn't have mattered even if I *had* tried to find a way to get on his radar. High school boys go after girls who think flirting is part of the curriculum, the ones who develop boobs early and drive down the mountain to buy makeup on the weekends and know how to throw their hair over their shoulders with a seductive smile.

By the time I hit the ninth grade, I was taller than most of the boys in my class. Nobody teaches you how to be the bean-stalk, and I struggled with some insecurities that I dealt with by keeping to the outskirts, choosing things that were a little nerd-ier and a lot more autonomous.

Working at the library.

Running on the cross country team.

Volunteering at the nursing home.

If nobody looked my way, I could avoid the attention I so desperately did *not* want.

Eventually, I got over that incredibly awkward stage once I left for college. That long-ago interest in Andy, though…it hasn't ever faded away. Not when I had that weasel of a boyfriend in high school. Not when I moved away for college. Not even when I moved in with and then got engaged to my ex, Chad.

Andy might not be a person I think about often, but he can still cause a pretty hefty swoop in my stomach when he comes to mind, that sensation you get when you accidentally step off a curb.

Sometime back in college, after having a few of my own shitty experiences with men and watching many of my friends go through the same, I began to realize I'm not a big fan of that heart-in-your-throat kind of feeling. It always seemed to lead to nothing but heartache.

Unfortunately, that perspective doesn't seem to stop my mind and body from reacting whenever I see Andy Marshall.

Like now, as he walks toward me wearing a pair of well-worn jeans and a dark red polo with the One Stop logo on the left sleeve. Damn if he doesn't look like he could grace the cover of a magazine. Strong jaw, artfully messy hair, and a little bit of stubble. All of that topping off a long, lean frame that looks both strong and soft at the same time.

I look away from him, embarrassed by my train of thought.

Strong and soft? I can't remember *ever* thinking about a man like that before. Certainly not Chad, that's for sure. My ex is a nice-looking guy, but he never elicited those kinds of feelings in me at just a glance, even back in the beginning. And I preferred it that way.

I clear my throat and try to shove my weird thoughts to the side. Ogling Andy is the last thing I need to be doing in this moment. I'm here to get a job, and I'd do well to remember that.

"Briar Mitchell," he says once he's finally a few feet away from me, tucking his hands into the pockets of his worn Levi's. "Long time, no see."

I try to give him a friendly smile that doesn't hint at where my mind was roving just a second ago, though I'm sure whatever expression I'm wearing looks less easygoing and more *What's that smell?*

Relaxed conversation has never been my strong suit.

"Hey, Andy."

"Good to see you. How's the fam?"

I lift a shoulder. "Pretty good. Same old, you know."

"Ah, that's not what I hear," he responds, that grin on his face growing slightly. "Word around town is that you've moved back."

I nibble on the inside of my cheek, wishing people weren't so damn talkative.

"Yeah," is all I offer as an explanation, choosing to sidestep any gossip that might arise from going into further detail. I don't need the town tongues to start wagging any more than they probably already are. "And I'm looking for a job, if you haven't filled that cashier position."

His eyebrows rise and he rocks back on his heels, as if I've stunned him.

"Briar Mitchell wants to work at One Stop?" he says, surprise and disbelief coloring his voice. "Never thought I'd see something like *that* happen."

I frown, his words hitting a place in my chest that I don't like.

"What's that supposed to mean?"

Andy lets out a laugh that's one part humor and much more than a dash of condescension, his laidback demeanor shifting away from friendly as he crosses his arms over his chest. "You don't have somewhere better to be than bagging groceries for the little people of Cedar Point?"

My nostrils flare, but I push back my irritation at how quickly he's decided to put me into a box he thinks he understands.

"I came in here looking for a job," I reply, my voice low even though the store is completely empty apart from the two of us and Lois, the sixty-something-year-old cashier who was reading *The National Enquirer* at her check stand when I walked in the front a few minutes ago. "Is it company policy to mock potential employees?"

He drops his hands down to his hips and pins me with a look that dismisses me outright. "You're not a potential employee, Briar. You're bored and looking for a way to get your parents off your back. I'm not looking to hire someone who will just waste my time, require a bunch of training and handholding, and then quit once she's bored."

My entire body bristles at his words.

I don't know what I've ever done to deserve Andy's ire. As far back as I can remember, he's always been approachable and warm. At the very least, I assumed being the younger sister of one of his best friends from high school would assure me some sort of friendliness, as surface level as it might be.

Clearly, I was wrong on all accounts.

My face is flushed red, and his sharp barbs have lanced me with embarrassment, not only regarding the fact that I've had to move home, but also due to what seems to be his opinion that I'm a lazy snob who thinks she's too good for a minimum-wage cashier position.

I should tell him exactly what I think. I should tell him he should give me a chance before judging me so harshly. That he's wrong in his assumptions. That he has no idea what the hell he's talking about.

But I've never been good with my words, so I don't do any of those things.

Instead, I turn away and march out of the store, flight being my chosen response when faced with the choice between being belittled in the middle of the grocery store or hightailing it out of the line of fire.

I'm normally really good at regulating my emotions. It's rare for me to be in a position that causes me to feel a significant emotional surge—positive or negative—that I'm not expecting.

And because I'm usually really good at anticipating things, I'm able to avoid letting my emotions get the best of me in situations like my interaction with Andy.

But never in my wildest dreams could I have imagined those statements coming out of Andy Marshall's mouth, completely unprovoked.

What the hell did I ever do to him?

When I moved back to Cedar Point, I assumed I'd be leaving my feelings of unhappiness and inadequacy behind, not storming out of the grocery store, swallowing down the same kinds of sensations my ex elicited from me for so long.

Maybe I'm overreacting. Maybe I'm reading too much into what Andy said. But I swore to myself when I moved home not too long ago that I'd never allow myself to feel small ever again.

Oh, how quickly I was proven wrong.

CHAPTER TWO

Andy

"You're still here?"

I turn my head at the sound of Lois' voice, giving her a tired smile that requires all of my effort.

"That's what happens when you're the boss," I say, trying to infuse some levity into my tone even knowing the joke will fall flat.

As expected, Lois gives me a sympathetic look, the wrinkles around her eyes becoming more pronounced as she watches me.

"How's your dad doin'?"

The inevitable question.

It's the same one just about everybody I know asks me on a daily basis. I want to tell them all the truth—that he's a shell of his former self and I'm barely keeping it all together—but I know my father would never forgive me if I told anyone what's really going on at home.

So instead of being honest, I just bob my head and keep that smile on my face, returning my eyes to the computer screen that's been making my vision blur for the past few hours.

"He's alright, Lois. Doing a lot better."

She nods and gives me another look that says she wishes there were something she could do.

But there isn't. There isn't anything anyone can do.

"I'll lock the front on my way out," she tells me, giving a little wave as she heads down the hallway leading out of the stockroom and offices at the back of One Stop.

Once she's gone, I let out a long sigh and push my hands through my hair, which is badly in need of a trim, then I lean back in my seat, trying to give my body a good stretch. I've been sitting here for hours looking over the numbers, and it doesn't seem to matter how I break things down or move them around.

We're just in a shit situation.

I told my dad I wasn't sure building out the store was the right thing to do. Cedar Point is a small town and has only grown by about a hundred residents in the past decade. Some new residents, sure, but mostly current residents having babies. And babies don't buy groceries.

Somehow, though, he got it in his head that having more space meant more options, and more options meant customers would spend more money.

The plan was to build out the north-facing wall, adding an additional thousand square feet to our building.

"Something for us to build together," he'd told me. "You'll make your own mark on the store."

A week after that first wall came down, he had a heart attack.

That was four months ago, and I'm only just now finishing what my dad and I started together because I finally broke down this summer and asked some locals for help putting up the framing and exterior walls. Then I spent three weeks finishing up the interior. Insulation, electrical, drywall, painting—all things I had just enough knowledge of to do wrong the first time, backtrack, do some research, and then try again.

Now that the buildout is finally finished and all the new shelving is getting installed, it's time to order all the boxed and canned goods to fill the space. The problem, though, is that I don't know where my dad's mind was at when he made his decision, because by *my* calculations and forecasts, there's pretty much no flexing our budget to make the purchases to fill the new shelves unless I want to open a new credit card and incur some debt.

Add to that the fact that we're in desperate need of at least one new full-time cashier, possibly one or two new baggers, and the piping in the bathroom is due for a compliance upgrade, and the numbers on the screen in front of me are just enough to make me want to pick up the computer and chuck it in the bin.

I let out another long sigh, stretching my neck from left to right and then shaking out my arms.

Come on, Andy. Keep it positive. Don't let yourself get down.

Instead of shutting things off and flipping the lights so I can head home to my dog and my bed, I decide to renew my efforts and take another crack at sorting out the budget that has been so difficult to navigate today.

There has to be a way to make this work, something I'm not seeing, a workaround that will help me find the funds to do the thing my dad thought would be a great decision for the family business.

If only he were back to being his normal self, maybe this wouldn't feel so damn daunting. I'd be able to sit him down and ask him to go through the budget with me, to point out what I'm so clearly missing.

Then I want to kick myself for even thinking that in the first place. It isn't dad's fault he isn't 'back to normal' yet. A heart attack will knock the wind out of anybody's sails for a while. I'm lucky he's even alive, and I'd do well to remind myself of that.

Sure, his recovery isn't going as well as I would like. He might be facing some additional…challenges that neither of us were expecting, but eventually, he'll get there.

I hope.

And it's not like I'm only working at One Stop because he's laid up at home. I've been working here since I was in high school. I was going to take over from him at some point. I've always known it, and I'm happy to do it. One Stop Shop is my family legacy, and I'm proud to be part of a business that serves the community where I was born and raised.

I love Cedar Point. I've lived here my entire life, and there's nowhere else I'd rather be. Sure, there are some pretty spectacular places around the world that are probably great places to live. I like traveling and exploring God's green earth just as much as the next guy.

But Cedar Point is that spectacular place for me, and I've always liked the idea of working with my old man then taking over from him someday. Having a family and raising them here, so they can get the same awesome small-town experience I did.

Stepping into my dad's shoes in the wake of his health complications happened a lot faster than I was expecting, though. And if I'm completely honest with myself—because hell if I'm gonna say this to anybody else—I know I'm not entirely ready to manage everything on my own just yet, at least not to the standard my dad has. There are a lot of things I've been navigating that I never would have thought to prepare for.

Like the buildout. Like finding space in the budget for new

employees and plumbing improvements. Like wondering how we're going to stock our new shelves.

But I guess that's the thing about life—it continues to happen whether you're ready or not. You just have to roll up your sleeves and dig in to whatever comes your way.

I click through the spreadsheet again, trying to make myself think outside the box. Maybe if I move…those funds from there over to…nope. Still not going to work.

It's times like these when I wish I'd actually gone to school and gotten that degree like my mom always wanted me to do. She used to tell me getting college experience and spending a few more years learning from business-savvy minds would benefit me in the long run.

As a person who never enjoyed the academic part of being a student, I had plenty of excuses for why that wasn't the right decision for me. Mostly, though, I was convinced that there was nobody better to teach me than my old man. He's been working at One Stop since *he* was in high school. Nobody knows it better than him.

Now I'm realizing just how shortsighted I was to assume my dad would always be around to talk to, and how many things I don't know that will be hard for him to teach me without some of the knowledge a business degree might have provided.

Every so often, I consider going back. Maybe online, so I don't have to leave town to do it. But right now just isn't a good time, especially with how difficult things have been. With the buildout, the employee transition, regular operations, *and* how much work it is to take care of dad, there's no way I could pick up college coursework as well.

Another hour crawls by and proves completely fruitless, so I tell myself it's okay to take a break for the night, choosing to give my mind a much-needed breather rather than suffer alone any longer.

I go through the routine of shutting everything down in my office and the stockroom then make my way through the store toward the front, eyeing the cooler we had repaired last week to make sure I don't spy any new leaks.

A million little things that constantly need my attention.

Leaving work was supposed to give my mind a break, but when I unlock the front door, step outside, and turn to lock it again, my eyes fall on the sign announcing that we're hiring a new cashier. My shoulders fall, remembering my conversation earlier today with Briar Mitchell.

Damn if she wasn't a blast from the past.

I don't remember Boyd's younger sister being such a knock-out. Sure, I've seen her a few times since high school, here and there over the years when she'd come back to town to visit her family. I mean, she's a Mitchell—their family literally founded the town, so everybody knows who they are. Our families have been friends for years, and Boyd and I have been pretty damn close since before I can even remember.

But I haven't actually *talked* to Briar since…well, damn, it's been an entire decade since we've said more than a few words to each other in passing.

And pretty much the first thing I did was insult and belittle her when she came to apply for a job.

I wince at my own assholery and finish locking up then start the short walk around the building to the parking lot in the back.

My memories of Briar are pretty patchy. I just remember her being kind of a Bambi: wide eyes and long, wobbly legs she never looked too confident on, pretty skittish, always rushing out of the room whenever Boyd would have a group of us over.

Well, the long legs part is still true, as are the eyes. But damn if I didn't feel a little bowled over when I came out to the front and saw her standing there, waiting for me.

I wasn't sure who she was at first since she was slightly turned away, facing the cooler at the front we keep stocked with flowers and cakes for special occasions. Then she turned to look at me, and it felt like a slow-rolling wave of realization. It started in my mind then kicked up my pulse and sent a wave of heat through my entire body.

Briar was a surprise today, that's for sure.

Shaking my head, I tap once on the back of my Jeep before yanking the door open and climbing inside. Then I crank up some country and make the ten-minute drive home, enjoying the way the wind hits me as I cruise alongside the lake and try to sort through what the hell happened earlier today.

I don't know what's going on in *her* life right now that's caused her to move home and need a minimum-wage job working as a grocery store cashier, but no matter what it is, I'm sure my words didn't make anything easier.

As the music plays and I enjoy the evening breeze in my face, I try to think over what I actually remember about Briar Mitchell.

I'm pretty sure I remember Boyd saying something about her working at the old library back when we were younger, but I can't be sure if that was Briar or someone else. I know she likes to run and she moved away for college in San Francisco, but that's pretty much the extent of my knowledge about my old friend's younger sister—*one* of his younger sisters.

The only real memory I have of Briar that I can play back in my head as if it were happening on a movie screen is from the day she left Cedar Point. She and one of her friends—the one she left town with—stopped in at One Stop to grab some snacks for their drive to San Francisco.

I was still bagging groceries at the time, and I was putting their chips and sodas into paper sacks. Her friend was flirting with me—far too obviously—when I overheard her say something about the two of them moving away.

"Oh, that's right. You're moving to college," I said to Briar, having heard bits and pieces about it from her mom, Patty, during her weekly shopping trips over the summer. "You excited?"

Briar kind of stared at me for a second before she answered, her face an odd combination of wariness and determination. "Yes."

"You sure you don't wanna stick around here instead?" I teased. "I bet I could get you a job working here with me and Lois. It's incredibly glamorous."

At my joke, Briar's face pinched, like she'd swallowed something sour. "That sounds like my worst nightmare. I'll pass."

I remember feeling almost shocked by her response. I knew Boyd had been eager to leave, to move away and spread his wings, but it always seemed like small-town life would be a good fit for Briar. I didn't know her *that* well, but I couldn't picture her enjoying a big city or major university. She'd get lost, surely.

"Neither of us want to stick around this hellhole," Briar's friend said. "We're trying to get out of here, and you couldn't pay us enough to stick around and bag groceries."

Briar nudged her friend, then, hissing her name. Rebecca, I think it might have been.

She rolled her eyes, grabbed the paper bag out of my hands, and then threw up two fingers. "Peace out, bag boy. See you

21

never."

"Sorry about that," Briar said as her friend went out to their car without her. "Rebecca hates it here, and she can be a little intense."

Lois snorted. "That's an understatement."

I don't remember what prompted me to ask, but I felt compelled to get an answer. "You hate it here, too?"

She stood straight then, looking me right in the eye. "I don't want to be stuck here for my whole life."

If anything was said after that, I can't remember what it was. All I know for sure is that it was one of the first times I'd actually felt irritation at someone for not feeling the same way about Cedar Point as I always had. Why it happened with Briar, I have no idea. We were friendly, I thought, but we weren't friends. It shouldn't have mattered if she felt like all of Cedar Point should burn to the ground.

But it did matter.

So maybe that's what my little asshole moment earlier today was about, some sort of internalized resentment toward a person who wanted to move away ten years ago.

I roll my eyes as I make the turn onto Brooks Road. Good to know I was a dick to someone because they had an opinion that had exactly nothing to do with me.

Today must have just been a shitty day, because I am *not* a guy who holds grudges. I'm normally easygoing and friendly. The only thing I can assume is that the stress at home is making me feel a bit more on edge about everything else, maybe a little more bitter and resentful than usual.

That said, my own internal issues don't give me an excuse to be an asshole, and that's exactly what I was—an asshole. I was rude, and possibly even hurtful, two things I don't stand for.

And two things Briar didn't deserve.

When I pull down our driveway and along the stretch of dirt that leads toward the garage, I can see there aren't any lights on at the main house, and my shoulders fall. Glancing at the clock, I see it's barely past eight. He's been doing this a lot, getting into bed before it's completely dark, his sleeping patterns getting longer and more dysfunctional as time goes on.

I'm starting to get legitimately concerned. I've read that anxiety and depression are common during recovery from a heart attack, but I assumed it would be a little less laughter or a bit more stress. This lack of interest in anything, this kind of checked-out behavior and inability to muster up the energy for getting up and moving around…it's scary. It's a mental challenge he's facing that I don't understand or know how to help with.

As much as I take after my dad and have that same constant positivity that usually defines him, it's gotten harder and harder to muster up a smile when I know he's at home struggling to find the energy to bathe for the first time in a week.

It's just a lot. A lot to take in, a lot to handle, a lot to work through. Mentally and physically and emotionally.

Like now. What I want to do is go inside my own place, throw on a ball game I've recorded, and just chill with a beer. Take a break from the growing stress at work. But I know I need to go over to my dad's and pick up the mess he's left around the house, do his dishes, start a load of laundry for him, and feed Percival. I need to make sure my dad is okay, and just that knowledge makes me want to sink down into the ground and never get up.

Because it's been four months of this. Four months of my jovial, perky father—who has weathered some of life's shittier storms—being the absolute antithesis of himself.

And handling it alone…handling *everything* alone just feels like too much.

"Hey dad, you awake?" I call out as I walk in his front door.

In the first few months, I used to be really quiet when I came over, not wanting to disturb him. Tiptoeing around to make sure he got all the rest he wanted. Now though, I feel like I need to make noise and inject life into this house again.

What I'd like to do is crank the stereo up to full volume, but that might be pushing things a little too far. I don't want to give the man *another* heart attack.

Flipping on the lights, I let out a long, sad sigh at the sight before me. Plates of barely eaten food on the coffee table, empty cans of soda and beer scattered throughout the room, some of them crumpled and on the carpet. All the blinds are pulled closed, and the room is musty with a faint hint of body odor.

Percival stands and stretches along the back of the old checkered couch that has been in the same spot since before I can remember, yawning and letting out a little meow.

"Hey buddy," I say, walking over and giving him a good scratch behind the ears. "I'll feed you in a minute, okay?"

He meows again then hops off the couch, heading for the kitchen in anticipation of the meal coming his way. I walk through the living room and down the hall, continuing to turn the lights on as I go and wishing the brightness could do something to help put the light back into my old man, even though I know it won't.

"Dad?" I say, knocking once on his bedroom door. "You awake?"

Pushing it open, I watch as the light from the hall stretches across the floor until it hits where he rests in his bed, curled on his side and snuggling the same pillow he's had next to him since mom died.

It always breaks something inside of me when I see him like that. Obviously, I miss my mother. She was an amazing person, kind and caring and teasing and loving.

But she and my dad were best friends. They had the kind of love you read about, the kind I can only hope exists in my future somewhere. I know living in a world without her in it is hard for him in a way I just don't understand.

Which is why I think the heart attack—and being holed up in the hospital for a few days when it happened—has had such a negative effect on him. I think it reminded him of losing her, made him remember the weeks spent in a hospital room just like his, at her side. It reiterated that she's not here anymore.

I think it made him wish he was with her instead.

The light on his face is enough to have him shifting a bit, his eyes peeking open to look at me before he shuts them again and tucks his face into the pillow.

"Hey, old man," I say, infusing as much enthusiasm into my words as I can. "Let's get you some dinner."

"Not hungry," he mumbles.

"I know you're not, but we both know you need to eat something. You didn't eat even half of your lunch."

There's a long silence before I see him start to move around in a way that tells me he's going to join me. It's a relief knowing I won't have to argue with him about getting out of bed, though I'll have to wait and see if he actually eats anything when he sits down for dinner.

"I'll be in the kitchen," I say, knowing it'll take at least ten minutes for him to muster the energy to get out of bed and out to the table.

I head down the hall and back to the living area, making

quick work of picking up the plates and trash scattered around, opting to drop all of the leftovers into the trash instead of putting them in the fridge. I made a tuna casserole last night—one of mom's old recipes—and came by at lunch to heat up some leftovers for him. He left it almost completely untouched on the plate.

Maybe resorting to mom's cookbook was a mistake, but I'm desperate to get him out of this funk and back to the functioning world, and I'm willing to try just about anything.

By the time my dad drops heavily into the wooden chair at the small round dining table that's seen better days, twenty minutes have passed. I've changed over a load of laundry, picked up the living room, wiped down the kitchen, fed and watered Percival, and boiled some noodles to make garlic and butter pasta, one of my favorites as a kid and an easy dinner on a night when I just don't have the energy to make something more complicated.

"Smell good?" I ask, setting a bowl and fork in front of him, along with a glass of water.

My dad just blinks and stares at it, not responding.

We used to talk about everything. Work. Friends. We had dinner together several nights a week and spent hours laughing and shooting the shit. He'd tease me about whatever girl I was dating at the time, and I'd razz him about finding a new woman to spend the rest of his own life with.

Now, it's work just getting him to give one-word responses.

He takes a few bites, mostly just moving the pasta around in his bowl before he gets up without saying anything and heads back to his room.

Back to the dark hole where he likes to hide.

I finish up my meal as quickly as I can, barely even tasting it through the frustration and helplessness that coats every inch of my body, then make quick work of washing up the few dishes I used.

"Hey dad, I'm heading back to my place, okay?" I say, cracking open his bedroom door again.

I'm met with the soft sound of his snoring.

Well, at least he's actually asleep and not just lying there staring at the wall.

I give Percival another scratch, wishing my dad's cat got along better with my dog Quincy so I could bring him over to my place for a while. I know there's no way the cat is getting the attention he's accustomed to.

Or who knows? Maybe Percival is the one living creature that's actually happy about the fact that my dad has basically shut himself away. Cats are weirdos like that.

I always wanted to move out when I was younger, envisioning a roommate or two and a party here or there. Ultimately, I decided to stick around the fifteen-acre lot at the end of Brooks Road, opting to move into the apartment over my parents' garage instead of moving into a house that belongs to someone else.

Sure, living only a football field away from my childhood home has a few cons, not as much privacy being the main one, but the benefits are plenty.

My rent money goes to my dad, who is hoping to retire in the next few years. I still get the independence of being in a separate unit since the garage is detached, and now that my dad has been dealing with these health issues, it makes it easier for me to be around and helpful without having to drive if he needs me for something urgent.

I don't intend to live here forever. At some point, I'd like to settle down, have a family, purchase my own home. But for now, this works.

Besides, it's not like I've had much free time to go out and try to meet anybody. Hell, I've barely even had more than a few nights when I felt like going out with friends. All of my time has been spent either at work or with dad or trying to get just a single minute to myself.

I shake my head, realizing I am in serious need of getting my butt out of the house and to The Mitch to interact with someone besides my dad and the people at work. Cracking open a beer at the town dive bar with Rusty, one of my friends from high school, might be just what the doctor ordered.

When I finally make it through my own front door, I'm just about knocked over by Quincy, my four-year-old Boykin Spaniel.

"Hey, sweet girl," I say, dropping down and giving her some pets, laughing at the intense licks she gives my face. "Let's take you out for a little bit, yeah?"

I grab her lead just in case I need it then head out to the lot along the back of our house, Quincy bounding down the steps with a quickness and grace only a dog can manage. The stretch of land behind the garage is covered in damp forest floor and filled with the beautiful incense cedars that provide Cedar Point and Cedar Lake with their names.

Quincy charges out into the darkness, farther than I can see, probably taking care of her business and enjoying the fresh air after being inside since I came home at lunch time to feed dad and let her out.

As I wait for my girl to sniff around and chase after squirrels, my mind wanders back to my conversation with Briar earlier today, still unable to let go of how it went.

The way she looked at me when I said that last bit, about the handholding and her getting bored...she looked like I'd about smacked her in the face. Surprise, yes, but a wounded look in her eyes that I doubt I'll be able to forget any time soon. Just thinking it over, that pit in my stomach grows, tightens.

I kick at a fallen branch with the tip of my shoe, knowing I need to do some backtracking but unsure of exactly how to go about it. Briar isn't the same kid she was ten years ago, that kind of skittish energy seeming to be long gone. Still, that doesn't mean she's likely to come back to One Stop any time soon.

No. If I want to apologize and explain myself, I'm going to have to go to her.

It's been a while since the last time I went by the Mitchells' house, but the place is as familiar to me as my own home, having spent many of my teenage years running in and out and down to the lake with Boyd. It should only take about ten minutes to get there, and when I look at my watch, I decide it's not too late to try to get this done tonight.

Never go to bed without clearing your conscience. That's what my mom always told me, and I'll find it hard to settle down for the night, remembering that look on Briar's face and knowing what I said has gone uncorrected.

I rub at my arms, the late-summer evening air beginning to chill slightly, just enough to think it's time to start bringing a jacket with me when I go into work.

"Come on, Quincy," I call out, smiling softly to myself when I hear the sound of her paws racing through the woods as she returns to me. "I have some crow I need to eat."

CHAPTER THREE

Briar

It's after ten when I see bright lights flash across my bedroom wall, followed by the sound of tires rolling over the gravel drive outside.

I set my pen down on the desk and cross the room, my fingers shifting the sheer curtains to the side so I can peer out the window. I have no idea who would be coming to the house so late, which is why surprise rolls through me when I see an old, forest green Jeep I haven't seen in years pull to a stop next to my dad's car.

Is that...Andy?

Sure enough, the door pops open and Andy Marshall steps out, wearing the same outfit he had on earlier, followed by a dog that happily hops onto the grass.

My eyes narrow, even as confusion wars with my emotions.

Why is he here?

I pull the curtain even farther to the side, unlatching my window and lifting it up so I can get his attention. I have no interest in waiting around for Andy to knock on the front door and inevitably wake up my parents, who are apparently in their late nineties if the fact that they get into bed around nine every night is any indicator.

Calling out his name, making sure to keep my voice fairly quiet so as not to wake anybody, I watch as his eyes rise and scan the road-facing wall of our house until he spots me.

"Hey," he says, smiling with something that looks oddly sheepish and stepping a few feet closer to my window. "Can I talk to you for a minute?"

"About what?"

He looks off to the side for a second before looking back up at me. "Just... Can you come down? It won't take that long."

I weigh it in my mind for a second, ultimately deciding I should at least try to avoid having whatever this awkward conversation will be through my window.

"I'll be down in a second. Go around to the deck."

He nods then calls out to his dog and walks toward the side of the house that will lead him around to the lake-facing deck and lawn.

I re-close my window, briefly trying to remember if I've ever had occasion to open it for anything other than catching a breeze. I know Boyd used to sneak his high school girlfriend in and out through his, à la *Dawson's Creek*, but I didn't have any reason to do such a thing—though I'm sure my high school boyfriend would have liked it if I'd initiated such a thing.

I roll my eyes at the thought of Nick Riley, the only guy I've ever cried over in my entire life. He was definitely a mistake I decided I would never make again.

Setting aside my thoughts about my one shitty high school relationship, I remind myself that Andy Marshall is waiting downstairs for me—words I *never* thought I'd say, regardless of the circumstances.

I glance down at my attire—flannel pajama bottoms and a zip-up hoodie—then quickly remind myself that I'm not in the market for male attention right now so it doesn't matter what the hell I look like. Then I slip out of my bedroom and move quietly down the hall, careful not to let my feet pad too heavily on the landing at the top where my sister's bedroom is.

I can see light coming out from under her door, and I have no intention of explaining why I'm creeping down the stairs so late. I might be 27, but that doesn't mean it's easy to dismiss the rules of my parents' house.

Once I reach the sliding door off the kitchen that leads out toward the lake, I stop for a second, just watching as Andy sits in one of the padded chairs, his adorable dog waiting excitedly between his legs as Andy gives it some ear scratches.

Something about seeing him with an animal has my hackles lowering, the part of me that was so enamored with Andy when I was younger fighting to crawl to the surface. It's hard to look at a man you used to secretly obsess over as he loves on his dog and *not* swoon.

But I manage.

When I pull the sliding door open and slip outside, Andy's head turns in my direction at the sound. I close it behind me, then tuck my hands in my hoodie pockets and set my shoulders, waiting for him to say whatever he came here for.

I want to ask him why he's here, why he would ever come here so late at night to talk to me, but I stay quiet. He doesn't need to know I'm eager for that information, doesn't need to be made aware that a little voice inside of me is praying he can somehow take back his earlier words so the younger me can go back to quietly admiring him from afar.

Another long beat passes before he drops his eyes down and looks at his dog.

"Have you ever met Quincy?"

My brow furrows, wondering how his dog has anything to do with why he's here.

"No."

Andy shakes his head. "I didn't think so. I only got her two years ago, and I don't think I've really talked to you at all in a long time."

I stay silent, choosing not to comment on the fact that I can't remember us *ever* having any kind of conversation.

The things I remember about Andy are the way it made me feel to watch him walk around shirtless in our house, the fact that he was *always* incredibly respectful of my parents, and the way he'd wink at me as I looked back at him before fleeing whatever room he'd just entered.

And his laugh.

I used to love the sound of his laugh.

It's crazy how I've had so few real interactions with him, and yet it still feels like he used to be such a big part of my life based solely on how he made me feel.

"Her name's Quincy?" I ask, crouching down and putting my hand out.

"Yeah," he answers as his chocolate-colored sweetie sniffs my hand then leans into it, practically begging me to give her some affection. "My mom was really into American history, and when I was a kid, she got on this kick about John Hancock. She *loved* the name Dorothy."

When my brow furrows, my own familiarity with history I haven't thought of since high school much more lacking than

Andy's, he chuckles, giving me a hint of that laugh I used to love so much.

"Don't worry, most people have no idea what I'm talking about. That was John Hancock's wife—Dorothy Quincy. Mom always told me she would have named her daughter Dorothy if she'd ever had one, but they tried for a long time to have more kids without any luck."

He pauses and clears his throat, watching Quincy with his lips turned up as she lies on the hard wood of the deck and rolls to her back. I take a seat on the ground with my legs crossed and begin to stroke the soft hairs along her tummy.

"Anyway, eventually I think she gave up on the idea of having a bigger family, but a few years before she died, she adopted an older dog from a shelter down the mountain and named her Dorothy."

He stands from his chair and moves over to sit opposite me on the deck then reaches out and starts to stroke Quincy's ears.

"Dorothy was pretty old when we got her, and she ended up passing away just a few months after my mom. So when I found this little nugget at the same exact shelter we got Dorothy—same breed, same coat, same eyes—I knew it was fate. It just seemed right to give her a name that had to do with the same woman."

My heart has been pinching tight inside of my chest since he first mentioned his mother, but now, watching him look at his dog with the kind of love and adoration that's currently shining in his eyes, my heart breaks.

"I'm sorry about your mom," I say, knowing my words don't actually help anything but feeling compelled to say them anyway. It's been years since she died, but for some reason, I want him to know just how sad I was to hear about what happened. "I heard about it back then. I thought about sending flowers, but I remember her saying she hated them."

Andy laughs, an odd mixture of emotions in his tone. "She did. Always said the last thing she wanted for a birthday or holiday was to be stuck with something she had to take care of that would just end up dying anyway."

I chuckle, remembering the one time I heard Evelyn speak words that were very similar to that.

"She was something else," he continues. "When I first got Quincy, I had all these emotions related to my mom every time I saw her. Then a few weeks into being a dog owner, my dad slapped me on the back of the head and told me I was being an asshole."

I nibble on the inside of my lip and keep my eyes on the pup in front of me, finally understanding where this conversation is going.

"I was taking the shit in my mind, some stuff about my mom that I'd been processing again without realizing it, and carrying it around with me everywhere. I was surly at work and I kept biting people's heads off. I don't want to make excuses, because I was a dick earlier and I shouldn't have been, but I've been going through some stuff with my dad and...I don't know. I think I've been testier than usual."

This time, I'm the one shaking my head. "Andy—"

"No, I need to say this, Briar. My attitude earlier was completely uncalled for. You came in looking for a job, and I knocked the wind out of your sails. Actually, I was flat-out rude and unkind. You didn't deserve that at all, so I just wanted to say...I'm sorry."

I look at him for a long moment, surprised by how earnest he looks, almost like he's desperate to make this right. "Thanks,"

I finally murmur, not having much else to say.

Even though he was definitely a dick earlier today, I'm sure there have been plenty of instances in life when I've said things I regret because something else was bothering me. I might not put a lot of stock in the things men say, but I'm finding it easier than normal to give Andy the benefit of the doubt.

I give Quincy another few strokes before I push myself back up to standing, ready to get Andy on his way and head back inside.

"And if you want the job, it's yours," he says.

I let out a long breath and set my hands on my hips, wishing he'd just let things end at the apology. I already resigned myself to the idea of working at Ugly Mug, even though part-time at a coffee shop is not as enticing as it would be to the high school girls who would love to get an employee discount on their soy chai venti half-caf mochaccino lattes, or whatever other kind of incredibly complicated drink they like to order.

But I'm resourceful. In fact, that's what I was working on when Andy pulled up earlier: a list of ideas for how I can make some side-hustle money until a job with better pay or more hours opens up in town. Granted, that list was pretty limited, but still—it was a first attempt at gathering ideas, and I know it will grow if I just set my mind to it.

"I appreciate it," I say, even though I don't. "But I don't need a sympathy job. Handouts aren't my thing."

Andy pushes up so he's standing as well, his tall frame towering over me as he mirrors my stance, his hands resting on his hips.

"It's not a handout, Briar. We need another cashier on the roster so Lois can take care of her granddaughter. And with the new buildout, we're expecting some scheduling and hour changes that…" He pauses and chuckles a little under his breath, seemingly at himself. Then he shakes his head. "That's boring business stuff. Sorry, I forget that not everyone cares about the logistics the way I do. I'm just saying we really need somebody. And soon."

I tuck my hands back into my hoodie pockets, knowing I should be jumping up and down to accept Andy's offer. It's exactly what I wanted earlier today—full-time work, even if minimum wage is a bit of a step down from what I was making at my old job.

But now there's something sour about it, like I'm only getting the position because he feels bad or because he's desperate. I don't want to have something just *handed* to me. If I wanted something like that, I could have talked to my dad.

No. I want to earn it. To deserve it. So just telling me *You're hired* isn't going to work for me.

"When can I interview?" I ask.

Andy's full-blown smile covers his face, reminding me just how much I like seeing it, even if I don't smile in return.

"You'll take the job?"

"I'll interview for it."

He bites his lip, the humor in his expression not disappearing even though I can tell he's trying to hide it. He clears his throat and drops the smile.

"Great. Can you come in at noon tomorrow?" he asks.

I nod. "Yes. Thank you for the opportunity."

The smile comes back and Andy shakes his head. "Briar, you are…something else. I don't remember you being this ornery when you were younger."

"A lot has changed since I was 17, Andy."

"Clearly."

His voice dips lower when he says it, and a little thrill races down my spine. It feels like a loaded word, but there's no way he meant it the way my ears heard it. Unsure of how to respond, I nod my head and take a step backward.

"See you at 12 tomorrow," I say, reaching for the sliding door, eager to get back to the safety of my bedroom and leave the fluttering in my belly that Andy seems to incite behind.

He nods again. "Sounds good."

I turn and head inside, pulling the door behind me as I go. But Andy continues to stand there, watching me for a moment longer, before he finally gives me a wave and walks back to the side of the house with Quincy hot on his heels.

It's been a long time since I've had a man's eyes watch me like that. I doubt Chad *ever* looked at me the way Andy just did. My ex's eyes were rarely looking in my direction, whenever he happened to be around, usually focusing instead on his own work.

Andy's eyes, though…there's a lightness to them, almost like he's laughing. But not *at* me. It's kind of like he's trying to laugh *with* me, even though I'm not in on the joke.

The way it makes me feel is unfamiliar, and I'm not sure I like it.

But I do know for sure that it's the last thing I need.

"You look nice," my mother says as I come into the kitchen the following morning in one of the outfits I used to wear when

I needed to dress professionally at my old job.

It's nothing special, just a pair of tan slacks and a flowy blouse. Being a florist meant that most days, I wore black pants and a work polo, but there were also days when the shop owner, Holly, and I would go to do setup at a professional event—a wedding, a funeral, a conference—and on those days, I wore this kind of outfit.

It never made sense to me. Why would I wear something nice on a day when I'm going to get sweaty and covered in damp spots and leaves and light green stains from lugging around tons of plants and flower arrangements in a banquet hall or wedding venue? But that was how Holly did things, and I wasn't about to argue with the woman I looked up to so much.

When I graduated from college, I moved with Chad to Sacramento. He got a job in sales with a pharmaceutical company, and, as horrible as it might sound, I still didn't know what I wanted to do, so I chose to follow him rather than face the fact that I didn't have any plans of my own.

What nobody tells you is that a bachelor's degree in business doesn't mean much on its own, and it's hard to find work during a recession that makes those four years at university feel worth it. So I got what I thought would be a temporary 'throwaway' job working at Holly's Flowers, assuming that in my off time, I could look for something more long-term.

I worked there for five years, and I loved just about every minute of it, though not because I've always wanted to arrange flowers for a living. I mean, yeah, it's fun to be creative and make things that are beautiful, but what I *really* loved was working for Holly.

She's one of those self-made women. Works her ass off, never given a leg up, kind of had the world against her. It took her nearly ten years to do all of her schoolwork. The entire time, she worked two jobs and saved every penny so she could start her business.

She was the inspiration that led me to go back to school. We were setting up some minor flower arrangements for an admissions event at a major hotel—one of those things where potential future students wander through rows of tables for various universities—and it was specifically for MBA programs. When I picked up one of the brochures, Holly told me I should stay and attend the event.

That day, as I wandered through the tables, picking up informational packets and brochure after brochure, I started to create a little dream. It's a little something I still keep tucked away, just for me, something I don't think will ever happen but is still fun to fantasize about.

The dream of opening a bookstore.

Maybe it's a stupid idea. Maybe opening a bookstore in a world where everyone wants to get their books online or from big box stores is just a recipe for failure, but something small that gives people a chance to escape into new worlds when they're not happy with their own…well, that idea grew and grew until I was finally convinced that going back to school was what I should do.

And then Chad shot it down, giving me plenty of reasons why my very good idea was actually a very bad idea.

It was too expensive.

There wasn't enough time in the day to work *and* take classes.

I already had a job—what would another degree do?

And, how could taking out student loans and going into debt help me save money to open a business?

With every pointed observation of all the hurdles I'd be facing, Chad's opinion began to snuff out the little sparks of the dream I'd been cultivating, and ultimately, I let him make the decision for me.

But Holly wouldn't let it go.

"If you're going to be successful, you can't let the small minds of negative people drag you away from what you want. You have to grab on to your dream with every bit of your energy and never *ever* let go, no matter who is rooting against you."

Then she told me Chad could fuck right off for not supporting what I wanted to do with my life, regardless of his reasoning.

It wasn't the first time I'd heard someone's negative opinion of the man I thought I was going to marry, but it *was* the first time I decided to heed the advice I was given.

I applied to a school in the area, and when I was admitted, Holly shocked the hell out of me by saying she wanted to cover my tuition as an employee benefit. It took me three years part-time, but I did it. I got my MBA.

Looking back, the fact that I did something Chad so intensely disagreed with was the beginning of the end. I even think his proposal, after I graduated, was an attempt at getting me to just settle back into my job at Holly's and plan a wedding rather than look for something that would allow me to use my degree.

During those three years in my master's program, I started learning more about myself, dreaming bigger, imagining something different for my future. Unfortunately, Chad had his *own* vision for who I was supposed to be, a vision that *didn't* include me starting my own business or being anything other than a woman who took care of his house and warmed his bed and eventually mothered his children.

When I graduated, I should have looked for a new job, but

I loved working for Holly and wasn't ready to fight with Chad about a future that felt so far away. I still thought things might be salvageable, so I pushed off my dreams and continued my work as a florist. Maybe I'd open up my own shop, but at that moment, I was content working for my friend and dreaming about the future.

Though it wasn't that much longer before I couldn't keep up the façade of a happy life any longer.

"Where are you off to?" my mom asks, spreading butter onto a piece of bread then dropping it into a pan on the stove.

"I'm interviewing at One Stop. They have a cashier position."

This morning, I resigned myself to the fact that I would need to tell my family about my plans to get a job. I know it shouldn't be a big deal, but there's a part of me that feels like I'm letting everyone down by moving home and working at a grocery store.

My parents, who wanted me to go off and get my degree.

My siblings, who were all shocked when I announced I was moving home last month.

Myself, for not actually using the MBA I worked so hard and so long to get.

But the more I think about it, the more I'm trying to remind myself of what Holly told me when I asked her why it took her ten years to get her bachelor's.

"Everyone's path looks different," she said. "Some people can get on a plane and get to their destination in a shorter amount of time. Others take a road trip all over before reaching where they want to be, and maybe they get in a fender bender on the way and they have to stop for a while. That doesn't make it any less important to get to that goal. If anything, it provides life experiences the person on the plane didn't get."

I'm trying to see my life that way, trying to take my mistakes—my fender benders—and turn them into lessons learned in my mind. The fact that I'm back in Cedar Point means I'm making a little pit stop on my path, and I need to figure out a way *not* to be ashamed of that at every turn.

"That's great, honey," mom says, giving me a big smile. "I didn't realize you were job-searching in town."

I know she wants to ask me. She wants to ask what my plans are. Why I moved home. How long I'm staying. What happened between me and Chad.

But she doesn't.

And I love her for that.

Out of my whole family, I'm closest with my brother, Boyd. He's the one I'm usually willing to share things with if I'm feeling like talking to someone.

But my mom is the person who knows me the best, and she knows I struggle to talk about myself, knows I like to keep my personal life private, even from the people I love the most.

So she waits patiently, even though I know she wishes I'd word-vomit all over her like my sisters do.

"My interview is in thirty minutes, so I need to head out," I say, giving her a smile and then wrapping my arms around her. "I love you, mama."

She kisses me on the temple and pats my hands with hers.

"Love you too, baby."

CHAPTER FOUR

Briar

When I walk through the front door of One Stop, I'm immediately pounced on by Lois.

"I heard you're interviewing," she says, giving me a much bigger smile today than yesterday.

"I am." I give her a small smile in return. "And *I* heard Marie had a baby?"

Lois' head bobs and she excitedly pulls out her phone to show me a picture of her daughter Marie's new baby girl.

"Nina turns two months next week," she says, swiping through picture after picture. "I can already tell she's going to be a little spitfire, just like her mama."

"She's beautiful," I say. "She looks just like you."

Lois beams. Her eyes never leave her phone, but I can see clearly on her face just how enchanted she is by her new grandchild.

"Would you mind calling Andy up here for me?" I ask, knowing she'll keep me flipping through photos for the next hour if I don't get to the reason why I'm here. "I don't want him to think I'm late."

"Oh!" she says, tucking her phone away. "Yes. One second."

I step away from the check stand and scan my eyes over the interior of One Stop as Lois calls Andy up to the front.

It's the only grocery in Cedar Point, has been since before I was born. If I remember correctly, Andy's grandfather was the one who opened it, with Andy's dad taking the helm and now Andy in the wake of his dad's heart attack.

He didn't mention it directly last night, only alluding to his father when he told me he had some stuff going on with his family that's been on his mind, but what else could he be referring to? As far as I know, he doesn't have any other family, his mom having passed away a few years after I graduated and left town.

Cancer.

One of those unfathomable things where she went in to see the doctor for 'just a cough' and died three months later.

I get a shiver just thinking about it. I might be the oddball in my family, and the whole lot of them might seriously get on my nerves with how much they like to poke at me and try to rile me up, but I can't imagine losing a single one of them.

My older brother, Boyd, is like my rock. The two of us are really close—well, as close as I'm willing to let anyone get. I'm closer with him than I was with my ex, that's for sure, and Chad was supposed to be the man I was going to marry. Boyd lives on the east coast and neither of us really enjoy talking on the phone so it's been a little more challenging to stay connected as adults over the years, but we do our best.

Bellamy is six years younger than me. She and her twin brother Bishop are like two peas in a pod—seriously. They're both outgoing and easily liked by just about everyone. Both are in their final year of college, with Bellamy going to school online and Bishop on a full-ride baseball scholarship at Whitney College down the mountain.

And then my youngest sister, Busy…she's the baby of the family at 19 and just starting her sophomore year of college in Southern California. She's super artistic and really sarcastic. Out of all of us, she's the one I think gets my sense of humor the best, especially since she's the only one who thinks I even *have* a sense of humor.

My parents are great, too. Caring and thoughtful and always there for us. My mom's one of those loveable loud women who always has a hug to spare and is the consummate host. I take more after my dad, being fairly quiet and reserved, but he's a loving guy, too.

I wrinkle my nose, wishing things between me and my family were different…better. I left as soon as I could, and I think my parents tried to be supportive even though they were hurt by how dismissive I was of the idea of ever wanting to live in Cedar Point again. Even though I try to keep up with my brothers and sisters, it's just…tough.

Thinking about my family in relation to the fact that Andy lost his mom so quickly…it must have been devastating, and just the idea reminds me of how lucky I am to have the family I do.

"Briar."

The sound of my name yanks me out of where I've been standing and staring blankly at a rack of greeting cards near the front door, lost in my thoughts about my siblings and the past.

I give Andy a smile, putting on my 'professional' hat as I remind myself that I'm not hired yet and I really need a job.

"Thanks for taking the time to meet with me."

He smiles, and I'm hit with that same little shiver in my spine that rippled through me the last time he looked at me that way.

It really is incredibly inconvenient.

"Absolutely. Do you want to come with me back to the office? We'll be interviewing there."

I nod and fall in line beside him, struggling to come up with something to say.

Thankfully, Andy handles that for me, his naturally sociable personality making casual conversation a lot easier for him than it has ever been for me.

"Have you been enjoying being back in town?"

I nod. "I have, actually. It's been good to spend some time with my family."

"I know everybody was back last month. Who's living at home right now? Just you and Bells?"

"Yeah."

"Must be weird living with a sibling again, huh?"

I shrug a shoulder. "In some ways. In others it doesn't feel that much different from living with my ex."

I glance up at Andy just as we get to the double swinging doors that lead to the back room, catching his eyes on me.

"That's the reason you moved back?" he asks.

I grimace, realizing my faux pas. "Kind of," I say, hoping we leave it at that.

Thankfully, Andy doesn't stick on that conversation topic.

"Here we are," he says as we step into his office. "Go ahead and take a seat."

As Andy flips open the file sitting on the center of his desk, my eyes do a quick glance around the room, taking everything in. You can learn a lot about a person based on how organized they are—or aren't. I can't tell whether the messy office is because of Andy or his dad. Either way, the disorganization makes me antsy.

"Sorry about the mess," Andy interjects, and when I look back at him, I see he's watching me as my eyes wander the room. "My dad hasn't ever been good at managing the office stuff, so this place has looked like a tornado hit it since I was a kid."

I smile, feeling a little embarrassed that I was caught. "Sorry. I'm a bit of a neat freak. Spaces like this make me want to start sorting and organizing."

He laughs. "Well, maybe I can pay you some overtime to come in and handle it all for me, then." He clicks the end of his pen. "Alright, we can get started, if you're ready?"

I nod, and Andy dives right in, asking questions in rapid succession, about my work history and how I handle problems and what I do with difficult customers. It's been a long time since my last interview, but it feels fairly standard. Nothing out of the ordinary, and before I know it, we're done.

"Well, I think the only question I have left is how long you'll be in town," he says as we're wrapping things up.

"I'm not sure yet," I reply, trying to be as honest as I can.

He nods and twiddles his pen. "Six months? A year?"

"God, I hope not," I say, before I can stop myself.

It's unusual for me to blurt out something like that, but just the idea of being stuck in my parents' house for a year, living off of them and not being able to truly take care of myself…well, it sounds like everything a nightmare is made of.

I need more freedom than that, more independence. I might be fresh off of a breakup and nursing some wounds that are far from healed, but what I *need* is to relearn how to be on my own. Relying on my parents to take care of me does the exact opposite of that.

"I'm home because of life circumstances," I continue, trying to backtrack a little bit and not sound like such a bitch, "but I don't plan to stay forever. I need to get a job that will help me get back on my feet, and I just don't know how long that will take."

Andy nods, clicking the end of his pen and making another note on his paperwork. Then he sets both the paper and pen down and leans forward, resting his arms on the desk and linking his fingers together.

"Well, Briar, I'm going to be honest. I'd like to hire someone who can commit to at least six months of employment. Preferably a year, but I'm willing to be flexible for you."

I twist my lips. "I can commit to six months," I say, wishing it wasn't something I had to do but knowing there's no way *any* job would get me up and on my own again in less time than that.

But hell if I'll commit to a year. That's pushing too far.

"Well then, I'd like to hire you."

Smiling, I nod my head. "That's great."

"It should take about two weeks to train you before you can be in the store alone, and with you replacing Lois as a full-time cashier, you'll need to be able to handle things independently. Opening, closing, receiving deliveries, managing things when I'm not around."

I nod, liking the sound of having a little more authority than I'd originally thought the position would have. I'm not power hungry by any means, but I *would* like to think I'm more capable than a kid in high school.

"Let's have you fill out some HR paperwork and then we can put together a training schedule with me and Lois to make sure we get you up to speed as quickly as possible."

I smile, the first genuine feeling of happiness creeping into my body since I moved back to town.

Maybe I'm still broke. Maybe I'm still not sure what's next in my life. Maybe I'm single and feeling a little lonely and insecure about myself.

But I've taken the first step to putting my life back together again, and that's a great place to start.

When I get back to the house, my mom is gone, probably off volunteering somewhere or helping a friend or something else altruistic because that's the very essence of who she is. I might be a lot more like my dad when it comes to my personality, but I like to think I got my heart for volunteer work from her.

In high school, outside of my job at the library and the days I spent at cross country practice, I volunteered at The Pines, the nursing home on South Bank Road. It wasn't anything too crazy, mostly playing games with residents and chatting with them over meals, but there were plenty of times when I worked late and helped the nurses with some of the more complicated tasks that come along with patient needs.

I've given my time to various volunteer positions over the past decade. A crisis response center in college. A senior citizen center in Sacramento. One-off positions here and there, like at races for my old running club or at food drives near our house. I really do have a heart for serving others, and I definitely get that from my mama.

Jogging up to my room, I change out of my slacks and

blouse, tugging on a pair of stretchy leggings and a racerback tank, desperate to get outside and move my body.

Routines make me happy, and it's been hard to find any kind of rhythm or routine since I've been back in Cedar Point. It's mostly because there isn't any kind of consistency to my days, what with being unemployed and unsure of what I need to be doing with my time, but also because I was in a relationship for seven years where almost every day was the same.

I woke up and went on a run, got ready for the day and made us breakfast, then went to work. When I got home for the day, I made dinner—usually for just me, but also for Chad if he wasn't working late. Sometimes, I volunteered on nights or weekends, but that was pretty much the only variation to my schedule. It was a very solitary life, I guess, and part of me liked it that way. Especially toward the end, as things between Chad and me really started to deteriorate.

Being back with my parents and living with a sibling again makes it hard to keep everything straight. I never know when I'll get the much-needed moments to myself or if tonight is a night when friends of my parents will be coming over for dinner.

Bellamy also has the habit of popping up all the time at completely random moments, wanting to hang out with me. It's nice in some ways but slightly strange in others, especially since we were never close growing up and she spent most of her time with Bishop and Busy. I was out of the house before she even started wearing a training bra, so that sisterly bond isn't as deep as it could be.

Boyd was always better at navigating the age gap than I was, taking our younger siblings on dates when he came back to town or going on little road trips down the mountain together. I always felt like an idiot, like I was trying to speak a new language everyone else expected me to pick up quickly and I just kept bumbling along saying the same few phrases over and over again.

Now that I'm back in town, I'm enjoying the random moments I'm getting with my sister. I feel like I'm getting to know her in a completely different way than I ever have before, especially since she likes to sit down next to me and share just about anything that's on her mind at any given moment. I remember her being talkative like that when we were kids, too. She has that same kind of knack Andy does, able to strike up a conversation with anybody.

That kind of warm affability is something I've always envied.

I unfurl a yoga mat on the grass facing the lake and click through my phone to find a video to watch online.

Being back in Cedar Point has forced me to step outside of the routine I've found comfort in over the years and find new ways to do things. Never in my life have I enjoyed anything other than going on a run for exercise. It was a straightforward way to get in some physical activity, didn't take a ton of time, and allowed me the ability to track myself to log improvements.

But yoga?

The first time I even did this was about a month ago with Boyd's girlfriend Ruby leading me and my siblings in a little class out here on the grass. It was so ridiculous, with my brother Bishop bent over and farting in my face, Boyd constantly checking out Ruby's ass as she led us through a number of movements that had me feeling muscles I didn't know existed.

It felt good, though, good in a way I hadn't been expecting. It wasn't about tracking myself and just getting the exercise out of the way, and, surprisingly, I liked that. I enjoyed the change from doing something for a logical reason, instead doing it for a mental and emotional one, which is definitely not my norm.

As I've been home for the past month, I've started to prioritize this outside time, whether it's doing yoga or swimming in the water or just lying in the grass while I read a book. It's become less about the obligation of fitness and more about giving myself the time and space to stretch and move my body, giving myself permission to exist in the world and shift and change in whatever way feels best.

Now, I do this a few times a week as a way to love my body, but also as a way to clear my mind, like a meditation.

"Can I join you?"

My head whips around and I spot my sister heading down to me, her own yoga mat tucked under her arm and a similar outfit on her body.

I give her a smile and nod. I may have originally planned to have some time alone to think over my interview—and, if I'm honest, maybe replay my interactions with Andy—but spending some time with my sister is a welcome distraction from the man who keeps popping into my mind.

"Sure."

She throws down her mat and takes a seat next to me. "God, I need this. My back is killing me."

I click around on my phone, still searching for a video to lead us through a routine.

"How come?"

"Ugh," she says, leaning back so she's flat on her mat. "I've been working too many shifts. Did I tell you I picked up some hours at The Mitch?"

I turn to glance at where she lies on her back, one leg pulled across her body as she stretches, and shake my head. I knew my sister was working waitressing shifts at Lucky's, the townie nickname we have for Dock 7, but I didn't know she was working a second job at the other bar in town.

"Yeah. Emily broke her ankle and they were down a bar-tender, so I said I'd help them out."

"That's nice of you."

"Thanks," she says, letting out a little huff as she pushes her-self up to sitting, leaning back on her hands. "It's not nice on my back, though." She eyes me for a second before she adds, "Maybe you could take over those shifts."

I snort, the action uncharacteristic of me. "I don't know how to mix drinks," I say. "Besides, I got a job working at One Stop."

Bellamy's eyebrows fly up. "Oh really? That's great! You tak-ing the spot from Lois?"

I nod.

"Very cool. Time to hook me up with your employee dis-count so I don't waste half my paycheck on chips and salsa," she says, giggling at herself. "So, does that mean you'll be sticking around town for a while then?"

I nibble on the inside of my cheek, just giving her a shrug. "I don't know."

Not wanting to let that vein of conversation go any further, I set my phone at the end of my yoga mat and click play.

My sister takes the hint that I'm done chitchatting, follow-ing my lead as I begin moving my body with the instructor on the screen.

Eventually, even though I try hard not to let my mind fall back to thinking about the handsome man I've known since childhood, I start to wonder what I should expect from working at One Stop…from working with Andy.

If I'm completely honest with myself, I'm a little nervous about being around my brother's old friend. He's just so…much. Tall and attractive and muscular, with those eyes that seem to watch me with an intensity I'm not familiar with.

I thought I'd put most of this teenage crush to bed, and I'm afraid being around Andy—spending any kind of time with a man who seems to unsettle me so easily—will create feelings I know will never have any kind of payoff.

The last thing a girl like me needs is a man who stirs up big emotions. Big emotions just lead to big heartbreak, and I don't have any intention of getting caught up in a storm like I know Andy could bring into my life and heart.

A man like him is dangerous, so the best thing I can do is keep my head down and my eyes away from that charming smile of his.

Besides, I was in a relationship with Chad for seven years. I'm still processing the fact that it's over and learning to let go of the things I was so used to. Any kind of relationship right now, even a crush, will distract me from my goal of sorting through the past seven years and figuring out what I want to do next.

I just wish I wasn't so...*aware* of him when he's around. It's incredibly frustrating.

Pretty soon, thirty minutes have gone by, though my mind doesn't feel as clear as I'd hoped, my thought process unable to sort Andy Marshall into the discard pile I so desperately wish he would fall into.

"That was great," Bells says from where she's lying flat on her back next to me. "I know we gave Boyd shit about it when he said he enjoyed yoga with Ruby, but maybe he's onto something."

I smile, staring up at the sky and the trees that sway in the light breeze above us. We both lie there for a while, just enjoying the outside time and the beautiful weather.

"Hey, B?"

When I feel her hand slip into mine, I look over and find my sister watching me, her light brown eyes narrowed with concern.

"I know I'm not Boyd," she tells me, "and I know I'm younger than you and you've never really, you know, *talked* to me about your life in any kind of real way…but I just want you to know I'm here for you if you need somebody."

Something thick settles in my throat, something that feels oddly like the sensation right before tears. I work hard to swallow it down.

"Like if you want to talk about what happened with Chad, or…"

I pull my body up so I'm no longer lying on my back, letting go of my sister's hand in the process.

"Thanks, but I'm good."

I know my words aren't what Bellamy wants to hear. She's the definition of being our mother's daughter—outgoing, friendly, and above all, has a strong desire to talk about things.

But I don't want to talk about Chad. I don't want to talk about my life with him where I felt so unhappy. I think about it enough on my own.

Nobody else needs to hear about the mistakes I made. Nobody else needs to know about all the times I let myself down.

Because that's really the reason I left Chad.

He didn't cheat on me. He didn't hit me or hurt me. Sure, he might not have been the biggest supporter of me going after things I wanted, and yeah, he basically just wanted me to be a woman who took care of him and slept with him and didn't cause a fuss.

But I left because I was disappointed in myself.

I had all those big plans, big plans and big ideas for my big life in the big city, and I let myself get made small. I let myself get dismissed, settling into a life that made me so unhappy I hardly knew what to do with myself.

I'm ashamed of who I became. I didn't recognize the woman in the mirror anymore, having allowed the man in my life to warp what I saw until I finally smashed my reflection to pieces.

How am I supposed to talk about that with my younger sister? She's supposed to be able to look up to me, and all she'll see if I tell her about Chad and my life down the mountain is someone who failed.

So I do the thing I know how to do.

I give her a smile and pull away, keeping the broken and ugly bits of myself tucked away safely inside.

Nobody really wants to see those parts anyway.

CHAPTER FIVE

Andy

When my alarm goes off on Monday morning, I reach over and slap at my phone to shut it off.

I've already been up for an hour, my normal inclination to want to sleep late not even on my radar today.

Even though I'm trying not to dwell on it too much, I can't help but let my thoughts drift to the place I've been trying to avoid for the past few days.

Briar's first day at One Stop.

The fact that I've been thinking about it this much is…different. Not necessarily unwelcome, but just…different. Maybe because I wasn't expecting my friend's younger sister to occupy this much space in my mind.

And by 'this much space' I mean it's all I've been thinking about as I've gone about my work, as I've kept an eye on dad, as I've walked Quincy and swam the lake.

I'd like to be able to say something like 'I'm a guy—thinking about a beautiful woman is just how my brain works,' but I long ago got sick of the phrase 'Boys will be boys.' I know things might pop into my mind without warning, but I'm completely in control of what I choose to ruminate on.

And yet I feel completely powerless in the face of how regularly and quickly Briar seems to come to mind. I've been trying to think back to the girl I knew in high school, the girl I knew existed but didn't really know as a person, but all I can see is the absolutely gorgeous woman she is today.

All that thick hair she likes to keep braided and pulled off her face, though wispy strands kept falling loose during her interview and distracting me.

Those long legs she has definitely gotten used to walking on if the way she sways her hips is anything to go off.

The beautiful hazel eyes I used to think always looked intimidated when we were younger now seem to swallow me whole.

I even went so far as to yank out my high school yearbooks from the dusty shelf in my dad's living room, flipping through to find photos of Briar as a freshman, her hair in pigtails and her teeth covered in braces. Then in the next book as a sophomore with almost the exact same look. Her junior year photo, though—my senior year—made me feel like a creep. She's gorgeous, her hair down, all thick and wild, no braces in sight.

How did I never notice her back then?

I mean, logically I can assume it was because she fled the room every time our group of friends came around. She wasn't really there for me to notice. And again, she's my friend's sister. It's a good thing I didn't notice her back then.

But still, I'm surprised I didn't at least mentally acknowledge how…just, damn beautiful she was.

It doesn't matter though. In the grand scheme of things, it doesn't matter whether I find her attractive now or didn't see it back then, because Briar and I could not be more opposite.

She's restless, and I'm settled. She's closed off; I'm an open book. She can't wait to get out of this little town, while the idea of living here for the rest of my life couldn't make me any happier. Attraction isn't enough for me. There has to be compatibility, and with Briar, I just can't imagine there being a connection when we see the world—both physically and metaphorically— in such a different way.

I shake my head, feeling like an idiot for even allowing that thought to come to mind in the first place.

It doesn't *matter* if Briar and I are compatible. She shouldn't even be on the list of people I think about when I think about the word compatible.

Boyd and I might not be as close as we used to be—life just gets in the way sometimes—but I'd still consider him one of my oldest friends. We usually get together when he's in town to shoot the shit and catch up, and it doesn't take long before we slip back into a competitive comradery only decades of friendship can provide. So, it feels like I'm breaking some kind of unspoken bro code agreement that says it's not okay to be attracted to your friend's younger sister.

Finishing up my breakfast of granola and yogurt, I try *again* to set my thoughts about Briar aside then let Quincy out for a roam and head over to dad's.

"Morning!" I call out, not seeing any signs of life as I enter through the front door. "You awake?"

It feels like I'm always asking that, always wondering if he's managed to pull himself up out of the bed that has become his life. Just like every other day, all I hear is silence.

I make quick work of getting my father out of bed and to the kitchen table for breakfast. I'm able to convince him to take a shower and change, which feels like a big win considering how often I try and he doesn't respond.

While he cleans himself up, I strip his sheets and put them in the wash, then I remake his bed with a spare set and open the blinds through the entire house. He'll hate me for doing that, but at least he'll have to get up and move around a little bit to reclose them all.

Once he's settled into his recliner in the living room and I've put out a big bottle of water I know he's likely to pass up in favor of beer, I give him a wave and head out. After feeding and watering Quincy, I finally climb into my Jeep and head to work.

I expect to be the first one there, which is why I'm surprised when I walk around the corner from parking my car and find the very object of my earlier musings sitting on a bench out front, sipping on a cup of coffee.

Her head turns, her eyes meeting mine as I approach, and I know I'm not imagining the way her lips turn up at the sight of me, or the way just that little movement has my steps stuttering.

"Morning," I say, my voice coming out a little raspy. Clearing my throat, I try again. "How come you're here so early?"

Briar's eyebrows dip and she glances at her watch, which should tell her that it's only seven.

"Aren't I supposed to be here?" she asks.

I shake my head. "We don't open until eight."

She stands as I unlock the front door. "But if I'm going to be working alone, I need to get familiar with what happens before we open, right?"

Grinning, I push through and hold the door open, motioning for Briar to follow me.

"You make an excellent point."

"Good. I don't want to be accused of needing handholding."

I wince, my words from last week coming back to haunt me. I don't know what the hell I was thinking, saying that shit to her.

"Briar…" I say, twiddling with my keys and pausing to try to put together the right thing to say.

"No, I'm sorry. That was uncalled for."

"No, it was completely called for," I respond, letting out a sigh, my earlier mood deflating like a popped balloon. "I was out of line last week."

"And you apologized," she interjects. "You apologized and I accepted it. I shouldn't have brought it up again."

We stare at each other for a long minute, and I know I'm not imagining things when I see the bit of frostiness that regularly colors Briar's expressions melt away into something a little more vulnerable and open.

I blink, turning away when I realize I've been staring at her in silence. "Okay then," I say, and then start walking through the dark store with Briar in my wake, only the light from the front doors and the bright red emergency exit signs guiding us. "When you work an opening shift, you'll want to get here thirty minutes before we unlock the doors. I'm usually already here, but the assumption should be that you're coming in alone."

I push through the double doors in the back and lead Briar to the large office space she interviewed in last week.

"We've got two offices back here. One is mine, and the other is the finance space, which is where we keep the safe and financial records, along with the tills and tools for counting money. There's also a break room over there," I add, pointing to the doorless area outfitted with a few lockers and a picnic table, "and a bathroom next to it that's also available for customer use."

I unlock my office and chuck my bag and phone onto my seat, booting up my computer then returning my attention to

Briar.

"Let's do a full tour, and then Lois can show you what opening looks like when she gets here in a little bit."

Briar and I spend about twenty minutes wandering around One Stop. It isn't massive like the grocery stores down the mountain, but there is still a lot to know. We go through produce and then I show her the deli and frozen section, making sure to point out the cold fridge where we house special cakes and flower arrangements.

Next I walk her through each of the major areas—dairy, bread, drinks and snacks, pasta, alcohol, as well as the new build-out filled with half-finished shelving and no products—before leading her into the stockroom and loading bay.

"We've got five cashiers, three full-time and two part-time, and four baggers that work the rush shifts. There are also a handful of full-time departmental employees. Someone who puts out and monitors the produce, someone who fills and takes care of the deli, stuff like that," I say as we come to a stop outside my office. "Only full-time employees are allowed to receive deliveries. I'm normally the one to handle them, but you'll be taught how to manage that during your training as well."

"I don't think I ever realized how much work goes into keeping this place moving," she says, her eyes wandering around the back room and taking in the pallets of packaged product waiting to be unwrapped and put up on shelves.

"Yeah. I didn't either," I say, lifting a shoulder. "I started working here when I was a junior in high school, but I had *no* idea until I started handling it on my own."

"Your dad made you start at the bottom?" she asks, and I can see her lips tilted up, a little hint of teasing in her eyes.

I grin. "Absolutely. Maybe lots of dads would want their

kid to learn the business side straight off the bat, but not my old man. His opinion is that you have to know how to do every single job in the store if you're going to be a good owner."

"So you were, what…a bag boy?"

"That would have been great," I say with a chuckle, though I'm shaking my head. "I started in janitorial."

Her mouth drops open and her eyes go wide. "Your dad made you clean the toilets?" she asks, and I can hear the hint of laughter and enjoyment in her voice.

I nod, though I can't seem to get any words out of my mouth for a moment. I'm frozen by the way she's looking at me, the big smile on her face lighting up her entire being in a way I've never seen before.

"You *would* find it funny. Just be glad you're starting in a primo position, Ms. Mitchell."

She lets out a quiet laugh, and I can't help but enjoy the little tremor that slides along my spine at the sound.

"No toilet scrubbing for me. *Please*."

We're both smiling when the double doors open from the storefront, and I turn to find Lois walking in with her purse slung over her shoulder.

"Morning, Lo," I say, lifting a hand in greeting.

When I turn back to Briar to continue our conversation, I find her expression has returned to something more neutral, that lightness between us buried underneath a professional and poised exterior.

I clear my throat, following her lead and setting aside the bit of silly energy that passed between us.

"Lois has been teaching new employees for the past few years," I tell Briar, knowing that the best thing to do is hand her off to the woman who has worked here longer than I have. "Let me know if you need anything, okay?"

She nods, and I see her mouth move slightly, as if she's nibbling on the inside of her cheek.

When I realize I'm standing there looking at Briar's lips, my eyes fly up, finding her watching me with tilted brows. Clearing my throat again, I take a step back.

"Let's meet at the end of your day to go over everything and wrap up some paperwork," I say, my voice coming out slightly choked.

And then I spin on my heels and stride into my office, closing the door behind me.

I scrub my hands over my face, wondering what the hell is wrong with me, wishing I'd kept my damn eyes to myself. Now I'm worried I've made her uncomfortable on her first day by staring at her mouth, at those light pink lips I'm starting to wonder more about…

How they taste.

How soft they feel.

What they'll look like wrapped around my…

I let my head fall back, my eyes closed as I try to think of other things. Baseball stats and naked grandmothers, right? Isn't that what's supposed to help?

God, I haven't had to do this in years. It feels ridiculous to be sitting in my office trying to get rid of the hardness that's growing in my pants at the thought of Briar on her knees. What am I, a teenager? Getting turned on at just the thought of a beautiful woman?

And it's not just any woman. It's Briar Mitchell.

Boyd's sister. My new employee.

But now that the door has been opened, I'm unable to close it, and my mind begins to ramble through the weeds. Thinking about her thick hair and beautiful eyes, the small swell on her chest and those slender hips that lead to legs that are a mile long.

Maybe most guys wouldn't blink at allowing a momentary daydream like the ones that keep popping into my mind about Briar, but I've never made a habit of spending too much time dwelling on women I know aren't for me.

I know what I want in life. I want to find someone to settle down with. Someone to have a family with. Here, in Cedar Point. Briar is not that woman, and the fact that I can't seem to get that through my head is just…it's infuriating.

But damn if the idea of something short and sweet with Briar isn't enough to get the heat climbing up my neck, making me wonder whether having a little bit of fun couldn't be something to enjoy, at least while she's in town.

Though even thinking that kind of thing about my new employee would have my dad finally sitting up and barking at me.

Huh. Maybe if I tell him about my sudden interest in Briar, he'll be pissed enough to get out of this funk he's been in.

That actually makes me laugh a little bit, and I finally manage to shake out my tense shoulders and turn my attention to the work in front of me.

I take all of my thoughts of Briar—the friendly ones and the dirty ones in kind—and place them firmly on the *to handle later* shelf in my mind.

It will still be there to ponder when the day is done.

"How was it?" I ask as Briar drops herself into the chair across from my desk after we close at 7, looking a bit like a wilted flower but no less beautiful because of it.

"Good."

I narrow my eyes at her, though my expression stays playful. "How was it *really*?"

She examines me for a second, scanning my face for something. Whatever it is, she must find it, because her shoulders sag and she slumps even farther into her chair. "I forgot what it's like to start a new job," she says.

"Overwhelming?"

She shakes her head. "No. Just...tiring."

I nod. "It'll get easier. The only reason you're starting on such long shifts is because we're being really aggressive with your training, right? Once that's over, you'll be working less hours a day and it won't feel so stressful."

"I know. I just don't want to let anyone down."

The minute she says the words, I can physically see Briar's entire body tense up, as if she said that on accident.

"You won't," I say, unsure what's going through her mind but certain something encouraging has to be the right thing to say. "You're smart, Briar. You're going to blow through Lois' training and then come out the other side teaching *me* things."

Something vulnerable shows up in the way she looks at me, in the way her eyes search mine.

"You think?"

"I know."

She nods slowly and does that nibble thing with her mouth, clearly a nervous habit.

Something inside of Briar is uneasy. Unsettled. Even though I don't know her more than just the bits and scraps I was able to cobble together the other day, I have a few guesses as to what it might be.

She's back in her hometown when she was desperate to leave.

She mentioned an ex earlier, and she's working at a grocery store when she has a master's in business, which I can only assume isn't what she'd planned.

Which makes me think of a question I've been wanting an answer to ever since I saw her resume.

"Can I ask you something?"

She considers it for a second before she gives me what looks to be a reluctant nod.

"Why aren't you using your MBA?"

Her chin tilts up slightly, and that frostiness from earlier shutters over her eyes. I can physically *see* her closing me off.

"Trying to get rid of me already?" she says.

There's something strained about her tone, like she's trying to make a joke but knows she didn't hit the delivery.

I shake my head. "Not in the slightest," I say, trying to get us back to where we were just a few minutes ago when she smiled at me. "I just remember you telling me One Stop was the last place you wanted to work. So I'm curious—especially since you're clearly qualified for a job that would pay you a lot more—why you're *here* and not doing something more important out *there*."

Her brow furrows. "What are you talking about?"

I curse inwardly, realizing my mistake. I didn't mean to bring up the day Briar moved away, but I can't lie and say I'm not curious about what has brought her full circle back to the place she seemed to detest so much.

"The day you moved away to college, when you and your friend came through the store—do you not remember that?"

She shakes her head.

"I joked about you staying in town and bagging groceries with me, and you said it sounded like your worst nightmare."

Briar nibbles on her cheek again and looks off to the side. "I can't believe you remember that," she finally says. "I totally forgot that happened."

I shrug a shoulder. "It isn't a big deal if you don't want to talk about it. It just seems like you worked really hard on a big-time degree, only to come back to the place you were so desperate to leave behind."

Briar takes a minute to respond, and when she does, her answer about knocks me off my feet.

"When you're lost, sometimes it seems like a better idea to keep moving, even if you're going in the wrong direction," she tells me. "I think that's where I am right now."

There's a long silence between us, and I can tell with every atom of my being that Briar is going through…something big. Something profound and painful and deep.

Suddenly, I understand why I haven't been able to get her off my mind. Yes, she's beautiful. Yes, I'm attracted to her.

But what I see when I look at her is a kindred spirit. Not because we're particularly alike, but because I'm going through my own painful moments at home, and I know what it feels like to wonder if there's anything beyond the current wall that feels impossible to climb over.

And because I feel that way, I'm also desperate for an escape, for anything that will bring levity to what's currently weighing me down. Maybe she feels that way, too.

"Well, I can think of a better place to be," I tell her, hoping like hell she'll go along with my idea. "The Mitch."

Briar groans and huffs out a laugh that's still shrouded in misery, but not completely, which I'm choosing to see as a positive.

"Really?"

I nod. "A celebratory drink after your first day," I say, giving her my most charming smile. "My treat."

Her lips turn up just slightly. "It better be your treat—I haven't gotten paid yet."

At that, I bark out a laugh, knowing that whatever happens tonight, I will have at least gotten her to tease me, to smile just a little bit.

And that's enough for now.

CHAPTER SIX

Briar

It's been years since I've been to The Mitch, the townie bar along the banks of Cedar Lake. It's a quintessential dive that mostly serves water masquerading as big-name beer, and when Andy and I walk into the dark and musty interior of the bar adorned with my family's namesake, it feels like a total blast from the past.

I forgot just how fun and funky this little place can be with its wooden walls covered in tchotchkes and the jukebox that still only plays the Red Hot Chili Peppers if the sound of *Californication* coming through the speakers is any indicator. As we sidle up to the bar, taking two empty seats side by side at the end, I can totally picture Bellamy working here, her sassy and friendly personality an absolute fit.

"What sounds good?" Andy asks me, his fingers drumming along the long stretch of maple wood that has certainly seen better days.

"Just a beer," I answer. "Maybe one of Rusty's?"

Andy nods at my reference to another one of Boyd's friends from high school who brews and bottles beer here in town. Cedar Cider is really popular locally and has been making its way into stores down the mountain as well. Chad never liked it, preferring to stick with liquor neat on the rare occasions we'd go out with colleagues of his from work, but I always grabbed one whenever I saw it, no matter where we were.

I might have moved out of town, but there's always been a little voice telling me it's still important to support the people who make their life here.

"Hey, Andy."

Keegan Pruitt slides up to us on the other side of the bar, wearing the uniform top the all-female bartending staff has worn for at least as long as I've been allowed in here. Tight and low-cut, the words *Mitch Bitch* stretched across the chest.

My uncle may have sold this bar off a while back, but he sure did think the new uniform was hilarious.

"Hey, Keegan. Can I get two Cedar Ciders? An IPA and a pilsner."

She gives him a wink and bites her lip. "You got it, baby," she says, her voice low and throaty.

I almost roll my eyes as I see her bend over to grab the bottles, her jean cutoffs short enough to show off her pockets in the front and the bottom of her ass cheeks in the back.

Keegan and Andy were together briefly in high school, though I don't know whether they were dating or just fooling around. I didn't pay a lot of attention to what most of the other girls in my class did back in the day, but I'm pretty sure they were together during their senior year—my junior year—since they were crowned prom king and queen.

I went with Nick and we broke up the next day, so my

memories of that night are a little tinged with the heartache of a young relationship coming to the end. Even so, I do remember Boyd and Andy and their whole crowd showing up at our house after everything had wrapped up at the school gym, sitting out by the fire and toasting drinks to celebrate the end of their high school years.

I might have been dating Nick at the time, but I was enamored by the way Andy looked in his tux, and maybe a little bit jealous that a girl like Keegan was on his arm.

It's a pretty damn similar feeling to what I get when I watch the way she eyes him now as she slides our drinks across the bar, and it's certainly not something I'm expecting.

I'm not prepared for the little jealousy monkey climbing up onto my back and glaring at her like she's doing us dirty. She's not doing anything other than her job, even if she *is* being a bit of a flirt. Andy's single, I think—I should be cheering her on, giving her a thumbs-up for having the courage to put herself so boldly in his path when someone like me would never do it in a million years.

"What should we cheers to?"

My eyes snap to Andy's, finding him looking at me and holding his bottle up.

I reach out and pick up my own, lifting it up to match his in height, though I don't clink them together yet as I think it over.

"I'm not sure," I reply, my mind still struggling to crawl out of my memories from high school mixed with my sudden awareness of my irrational jealousy over Keegan's history with Andy.

He hums for a second, seeming to mull it over.

"I know," he finally says, moving his glass closer to mine, his eyes never straying away. "To getting lost on the way to finding happiness."

I swallow down the sudden welling of emotion that wants to surge out of me at his sentiment and nod, repeating it back to him.

"To getting lost on the way to finding happiness."

Then we clink our bottles together, tap the bottoms on the bar, and each take a long pull.

"What are you up to tonight?" Keegan asks, her hands planted wide on the old wooden bar and her body leaning forward in a way that couldn't be misconstrued as anything other than an invitation.

"Spending time with Briar," Andy replies easily. "You remember Briar Mitchell, right?"

Keegan's eyes flick to mine briefly then go back to Andy, dismissing me quickly in that way I always tried to avoid when we were younger.

It's a look that communicates in less than a second that I'm not worthy of her time, and damn if that doesn't just hit me in a weak spot.

"Yeah, Boyd's little sister. You're the one who always hid when we'd come over to your house, right?"

That feeling of sour discomfort continues to grow, and I can feel a rush of heat sliding up my neck.

"I wasn't *hiding*," I reply, sitting up straighter, my tone a little less than friendly. "I'm just not a fan of big groups."

Keegan laughs and gives a little eyeroll that says she thinks I'm full of shit. "Okay."

My nostrils flare, but I stay quiet, desperately trying to let her comment roll off my back.

"Well, it was good to see you, Keegan."

At his tone, I look over to Andy, surprise rolling through me at the way his eyes are narrowed and pinning Keegan in place.

She giggles a little bit, looking back and forth between us before her smile falls and she rolls her eyes again.

"Whatever," she mumbles, then wanders off to the other end of the bar.

"Sorry about that," Andy says, his expression still flat as he watches her walk away for a moment before returning his attention to me.

"It's not your fault."

He shakes his head. "Yeah, but I didn't think about the fact that she works here when I invited you out," he clarifies. "Any time I come in here with a woman—a friend or otherwise—Keegan gets a little territorial. I don't know if you remember, but we dated for a while back in high school, and then again a few years later, so…"

"You don't have to explain yourself," I interrupt. "There's a history there. We all have them."

"Yeah, I guess you're right. Unfortunately, we're guided mostly by our lower half when we're young, even though that's not an excuse."

At that, I can't help but laugh a little bit.

"Was that a laugh?" Andy says, his eyes widening before he looks around dramatically.

I roll my eyes. "Come on. I laugh."

"Not often enough."

Taking a sip of my drink, I think it over. "Okay, you're right. I don't—but I would counter your statement with an argument that most people laugh too often."

At that, Andy bursts into a deep laughter that carries across the bar, rippling through my chest. I instantly want to take my words back. In this moment, I know Andy Marshall could spend the rest of his life laughing next to me and I'd never get tired of the sound.

"Oh, Briar," he says, shaking his head. "If you think that's true, we need to find ways to get you to laugh and smile more often. It's just…good for the soul."

I nibble on the inside of my cheek, wishing it were that easy.

"Here, watch. Tell me something funny. I'll show you how much fun it is to laugh."

Rolling my eyes, I look back at my beer bottle, deciding to play whatever game he's getting at.

"Alright. I'm not sure if you'll laugh at this, but I'm pretty sure you'll be shocked. You know how Boyd bought all those beers to celebrate your win as prom king?"

Andy nods. "Yeah. That night was a blast."

I grin at him. "Boyd thought *he* was gonna win. He got all that stuff because he thought he was going to be hosting his own celebration party."

Andy's eyes widen in shock, and he's silent for a split second before he's leaning on the bar, his face tucked into his elbow as he cackles away.

It's hard to hold back my own laughter, and for a beat, I wonder if Andy's right. If laughter and smiling are good for the soul.

When he sits up straight again, his eyes are bright and his cheeks are slightly red.

"Briar, you have absolutely made my night. I'm going to be calling him tomorrow to give him all kinds of shit about that."

We settle into a comfortable silence for a few minutes, and I realize it's been a long time since I've really enjoyed a conversation with a guy like this. Chad and I used to talk so rarely, and when that's the way you live your life for so long, enough time goes by and it starts to feel normal to never say anything.

Talking with Andy feels like peeling back a layer of carpet over wooden floors, revealing something I didn't realize was there.

"Okay, I'm gonna ask you a question, but I want you to know that you don't have to answer it," he says.

Instantly I'm put on alert.

"What is it about Cedar Point that makes you dislike it so much?"

"What is it about Cedar Point that makes you *like* it so much?" I counter, trying to deflect so I don't have to respond.

"The people, the weather, being close to my dad, having friends I've known for decades, living near a lake, getting to swim for exercise, slower pace of life, no traffic, clean air—"

"Okay, okay," I say, grabbing the hand he was using to count off all the reasons he loves living here. "I get your point."

Then I quickly drop his hand, belatedly realizing just my skin on his is enough to get my heart racing.

"Seriously, Briar. I'm not gonna judge. I just...obviously I love it here. I'm just trying to understand why you don't."

I take in a deep breath and let out a long sigh, trying to decide exactly what to say.

"I don't know that there's one thing," I say.

"So it's everything?" Andy jokes.

I huff out a breath of laughter, unable to help myself.

"It's not *everything*," I say. "It's just...a lot of little things, I guess. I've never really thought it all the way through before."

He shrugs a shoulder and takes a pull from his beer. "So, walk me through it. I've got time."

I nibble on my cheek. "Okay, well...for starters, it's hard being a Mitchell here. When I was younger, it felt like everyone was watching me all the time, and that feeling hasn't ever gone away as I've gotten older."

"Can I tell you a secret?"

I nod.

"That's because everyone *does* watch you."

My eyes widen.

"But they watch me, too. And Rusty, and Lois, and my dad. Everybody watches everybody and everything. So, yeah, you weren't wrong."

"And it doesn't bother you?" I ask. "Doesn't it make you feel like everyone's in your business?"

Andy shakes his head. "Nah. When I was a kid and trying to get away with things, it was frustrating, for sure"—he laughs—"but eventually I just decided not to let it bother me anymore. It's one of those things I don't let get under my skin. For the most part." A long pause goes by before he speaks again. "So what else?"

I blow out another breath, feeling a little put on the spot. "I don't know. I'll have to think about it."

He nods his head then drains the last sip of his beer, sets it on the bar with a *thunk*.

"Here's what I think, Briar," he says, eyeing me with seriousness. "I think you don't really know why you don't like it here, and I will bet you a million dollars that if you give me a chance, I can show you all the things that make this town so great."

I pin him with an incredulous look. "A million dollars?"

He shrugs. "Monopoly dollars, but yes, a million."

Unable to help my smile, I shake my head. "You're ridiculous."

"Maybe, but I'm also serious."

Pursing my lips, I just stare at him.

"You're back in town for a while, right? I mean, you promised me you're here for at least six months. At the very least, I bet I can get you not to *hate* it here."

I lift an eyebrow. "I feel like you're making a bet with me."

"Maybe I am."

"Well, what's in it for me? What happens if you *don't* convince me that Cedar Point is the greatest place in the world?"

He shrugs then winks at me, giving me that same tummy-swooping feeling he used to give me in high school. "I guess you'll just have to give it a shot to find out."

"Thanks for the drink and for celebrating my first day," I say once he finally pulls into the drive at my house to drop me off.

"It was a good time," he says. "Hanging out at The Mitch—just one of the many *amazing* things about Cedar Point."

I snort and roll my eyes. "Dealing with bitchy Keegan—one of the many things to *dislike* about Cedar Point."

Andy laughs. "Ah, you have me there," he says, his eyes roving over my face for a long moment.

A very long moment where we're both kind of just staring at each other...and I don't think I'm imagining it when I catch something that looks a lot like interest in Andy's eyes.

Swallowing thickly, I look away.

"I'll see you at work tomorrow," I say, shoving my door open and hopping down to the ground.

"Briar," Andy says, right before I close the door.

When I stop and look at him, he opens his mouth, and then

closes it again. Like he has something he wants to say and doesn't know whether or not to say it.

Ultimately, he looks forward and clears his throat.

"I'll wait until you get inside."

I nod then shut the car door, walking quickly to my house and stepping inside, only peeking back out once I've closed the front door and locked it. Through the side window, I watch as Andy's car idles there for another minute before it finally backs up and races down the road.

"Oh my gosh!"

The bubbly voice is enough to have my head turning, but it's the big shit-eating grin aimed my way that has me breaking into my own real, honest-to-goodness smile.

"Briar!"

Before I can even formulate a response, Abby Fuller's body collides with mine, her little frame wrapping around me without any care that I'm standing at my check stand, trying to work.

"Hey, Abs," I say, wrapping my arms around her and giving her a snug squeeze. "Good to see you, lady."

My longtime friend pulls back and looks at me with wide eyes and that same elated expression. Knowing how happy she is to see me makes me feel like I stand just a little bit taller.

Not that I need the extra height.

"You, too!" she enthuses, her smile never waning. "I didn't realize you were still in town. I thought I'd miss out on seeing you because I was gone for August."

Abby is a few years younger than me, but she was my closest friend when I was growing up, our families having been friends for ages. Her older brother, Rusty, is the guy who makes the awesome beer. I don't have many friends in general—even fewer in Cedar Point—but Abby would definitely be considered my best friend out of the whole lot.

Something about her genuinely happy disposition in contrast to my generally muted personality just makes for a good mix.

I only come home a few times a year, but I'm always back for our mandatory, last-two-weeks-of-August family 'reunion.' It's the one period of time when my mom and dad are able to get all the Mitchell kids home together. We spend time on the water and have regular family dinners, do a two-day hike, and have endless bonfires out on the deck.

They'd never get me to admit it, but it's my favorite time of year. Even more than I love autumn, I love spending time with my family, although being with my siblings all at once is just a recipe for obnoxious behaviors and ceaseless teasing and poking fun.

Normally when I'm home, I spend some quality time with Abby, but she went to help her grandmother transition into an assisted living facility in Southern California last month, so we haven't seen each other since…I think it was April, when I came home for a few days to celebrate Easter.

And because we haven't had the chance to catch up, I haven't told her that I've moved home or what's been going on with me and Chad, so it makes sense for her to be shocked to see me scanning groceries at One Stop with Lois at my side. As far as she knew, I was back down the mountain, not still in Cedar Point, working a full-time job and living with my parents.

"No, I'm still here," I say, enjoying the belated realization that talking with Abby about what's been going on in my life is exactly what I need.

I might not be a person who wants to share every thought and emotion I have, but breaking up with Chad and moving home was a huge life change. Rehashing everything might not be fun, but it certainly will be good to get her thoughts.

"Are you like...*back*, back? Or..."

I wiggle my hand. "For a little while."

She squeals, her joy at the news making me smile.

"This is seriously the best news ever, ever, ever!"

I laugh. "I don't know about *that*, but I do think it will be fun to get together soon."

Abby's head bobbles. "Yes, please! Let me do some shopping really quick and then we can plan a date."

She waves at me and apologizes to Lois before shooting off into the store in search of whatever it is she came for.

I've never been a fan of the phrase 'adopt an introvert,' as if those of us who are not energized by being around people are deficient in something that makes life enjoyable, and Abby never bought into that either. She didn't make it her life's goal to push me into situations that didn't feel comfortable. Even though she liked hanging out around town and occasionally was able to talk me into going to do social things with some of our other friends, she was still really good at respecting my need for alone and quiet time, often bringing over her homework or a book to be quiet *with* me.

I think that's why we became so close, why I think she's so fantastic. Even though we are as different as can be, she didn't try to change a fundamental part of who I am. She just leaned into it.

"Are you listening?"

My eyes fly to Lois. "What?"

"Well, there's my answer," she says, though there isn't any heat to her words. "Pay attention, girly. I don't want to have to train you for any longer than we have on the schedule."

I bob my head and return my focus to the checkout screen, watching attentively as she walks me through the complicated steps for accepting checks.

Eventually, Abby comes through the line, dumping a ton of baking ingredients onto the conveyor belt with a grin.

Abby is an amazing baker, so I'm unsurprised to see what she's purchasing.

"Brownies?" I guess, dragging a package of cocoa powder across the scanner.

"Not just *any* brownies," she says. "Slutty brownies."

Lois barks out a laugh. "Last time I had brownies that turned me into a slut, I found out my friend Barb used a recipe with hooch in it."

I freeze, my hand reaching out for a bag of chocolate chips, and when I look at Lois, she grins at me.

"What?" she asks. "I was young once, too."

Abby and I break into a fit of giggles, and it requires effort for me to wipe my eyes and keep scanning.

"You're too much, Lo," Abby says once she's finally calmed down and caught her breath. "These are definitely not weed brownies, although that does sound like a fun idea to experiment with."

I roll my eyes, knowing she's full of shit. Abby likes to talk about stuff like weed brownies and breaking the rules, but she's just as big of a nerdy rule-follower as I am.

"It's a cookie and brownie combo, but I add in a little something extra."

"Is the something extra what makes them so slutty?" Lois asks, and I look at her just in time to see her wiggling her eyebrows up and down.

"You'll just have to wait and see," Abby taunts. Then her eyes find mine. "You're coming over tonight to help me make them."

"I can't," I tell her as I finish scanning her last items. "I just started an hour ago and I'm working late to learn how to receive deliveries."

My friend's shoulders fall. "Call in sick."

I snort. "Sure. I'll get right on that."

"Tomorrow then? I can wait to make the brownies, but they have to be ready by tomorrow night."

"Yeah, I can do tomorrow," I say, clicking a few buttons on the screen to ring up Abby's total.

"Good, because I have so much to tell you."

I narrow my eyes. "Like what?"

Abby swipes her card in the reader, giving me a sneaky little grin. "You'll just have to wait and see."

Once Abby's paid, she rounds the check stand, gives me another hug, and tells me to expect a text from her before heading out the door.

Lois and I get back to training, though it isn't much longer before the end of her shift and she leaves me for my first few hours working alone and closing by myself. The stream of customers is slow, and my mind begins to wander.

After spending a little time thinking about Abby and the conversation we're going to have tomorrow night about Chad, my mind circles back to my night at The Mitch with Andy last

Monday.

It's been over a week since we went out for drinks, and I've tried my hardest not to think so much about it. My efforts have been in vain, though, as I've spent many evenings staring up at the ceiling and thinking about everything. The easy conversation, the little bit of flirtation, the way I feel when he laughs.

That little moment at the end of the night, as we stared at each other across the console in his Jeep…

What the hell *was* that?

Did I imagine the way he was looking at me?

I keep telling myself I shouldn't be thinking about *any* guy the way he's been on my mind. Logically, I know I need time to process what happened with Chad and shouldn't waste time on a man when I need to be planning what's next in my life.

But even with that internal mantra, I can't get my mind off of Andy. Even now, he lingers there in the back of my thoughts over the next hour or so, until the store is about to close. And then, almost like I conjured him up with my mind, Andy walks out to the front, my eyes studiously avoiding him the minute I see him walking down the long aisle from the back.

Funny. A decade has passed, and somehow I'm still that teenager who flees the room whenever he comes around.

"You ready?" he asks.

I know logically he's talking about closing up and spending the evening receiving deliveries, doing the very work-related things I'm supposed to be doing.

But I can't seem to quiet the little voice that wishes he were talking about anything else.

Grabbing another drink.

Heading out to dinner.

Going back to his place for something a little more private.

I clear my throat and try to swallow that down, but I'm sure my face and neck are flushing even though he can't see my thoughts.

"Yeah," I say. "I'll close up and meet you back there."

He nods his head, his eyes scanning my face for a few seconds before he turns and heads back to the stockroom.

My shoulders fall and I turn to grab the keys out of my register, then practically storm over to the front door to lock up, infuriated at myself.

The way Andy looks at me...it's hard to explain and unlike anything I've experienced before.

When Chad used to look at me, there was expectation. Either he had a question he wanted answered or a desire he wanted fulfilled.

When Andy looks at me, there's anticipation. As if he's been waiting to see me, or talk to me, or hear the next thing out of my mouth.

The difference between those two words—expectation and anticipation—is so minute, and yet so colossal at the same time.

Maybe I'm just imagining it. Maybe what I'm seeing is just the same thing on a different face.

But it doesn't feel that way.

As I walk through One Stop and head to the back, where I know I'll be spending the next few hours alone with Andy, I try for what feels like the thousandth time to remind myself that my focus in life shouldn't include a man.

Especially one who manages to fluster me as much as Andy Marshall does.

CHAPTER SEVEN

Andy

Over a week has gone by since the night I took Briar out for drinks, and I've found it even more difficult to get her off my mind than before.

I'm still going through my regular routine—taking care of dad, working long hours, swimming as often as I can—but I'm starting to observe nearly everything in and around town with a critical eye.

Would Briar like swimming in this section of the lake?

Does Briar know Ruthie opened her own bakery?

Has Briar ever taken the time to enjoy the little farm Melvin Kinny has on the lot behind his house?

It's exhausting.

And also rejuvenating in a way I could never have expected.

I've been so overwhelmed with the day-to-day of keeping my dad and the family business afloat that I hardly take any time for myself anymore. Somehow, distracting my mind with thoughts of Briar is the exact kind of escape I've been needing.

There's an element of excitement, of anticipation when I come to work every day knowing she's here, training with Lois. It's taken everything in me not to ask her out for another drink at the end of every evening when she stops by my office to let me know she's leaving, her eyes tired.

Although, I *have* been putting together a list of ideas for what we could do to remind Briar of all the reasons why Cedar Point is a great place to live.

Just in case an opportunity presents itself.

"Alright, I'm ready."

Briar's voice has me looking up from where I'm staring blankly at the incoming shipment logs for the two deliveries we're expecting tonight.

"Awesome," I say, refocusing my attention on work and the reason Briar is working a late shift tonight. "Let's jump right in. The first delivery should be here in the next fifteen minutes, and there's a lot to go over before they get here."

I take Briar over to the wall next to the office, where a handful of clipboards are hanging on nails, side by side. We go over what each one is for, and I explain the system I helped my dad develop to make sure everything's done on schedule.

Then I hand her the delivery slip for the first expected order, explaining what all the information means. Since most shipping companies use codes to reference product, I show her how to find out what code connects with what product on one of the other lists.

Finally, I walk her through the stockroom and review the areas where tonight's shipments need to be stored. Since the first one is all non-perishables in cans and jars, it goes out on shelves. The second delivery, a restock of dairy products, will need to go in the cooler.

"It's so cold in here," she says as we step into the walk-in fridge in the back corner of the stockroom.

When I look at her, I catch her rolling her eyes then chuckling quietly at herself.

"I get that it's a fridge," she clarifies. "Obviously. I just wasn't expecting it to be *this* cold."

I grin along with her. "You'll definitely want to bring a coat on the days you're scheduled to do expiration checks. Once a week we do a product fresh check to make sure none of the perishables, like the stuff in here, have expired."

She nods, her eyes flitting over the shelves. "Is there only one brand of milk?" she asks, scanning across the left wall, where all the gallon and half-gallon containers are stored.

"We have an exclusive contract with Betty Farms. It covers all of our dairy," I say, referencing the small farm in Central California my dad signed with a few years ago.

She hums and bobs her head, but when she doesn't say anything else, my curiosity is piqued.

"Why?"

Briar looks up at me and lifts a shoulder. "No reason."

I grin. "Oh, come on. I feel like there's a big sign on your forehead saying you have an opinion you're keeping to yourself."

She wiggles her nose a little bit, like she's weighing her words, before she finally shrugs. "It just seems like signing a contract with a supplier that restricts you from offering other brands locks you in to their pricing. It doesn't allow you to use a different product if you find something more competitive."

I nod, having heard that argument before—out of my own mouth when my dad decided to sign with Orwin Betty. I had lots of reasons I thought were valid, and my dad listened to them all before explaining his decision-making process. I give the same information to Briar.

"You're absolutely right," I say. "We could get a cheaper product from a different farm. We could offer a variety to make sure the pricing stays competitive, but my father believes in small towns and small businesses, and how they support and take care of families. He signed a contract with Betty Farms because he wanted to give their small business the reassurance that we wouldn't try to get them to drop their prices to the point where they couldn't afford to supply us anymore."

Briar nibbles on the inside of her cheek, that same nervous habit I've seen from her so much since she's been working here. Did she do that when she was younger? Part of me wishes I knew, wishes I'd paid more attention back then.

"That's really...noble," she responds.

"And expensive and not very business-minded," I add with a laugh, enjoying the look of surprise on Briar's face. "It's true. And I know, because I had this exact conversation with my dad a few years ago when he told me he was signing the contract, but not every decision he's made over the years has been about the business's bottom line. Sometimes, it's about doing what feels right, and for him, sacrificing a little bit of profit in the long run is worth it to know he's standing by his values. That includes supporting small businesses."

A grin spreads on her face and she nods her head.

"I don't remember your dad much, but I'm pretty sure I'd really like him."

"I think he'll like you, too."

We both stand in silence, just staring at each other for a long moment, the air between us filled with little puffs of fog from the heat of our breath in the cold room.

"Thanks again, for the drink last week," she says, shuffling on her feet and rubbing her arms. "I had fun."

I smile. "Me too. It's been a long time since I've gone out to do something fun, so…thanks for letting me treat you."

"Maybe…we could do something again," she says, surprising me. "If you want."

My mind instantly starts sorting through the list of things we can do together. Hiking, swimming, enjoying downtown. Camping and stargazing and the Saturday morning market, not to mention all the fall festivities in the near future.

"We should go hiking," I say, "or swimming. Something outdoorsy before the weather gets too cold."

Briar grins. "That could be fun."

"Ah, be careful," I tease. "I don't want you to risk having *too* much fun in lame-ass Cedar Point."

She rolls her eyes but doesn't stop smiling. "You know, you're a lot different than I thought you'd be," she tells me.

My eyebrows rise. "Oh? How did you think I'd be?"

Her eyes rove over my face before they dip to my mouth, just for a second, so quickly I think I misread it. But then her eyes widen and she looks away.

Before either of us can say or do anything else, the buzzer goes off to signal that a truck has pulled up to the back.

"Come on." Pushing the fridge door open, I wave my hand to have Briar walk out first. "Let's teach you how to receive an order."

Forty-five minutes later, we've stacked the pallets of canned goods in the right spot in the stockroom and sent the delivery guy on his way to the next store on his list.

"I think I understand why you do deliveries at night," Briar tells me, her eyes following the big rig as it backs ever so slowly out of the One Stop parking lot.

"Oh? Why's that?"

"Because you don't have to worry about there being any cars in the parking lot to get in the way when they pull in."

I point a finger at her like a gun and pull the trigger. "Bingo."

She grins and we both turn to head back inside.

"The second delivery should be here in the next thirty minutes. This one is all dairy." I walk Briar over to the wall of clipboards. "Pretend you're going to be receiving this order by yourself. Walk me through how you'd go about it, step by step."

Briar takes a deep breath and blows it out, her cheeks puffing up slightly, the gust of air blowing the loose strands of hair away from her face.

Then she picks up the clipboard she needs and walks me through it, from explaining how she'd find out there was a delivery during her shift through meeting with the truck driver, into how she'll direct the delivery to be stacked and put away in the walk-in.

She nails every single step.

"And then once we're done putting the last containers on the shelves, I'll have the driver wait while I do a final count to confirm the product on the shelf matches the invoice. Then I'll have them sign our slip, and I'll sign his slip and walk the driver out to their truck."

I cross my arms and narrow my eyes at her. "And?"

Briar's eyes widen, and she looks down at the paperwork in her hand then around the walk-in, her sudden worry about having missed something apparent on her face.

"And…" she says, stretching the word out. "I'll tell them to have a nice night?"

At that, I start laughing.

"Awesome job, Briar," I tell her, still chuckling a little bit. "Really. You did the whole thing 100% correct."

She scrunches up her nose and playfully smacks me with the back of the clipboard, but I can see the smile in her eyes.

"You jerk," she mumbles. "I thought I got something wrong."

"Briar Mitchell? Get something wrong?" I scoff. "Not a chance, sweetheart—not with a brain like yours. I wouldn't be surprised if I found out you graduated college with honors."

My eyes drop to her lips when she twists them to the side, and I see a bit of red peek out from under her shirt at her neck, the telltale sign of embarrassment.

"I'm right, aren't I?"

She sighs, like talking about how smart she is could be something humiliating.

"Tell me."

"I graduated summa cum laude."

"And that means?"

"It's a GPA of 3.8 or higher, so…I mean it's not like I was valedictorian or anything."

"So what you're saying is you're a genius."

Briar just shakes her head at me, her eyes crinkling at the corners from her smile.

I love seeing that on her face. She doesn't seem to smile very often—not often enough, by my standards—so whenever I see it, I feel like it's a gift.

"You have a great smile."

I watch as the pink on Briar's cheeks grows even more pronounced. She swallows, the movement visible on her long, slender neck.

I know I should take a step back, take a step away. I should remind myself of the fact that Briar is my employee, Boyd's sister, not the woman I'm going to end up with—all the reasons I've given myself before to keep from eyeing her with the kind of attraction and interest that has me feeling like I'm balancing on a razor's edge. But I just can't seem to do it.

There's something about her that I'm drawn to, a feeling I can't manage to push away, no matter how much I wish I could.

"Thanks," she says, the single word coming out breathy and creating a tiny cloud of fog between us. After an elongated pause, she adds, "I've always loved your laugh."

I'm caught by surprise at her words. "Always?"

Briar's eyes widen, and she starts to nibble on that cheek of hers, the one she bites when she's nervous.

A thought comes to mind, something I've never considered before. The skittish girl she used to be, always racing out of the room when I was over at her house and hanging out with her brother. Could it... Was there more to that?

"Yeah," she finally says. "It's a good laugh. Thick and, you know...deep."

Something dirty must cross her mind because Briar suddenly looks even more flustered at herself.

"I mean...you know, the tone of it. Your laugh. I'm talking about your laugh."

I can't help but grin at her. "What else would you have meant?" I ask, knowing I'm ruffling her feathers a little bit.

Briar shakes her head, her eyes narrowing, but a little smile still sits on her lips.

"I feel like you like getting me flustered," she says, her voice low.

"Maybe I do."

Almost as if it has a life of its own, my hand rises, taking some of the loose strands of hair at Briar's temple and tucking them back behind her ear. I about lose my mind when I see her entire body shiver. Somehow, just that simple movement alone has shifted the feeling in the room.

We stare at each other for another long moment, and I wonder what it would be like if I gave in to the urge sweeping through my body, the one that's telling me I'm an idiot *not* to kiss the mouth that has been holding me captive since the moment I first saw her two weeks ago.

Then, before I even realize what's happening, Briar's lips are suddenly against mine. Warm and soft and just about every damn thing I thought they would be as I imagined kissing her over and over again.

But just as quickly, she pulls back, and I watch as her hand comes to her mouth and her eyes go wide.

"Oh my god," she whispers against her fingers.

Then she closes her eyes and presses her hand against her whole face.

"Oh my god, I'm so sorry. I don't know what I was thinking, I just kissed you and it came out of nowhere. I just…"

Before she can convince herself that she did something wrong, I push her hand away from her face and step into her so her back is pressed against the rear wall of the fridge.

She gasps. Partly at the cold, surely, but definitely at me, at the heat of my body and the way I drop my mouth so close I can almost taste her.

"Don't ever apologize for kissing me again," I say.

Her eyes widen momentarily, but then my lips touch hers and we're both lost.

She opens for me immediately, almost like she was desperate for me to do it, our tongues flirting and twisting and stroking each other.

God, it feels so good. So warm, so wet, and I love the way she's responding to me. Slowly, tentatively, yes, but also like the slow pace is exactly what's hitting her in the right spot.

I hear her moan as my hands pull her closer to me, as I grip her hip with one hand and wrap my arm around her back with the other, and I feel myself growing hard beneath my zipper. Just that little moan, that little blip of desire has my heart racing in a way I haven't felt...ever.

"Shit," I say, pulling back just slightly, my breaths panting between us as if I've just run a marathon.

"I know," she says, and then she wraps her arms around my neck and yanks my mouth back down to hers, like she can't get enough.

Well then.

We kiss for who knows how long. Maybe minutes. Maybe hours. I don't care, though, losing myself in what is quite possibly the most delicious, tantalizing kiss I've ever had in my life. The way she tastes, the way she feels pressed against me, the way her arms are wrapped around me, holding me close as if she never wants to let me go.

My hands are holding her hips and sliding back to her ass, desperate to touch and grab anything I can, wanting her snug against my body, wishing we were anywhere else but here so I could strip these pesky clothes off of us and get to all the fun underneath.

When I hear the sound of the buzzer that means the second delivery has pulled up outside, both of us yank back, startled, as if we've been caught doing something we shouldn't.

Briar's eyes are wide as her hand reaches back up to touch her lips, almost like she can't believe what just happened between us.

I like that look of dazed confusion on her face, like kissing me was just as intoxicating for her as kissing her was for me.

"We should go handle that," I say.

She nods, stepping back and taking all that delicious body heat with her.

"I'll go first," she says, her eyes dropping to my lower half. "Give you a minute to sort yourself."

I grin, unable to hide my enjoyment that she's teasing me. "I'll be out in a second."

She nods her head then scurries away, glancing back at me as she nibbles on the inside of her mouth again. She only stares at me for a second before she pushes through the door and leaves me standing alone in the walk-in fridge with the most intense hard-on I've ever had.

I quickly strip off my shirt, hoping releasing my body heat will do the trick and cool me down enough that the blood rushes to other places in my body. A minute later, I tug my shirt back on and exit the fridge, finding Briar talking with the truck driver.

Instead of heading over to monitor what she's doing, I take a step back and retreat into my office, wanting to give us a moment apart, as well as provide Briar an opportunity to shine without me hovering in the background.

I'd be lying, though, if I didn't admit I also want a second to myself so I can replay what just happened between us.

Because holy shit.

Never in my wildest dreams would I have expected a steamy little make-out session with Briar Mitchell to be on the docket this evening.

Deliveries? Yes.

Devouring Briar? No.

But damn if it wasn't everything I was anticipating it could be. I almost laugh at myself when I realize I'm touching my lips like she was, as if I've never been kissed before, enjoying that little remnant of how she tastes on my tongue…peppermint and chocolate and something distinctly Briar that I can't place.

It's been a long time since I've kissed someone I'm not actively dating, and normally, I don't go that route. I may have played around a little bit in and after high school, just having fun, but it's been years since I've been that guy, instead putting my energy into dating, even if I haven't been successful in finding anything long-term.

Which is why this kind of thing happening with Briar feels like quite a mistake in the making.

Hell if it wasn't a delicious surprise, though.

After about twenty minutes go by, I poke my head out to see how she's coming along, unsurprised to see she's already sending the truck driver on his way with a wave.

When she turns to press the button that lowers the delivery door, I catch the little glimpse of pride in her expression that I'd bet she wouldn't ever show if she thought someone was watching. My guess is confirmed when she wipes her face clean the instant she sees me standing off to the side.

"All done?" I ask.

She nods her head. "Do you want to take a look?"

I shake my head. "Nah. I don't doubt you did it perfectly."

Briar grins at me then twists her fingers together. "Anything else?" she asks. "Or is that it for the night?"

Part of me wants to say *Hell yes there's something else*, sweep her into my arms, and convince her to let me take her home, to spend the night allowing me to worship her gorgeous body.

But even though kissing Briar was exactly what I've been daydreaming about for weeks, there are too many reasons why something like that can't happen again.

So instead of suggesting we go out for a drink, I force my mind to focus on work.

"I think that's everything," I reply. "Awesome job tonight, Briar. Really. You nailed it."

She blushes at my praise but doesn't say anything else, just taking my words as an indicator that she should gather her belongings from the staff lockers and clear out.

Her movements are slow, though. Unhurried in a way that makes me think she wants me to walk her out. So I shut down my computer and all the back lights just as she walks out with her purse.

"Are you ready?" I ask.

She nods, her lips tipping up at the sides. "Definitely."

We stride through One Stop and out through the front door then walk around the building to the lot in the back.

"So," I begin, once we're standing between two cars, my Jeep and an older, black RAV4.

"So," she echoes, standing a few feet away from me. "Thanks for taking the time to teach me tonight."

I nod. "Thanks for being a great student."

She licks her lips. "Alright, well…I guess I'll just, see you around?"

"Yeah." I pause, and then before I can help myself, I blurt

out the only thing on my mind. "Maybe…this weekend, we could see each other around at the Saturday market?"

Briar chews on the inside of her cheek, trying to hide her smile but failing spectacularly.

"Sure. Maybe I'll be there around 9?"

I grin. "I might be there at 9, too."

She bobs her head then steps backward. "Alright, then. I'll… see you around," she says, actually meaning it this time.

"See you, Briar."

Then she climbs into her car and gives me a wave before pulling out of the parking lot and heading off. Back to her parents' house, to the place she's staying in temporarily until she decides what's next.

I take a deep breath and let it out, long and slow.

What the hell am I doing?

CHAPTER EIGHT

Briar

"I want to have the Perrys over for dinner tonight. Do you want to have pasta or should I do something else?"

When I don't hear anything else, I look over at my mother holding her mug of coffee close to her chest, realizing she's talking to me.

"Oh," I say. "Sorry. I have plans tonight. I can't do dinner."

Her expression falls, but in a way that makes me laugh. My mom knows how to pout like a child better than any kid I know. Her shoulders droop and her body sags and her mouth fully turns into a frown. It's actually pretty adorable, even if I know she's completely serious.

"Abby's back from her grandmother's," I add.

At that piece of information, my mom's face morphs into something completely different. Her smile stretches wide, her eyebrows rise, and her dimples pop out.

"Oh that's wonderful!" she says. "I just love that Abby."

I snort into my own cup of coffee.

Every *single* time I mention her, my mother says those exact words. *I just love that Abby.*

"What? I do! And Rusty, too. They're both such sweethearts. It's so wonderful how the two of them have bonded together in the wake of…well, everything."

The *everything* she's not articulating is the fact that Rusty and Abby's parents passed away when Abby was still in high school. A drunk driving accident that left the town reeling. I'd left for college the year before, and I did everything I could. But I've always wished I had been around during that time to be a support to my friend during the most difficult time of her life.

Thankfully, Rusty was able to convince a judge that he should be able to take care of her for the last two years before she turned 18, and she never had to leave Cedar Point or move into the system. She eventually moved away for college but went right back to Rusty's after she graduated, preferring to be in her childhood home rather than trying to forge her own path.

But any time we talk about her life here, she always hints at the idea that she might like to move away eventually, try something new. I don't push that on her, though. I can be supportive of her ideas and talk her through pros and cons without telling her moving away is the best thing she could ever do for herself. That's something she'll have to figure out—and decide—on her own.

"So what are you two going to get up to tonight?" my mom prods. "Lots of trouble and mischief?"

I roll my eyes, reading the sarcasm in her voice.

It's one of her favorite things to do. Joke about me—the quintessential quiet girl—and Abby—the consummate rule-follower—going out and being bad girls.

I'd like to say it gets old, but it's funny because it's true.

"We're going to bake slutty brownies."

My mother's eyebrows turn into one caterpillar with how deeply concerned her facial expression becomes.

"I don't like that word."

"I know, which is why you're not allowed to have any brownies."

She rolls her eyes then takes another sip of her coffee.

We sit in silence for a minute, the two of us just enjoying our morning caffeine intake and the silence. While we do that, my mind drifts off to a faraway place I like to call 'The Curious World of Andy Marshall.'

We kissed last night—and not a little smooch, either. There wasn't anything tiny about it. Not in size, not in length, not in the depth of lust and desire it made me feel.

I could have made a million bets on what was going to happen last night, and not a single one of them would have ended with the two of us wrapped together like vines growing up the shelving in the walk-in. And yet, that's exactly what happened.

As I relive that memory, I can't help but let a little smile come across my face…not just due to how his mouth on mine made me feel, but also because of how proud I was at his praise of my work. It's something I've noticed about him a lot during my training; he's constantly telling everyone when they're doing a good job. I haven't seen more than a few hours go by without him popping into the front of the store to check in with me and Lois and whoever else is working. Other cashiers, baggers—it doesn't matter. He's constantly praising the little things, acknowledging the good.

It's incredibly refreshing. When I was younger, I didn't *know* Andy; I just had a crush on him. All my emotions and feelings were wrapped up in the simple yet very big feelings of attraction.

Now, having spent the past week or so watching him actually manage people, I'm starting to realize he's just…a kind person. An honest-to-goodness good guy. Real, in a world filled with fakes.

Like I said: refreshing.

And intoxicating, if the way I threw myself at him is any indicator.

I still can't believe I kissed him first. I've never been that forward in my life, but I guess it's too late now to be embarrassed. Now, I get to just enjoy the memory of making out with Andy Marshall.

"What's that face for?"

I look over at my mother, my smile wiping clean in an instant.

"What?"

"That smile," she says, her own creeping across her face. "I haven't seen you smile like *that* in…well, in a long damn time."

Nibbling at my cheek, I try to think of something to say—something that *isn't* about my tongue in Andy's mouth while we were at work. Something tells me she wouldn't be too pleased to find out I kissed my boss.

But nothing comes to mind, nothing that would be convincing enough, anyway. So I just decide to do what I always do.

Close off.

"It's nothing," I finally say, though I hate the little bit of disappointment she tries to hide from me when she realizes I'm not going to share.

I'm not ready to talk with my mom about something like what happened between me and Andy. I like to keep my private life private, which is why I also haven't ever talked a lot about my relationship with Chad.

But that doesn't mean I enjoy disappointing my mother.

She's the most important woman in my life. I want her to know me, and love me and be proud of me. For some reason, though, I just struggle to open up about men. About love.

Maybe it's because I've spent my entire life watching her relationship with my dad. They're so perfect together, so loving and caring and supportive.

The idea of telling her about all my relationship failures just makes me feel like…trash. Like I'm broken or defective. Like I didn't love myself enough to want the happily ever after the two of them have shown me exists in the world.

"Well, if you ever want to share," she says, giving me those kind eyes as she rounds the counter and comes up to my side, "I'm always here for you."

Then she places a kiss on my forehead and squeezes my shoulder before heading out of the kitchen, taking her coffee mug with her.

"Shut. Up!"

I take another long swig of my wine and try to burrow deeper into the corner of the couch as Abby's eyes fly wide.

She's been storming around the kitchen for the past fifteen minutes as I try to recap my breakup with Chad in as few words as possible.

"So, to kind of…wrap this up," I continue, "I told him I wasn't happy, said it felt like he just wanted me to be his little woman who stays home and takes care of him and that's not what I wanted to be."

"And what did he say to that?"

I pause, nibbling on my cheek. "He said that was exactly what he wanted and all I was good for anyway."

I can see Abby's nostrils flare from across the room.

"I was already supposed to come home a week later, so I just packed more thoroughly, and when I left, I handed Chad my ring. He rolled his eyes at me and said he was surprised I had the decency not to take it. Then he said something about how he knew I'd be back, but I was so upset by that point, I don't even remember."

Abby slams a cabinet door after pulling out a bag of chocolate chips then returns to the kitchen island.

"Well, I for one will tell you that moving on to bigger and better is absolutely the right move," she says, ripping the bag open and chucking a handful of morsels into the bowl of dough she's been working on.

"Hey," I call out. "They're called slutty brownies, not angry brownies."

Abby snorts. "Maybe they *should* be angry brownies. Maybe I'll invent them myself. They can be mixed with red velvet cake and extra dark chocolate and I'll yell at them while I bake."

"Sounds delicious," I say, giggling as I take another sip of my wine.

"You know what's delicious?" she says, grabbing her spatula off the counter and using it to mix in the chips. "Giving your ex the middle finger and leaving him behind when you finally realize he isn't treating you like the goddess you are."

I huff out a little laugh through my nose but don't add my own two cents. Abby always flies off the handle when I talk about

Chad. She's been telling me for years that I should move on, and I've agreed with her for a lot longer than I'd like to admit.

But there's something hard about leaving behind a relationship you've invested so much time in. You start to convince yourself that the other person might change if you give it a little more time. A little more energy. A little more effort.

Obviously, *now* I can look back and say there were a lot more problems than positives. *Now* I can identify all the ways we weren't compatible. But in the moment, I was so sure we could make it work, so certain that if he just changed a little or I just flexed a bit, we would figure it out and things would get better.

Looking back, I know I waited around entirely too long for a man I wasn't even in love with. Though, I guess back then, that was actually preferable.

There really was a time in the beginning when I cared deeply for Chad, but somewhere along the way, the things we wanted out of a relationship just became too different. Leaving wasn't my only option. I could have stayed, could have continued being the woman he wanted me to be.

But I wouldn't have been happy. *Nothing* about my life with Chad made me happy. I'm not sure it ever did.

"I still don't think you should have left so much of your stuff," Abby says. "I mean, I get the empowerment part of being like *Hey dick, I'm outta here* and just leaving it all behind, but I also think it can make it too easy to go back."

"I'm never going back," I say, taking a deep breath. "Chad isn't for me. And who knows? Maybe I never find a man who *is* for me. Maybe a guy who can be my friend *and* give me good orgasms doesn't exist in the world, but I know for damn sure Chad is not that man."

Abby looks at me with wide eyes. "Look at *you*, Miss Sassypants with your attitude and 'I know for damn sure' declarations."

I giggle, holding up my wine glass. "You know red wine makes me a little feisty."

"Which is why I told you you're not allowed more than the one glass," she replies. "I don't need to peel a hungover Briar off my couch tomorrow morning."

I smirk, stretching my long legs out along the L-shaped sectional in Rusty and Abby's living room. It's technically their parents' house, I guess, though nothing inside is the same as it was when they were younger. When I came home the summer after their parents died, I found Abby and Rusty living on air mattresses. The entire house had been emptied, from the kitchenware to the art on the walls and all the furniture.

They'd moved it to storage, each of them struggling to cope with the loss of their parents while living in the house they'd lived in together as one big happy family.

New furniture would pop up every time I came to town as they purchased pieces from thrift stores or accepted castoffs from other Cedar Point residents posting their freebies on the *Take It or Leave It* bulletin board at the community center.

It's taken them years to make this house into a place that feels like a completely different home than what they remember, but even so, I think Abby's desperate to move out on her own. She's mentioned it a few times over the past two years but always says it's not realistic because her job at the craft store isn't enough to live on.

"How's work?" I ask, trying to remember the last thing she told me about working at Uncle Ben's Crafts. Something about a new quilt-making workshop leaving her with bloody fingers, I think. "Still loving it?"

"Oh, no. I quit."

I pop up on the couch, leaning forward against the back so I can watch Abby as she makes her brownies.

"What? When did that happen?"

"Before I left for Gam's," she says. Then she sets down the bowl she's been mixing everything in and gives me a big grin. "I started working at Ruthie's."

My eyes go wide. "You serious?"

She nods, her expression lighting up the entire room. "That's why I'm working on these brownies. Ruth told me she wants to mix up her menu and make it a little more fun."

I smile. "Wow, Abby. That's so great."

For as long as I can remember, Abby has loved baking, and she's always had a flair for creating fun concoctions, like the angry brownies idea. She's waffled with the idea of making her own company or doing something with her baking on social media, but she always seems to get bogged down in all the business-y details. Knowing she's finally going after her dream makes me happy for her.

Maybe a tiny bit jealous, since I can't seem to figure out what the hell I want to do, but mostly happy.

We spend a while talking about the bakery and some of Abby's ideas before we loop back around to Chad and the breakup and moving back home.

"So, how's working at One Stop going?"

My mind instantly goes to Andy and our *phenomenal* kiss last night in the walk-in. It's all that's been filling my head all day, and it's been active work not thinking about it while I've been here. Of course, that's now flown out the window.

"What's with the face?"

I glance at Abby, cursing the fact that my expressions have

been so transparent today. I'd blame the wine, but I'm starting to think it's Andy. First the romanticized daydreaming earlier in front of my mom, and now this.

"And don't say nothing," Abby continues, pointing her spatula at me with enough oomph to send a few chocolate chips flying in my direction. "I can see that something is going on in that head of yours. If you don't want to talk about it, say that, but don't pretend there's nothing up."

Sighing, I lie back on the couch, actually enjoying the fact that the wine in my system is loosening my tongue with every second that passes.

This is Abby, I tell myself. *You can talk to her about it.*

"I kissed Andy."

The minute I say it, I slap my hands over my face, wishing I could suck the words back in and tell nobody.

There's a long pause, and then I hear a clatter a few seconds before Abby rounds the couch and plops down next to my feet, her eyes wide and the biggest shit-eating grin on her face.

"Tell. Me. *Everything.*"

I can't help but laugh at how ridiculous she is, and then I laugh even harder when she starts poking at me to say I shouldn't laugh at her.

Eventually, I get control over myself and just spit it out, all of it. The way things were with him at The Mitch last week and how I spent a week trying not to think about him every second. The fact that I kissed him first and then how he pressed me up against the wall and demanded I never apologize for kissing him. And how we have plans to get together at the Saturday market this weekend. By the time I'm done, Abby's fanning her face.

"You should absolutely sleep with him," she says.

"What? No! That's ridiculous."

"How is that ridiculous?" she says. "You're fresh off a break-up, and getting some from the—can I say it? Yeah, I'm gonna say it—fucking *scrumptious* Andy Marshall? I mean, talk about a huge step up from fucking *Chad*, amiright?"

I roll my eyes. "I'm not sleeping with Andy," I tell her. "I'm not even sure I should be entertaining this whole…flirtation and kissing thing. I'm trying to figure out my life right now, not distract myself with another guy."

"Which is why it's perfect."

My eyebrows scrunch in slight tipsiness and confusion.

"Think about it this way: you're newly single and focusing on you, right? Andy Marshall is a super charming guy who wants to help you learn how to have fun in Cedar Point. So?" She spreads her arms out and wiggles her eyebrows. "Have a little fun—but in his pants."

I giggle and roll my eyes. "You're ridiculous."

"You already said that, and saying it again doesn't make it true. It is categorically false. Tonight, you're going to think about this while you lie in bed, daydreaming about your new sexy hunk, and tomorrow you'll realize how right I am. You can focus on yourself and figure out what's next for you *and* take care of your vagina at the same time. They're not mutually exclusive."

"When did you become a psychic?" I tease, only to be met with a pillow to the face.

"Mark my words," she tells me. "Tomorrow, you're going to be thinking all about Andy Marshall and his dick."

Twelve hours later, as I sit in my kitchen and eat breakfast before leaving for my last training shift at One Stop, I am *indeed* thinking about Andy Marshall and his dick.

Jesus. I'd like to blame Abby and say it's just her crazy ideas that are guiding my train of thought, but I can't place it all entirely on her.

Not when I crawled into bed last night and slipped my fingers between my thighs, the wine in my system easing me back to the way it felt when Andy had me pressed against the wall in the walk-in. The way his hardness was so intense against my softness. The passionate way he kissed me in such stark contrast to the lukewarm feelings between myself and Chad.

I came quietly, a little ripple of something that rolled through me in slow waves and had me falling asleep almost instantly.

Now that my light buzz has worn off, I'm left with a little bit of a headache and a lotta bit of curiosity.

I've been so closed off to the idea of a new relationship with any man that I never even considered the 'just have a little fun' approach Abby suggested last night.

Could I do something like that?

My sexual experiences have been pretty good. A few college boys back before Chad who knew what they were doing, and then Chad himself was decent enough in bed to get me off until he stopped putting any effort in.

I can admit it's been at least a few years since the last time a man was the reason I orgasmed. Normally, I'd make sure Chad came and then he'd fall asleep. I'd like to say I grabbed a vibrator and at least satisfied myself, but toward the end, I couldn't even be bothered with that.

I don't know when he stopped caring about making me feel good, or why. All I know is that what I felt last night, beneath my covers and at the memory of Andy Marshall, is the highest sexual peak I've seen in quite a while. Knowing what it was like just to kiss him yesterday and to fantasize about him last night, I can't imagine what it would be like to actually *sleep* with him.

Which makes his inability to leave my thoughts completely understandable.

Though, the fact that it's understandable doesn't make it any easier when I finally arrive at One Stop and go through the motions of opening the store. Especially when Andy walks in and finds me reorganizing the floral arrangements near the front.

"Morning, Briar."

His deep voice hits me in the stomach, pooling warmth low in my waist and reminding me of what it felt like last night to come with his name on my lips.

"Morning," I say, blushing and closing the cooler door.

We haven't seen each other since we kissed in the walk-in, as yesterday was my day off. Now that I've spent a night fantasizing about him, I feel like I can barely look him in the eye.

"Have a good day off?"

I nod. "Yeah. Hung out with my friend Abby."

"Abby Fuller? Last night?" When I nod again, he chuckles. "Funny—I was out with Rusty last night."

I grin, remembering that Rusty and Andy are just as close with each other as they are with Boyd. "What did you guys get up to?"

"We had a few drinks at Lucky's, and then we went out to Carson's dad's dock and fished for a while."

"Sounds like a quintessential guy's night," I joke.

Andy nods. "It definitely was. It's been too long since the last time I got together with them, so…" He trails off, shrugging a shoulder.

We stand there for a few minutes, just looking at each other, before Andy takes a step closer. I follow his lead, bringing my body just a few inches from his.

And then we're both reaching out, like moths to each other's flame, our mouths pressing together as if it's the most natural thing in the world.

This moment makes the last one between us feel like it was the beginning of something fun and delicious and, like Abby said, possibly exactly what I need.

Andy's arms wrap around my waist, pulling me firmly against his chest, and I moan, wanting nothing more than to be nestled in against him where I can feel the hard planes of his body. But before I can get too lost in the way our mouths are dueling against each other, he pulls back and presses his forehead against mine.

"We have to work," he says. "We shouldn't start something we can't…"

When he trails off again, heat flushes up along my neck as I envision the two of us starting something we *can* finish.

But I clear my throat and lick my lips, knowing he's absolutely right.

Andy softly kisses my lips again then steps away from me, though he grabs my hand and links our fingers together.

"I know we talked about meeting up at the market this weekend but…are you busy tonight?"

I shake my head. "No."

Andy grins and lifts my hand to his mouth, pressing his lips against the inside of my wrist.

"Dinner at mine?"

All I can manage to do is nod my head, but Andy must accept that answer as good enough, because he smiles then turns to head back to his office. My eyes follow him all the way down the aisle before he walks through the double doors at the back.

As I go through the motions of my final training day with Lois, learning the last few things she thinks are imperative for my knowledge bank before she drops to part-time, my mind continues to wander off toward the back of the building, to where I know Andy is sitting in his office, doing whatever managerial things he needs to do.

I try to decide whether or not I'm making the right choice by going to his place tonight, try to decide if I'm making a mistake.

And I just can't seem to muster up the energy to care.

CHAPTER NINE

Andy

Looking around my place, I try to find anything else I should do before Briar gets here, but I think my mother would actually be proud of how it looks on a night when I've invited a woman over.

Of course, I had to rush around today to make sure I had enough time, wrapping up work earlier than usual so I could get home, check in on dad and get him sorted, not to mention have a little bit of time to pick up and shower.

For my date. With Briar Mitchell.

I shake my head and walk back to my bathroom, slapping the handle on the wall to turn on the water.

Part of me worries I'm making a mistake by inviting her over. As much as I've been enjoying the way my thoughts of her have been a distraction from the more depressing parts of my life, there's still a niggling voice in the back of my mind telling me not to get involved with someone who has no intentions of sticking around.

I shower quickly, style my hair a little bit, and throw on a pair of dark green pants and a black button-up. I check my reflection in the mirror when I hear tires rolling along the gravel outside and try not to focus on that little voice. Instead, I remind myself that my smile has been a lot more genuine today. It doesn't matter what Briar wants long-term; that should be more than enough.

"Hey," she says when I open the door a few minutes after seven. "Sorry I'm a little late. It took me forever to get out of the house."

I pull back the door even wider and wave her in. "No worries. I had a few things to take care of when I got home, so it's actually perfect timing."

As she steps past me, I can smell the subtle hints of her perfume, the same floral notes I caught when my lips were pressed to hers this morning. As she walks past me and places her purse next to the side of the couch, I can't help the way my eyes drop to appreciate what she looks like from behind.

The way she wears those jeans is something else, the faded denim cupping her perfectly and making her legs look a mile long.

"It's amazing the reaction my parents had when I told them I was going out tonight but wouldn't say with who."

At her words, my eyes fly up just in time to catch her turning to look back at me. That's when I realize what she's just said.

"Oh?"

Briar nods. "I said I had plans and my mom would not let it go. She was still asking as I pulled out of the driveway."

I know I should be thankful she's not broadcasting our date to her parents, especially when I see them in the store at least once a week. But I feel like a total hypocrite, because I can't help feeling a little put off by the fact that she didn't tell her family where she was going.

"I was just about to grab a beer," I say, shaking off that thought. "Do you want some wine?"

Briar shakes her head. "No. Wine isn't a good idea for me. Makes me do things I wouldn't normally do."

The minute she says it, a hint of red stains her cheeks, and it makes me wonder about the things she's gotten up to in the past while drinking a little too much vino.

"I feel like there's a story there. Care to share?"

She twists her lips. "Not particularly."

I nod and walk into the kitchen. "How about a beer then? Maybe that's a safer choice?"

"Sure."

I pull two bottles of Cedar Cider pilsner out of the fridge, pop the tops off, and hand one to Briar, each of us taking long pulls without looking away from the other.

"So, what's for dinner?" she asks. "It smells delicious."

"Italian chicken," I say, holding up a finger as I pop the oven open to take a look at the meat I prepared when I got home and put in when I heard Briar pull up a few minutes ago.

"I didn't realize chickens could speak Italian."

It takes me half a second before I jerk my head over to find a funny smile on Briar's face that I can barely see because she's hiding it slightly behind the neck of her beer.

"Was that a joke?"

She lifts a shoulder. "I know how to joke."

"Clearly. I liked it."

Closing the oven, I pick my beer back up and gesture for Briar to take a seat at the island. Once she's settled, I post up across from her, my hip leaning against the cabinets.

"Italian chicken is kind of like a pizza but without the bread," I clarify. "Some recipes have cheese and some don't. I'd say it's like a cross between regular chicken and chicken parmesan."

"Sounds as delicious as it smells."

"Well, I'm not the cook in the family. That was always my mom, but she taught me a few things, and chicken was her favorite thing to experiment with."

Briar's eyes soften, and I instantly regret bringing my mother into the conversation. We don't need any kind of sadness infused into our evening, and as much as I know I can think about my mother and have feelings other than sadness, most people who haven't lost a parent assume it's the only emotion there is.

"I always loved cooking with my mom," Briar says, taking the thread of conversation and shifting it away from *my* mother, for which I'm very grateful. "I don't know how well you remember me from when I was younger, but I was kind of a quiet homebody."

I chuckle. "You don't say."

She takes my words as the good-natured teasing they're intended to be, rolling her eyes playfully.

"I'm not a big talker, but I think my mom figured out that if she got me in the kitchen, I'd open up a little bit more."

"Sneaky."

"Exactly. So, of course, I ruined it by telling her I didn't want to cook with her anymore. I've always regretted that."

"It's never too late to get back in the kitchen with her," I say. "I'd give anything to have my mom teach me another recipe or cooking technique. You're back home for the first time in a long while, and I bet she'd love it if you would make something with her again."

Briar nods, her expression thoughtful as she rolls her beer

119

bottle back and forth between her hands.

"Maybe I will," she finally says.

There's something I really enjoy about Briar's mind, even though I feel like I'm just barely getting to know her. She moves slowly and methodically when it comes to making decisions, never jumping into anything without being cautious and thorough.

I think I kind of like it.

I think I kind of like *her*.

A few minutes later, I pull the pan of chicken out of the oven, getting to work on putting together our plates while Briar stays seated at the island, telling me about her brother Boyd and his new girlfriend and how she made Briar like yoga.

"Boyd doing yoga?" I ask, chuckling to myself as I get everything plated. "Will you grab me another beer?"

Briar pulls a bottle from the fridge then follows behind me as I carry our plates out to the small table. "It really was hilarious. As much as he would probably claim he was just doing it to impress Ruby, I think he actually enjoyed it. I caught him doing it on his own a few times before he left town."

I chuckle as we both take our seats.

"Well, there's nothing wrong with trying new things, huh?" I say, popping the cap off my bottle with a lighter. Then I light the little candle I have sitting in the middle of the table. "Alright, dig in. Let me know what you think, and it's totally okay if you hate it."

Briar takes a bite then wipes her mouth with a napkin, bobbing her head up and down.

"This really is as delicious as it smells."

I grin, silently thanking my mother for taking the time to teach me a few things in the kitchen, then I dig in myself.

We spend a little while eating and talking about things that sit somewhere between surface level and a little bit deeper, our topics mostly revolving around shared knowledge of people and places that comes along with growing up in the same small town.

Eventually we finish our meals and move back into the kitchen, though Briar makes me sit at the island while she washes the dishes, telling me it's only fair for her to clean since I cooked.

"The only job I ever loved more than working at the library was when I started working for Holly," she says, our conversation bunny-trailing from who is still living in town to what her old boss from the library is doing now—teaching—and then on to her job working for a woman named Holly.

"That was the flower place?"

She nods as she scrubs a soaped-up sponge along the tray I used to bake the chicken, her eyes focused on her hands.

"Yeah. Holly's Flowers."

"We talked about that a little during your interview, but I never fully understood why you loved it so much."

"Because of Holly," she answers. "She was like…I don't know, an older sister and mentor and mother figure all rolled into one." Then she looks up at me. "Not that I needed a mother figure. I mean, my mom is great. But, I don't know…I guess I was just at a time in my life when I wanted advice and support without having to ask my parents for anything. Holly taught me a lot about business and hard work." She looks up at me again. "And ethics, like your dad taught you."

I grin, thinking back to our conversation in the walk-in.

"Sounds like Holly was a great boss."

"You have no idea."

She pauses, both her words and her hands, glancing at me briefly as she considers what she wants to say next. It almost surprises me that I'm recognizing her little facial expressions so easily, and so quickly. The way Briar looks, the creases on her face and little twitches of her eyes and lips—it feels like she's an open book to me, though I don't think she would particularly enjoy knowing I'm learning to read her so easily.

"She actually...paid for my MBA," she finally says. "As an employee benefit."

My eyebrows rise. "Wow. That is quite a gift."

Briar nods. "Yeah. I told her no at first—I didn't want to feel indebted—but she was very convincing, and honestly, it was the best decision. She got to write it off, and I'm not saddled with crazy student debt, which I *so* appreciate."

"Any thoughts on what you want to do with it?" I ask, watching as she finishes up with the last dish and sets it in my drying rack.

She pauses again, drying her hands on a dish rag.

"I thought...I thought about maybe, if I can figure it all out...opening a bookstore?"

Now that Briar has put that vision in my mind, I can't imagine anything more perfect for her. The way she talked earlier about her love for working at the library and then discussing how much she enjoyed working for a small business down the mountain, a bookstore sounds like an amazing decision.

"I don't know though. I mean, I doubt I'll ever have the kind of plan or money to put something like that into the works."

I shake my head. "Don't act like you aren't smart enough to figure it all out," I tell her. "If it's important to you, I know you can make it happen."

She blushes, looking down at the empty sink.

"Have you ever considered asking your parents to invest in something like that?"

Her shoulders straighten at my words, and I see that old, familiar bit of frostiness in her expression.

"I don't consider my parents to be a money pit," she tells me, irritation coloring her tone. "They've always raised us to expect little financial support from them."

"I love that," I say, realizing I need to be careful about the next words I say, having clearly struck a nerve. "That they never made you feel like you were dependent on them for the resources to achieve your dreams. My comment wasn't about you not being able to figure out a way to make your bookstore happen without them, but simply about the fact that your parents have invested in several newer businesses in town to help them get off their feet."

I watch as Briar's shoulders begin to lower. "Really?" she says. "I didn't realize they did stuff like that."

I nod, though I wait, giving her the chance to process.

"How do *you* know about it?" she asks.

"It was a town hall meeting a few years back," I tell her, "after the library was demolished and those new storefronts were built. Roy Grove was the developer for that project, but once it was done, he couldn't get more than a few of the little shops rented and he was gonna go belly up. Your parents announced a small business project that would allow young entrepreneurs a chance to get things going without having to take loans out with banks that might not approve a new small business or first-time owner."

Briar looks almost stunned. "Wow. I didn't know about any of that. And all those shops on Main Street look like they're doing so well."

"They are," I continue. "They just needed a little help getting things going, and there's no shame in that."

A long moment goes by before I realize it's time for a change in topic. As much as I want to know Briar on a deeper level, I can tell the direction this chat is going is maybe a bit more emotional for her than I had intended.

"I need to let Quincy out. You wanna take a little walk outside?"

Briar smiles. "Absolutely."

I make quick work of grabbing Quincy's lead then letting her out of where she's been hanging out on her bed in the corner of my bedroom.

She races through the house, and when I round the corner for the living room, I laugh when I find Briar flat on her back and Quincy furiously licking her face, giggling.

"Quincy," I scold, though there's no heat in my tone. "That's my job."

Briar lets out another laugh, her head falling back as I tug Quincy away from her. She gazes up at me, letting out a long sigh as her laughter finally starts to fade. Then she takes my extended hand, and I pull her up off the floor.

"Come on, beautiful. Let's give the dog her moment."

Twenty minutes later, we're leaning against the back of my Jeep while Quincy happily prances around in the woods, reminiscing about some of the more scandalous and ridiculous things that have happened in Cedar Point.

"That is *not* what happened," she says, shaking her head.

"You are completely misremembering."

I scoff. "Excuse me—which one of us was the 15-year-old hormonally driven boy at the time?" Then I point a finger at myself. "Definitely me. I think I'd have a better memory of the naked beach debacle than you."

"False," she assures me. "The fact that I wasn't clouded by lust at the sight of naked bodies makes me an impartial witness. I would *obviously* remember it better than you."

I narrow my eyes. "Okay, you might have a point."

She stretches her arms out wide and does a little bow. "Thank you."

We both laugh before settling into a silent moment as Quincy races over with a pine cone in her mouth. Taking it from her, I chuck it out past the tree line, watching as she races off to find it, lost in the middle of a dozen other pine cones.

"Thanks for dinner," Briar tells me. "It was delicious."

"I'm glad you enjoyed it," I reply. "When we head back in, I have some coffee and hot chocolate, if you want some."

She takes a deep breath as she watches me, and I think I'm seeing her try to decide whether she wants to stick around any longer. I'll be honest, it would be a lie if I said I wouldn't be disappointed if she decided to go.

I want more of her mouth against mine.

"Andy…" she starts, her voice trailing off.

"No pressure, though," I try to reassure her. "If you wanna head home, I totally understand."

"It's not that," she says, shaking her head. "I just…feel like I need to have a conversation with you that's kind of…awkward."

My eyebrows dip, and I adjust where I'm leaning back against the Jeep, turning to the side to give her my full focus.

"Okay."

There's a long pause before she speaks again. "I just got out of a really long relationship," she tells me. "And I'm trying to… figure myself out."

I nod my head, realizing where this is going. It's probably for the best, I tell myself. This way I won't get caught up in something that isn't going anywhere.

"So, I can only come inside if you know things would need to be strictly physical."

My head whips to the side, unsure I heard her correctly.

"I mean, I want to be friends, obviously. I really enjoy hanging out with you. You're easy to talk to, but any kind of emotional commitment is just more than what I can handle right now, so…" She shrugs a shoulder. "What do you think?"

I blink a few times, realizing I need to clarify this with her completely to make sure I'm not misunderstanding.

"Are you talking about being fuck buddies?"

Briar's nose wrinkles. "I prefer the term friends with benefits. It's a little less crass and focuses on the friends part. But yes, I guess…yeah, that's what I'm talking about."

I watch her for a minute as she shuffles from foot to foot, trying to remember what the hell I thought was going to happen tonight and wondering how we got here…to a place where we're talking about sex in a way that is *very* different than how I've ever talked about it before.

The part of me that thought dinner tonight was a mistake is crossing his arms with a glare and pointing at Briar with a kind of *See?* But the part of me that is insanely attracted to her is already trying to convince myself this could actually be perfect.

Maybe in my regular life, I wouldn't be interested in this kind of relationship, but I haven't been living my regular life in months—not since all this stuff with my dad has been going on.

Truth be told, I haven't smiled this much in a long while, and I feel like it's only fair to allow myself the ability to grab at whatever new thing is making me happy again.

Right now, that's Briar and the excitement I feel at seeing her at work, at the idea of reminding her of all the wonderful things Cedar Point has to offer, at the way my entire body surges with lust and desire when we kiss.

"Yes," I reply, before I can second-guess myself, before I can talk myself out of an offer that is absolutely going to bring me a lot of joy and satisfaction.

"Yeah?" she says, the slightly pinched, worried look on her face evaporating and getting replaced by a smile.

"Yeah."

Briar shuffles where she stands, her hands nervously fidgeting with the hem of her top, almost like she doesn't know what to do with herself now that I've agreed.

"I've never done this before," she finally tells me, confirming my suspicion. "And it took all my nerve to ask, so I'm gonna need you to take the lead on this, okay?"

At her bold honesty, I let out a deep laugh of relief. I hope she can always be this honest with me, especially if we're about to take this into the bedroom.

"I can do that," I tell her, reaching out and taking one of her hands in mine, then tugging her my way so she's standing between my legs.

Then I place my hands on either side of her face, enjoying the little look of nervous excitement she gives me.

"This is going to be fun," I whisper.

And then I pull her mouth to mine.

CHAPTER TEN

Briar

I don't know what I was expecting from this dinner at Andy Marshall's house, but suggesting friends with benefits was definitely not it. And it came out of *my* mouth.

But as he held my face between his strong, warm hands and kissed me senseless, I knew mustering up the nerve to just blurt it out was absolutely worth it.

I've been thinking about what's been happening between us since our kiss earlier this morning, stressing about my clear inability to keep Andy off of my mind, no matter how hard I try. As I stood in the shower after I got home from work, trying not to focus too much on why I wanted to clean up my body before dinner, Abby's voice popped into my mind again.

Although, this time, I really began to entertain her suggestion of just enjoying a little sexy fun. Nothing serious. Nothing crazy. Nothing that requires more than I'm comfortable giving.

But an only-sex relationship just didn't feel right. There were a few boys I slept with during college, one-night stands I thought would just be a little bit of fun. Each of those instances left me feeling sexually satisfied but unfulfilled, as if focusing on *only* the sex made it…less, somehow.

I also wasn't a fan of being one of many, knowing those guys were probably crawling into bed with someone else the next night. It made me a little squirmy, and not in the good way.

Which is why I started thinking maybe Andy's actually the perfect guy for something like this.

He's a good guy, someone who makes me laugh, and I enjoy his company. Definitely ticks the friend box, and I haven't heard anything floating around town about him being in and out of tourists' beds, unlike, say, Rusty. And then, of course, there's the fact that the younger version of me would love nothing more than a chance for things between us to move into the bedroom.

I'd been thinking about this whole idea off and on for our entire dinner, finally realizing my moment when he invited me in for coffee or hot chocolate, a very clear indicator of what he was hoping would happen.

And, god, am I glad I blurted it out, glad I was honest—and glad he's interested in the same thing.

We kissed for a few minutes outside, until Quincy kept whimpering for his attention. Cursing, Andy pulled back and looked down at his dog.

"Time to go inside, girl," he told her. Then he looked at me and grinned. "If you want to."

I laughed and he slipped his hand into mine, the two of us heading up the stairs and back into his house. Andy put Quincy in her bed and closed his bedroom door then came back out to where I was sitting on the couch, wondering what to do next.

Which is where we are now, just kind of smiling softly at each other, Andy holding my hand, tracing slow circles around my wrist.

I just watch, hypnotized as he strokes the pads of his pointer and middle fingers slightly up my forearm and then back down to my wrist. Onto the palm of my hand, circling the middle before tracing up and down each one of my fingers.

As goose bumps rise on my arms, I close my eyes, simply enjoying this delicious sensation and the nearly overwhelming feelings welling up in my body.

When I feel a hand gently touch my jaw, my eyes fly open, and I find Andy's face much closer than it was before, just inches from mine.

"I can take the lead, but I need to know what you're thinking, Briar," he says, his voice husky.

He leans even closer, his nose bumping mine, but his heavy-lidded eyes are still watching me when I feel his lips brush against me. Just the faintest kiss, but it feels like something different than before, like the fact that we're both on the same page means I don't have to stress or worry about or think through every single little thing. Instead, I can just enjoy what's happening between us.

"Kiss me," I whisper, wanting him to take that final step to push us over the ledge.

The words are barely out of my mouth and he's on me, his hands coming to each side of my face as his tongue plunders my mouth, stroking deep and dragging a moan out of me that I've never heard from myself before.

His hands hold me reverently, but his kisses are anything but. Long licks, deep thrusts of his tongue. I can't help but reach for him, wrapping my arms around his waist and dragging him closer, pulling his body up and over mine as I stretch back on the length of the couch.

It's a game changer, the way the warmth of his body feels as it presses me down into the soft cushion beneath me. The way his muscles feel under my hands as I slip my fingers underneath his button-up shirt, wanting to feel the dips and planes of a body he's clearly worked hard for.

All the while, he continues to kiss me, but his mouth moves…down against the soft skin of my neck, his tongue licking before he sucks on a spot beneath my ear that has me gasping and shifting my hips.

There are so many sensations. Almost too many, and yet not enough. Nothing feels like enough. Not enough closeness, or wetness or sucking or licking or rubbing. Damn does his body feel good against mine.

He pulls back and looks at me for just a moment before he sits up and unbuttons his shirt, yanking it back and then chucking it to the side. My hands instantly fly up, reaching out to touch and tease and explore the hard body and dusting of dark hairs that cross his pecs and lead a trail down beneath his pants.

"God, Briar," he says, his hands slipping under my top and stroking softly, desperately along the skin under my breasts.

With no prodding, I lift my arms, and Andy gives my blue top a tug up and over my head. When I'm lying in front of him, stretched out on the couch in the black lacy bra I put on earlier with the distant hope that he might see it, I revel in the way his eyes drink me in.

"You are…" he starts, shaking his head. "Damn."

His hands move over my breasts, stroking almost feather-light on my nipples through the material of my bra, and yet I feel it like he's tugged and twisted at me, the sensation shooting straight to my core and making me squirm, desperate for something I can't name.

"You, too," I manage to blurt out, knowing my words aren't enough to capture the way just looking at him seems to light up my insides, the pleasure pooling below my belly button.

His mouth returns to mine, our hands continuing to rove and touch and tease and explore. I love the way he moans when I grip his ass and squeeze, the way he gasps when I drag my fingernails up his back, the way he bites hard on my lip as he begins to flex his hips in a way that strokes him *just* right between my thighs, revving me up even further.

"Do you have a condom?" I ask, my hands reaching between us to unbutton his jeans.

I feel him nod and the relief soars through me. It took everything for me to ask that question, but I can't be stupid enough not to use protection for the first sex I've had other than Chad for the better part of a decade.

It's a struggle to get his pants off in this position, so Andy hops up and pulls them down, kicking off his shoes and dropping his pants and boxers in one go.

I'd begun the process of pulling my own pants off, my button undone and the zipper pulled down, my thumbs wedged between my skin and the fabric tight at my hips—but when I see him standing completely naked in front of me, I freeze, my mouth drying at the sight.

"Jesus," I say, my mouth agape as my eyes drink him in from head to toe, the sight of his gorgeous body clearly robbing me of any kind of filter.

From his bare feet and up his legs, which are strong and lean and braced wide in a stance that exudes power. Then along the length of him, which he currently has in his hand, his grip tight.

It's a no-joke dick, and just that thought has me laughing at myself a little bit.

Which, of course, is *not* the appropriate thing to do when looking at someone standing naked in front of you.

Andy's eyebrow quirks up, and I'm sure if my entire body wasn't already flushed red, it certainly is now.

"I'm so sorry," I stammer. "I wasn't laughing at you. I was laughing at your dick." I slap my hand on my forehead. "I mean, I was laughing because it's so great. Perfect. I called it a no-joke dick in my head and that's why I laughed."

"Briar."

I close my mouth and return my eyes to his, recognizing the humor in his expression and feeling instantly relieved that he didn't take my statement as an offense against his…manhood, or whatever.

"Sorry."

"Stop apologizing," he tells me, "and take your pants off. I've got a no-joke dick that's desperate to get inside you."

I bite my lip and snicker as I continue to wiggle my way out of my jeans, wishing I'd picked something easier to manage, like a dress or a skirt.

Only one foot is out of my pants before Andy's swatting my hands away and kneeling between my legs.

"What are you…"

But I don't say anything else. The only thing that comes out of me when Andy presses his mouth against my lower lips is a series of whimpers I can't seem to control at the feeling of one of the most amazing experiences of my life.

"Oh my god," I whisper, my hands flying to the back of his head and gripping firmly into his hair.

I've only had a mouth between my legs a few times in my life, a very long time ago, and it was *nothing* like *this*. Back then, it was a lazy attempt to encourage me to return the favor, but the way Andy focuses his attention on me...the way he absolutely worships me...I can barely think straight.

He spends long moments stroking his tongue along my core, up and down and around my clit, over and over again, though he never actually touches it. I feel like a jack-in-the-box, getting cranked tighter and tighter and pushed closer to the edge.

Right before I feel like I might pop, I feel him sliding his fingers inside me, stroking me deeply and rubbing against my inner walls in a way that has me threatening to burst at the seams.

"I can't" falls from my lips like a chant, and I'm wound impossibly tighter.

"You will," he tells me, the confidence in his tone as he looks at me quite possibly the sexiest thing I've ever heard.

His fingers stay within me, stroking and rubbing at a spot that has little flickers of light beginning to show up behind my closed eyes. And then, just as I'm about to tip over, just before I'm about to let him know I'm *right there*, he pulls his fingers out and leans away.

"What are you doing?" I ask, my eyes flying open at the idea that he might leave me like this.

He chuckles and I watch as he tugs his wallet from his jeans, pulling out a condom and holding it up for me to see.

"Grabbing something important," he answers.

I sink into the couch, both embarrassed by my outburst and desperate to have him inside me. I watch as he opens the condom with both hands then rolls it on with a practiced skill that should concern me but doesn't because *desperate*.

Then he's hovering over me, and I can feel that he's notched himself exactly where I want him. But he doesn't move. He just stays there, his eyes tracking between mine before they drop to my lips. Then he kisses me, something so much softer and sweeter than how frantic everything felt just seconds ago.

That's when he pushes inside, his thick dick slipping into me in one long, slow motion that makes me feel like I'm being slowly split in half. The sound he makes once he's fully seated, his hips pressed flush against mine with a long pause—it sounds torturous. The best kind of pleasure and the best kind of pain.

And I know exactly how he feels.

I whimper when he just stays there, my heart thundering aggressively in my chest, every cell and atom in my body attuned to the place where he's stretching me, where he's settled himself so deep inside me I can barely breathe.

"Please, Andy," I say, my words coming out choppy and awkward.

"What do you need, sweetheart?" he asks, pulling his upper body away slightly so he can look me in the eye.

"Fuck me."

My words come out in a way that's so desperate, so tawdry, so dirty, I can't believe they've come from my own mouth.

It's clear that I've stunned Andy as well, because his mouth falls open before his eyes roll back in his head, and he pulls his hips away then plunges back into me.

I cry out, the feeling of him slamming into me unlike anything I've ever experienced.

"Shit," he says, pulling back and thrusting forward, over and over and over again. "Fucking shit."

I know exactly how he feels, because it's the same for me. My nipples are peaked, my body is on fire, I'm sweaty and flushed and my heart is slamming inside of me with the same kind of intensity Andy embodies as he slams into me.

When he shifts his hips just slightly to the side, I can feel the telltale sign at the base of my spine and in the top of my hips, the feeling that lets me know I'm racing to the top of the mountain with no sign of slowing down.

"I'm gonna come," I say, and before I even get the words completely out, it feels like every muscle in my body constricts, every inch of me going rigid with a force that threatens to break me, inside and out.

Andy shouts out and tumbles over with me, his body rocking into me over and over and over before he stills. We both pant out our breaths as we try to calm ourselves, our bodies slowly coming down from the high we were just riding.

"Holy shit," I hear him whisper next to my ear, and I can't help but smile, wrapping my arms around his torso and holding him close to me, enjoying the way his naked body looks and feels, slicked with sweat and smelling of sex.

Andy peppers soft, slow kisses across my collarbone and up along my neck before he places a sensual one on my mouth, his tongue licking in with a type of intimacy I'm not expecting.

"That was amazing," he tells me, and all I can do is giggle.

I'm not normally a giggler. I don't laugh when I don't know what to say, usually just staying silent, but the feelings that are welling up within me after sex with Andy are not normal. The way I feel right now is so far outside of normal that I don't know how to describe it.

So I don't even allow myself to feel embarrassed by the weird little giggle that tumbles out of my lips unbidden. It just…is what it is.

We lie there for a while, relishing the feeling of being naked and warm and close to each other, before my entire body shivers.

"How are you cold?" he asks as he pulls back and begins to stand. "I'm burning up."

"I get cold really easily," I answer, shrugging a shoulder and taking the hand he extends to me. "It's why I love sweaters and scarves."

Andy chuckles, pulling me to standing, then reaching behind me to grab a blanket from a basket at the end of his couch. Without a word, he wraps it around my shoulders and crosses it in front of me.

"You'll get to wear a lot of those soon."

I nod. "I know. Autumn is my favorite time of year."

"You're one of those pumpkin-spice-obsessed people?"

"Absolutely."

Andy rolls his eyes, but I can tell he's just teasing.

"And I make an amazing pumpkin bread that you're going to love," I continue.

"Can't wait," he says, tugging off the condom and crossing the room to dispose of it in the trash.

The whole conversation feels so casual. So relaxed. So friendly. I wonder if this is what being friends with benefits is normally like for other people, or if we're doing it completely wrong altogether.

"You need something?" he asks as he pulls his boxers on, having caught me looking around the room as I try to decide what to do next.

I give him an awkward smile. "No, I just…I guess I thought through the beginning part, not the end, you know?"

Andy stands in nothing but his undies, watching me with an unreadable expression.

"Like, we just had sex and…I mean, I'm going home right?" I ask, my eyes looking around again, trying to catalogue where all my things are scattered on the floor.

When I look up at Andy, I realize *he's* the one struggling to say something this time.

"If that's what you want," he says, clearing his throat and turning to head into the kitchen. "Do you want any water?"

I shake my head, feeling like I did something wrong but not knowing exactly what it was.

"No thank you," I say, reaching down to put my other foot in my half-on pair of undies and jeans, keeping my body mostly hidden under the blanket Andy wrapped me in.

"This was fun," I say, trying to give off a casual air that makes this sound as casual as can be.

Yeah. Casual.

I tug my bra over my breasts and clip it together in the back.

"What's the rush?" Andy asks as I refold the blanket and put it at the end of the couch.

I shake my head and step back, tugging my shirt over my head. "No rush. I just need to get home. I open tomorrow, so…"

Andy watches me for another long minute, his brows down and his hands on his hips.

"Thanks for the…you know. The sex and stuff," I say, instantly wishing I could hit delete on those words.

At that, the expression on Andy's face breaks a little, his lips tipping up at the sides.

"Come here, you," he says, crossing the room to me and tugging me in against his chest. Then he drops a hard kiss against my lips. "This doesn't need to be weird, okay? This is where the friends part is supposed to kick in and make it easy and comfortable. Yeah?"

I grin, thankful that he took a moment to reassure me.

I might not want either of us to fall in love, but I do care about him and want things between us to be okay.

Following his lead, I pop up on my toes and kiss him back.

"Still on for the market on Saturday?" I ask.

Andy nods. "Definitely."

"Alright," I say. "See you then." With a final little wave, I head out the door.

I'm crawling into bed, post-shower, still feeling the sweet ache between my legs from the best sex of my entire life, when I get a text from Andy.

ANDY: JUST MAKING SURE YOU GOT HOME SAFE.

I flick off a response quickly, enjoying the fact that he thought to check in with me.

ME: YEAH, I'M HOME. THANKS.

Then I set my phone down on my nightstand, turn off the light, and roll over to stare at the wall.

I replay every single second of tonight in my mind, and I can't bring myself to regret it. It was amazing. Hot. Sexy. He was a considerate lover. I've never come so hard in my life.

There were some growing pains at the end as we both figured out what to do after the benefits part was done, but I'm thankful Andy decided to make the effort to remind me of the friends part.

This whole plan might be one of the greatest ideas I've ever had, and I can't wait to see what happens next.

CHAPTER ELEVEN

Andy

"Did you ever have Mrs. Schneider?"

Briar nods and chucks a rock out to the water, both of us stopping for a second to watch as it skips one, two, three, four times before sinking under the surface.

"Yeah. Junior year."

"Kris is her son," I say, referring to one of the bag boys who works a few shifts a week.

"Oh, seriously?" she asks, returning to the pile of rocks a few feet away to look for another good one. "I had no idea."

We've been out here for about half an hour, trying to one-up each other on who can skip stones the farthest out into the water and enjoying the last little bit of light before the glow from the other side of the trees finally disappears.

As it is, we can hardly see the rocks we're throwing anymore, but I'm not trying to push us to head inside just yet. We've been having an amazing day, and the last thing I want to do is bring it to an end any sooner than I need to.

This morning, we met up at the Saturday Market in town and spent a few hours perusing the little stands and popping in and out of the stores on Main Street. It's been a while since I've just *enjoyed* hanging out in town. Usually, I'm moving as fast as possible to get whatever I need and get home, trying to avoid talking with anyone or having to be out any longer than I absolutely have to.

After the market, I assumed we'd be done for the day, but somehow we keep parlaying what we're doing into the next thing.

Like purchasing food at the market and then going back to my house to make lunch together. Then taking that lunch out on the porch and playing with Quincy for a while before going on a long walk on the trail behind my house. Once we got back, we decided to go down to the little beach that's walking distance from my place and dip our feet in, which turned into a rock-throwing competition and a stone-skipping marathon.

All the while, the conversation between us has been easy. Not constant—there have been plenty of long, quiet moments when we both just enjoyed the sounds of the outdoors or allowed a natural lull between topics—but easy, definitely.

"You know, I found out that Marta Wolford married Kyle Erwin the other day, which totally blew my mind," Briar says, drawing me back.

"That pairing was *quite the scandal*," I say, mimicking the way Lois likes to get all uppity when she hears about something surprising in town.

Briar snickers as she walks back to the edge of the water and squats low, trying to get a good angle on her next throw. I, of course, just stay back and enjoy the view, of both the lake *and* Briar bending over.

"It's always surprising who people end up with," she continues. "Especially when it's someone completely outside that person's old social circle."

The way she says it makes me think of the two of us.

The quiet girl and the jock, though I would never actively label us as either of those things even if that's what our peers would have seen when we were younger.

"What was dating like for you back in school?" I ask, finally stepping up to the water as Briar finishes a skip that hits the surface five times. "I don't have any memories of you having a boyfriend or anything, but we've already established that I was super self-absorbed, so that's not saying much."

My joke hits the target, and I enjoy the way Briar's laugh sounds as it ripples along the lake.

"Ah, well, dating was a bit of a nosedive for me," she says just as I launch my rock out.

I turn to look at her and catch the way she's wrinkling her nose and shaking her head.

"How so?"

She takes her time with answering as she picks out a new rock and then crouches down at the water's edge to clean it off a little bit.

"Do you know Nick Riley?"

I tilt my head back and try to remember someone with that name. I used to feel like I knew most people in town, but it's becoming a lot more common for me to see people in the store I don't recognize or hear names I've never heard.

"Possibly. Can't picture a face, though."

"Thomas Riley's son."

"Oh," I exclaim, resting my hands on my hips as a picture comes to mind of the man who has served as the chair of the city council for the past few years and the son who attends all the meetings with him. "Yeah, I know Nick. Not personally, but I know who you're talking about."

Briar finally chucks her rock out into the water, this time throwing it way too high, both of us listening as it *thunks* into the water off in the distance, past where we can see now that the light is finally almost gone.

"We dated for most of my junior year," she tells me. "And broke up the day after prom."

I cringe. "Ouch. What happened?"

She shifts to the side, tucking her hands into her pockets and staring off past me, toward the little trail that leads off this small stretch of rocky beach and up to the main road.

For a minute, I wonder if she's going to answer me or keep her story to herself.

"Two things, actually," she finally says. "I wouldn't sleep with him, and then I found out that he didn't really want to date me. He just wanted an 'in' with the Mitchell family."

My jaws about falls off with how heavily it drops.

"What?"

She nods. "Yeah. It was…pretty mortifying, if I'm honest. He said something like *I knew this was a big waste of time. What's the point of dating the loser Mitchell if I can't even get anything out of it?* But it…might have been a little more colorful than that."

Even in the darkness of this spot by the lake, I can still see the embarrassment on her face, the patches of red that streak her neck as she shifts from one foot to the other. I honestly think the only reason she told me is because it's dark enough outside for her to hide her discomfort.

It makes me want to light this Nick asshole on fire.

"Briar, I'm…fuck, like, I want to say I'm sorry because I am, but I don't even know what to say."

"You don't have to say anything," she says, finally looking at me. "It's not your fault, and lots of guys are dicks. That's not on you. I was just…trying to be honest when talking about what dating was like for me. Long story short, it wasn't so great, so…"

She trails off, the toe of her tennis shoe nudging a rock in the soft earth until it pops out of the dirt.

"Well, I know I can't top that, but would you like me to share an embarrassing story of my own to even things out?" I joke.

I expect her to shake her head and say no, which is why I'm surprised when she grins and nods her head.

"Actually, yeah. It might make me feel better to know Andy Marshall hasn't had everything perfect over the years."

I chuckle, trying to think back to something that is embarrassing *enough* without scaring the shit out of her and sending her packing.

"Let's start to walk back. I'll think of something on the way."

We both leave the rocky beach behind, following the little trail to the main road and across to the long street that dead-ends at my place.

"Alright," I say, once we're walking up Brooks Road. "An embarrassing moment for Andy."

There have been quite a few over the years, but one stands out among the rest.

"During senior year, Keegan and I started hooking up. We weren't dating since her dad said she wasn't allowed to, but of course as teenagers we found ways around it that weren't technically breaking the rules."

Briar scoffs, but I can see the smile on her face at the mind of a teenage boy.

"We used to meet up around the corner from her place and then sneak down to the end of her neighbor's dock and make out. It was really dark, which was the point, since we didn't want to get caught, and we started making out and whatever, and when I pulled back, the moon caught on something shiny on her face."

I turn to look at Briar and see that she's watching me with curiosity.

"So I got out my phone and lit her up, and her face was covered in blood."

Briar gasps then barks out a laugh.

"Yeah. I used to get nosebleeds when I was younger, and apparently my nose had bled all over her face. She started screaming and it woke up her neighbors, and we were trying to run down the dock with my head tilted back so I didn't get more blood everywhere. Stop laughing!"

But my protestation is surrounded by my own bouts of laughter at the sight of Briar paused in the road, bent in half as she laughs her ass off at my embarrassing moment.

"Oh my god," she says, finally standing and wiping under her eyes, little giggles still falling from between her lips. "Please tell me you had to explain yourselves to someone."

I roll my eyes. "Well, that's the embarrassing part."

"What!?" she cries out. "The nosebleed wasn't it?"

I shake my head as we keep walking, gearing up to tell her the best—or worst—part.

"When we made it up the dock, Keegan's dad was standing there in his pajama pants and robe, arms crossed, ready to beat my ass for doing something that made his daughter scream and punch me in the face."

"Oh, no."

"So Keegan is trying to explain what happened and how it was just a nosebleed as her father has me pretty much pinned against the side of the house, and of course her mom comes running out to help stop the bleeding." I look Briar in the face. "With tampons."

At this point, she's basically wheezing she's laughing so hard as I tell her all about Keegan's mother shoving two massive tampons into my nostrils then calling my parents to come get me since they didn't think it was safe for me to be driving home.

"I hope you're enjoying yourself over there," I say, taking Briar's hand and basically dragging her along behind me as she tries to control her nearly hysterical laughter.

"Oh, I am—completely and entirely enjoying myself," she says as we make our way up the stairs that lead to my apartment above the garage. "Thanks for telling me that story."

"Well, hopefully it helps you feel like you aren't the only one with embarrassing shit in their past," I say, circling back to why I told her in the first place. "I've always tried to remind myself that we are who we are today because of the things that have happened to and around us, big or small."

She nods and hums to herself, wiping under her eyes to catch the tears that have fallen because she was laughing so hard..

"Plus, I'm always happy to share something that will get you to laugh like that."

"I will say, the whole 'laughter is good for the soul' thing? I might believe you a little bit, because my soul does feel lighter after that," she admits, grinning at me as we head inside.

Once we've each grabbed a beer and returned to the deck, I dust off the two patio chairs and we take a seat, clinking our bottles together. I don't have a straight view of the lake, but during the day, you can see pieces of it through the trees in the distance.

With the light completely gone now, all we can see is darkness behind the line of trees.

We both sit and enjoy the silence for a while as the sky fades from purple to an inky black, the sounds of the wind blowing softly through the trees and the little creatures roaming around for their nightly meals.

"I used to think I only missed having seasons," she says, looking over at me. "But I miss the quiet, too. It doesn't sound like this down the mountain. Everything is so…brash and intense all the time. There's nothing like enjoying the quiet lake and mountain at night."

"Definitely agree with that. It's one of the reasons I decided to rent this place instead of finding an apartment closer to town or taking someone's cabin. I love living at the end of this road with no neighbors for at least a mile."

"Yeah, there's definitely levels of quiet," she says. "It's really quiet at my parents' house, but we can still hear the hum of noise from the houses next door to us. Although it's still *much* better than the noise from next door at my apartment down the mountain."

She chuckles to herself and rolls her eyes.

"Chad and I could hear the couple next to us having sex through the wall, which isn't anything crazy except they had sex *all the time*. That's not the type of relationship we had, so it felt like it was just highlighting the fact that we were like…not doing anything."

I twist my beer on the armrest of my chair, wanting to tread softly since this is the first time she's brought up her ex on her own, unprompted.

"What kind of relationship *did* you have?"

She tilts her head from left to right, considering.

"A quiet one." Briar shifts in her chair so she's sitting sideways, her legs pulled up to her chest as she faces me. "That's honestly the best word to describe it. It was quiet and simple and we had routines. Outside of that…there wasn't really anything else."

I nod but keep my thoughts to myself—my thoughts that are convinced this guy was an idiot.

Briar might be a cautious person. She might move slowly through her decisions and be thoughtful in how she does things, but after the time we've spent together, I can't imagine her as a quiet person. I may not know her as well as someone who has been in her life a lot longer than I have, but Briar is a woman with a lot on her mind, even if she doesn't speak it all at once. I'm realizing quickly that if I give her the opportunity, if I ask the right questions, she'll open up to me, share with me those thoughts of hers that I love hearing.

So, yeah. Her ex was an idiot if the life they lived together kept her quiet.

"He liked our quiet little life and didn't want anything to change," she continues after another minute has passed. "So *I* changed until it got to the point where I didn't even recognize myself anymore. He didn't want me to get my MBA…have I told you that?"

I shake my head.

"Chad had all these excuses. It was too expensive, I didn't have the time, what would it really help…but honestly, he just didn't want me to go do something that would take me away from what *he* wanted. I did it anyway. For me," she says, staring off into the darkness, lost in thought. "And that's when I started to really realize we just wanted different things…different lives. He wanted me to be quiet and small."

Then she looks me in the eye and breaks my heart.

"I can honestly say to you that one of the most difficult things to experience is to be in a room, next to a person you're supposed to love, and feel like you're completely alone."

The way Briar talks about Chad, I wonder how the hell she could have stayed in a relationship with him for as long as she did. Obviously, everyone makes choices based on the information they have at the time, and I'm not blaming her by any measure. But I just want to drive down the mountain and set Chad straight. Clock him in the face for the way he's made her feel so small. Like what she wants doesn't matter.

Though I guess I should be thanking him for being a dick, because it was his ineptitude that sent Briar my way. She wouldn't be here with me if it wasn't for him.

I swallow something thick, trying to take that thought and tuck it back into a box, file it away in my mind. The way I just thought that makes it seem like I think…Briar belongs to me. Like she's my girlfriend or something.

"Do you want another beer?" I ask, hoping I can shake off this little mental funk that has popped up out of nowhere.

Briar nods, handing her empty bottle to me. "Sure."

When I get into the kitchen, I dump our empties into the recycling then take a minute to remind myself of what we're doing. I'm not *dating* Briar. We're hanging out. We're friends. We're enjoying time together and exploring town together and sleeping together.

I shake my head and let out a long sigh.

It sounds like dating to me, but what the hell do I know?

Grabbing two beers, I pop the tops off and head back outside.

CHAPTER TWELVE

Briar

"You got some dick."

My eyes about pop out of my skull at Abby's words, spoken much louder than I would prefer as we sit across from each other inside Ugly Mug Coffee Shop a week later.

When she called me a few days ago to say we needed to schedule some girl time, I assumed we would eventually touch on what's going on with me and Andy. I just never assumed those words would be the first ones out of her mouth, before I've even fully taken a seat.

"Abby," I hiss, "lower your voice."

She just crosses her arms and gives me a smirk. "So, it's true."

I roll my eyes and set my drink down then chuck my purse onto the empty seat next to me.

"I didn't say that. I would just prefer for you to *not* use a bullhorn to say something like that to all of Cedar Point, thank you."

But she shakes her head. "Nah. If it wasn't true, you would

have just rolled your eyes. But you don't want anyone to know that you—"

"Shhhhhh."

Okay, maybe I'm being a little dramatic about how much I want Abby to lower her voice. There are only a few other people in here right now, and the sound of one of the baristas turning beans into grounds is enough to drown out any potential eavesdropping.

Not that anyone in town would ever assume something interesting was going on in *my* life. It might always feel like someone's watching, but I'm definitely the least interesting Mitchell sibling. Boyd's the firstborn, the popular and athletic one. Bishop is probably going to be the famous one. Bellamy is the outgoing one who is friends with everyone, and Busy is the one with tons of attitude.

Hell, even Abby is more interesting than me.

When I say it that way, it makes me sound like a bitch, but all I mean is that Abby is a good girl. Her brother is the baddie, and he has definitely earned that reputation. Abby has mostly taken it upon herself to protect the Fuller name, as if her good deeds can somehow counterbalance her brother's poor choices.

Though I think it's fair to point out that those 'poor choices' are strictly female-related and not anything else. Cedar Cider is booming, and according to my dad, Rusty has been getting more involved in small business politics at the town hall meetings. He *has* been known to get into a few fights, and if rumors are true, they had to do with women he was sleeping with—women who were not entirely single.

So Abby, bless her heart, has been trying fruitlessly to keep the two of them in the town's good graces, which makes gossip about her basically a bragging contest about how wonderful she is. I personally love to feed into that kind of gossip, but I guess people want to hear the shady stuff more than the bright and fluffy.

"Before we get into the nasty details of your dicking, please tell me it wasn't with my brother."

My head pulls back and an absolutely mortified look crosses my face, followed by a slight gag.

"No thank you. You've told me enough stories about that man to make him forever on my Not To Do list."

Abby giggles. "That's funny. Also gross, because you're talking about my brother, but funny."

I break off a piece of the croissant I bought with my latte and pop it into my mouth just as Abby makes her next guess.

"So, it's Andy, then?"

Trying to respond quickly, I accidentally inhale the stupid bite of croissant, causing me to launch into a coughing fit that has all eyes in the room focused my way for half a second before looking away.

Good to know the people of this town are so concerned for me when I'm over here choking to death.

I cough a few more times then take a sip of my coffee, pat my chest, and clear my throat a few times.

"It's definitely Andy."

I glare at her, continuing to try to get past my choking fit.

"You are relentless," I finally say, taking another sip of my latte. "And yes, okay? Yes, I am sleeping with Andy Marshall."

Of course, the literal second before I say those words, the coffee grinder turns off, and I end up speaking at full volume, the sound of my voice carrying across the room. Just about every head turns my way again, and I swear, if I could sink into a hole in the ground right now, I would.

"Oh my god," I whisper, resting my elbows on the table and hiding my face in my hands.

"Well, no use hiding now, huh? You just told everybody."

I glare at Abby again, and she giggles.

"Oh come on, Bri," she says, reaching across and squeezing my forearm. "It's not a big deal. You're 27 years old, and that is some fine ass to be sleeping with. You could do a lot worse."

Shaking my head, I lean back, trying to let the embarrassment of the past few minutes fall away.

"So," she continues, drawing the word out and giving me excited eyes, "tell me all about it."

I roll my eyes but give in, telling her about what's been going on between the two of us since the last time I saw my friend when we made slutty brownies, describing what happened when he invited me over for dinner and the whole *friends with benefits* conversation we had.

"So was it just the one day? Come over, dinner, sex?"

I shake my head. "No, we spent Saturday together last weekend, too."

"Sex two days in a row?" she says, grinning at me. "Nice."

"Well, no we didn't have sex on Saturday. We just...hung out. The *friends* part."

Abby nods and takes a sip of her drink. "Good. Too much sex in a short time can cause too many emotions to get involved."

I snort. "When did you become the friends-with-benefits expert?" I ask.

"Hey, I drink wine, I read *Cosmo*, and I know things."

We both have a little giggle at that.

"You're having fun, though?" she asks.

"I am. Really. It feels like I can just *enjoy* myself instead of worrying about everything constantly. And you know what's crazy? It feels like we're actual friends. I was never friends with Nick. Definitely not with Chad. But Andy and I can sit and chat for hours."

Abby assesses me for a long moment. "Just…be careful."

I lift an eyebrow. "What do you mean?"

She shrugs. "I just worry you'll start seeing him as a possible relationship when a guy like Andy isn't what someone like you needs.

"What do you mean *someone like you*?" I ask. "What does someone like me need?"

"Oh, I didn't mean anything negative by it," she clarifies. "I just mean, you're not looking for a guy like Andy, you know?"

There's an extended pause where I just kind of stare at her, and she takes that for the direction it is—that she needs to continue clarifying, because no, I don't know.

"A lifer."

Another pause.

"Andy Marshall is One Stop for life, hon. That's awesome for him—stable, secure, local boy, taking over the family business for his dad—but he's never leaving here, and that's like, your number one goal. So, it's great that you're having fun, but when I tell you to be careful, it's because I know you don't want to be here forever, and your boy definitely does."

I sit up straighter in my chair. "You're the one who told me to just have a little fun," I say. "Where is this warning coming from? What changed so suddenly?"

Abby shakes her head. "Nothing changed. I just assumed you'd be the same with Andy as you were with Chad, and that's not the case."

"How was I with Chad?" I ask, not entirely sure I want the answer but knowing I probably need it.

My friend rotates her coffee cup between her palms, seemingly thinking her words over before she says anything.

"Chad was a guy who never made you happy, not from the very beginning, so you hardly ever talked about him. You'd bring him up here and there if I really asked questions, but for the most part, you kept it all to yourself."

"I only talked to you about Andy because you asked," I say, feeling a little defensive.

"No, it was different. You look like you're on cloud nine. And who knows? Maybe it really is just as simple as the fact that he's so great in bed. Maybe it really is just that he's easy to talk to. I'm not saying I know. What I'm saying is just as simple as what I meant. Be careful. Not just for you, but for him, too."

I only mull her words over for a second before I nod and we move on to another topic—taking out her dad's boat to go fishing soon—but I know I'm going to pocket what she's said and think about it later.

When I'm by myself, lying on my bed in the childhood home I can't wait to get out of, I finally think through everything she said again.

About the way I've gushed over Andy like he's a new boyfriend. About Andy being a lifer. About the difference between how I talked about him versus the way I used to talk about Chad.

Even though there might be some validity to what she's saying, I'm really enjoying sex and friendship with Andy right now. It's a much-needed break from the life I used to live, and I can honestly say that giving myself permission to enjoy time with Andy—instead of constantly berating myself for it—has released my mind in a way I hadn't truly anticipated.

Just this week alone, I've begun to put together a few legitimate ideas for jobs I'd like to apply for down the mountain, as well as spent some time perusing resources online that share information on how to get small businesses started when you don't have the financial capital. I'd like to look through some of my old textbooks, but those are back at Chad's and I'm not entirely sure I'm ready to go collect everything just yet.

Regardless of the fact that I feel like this thing with Andy is right, or at least *right for now*, Abby's words sow a seed of concern in the back of my mind…something that's hard to get rid of, no matter what kind of rational thinking I try to do.

"Okay, you were right. The view from up here really does make the sunset look more magical."

Andy grins at me. "Check mark for another amazing thing in Cedar Point."

"You act like you can only get sunsets here," I say in response, though I return his grin. "They literally exist everywhere else in the world."

He just lifts a shoulder and points at where the sun is dipping behind the trees in the distance. "Not *that* sunset."

When I pulled up in front of Andy's tonight in my brother Boyd's beat-up old truck, he hopped in, telling me the truck was a much better choice for where we were headed. Then he proceeded to take me the short drive down to the South Bank Resort, and up along a winding road that leads to a clearing.

"I still can't believe you actually brought me up to Easy Street," I tease, using the nickname other locals use to reference the known hookup spot in Cedar Point.

"Oh, like you've never been here before?" he jokes back.

His easy grin falls away, though, when I shake my head.

"I didn't date a lot, you know?" I tell him. "Besides, the only guy who would've brought me up here was Nick, and we both know his plans would have looked a little different than mine."

Andy's eyes narrow. "I still can't believe he said that shit to you."

I wave my hand, shifting where I'm reclined on the hood of the truck to get more comfortable. "I don't like to spend my time thinking about him," I say. "He was a mistake from the past, and I've more than moved on. The only thing I wish I could change is that he was my first kiss, you know?"

"You were a junior in high school for your first kiss?" Andy asks, surprise in his voice. I turn and narrow my eyes at him, and he raises a hand. "Sorry, I said that wrong. It made it sound like there was something wrong with *you*. All I'm saying is…I can't believe someone didn't try sooner."

"Maybe you don't remember what I looked like back in high school," I tell him, "but pigtails and braces aren't the typical look 15-year-old guys are interested in."

Andy chuckles and rubs at the stubble along his chin. "I, uh…actually do remember what you looked like," he tells me. "I may have… Okay, this is embarrassing to admit, but I may have gone through my old yearbooks after you interviewed for the job."

My eyes widen. "Oh, jeez."

"I was trying to remember what you were like back then because you just seemed so…different."

Shaking my head, I look off in the distance.

"So now you know why I was a junior before anyone wanted

to kiss me," I admit. "And why the only guy who *did* want to kiss me was just in it for shitty reasons."

Before I know it, Andy has shifted our bodies so we're no longer reclining next to each other but are pressed together. One arm wraps around my shoulders and the other hand takes my face so I'm looking straight into his eyes.

"I looked at all of your pictures," he tells me. "And do you know what I thought to myself?"

I shake my head.

"I thought, how the *hell* did I not notice her back then?"

Surprise must show on my face, because Andy nods, as if I've asked him a question.

"Your beauty didn't change," he tells me, dropping his gaze to look at my mouth as his thumb strokes lightly against my bottom lip. "It just sometimes takes guys a little bit longer to finally grow up and notice."

When my mouth tilts up at the side, he leans forward and presses his lips against that spot, kissing it softly and sending a wave of delight through my body.

Unable to help myself, I shift my head just slightly so we're better aligned, lip to lip, and then revel in Andy's deep moan when we open our mouths, tongues seeking and stroking.

It feels like everything I notice about Andy is monumentally different than how things were with Chad, even things as simple as kissing. I could stay here forever, just enjoying the way our lips are pressed together, my body wrapped in his arms. There's something freeing about knowing we're not in a rush, knowing getting off isn't always the goal. Instead, I get to just enjoy this, right now. Enjoy the feel of his solid chest beneath my palm, his work-roughened fingers against my face.

But then the thought pops into my mind. The stupid little

thing that tells me I should use this as a chance to really get the Cedar Point bucket list experience I never got when I was younger: a hookup at Easy Street.

"Andy," I whisper, pulling back then giggling as his mouth drops to lick and suck at my neck.

"Hmm."

"Let's get back in the truck."

It takes him a second to realize what I'm saying, but when he does, his entire body tenses before he pulls back and looks me in the eye.

"If you're gonna bring me to Easy Street," I tease, "you better plan to give me VIP treatment."

Andy's smile splits wide. "You know it."

Then he's tugging me down off the hood and ushering me quickly into the old truck I'm so glad I used to drive us up here.

"Thank god for blankets and bench seats," he tells me as he closes his door, and then his mouth is back on mine.

We kiss for a long time. A *long* time. Until the sky is dark enough that we don't have to worry about anybody else driving up here and possibly seeing us through the truck windows, though we do happen to be parked off to the side.

Our hands wander a lot, touching and teasing and dipping under clothes, exploring each other until I feel like my entire body is vibrating with need.

I told Andy I would let him take the lead on things, but I'm realizing I might be a little bit needier when it comes to sex than I'd assumed. Eventually I get to the point where I don't want to wait any longer, and I pull back, tugging my sweater and bralette over my head in one go.

Andy's eyes drop and stare at my breasts.

"These are just…perfect," he says, his warm hands cupping

159

me, his thumbs stroking over my nipples and sending sparks of lust through my body and down to my core.

He tugs me so I'm up on my knees on the blanket covered bench and leans in, sucking on one nipple then the other, his tongue circling around and flicking back and forth.

"I want to be inside you," he groans.

"Yes, me too."

We become a scramble of limbs and clothing, each of us trying to get undressed without knocking the other unconscious, and I can't help the little giggle that falls from my mouth.

"Come here," Andy says, yanking me against him once we're both naked.

As he kisses me, he lifts me so I'm straddling him, so I can feel his heat pressed along my body. His hands stroke along my bare back and down my sides, sending shivers skittering along my skin. Over my hips, down farther, until he brings one single finger to the very heart of me.

His thumb dips between my thighs, and he groans when he finds me wet. But he doesn't make a move to do anything other than this. He just stares at me, his lips parted and his breaths fast, as his thumb strokes back and forth and around the little nub that's aching for release.

Unable to help it, little whimpers of need begin to slip from my mouth as I climb closer and closer to the peak, as I shift my hips from side to side in desperation.

"Please," I whisper. "God, Andy, please."

I hear a crinkle, and when I open my eyes and look down, I watch as Andy manages to slip a condom on, all while never faltering in his movements against me.

I shift slightly, expecting to be able to slide down over him, but he holds me in place.

"I want to see you come first," he tells me, though he still notches the head of his dick against my opening. "Come for me."

My fingers grip his shoulders, my nails leaving little half-moons in his skin as I get higher and higher.

"Oh my god, it's right there," I whisper.

Andy moans and leans forward, his teeth biting just barely too hard into my neck, pushing me over the edge.

I cry out, gasping as pleasure races through me, and that's when Andy brings me down onto him, sliding himself into my pulsing core.

He shouts out his own pleasure, his hands moving to my thighs, his strong muscles lifting me up and slamming me back down, all while I wriggle and writhe on top of him, a mess of pleasure and desire as my orgasm continues to wash over me, all while I feel another begin to build.

My nipples rub against his bare chest, and his hot breath pants out against me as we chase whatever is on the other side of this mountain we're climbing together.

Andy's hands squeeze my hips as he moans, and then one hand slaps me on the ass.

"I'm gonna come again," I tell him. "I'm right there."

He nods, a bead of sweat dripping down the side of his face even though it's so cold. I press my mouth back to his, our kiss harder and more aggressive in this moment than any others have been before.

Then I feel his thumb slip back into that space between my thighs, stroking over my clit again and again, until I can't hold on any longer.

"Fuck," he grits out as I pulse around him, and then he falls over the brink as well.

Twenty minutes later, we've cooled down a bit and put our clothes back on, both of us unable to hide our grins.

"We should get you home, Ms. Mitchell," Andy teases. "I promised your mom I'd get you home before curfew."

I giggle, enjoying the little joke, the idea that we're two young kids fooling around on a high school date.

"Wouldn't want my parents to think we'd been doing anything…improper," I reply.

I back us out of the spot where we're parked and begin the slow drive down the windy switchbacks to get back to town.

"Just to be clear," Andy adds, "you definitely can't get that kind of sunset anywhere else."

I laugh pretty much the entire way home.

CHAPTER THIRTEEN

Briar

My favorite season is fall for about a million different reasons. The cooler air. The changing leaves. The sweaters and scarves and warm fires.

But above all, my favorite part of fall is the pumpkin and apple goodies that seem to flood the world, and there is nothing more perfect than having warm apple cinnamon donuts from Ruthie's.

For the longest time, Ruth Kower sold her famous treats out of the food stand window at Cedar Point High School events. Her three kids are around the same age as me and Boyd, and she used all the money she made to pay for their athletic uniforms and equipment.

Over the years, she moved from athletic events to town functions, popping up with her own little booth that always had a crazy line. Then, a few years ago, she finally opened her own bakery, Ruthie's, right in the heart of Main Street in one of the storefronts that replaced the old library. Now, years later and based on my conversation with Andy, I wonder if my parents had something to do with her ability to open her shop.

"Did you and dad give out small business loans a few years ago?" I ask my mom as she dunks her donut into her hot chocolate.

Surprise crosses her face. "Where did that question come from?" she asks before taking a bite.

I shrug as I break my own warm treat into a few pieces. "Andy and I were talking about small businesses and he mentioned that you guys did something like that. I mean, it was at a town hall, right? It wasn't a secret or anything."

My mom shakes her head. "No, it's not a secret, but we don't like to talk about those things with you kids since it impacts some of your friends and their families. Not everyone likes to have their information shared publicly, you know."

I nod at her pointed look. "I get that. I was just...curious."

"We've always wanted to do things to give back to the community, you know that," she says. "And sometimes, people need a helping hand to get started."

"That's what Andy said."

"Good. I'm glad he sees it that way, too."

We sit in silence for a little bit longer, both of us looking out the front window and watching the people passing by. It's not a particularly busy evening in town, but there are enough people scattered around to see that the lull from post-summer is truly starting to fade away.

From May to August, Cedar Point is slammed with tourists staying in cabins and at the resort and small bed and breakfasts, looking to enjoy fun on the lake. Once kids are back in school, those numbers take a sharp dive. Then in early October, it starts to pick back up again as people from down the mountain look for beautiful places to take breaks from life. And our little town is a great place to escape to.

We're barely halfway through the month and Halloween decorations are already starting to creep up on storefront windows. Pumpkins and cobwebs and witches, oh my! I have to admit, even though I was always happy to leave town, there does seem to be something magical about it as I look out and watch the shoppers go by, exploring the home goods store and the art gallery and the coffee shop. And of course, Ruthie's, the little bell dinging at the door every time someone new comes in.

"You've been spending a lot of time with Andy."

My head turns to look at my mother, both surprised and unsurprised that she brought it up.

"Yeah. We're…friends."

She gives me a little smile then looks down at her coffee.

"The kind of friends who spend the night?" she asks, popping a piece of her donut into her mouth.

I feel thankful that I'm not chewing anything or I might have inhaled and choked on it like I did at Ugly Mug yesterday with Abby.

"What?"

"Oh come on, Briar. You're 27. I might be your mom, but I'm also a woman who used to spend the night at your father's before we got married."

She laughs as I wince a little bit. I don't want to be one of those people who gags when her parents insinuate that they have a sex life, but I can't help having *some* kind of reaction.

"I'm only guessing about you and Andy, but it *is* based on seeing you guys together and hearing from a few others that they've seen you around town. The fact that you've not come home a few nights…" She lifts a shoulder. "I'm just curious."

I rotate my mug between my hands, the warmth from the hot chocolate dulling more the longer I let it sit.

"Yeah," I finally say, deciding I can share a little bit of this with my mom. "Yeah, we're…sleeping together."

My mom's eyes widen and she about flies back in her chair.

"What?" I say. "You asked."

"Yeah, but I didn't expect you to answer," she replies, laughing and putting her hands to her face. "I tease the others about their sex lives, but I've never had you give me anything to work with before. I don't know how I'm supposed to react."

I bite my lip, enjoying the laughter on my mom's face. It's rare that I'm the one who makes her smile, so I can't help but enjoy how good it makes me feel.

"Well, don't ask questions you don't want answers to," I tease.

"Okay, okay," she tells me. "So…you're having fun, though?"

I cover my face with my hands. "Did you really just ask that?"

My mother bursts into laughter. "I mean because you're dating. Are you having fun *dating*?" she clarifies, still giggling like she's a lot younger than mid-50s.

"Yes, we're having fun. But we're not dating."

Her head tilts to the side. "What?"

"We're having fun, but that's all we're having." I wait a second longer and take a deep breath, deciding to go all in. "We're friends with benefits."

At that, my mother covers her own face. "Okay, that might have been a little too much info."

I rub my lips together to hide a smile, though I do enjoy a bit of a giggle when her fingers part and she peeks at me through them. Then she finally drops her hand and takes another sip of her drink.

"No judgment, I promise, but I have to ask," she says, leaning forward and lowing her voice. "Is that enough for you?"

I nibble on my cheek, thinking over my answer. "It's enough for now."

She nods her head, a thoughtful expression on her face. "Okay then," she says, lifting a hand as if she's finally come to terms with it. "Well, Andy's wonderful. I love his little heart, and I love his father, so…you have my thumbs-up."

I smile then take a final bite of my donut.

"I'm surprised you're sharing so much. Does this mean I can ask you all the questions I want?" she asks, poking me with her finger.

I roll my eyes, but there's no heat to it. "You're always allowed to ask. I just don't like seeing how disappointed you are when I keep things to myself."

The teasing tone to our conversation falls away, and a seriousness replaces it. My mom tilts her head, her eyes tracking over my face.

"Is there a reason you don't feel like you can talk to me?" she asks. "Is there…something I've done to make you…"

Her voice fades, and for the first time, she's letting me see on her face how much it hurts her that I hide away from her, that I keep so much of my life to myself and don't let her in the way my other siblings do.

The hardest part is that I don't know how to explain it to her. I don't have an easy answer for why I don't like to share, why I share certain things and not others. Why I can talk to Abby or Boyd…why I'm now suddenly able to talk to Andy…but haven't ever been able to share with her.

But I do know if I don't find a way to make sure she knows

how much I love and appreciate her willingness to let me be the odd one out, I will regret it.

"Mom," I say, putting my hand over hers. "No. You've never done *anything* to make me close off. I promise."

She nods, but her brows stay furrowed as she watches me.

"I love you. You're an amazing mother, and you have no idea how much I appreciate how well you love me."

A tear tracks down her face.

"You've always been the one to defend my right to be the oddball, to keep things to myself. You've told the others to back off when their teasing got to be too much. You've respected my desire to be quiet and never tried to make me any different than I am. And I love you *so* much for that."

I pause. I might struggle with my words, but this I need to make sure I get right.

"I can't really explain why I don't want to talk about things. I don't have an easy answer, and I'm sorry. But I love you, and I'm so glad you're my mom."

She gives me a soft smile and squeezes my hand.

Even now, as she experiences some kind of pain inside that I can see on her face, she's still being the mom, still trying to comfort me and love me in a way only she knows how to do.

So I try to love her the way I know how as well.

I round the table and come up behind her, wrapping my arms around her shoulders and giving her my own squeeze.

It's all I have, and I hope it's enough.

We're walking out to the car when I hear my mom's name being called. When I turn, I'm surprised to see Thomas Riley striding toward us.

"Hi Thomas," my mom says, giving him a smile that's a lot less genuine than the one she gives most Cedar Point residents.

She's never been a fan of the Rileys, Thomas *or* Nick, and it's only partially due to the fact that Nick was such a little shit to me in high school.

I may not have told my mom what actually happened between him and me, but she knows I cried my eyes out for two solid days after we broke up, then vowed to never let a man make me cry ever again. My guess is that, for her, that was enough to place Nick firmly on her shit list.

"I'm glad I caught you. I was hoping to talk to you about one of the proposals that was brought to city council last week and…"

As Thomas talks to my mom, who also serves on the council, my eyes track over to One Stop Shop down the street. Andy's in there working. Like he does every day.

I know he's taking over for his dad and trying to keep things moving along, but it actually concerns me how much he works. Since the day I started working there about a month ago, he's hardly taken any days off.

I smile to myself, realizing one of those days was the one we spent at the market and down on the beach throwing stones last weekend. Clearly, I'm a force of good in his life, at least when it comes to taking a little time for himself. Maybe I need to come up with something for us to do that makes him want to take another day away from the store.

"I know that smile."

My head jerks when I realize Nick is standing next to me.

I glance around, wondering where the hell he came from and wishing I'd noticed him quick enough so I could be literally anywhere else.

The smile I previously had on falls away, something tight and uncomfortable covering my face.

"Nick."

"Oh, come on. Don't be so standoffish," he says, wrapping an arm around my shoulders that I immediately slip out from under, having no interest in being pressed up against him in any way.

"I'm not," I say, narrowing my eyes. "I don't want to be touched by you. That's a valid reaction to being touched by someone you don't like."

Normally, I'm more neutral with Nick—though I work my hardest never to be in the same space as him whenever I'm in town—but to have him come up on me when I was thinking about Andy was such a starkly opposite feeling that I'm having a hard time doing anything other than bristle.

He rolls his eyes, which he does a lot whenever I say something he doesn't like.

"Don't be so dramatic."

Instead of responding, I cross my arms and look over at where my mom has stepped to the side and is taking a look at some paperwork with Thomas, her glasses on.

"And I *do* know that face. You've been fucking the grocery boy," Nick says, and I'm pretty sure my neck about snaps off at how quickly I look at him, my eyes wide. "Slumming it a little, don't you think?"

I take a deep breath, my internal disgust climbing up the walls of my throat. Then I let it out, long and slow, resigning myself to treating him like a human and not the asshole he is.

But when I finally look back at his face, I see him staring at my breasts like a creep, and I nearly break my teeth with how tightly I grit my jaw.

"I don't know where you get off thinking you can say something like that to me," I say, my tone firm, my voice low. "But I'm telling you right now that you can't." Then I point a finger at him. "And just for the record, the only time I've ever been *slumming it* was when I was dating you."

Something nasty takes over his face, but before he can say anything else, his dad walks over and claps a hand on his shoulder.

"Briar! I heard you were living back at home. What a nice surprise that must have been for your parents."

I smile at Mr. Riley, but it's far from genuine. "Being home has been wonderful."

"We've loved having Briar home," my mom adds, wrapping an arm around my shoulders, and I lean into it, thankful that my mom is here to erase how gross Nick makes me feel.

"And working at the grocery store, huh? Just until something a little more refined comes along?"

I can feel my mom tense at Thomas' words, and I'm sure my own body is a reflection of hers as well.

I scratch at my chin and cross my arms. "You know, for a second, it sounded like you were speaking poorly of a small business owner," I say, pretending to be confused. "I probably didn't hear you correctly, City Councilman."

Thomas stands up a little straighter, his hand falling away from his son's shoulder.

"Thanks for your assistance, Patty," Thomas says, his eyes returning to my mother's. "I'll see you on the twenty-second, yes?"

"Yep. Have a nice day, Thomas."

My mom's voice is as firm as mine, and we watch as both of the Riley men turn and head down the street, my narrowed eyes following them for a lot longer than they should.

It's a bump from my mom's hip against mine that yanks my attention back to her.

"Huh?"

"Where did that spitfire attitude come from?" she asks me, a quizzical expression on her face. "*I probably didn't hear you correctly, City Councilman.*"

I snort. "I just didn't like his attitude. It's so…elitist."

"Yeah, he's been that way since we were kids," my mom says, rolling her eyes. "He used to tell your father he was slumming it by dating me."

"That's what Nick said about Andy," I tell her, the words just tumbling out of my mouth.

My mom's hand comes up and she tugs lightly on the end of my braid.

"Don't let him get to you. He doesn't know what the hell he's talking about."

We both turn and start walking down the street in the opposite direction, heading back to my mom's car.

"Why did he think *you* were slumming it?" I ask, though I'm pretty sure I can guess.

"Because your dad was a Mitchell and I was the janitor's daughter."

"So?"

My mom smiles and wraps her arm around my shoulders. "Exactly."

I remember hearing the story about my parents and how they started dating. I was in the second grade the first time they told it to me.

172

Being the daughter of the man who cleaned the toilets at the high school meant my mom had to deal with at least a handful of assholes who thought she was at the bottom of the totem pole.

But my dad fell head over heels for her when she asked him to go to the Sadie Hawkins dance during their junior year. It didn't matter what her dad did. It mattered who she was, and my dad fell hard for her big personality, amazing smile, and heart for helping others.

"Besides," my dad has always said, "no job is beneath you. Your job isn't what makes you who you are—your character is."

When I was younger, I always thought he was blowing smoke when he said stuff like that. But as I've gotten older, I've realized he really does mean it.

I've heard my dad tell the story enough times to know his words almost by heart, and I love that about them. Love that they love looking back on the thirty-six years they've been married and the three years before that spent dating, that they can still recall those memories like it was yesterday.

My parents are soulmates, without a doubt.

I've been thinking a lot about soulmates in the wake of my breakup with Chad, the idea that there's one person in the world who's meant for you. My brother Boyd told me you can't really believe in soulmates until you meet them, because anything else just feels too small to make it real.

Maybe that's why I have a hard time talking to my mom about my personal life. Just the idea of discussing the men I've been with in the past...I worry I'll let her down. If she knew how long I stayed with Chad when I was truly unhappy, her heart would break for me, and I don't want to be the one to cause that. I don't want my choice in partners to let them down.

First Nick, then Chad.

Andy seems to be a different story, though. He's a good man, I can tell, and like my mom said earlier, he has a great heart. It seemed to be a little easier to talk to my mom about him today, which surprised us both.

If I were looking for something long-term, maybe he'd be the guy for me.

But when I glance over my shoulder and look back at One Stop as I pull open the door to my mom's car, I remind myself that what I'm looking for isn't here in Cedar Point.

CHAPTER FOURTEEN

Andy

"What do you think about going on a walk this morning?"

My dad looks at me for a brief moment, and there's a split second where I think he might actually be considering it—but then his eyes return to the TV in front of him.

I nod my head, my lips pursed. "Right."

Pushing up from where I'm sitting on the coffee table, I head back into the kitchen and finish putting together a day's worth of food that my dad might or might not eat while I'm gone. Briar planned something for us to do today, telling me I needed a day off work. It took a few days for me to agree to it, but eventually I realized she's right. I *do* need a day off.

We'll be gone all day, and I've never been gone a full day without checking in on my dad at least once, not in the five months since his heart attack.

So, I'm prepping food in case he decides he wants to eat it. He's already had breakfast and now I'm putting together his lunch, a sandwich he can just eat without me coming by to get anything ready for him.

"Turkey and cheese," I tell him, holding up the brown sack as I stand in front of the TV, demanding his attention. "There's fruit and a cheese stick and a bag of chips, too. Do you want me to put a drink in here?"

I don't know why I ask. He clearly manages to get up off his butt to go to the kitchen for beers and sodas.

"I'm not a child, Andrew."

My dad's words, some of the few he's spoken to me in the past five months, twist something sour in my chest.

I clear my throat, wishing I could give in to the nasty little devil that lives somewhere inside everyone.

Because what I *want* to tell him is that if he's not a child, he shouldn't fucking act like one.

What I *want* to tell him is that he's right, he's not a child, so he needs to go to work like a damn adult and stop being such a weak asshole.

What I *want* to tell him is…

But I grit my teeth, ashamed of my building anger and resentment regarding my father's inability to get outside of this depression.

It's not his fault, I remind myself. *You're doing everything you can, and for now, that has to be enough.*

Instead of responding in anger, I take a deep breath and let it out slowly, then turn and place the bag on the coffee table so he can get it easily.

"Have a good day, old man," I say, trying to give him a smile as I turn and head out the door.

Then I pause at the threshold and make sure I say the thing I know he needs to hear.

"Love you."

When I pull up in front of the Mitchell house fifteen minutes later, I'm surprised to see Abby and Rusty leaning against the back of Rusty's red Chevy Blazer, shooting the shit.

"What have we here?" I say, grinning after I've parked and walked their way.

"I thought it would be more fun with a group," Briar says, coming out of the house with a bunch of fishing rods. "Besides, I haven't been fishing in a long time and thought it would be better to have someone with us who knows what they're doing."

"That's the only reason you invited me?" Rusty says, giving her a grin I've seen him use on female toursits at Lucky's. "I thought it was because I have a huge…boat."

When he finally looks at me, he winks, and I flip him the middle finger.

"Yes, it's the only reason you were invited," Abby said, rolling her eyes. "Don't be disgusting, Rus."

We spend a few minutes loading up Rusty's car with all the provisions Briar prepared—rods, bait, lures, beer, towels, bathing suits, sunscreen—then we all pile in, heading off to do some fishing, apparently.

Rusty and I have gone out fishing with some friends often over the years, heading off to some of the quieter areas of the lake, but that was at five or six in the morning. It's nearing ten, and I don't have the heart to tell Briar fish are less likely to bite later in the day.

She's so excited, a huge smile covering her face—well, huge for Briar, average for everyone else. Seeing her like that, seeing her happy as she tries to make me happy…it hits me square in the chest.

I wonder if that's how my mom would look at my dad when she would go with him to those car shows he used to love so much, if she looked at him with that kind of smile that was zeroed in on my dad's enjoyment.

My brows pull down and I look out the window as trees race past us and Kings of Leon plays on the radio. Am I comparing my mom and Briar? Is that…a thing now?

I shake my head. I've been noticing little things like that more and more recently. The small, day-to-day interactions that make me think I'm starting to wish things with Briar were a little less friendly and a little more…something else. What that something is, I'm not willing to spend too much time dwelling on.

Maybe I'm an idiot. I'm sure there are plenty of guys out there who would look at me and throw their hands in the air, wondering what the hell I'm thinking wishing my friends-with-bennies girl was…my girlfriend? Is that what I want?

But I don't know what to say in response to that. Should it be something stupid like *The heart wants what the heart wants*? Or how about something a bit more honest like, *I didn't expect to feel this way about Briar*? Because that's the truth.

As much as I thought I would be able to take my attraction for her and place it solidly in the friends category, I think I might have been kidding myself. I assumed I'd be able to separate my feelings from the physical, and I just don't think I'm built for that, try as I might.

The more time that passes, the more intimate we become, the more we share about our lives…I'm developing a clear awareness that the way I feel around Briar is different than I've felt around any of the other women I've dated.

And now, comparing her and me to my parents' relationship?

It worries me, makes me wonder if I should call this thing off. It's just supposed to be a little fun, right? The longer we stick this out, the deeper those feelings are going to get.

But then I look over at her, where she's sitting next to me, her hair tied back in that familiar braid and those loose tendrils and wispies flying around her face, and I know without a shadow of a doubt that when it comes time for things to end between us, it won't be me who makes it happen. That responsibility will rest firmly in Briar's court, because I doubt I'll ever be able to voluntarily let her go.

"Alright, guys. Let's unload."

We hop out at Drucker Landing, all of us grabbing handfuls and armfuls of supplies then walking the long stretch of dock out to where Rusty's family boat is moored.

There are two spots in Cedar Point where boats get permanent docking: South Bank Resort and Marina, which has space for 150 boats along 15 docks at the south end of the lake, and Drucker Landing, which has 30 boats on 3 docks, at the middle point of the lake. Other than that, you have to have a home *on* the lake with your own dock to have a boat, or keep it on a trailer in your drive and back it in every time you want to get out on the water.

My family hasn't ever owned any water toys, which is usually shocking to other people in town. Obviously, not everyone can afford a boat or a jet ski, or the maintenance and upkeep that come along with them. My dad always made it clear that he would only buy a boat if he knew he would use it at least once a week during the warmer seasons. For a guy who hardly ever took a day off because he loved his job so much, it was hard to see him ever doing that.

Luckily, as a person who enjoys all the different fun activities living on a lake provides—fishing, swimming, kayaking, wakeboarding, stand up paddle boarding, you name it—I was blessed with a number of friends who *do* want to own boats and use them regularly.

"Haven't been on David Buoy in a while," I say, referencing the name their dad gave the boat when they bought it a decade ago.

"Yeah, I haven't taken it out in a while," Rusty replies. "But Abby and I have been trying to do more things using their stuff, you know…"

He trails off, and I slap him on the back.

Rusty and Abby lost their parents a while back. Abby talks about them with so much enthusiasm and positivity, almost as if they're still alive, even though I know that's not what she thinks or feels.

Rusty, on the other hand, seems to have a hard time even mentioning them. It's been that way since everything happened. I get it, to some degree, having lost my mom, but at least I still have my dad, even if he's not exactly himself right now. I can't imagine what it would be like to have lost them both at once.

Once we've loaded up into David Buoy and Rusty has gone through the little list of checks that his dad left hanging next to the throttle, we back out of Drucker Landing and head north.

"Today's supposed to be one of the last semi-warm days of the year," Abby says, stretching her legs out where she sits across from me in the back of the boat. "Make sure to soak it up."

"Where are we going?" I ask, turning my attention to Briar.

She grins. "North Bay. I talked with Rodney and he said that would be the best spot to go fishing during this time of year."

My own smile splits my face. "You talked to Rodney Hamill about fishing?" I ask. "He actually talked to you?"

Rod is one of those recluse kinda guys who likes to live in the mountains because he doesn't want to talk to anybody. He's in his 60s and only comes into town to get groceries or to get fishing or hunting supplies. Otherwise he's at his cabin or off trying to catch something he can cook and eat later.

She shrugs a shoulder. "Yeah. Why?"

"That man has been coming in to grocery shop since I was a kid, and he's never said a single word to me."

"Well, did you ask him something about fishing?"

I snort. "That simple?"

Briar nods. "Talk to people about what matters to them, and they'll open up." Then she looks at me and winks. "Worked on me, didn't it?"

I rub a hand over my chest, her look and her words hitting me square on. She *does* talk to me. A lot. I think back to the way she used to flee the room when she was younger, and even the way she spoke to me when she first started working at One Stop. Tentative. Nervous. Uncertain. She may have been more confident in herself than she was as a kid, but she was still closed off to me.

The way she is now is just…maybe not a complete 180, but definitely moving in that direction. The conversations we've had over the past month of spending time together—about her relationships, her parents, her siblings—it blows my mind how much she's opened up to me.

In fact, now that I'm thinking about it, I realize she's being open and honest and vulnerable…and I'm not.

Even though we talk a lot, about just about everything under the sun, I still haven't told her what's going on with my dad, haven't said he's been at home for months, shut off from his life. Maybe I need to do that. Maybe Briar is actually the perfect person to talk to about it.

Rusty picks up speed as we get out of the no-wake zone, and I can't help but watch as Briar closes her eyes, tilting her face back and enjoying both the sun and the cool air as we race along Cedar Lake.

God she's beautiful. It really is something else to look at her.

When she opens her eyes, the wind still whipping her in the face, and peers over at me, she giggles when she finds me watching her.

I love that she's coming out of her shell with me, her personality starting to leak through the cracks I've been slowly putting in that shell she likes to keep herself so tightly wrapped in.

It feels like she's starting to trust me, and I get the feeling trust isn't something easy to come by with Briar.

I shift where I'm sitting, thinking about last night. We had sex in my office for the first time. She was reluctant when I first brought it up a while back, so I didn't try for it again, wanting to respect her boundaries.

Then she showed up in my office after everything shut down for the night, closing the door behind her and locking it before slinking across the room and hopping up on the desk. It was the most forward she's ever been with me, sexually speaking, and I don't know if I've ever been more turned on in my life as I was when she spread her legs and asked me to go down on her.

Which I did, happily, before I spun her around and fucked her into the desk so hard she came twice.

"You look at her like I've never seen you look at anybody."

I turn to Abby, who is sitting next to me, her eyes wide and curious. Then I look back at Briar, where she sits closer to the front of the boat, her head still tilted back and her eyes closed.

"That's because she's unlike anybody I've ever known."

"I want you in bed, gloriously naked," Briar says, flashing me a smile and whipping off her top.

"Wait, wait, wait," I say, pulling back to place my hands over hers. "Are you anti-Christmas?"

Briar's eyebrows furrow as she tries to understand what the hell I'm talking about.

"Huh?"

"Do you love Christmas?"

She shrugs a shoulder. "Who doesn't love Christmas?"

"Then you know more than half the joy of the holidays is the anticipation," I say, dropping a kiss to the skin of her neck. "The buildup." Another one on her collarbone. "The waiting."

Briar moans as my mouth moves to her bra, licking at her nipple through the fabric then sucking it lightly between my lips.

"Would it be any fun to wake up on Christmas morning…" I lick my way down her stomach. "And find out someone else had opened all your presents?"

I glance up at her as I trace my tongue around her belly button, and I can see when understanding dawns. Her hands release from where she was about to unbutton her jeans, and her eyes close as I trace along her exposed skin with my lips and fingers.

"Undressing you is like unwrapping a present, Briar," I say, my voice dipping low as I slowly pull her jeans down her legs, my hands touching all that smooth, creamy skin. "But unlike a kid who rips into the paper like a monster, I want to take my time."

A thought occurs to me and I stop my movements, leaving her jeans only partway removed so they're snug around her knees. Then I roll her onto her stomach, shifting her body so she's on her knees with her arms stretched out and her head on the bed.

God, her body is gorgeous, and I allow myself just a moment to enjoy the view of her sprawled out, her ass on display.

"And the best part," I continue, slipping my fingers into the lacy fabric of her thong and dragging it slowly down so I can see everything, "is when you finally get to see what you've been wanting so badly."

My mouth waters when I see the glisten between her thighs, and I lean in, sliding my tongue through her pussy lips. Briar makes a noise of surprise, but then she whimpers as I feast on her, my bit of stubble surely giving her cause to squirm.

I lick her over and over, up and down, focusing on her clit and then on her center. I love seeing her come, love hearing her cries of pleasure, and I'm relentless as I push her closer and closer to the edge.

"God, the way you taste," I say, and then I slip two fingers into her.

Briar lets out a restless moan, panting, her body shifting as she rocks against my hand.

"I want you inside me before I come," she says, her voice muffled from where she's pressed against the sheets.

Usually, I like to push her over once before I join her, but today, I feel needy. I want her entire body pressed against mine. I make quick work of yanking my own pants off, grabbing a condom from my bedside table, and getting it on.

And then I'm behind her, slipping my dick between her lower lips, stroking over her clit and unable to hold back my groan at how wet she is. Then I line myself up and slip into her in one long, smooth thrust that makes me feel like I'm going to burst out of my skin.

My hands grip her hips as I pull away then push inside again, over and over, my pace picking up. Briar lets out these choked noises, little whimpers I can barely hear but that still seem to twist something hot within me.

The friction is unreal, the warm wetness of her core as it sucks at me over and over again. I almost tip over when I catch sight of Briar's fingers clutching the sheets until I hear ripping noises.

I reach forward and pop the clasp of her bra, loosening the material just enough to allow my hand to move under the cup to take all that soft flesh in my palm.

"Fuck," I grit when I feel her clamp down on me. "When I do this you squeeze me so fucking good."

And then I prove my point by tugging on her nipple, my entire body flushing with heat as she clenches around me again.

"Briar," I pant out, not having any words to speak but feeling like I need to communicate…*something*. Anything. I need her to know I'm barreling toward the edge of a cliff at record speed, my entire body a train chugging toward blissful destruction.

"Tell me it feels good," I say, never slowing my pace.

"*So* good."

"Tell me how you want it."

"Just like this."

"Yeah?"

"Yeah."

But instead of continuing, I yank her up so her back is plastered to my front, wrapping one arm around her chest and slipping the other down between her thighs to flick and tug at her clit.

Apparently, that shift is the match that lights the fireworks, and only a few more thrusts go by before it feels like everything in her body compresses, constricting around me as she cries out her release.

I pump into her a few more times, trying to prolong it, wanting to keep going just a bit…

"Come in my mouth," she says.

My entire body freezes as a powerful orgasm slams into me. "Holy fuck." And then I groan, long and tortured as pleasure unlike anything hits every single nerve ending in my body, before I finally go still behind her.

We both collapse on top of the quilt, sweaty and exhausted and enjoying the little tingles of aftershocks that ripple through our bodies.

After I feel like I've caught my breath a little bit, I shift us around so we're naked and plastered against each other, our faces inches apart.

"Come in my *mouth*?" I ask her, still in disbelief that I heard those words from her.

She giggles then tucks her face against my chest, clearly a little embarrassed and unwilling to look me in the eye.

"That might have been the hottest fucking thing I've heard in my life," I add. "I couldn't hold on any longer."

I press a kiss against the top of her head then give her a little tug so she's forced to pull back and look at me.

"I guess we'll just have to save that for another night," she teases.

"You're a monster."

Shifting away, I crawl out of bed to dispose of the condom.

Then I climb back in next to her and pull her close, tucking her long body against mine.

"Stay," I tell her, not wanting this to be another night where she and I part ways after we're done being intimate.

She rests still in my arms for a long moment before she eventually nods.

At her agreement, it feels like everything inside of me settles, at least for a moment. Briar has stayed over a few times, but I always have to ask. Always have to try and convince her that I want her here in my bed for more than just getting off. Sometimes, I wish it was something *she* would ask for. And, not for the first time, I can't help but wish things between us felt more concrete.

As we snuggle close, I choose not to examine that thought any longer, instead enjoying the feel of her in my arms as we fade into sleep.

CHAPTER FIFTEEN

Briar

"Well someone looks nice today," I say, leaning against the doorjamb and crossing my arms, giving my eyes permission to rove over Andy Marshall, dressed to impress.

He looks over and grins, and it gives me that same wobbly-kneed feeling from the day I walked into One Stop looking for a job, the same kind of little heart palpitations I felt back when I was a freshman in high school and Boyd brought him home from school after swim practice, making my eyes about bug out of my head.

He's dressed in black pants and a white button-up shirt, a tie loose around his neck.

And *glasses*.

The same kind of thick-rimmed glasses he used to wear when we were in high school and he would study at our house. Seeing him wearing them now brings back all kinds of fluttery memories from when I was younger.

"I haven't seen you wear those in a long time," I add, gesturing to his face.

"You like my glasses?" he asks, and when I nod, he winks at me. "Maybe I need to start wearing them more often.

I nibble on my lip, imagining what that might look like. "You wouldn't hear me complaining."

Andy clicks one or two more times on his mouse then stands from his desk and begins to unbutton his shirt. That's when my eyes widen, heat flaring up along my neck as I see what he has on underneath.

"What do you think?" he asks, spreading his shirt wide enough that I can see the Superman logo underneath.

The smirk on his face says he knows *exactly* what he's doing to me, knows exactly how seeing the man in front of me dressed up like my favorite superhero makes me feel.

We got into a conversation the other night about Marvel versus DC, and I revealed that I'm a Marvel fan when it comes to the movies, telling him how mad I was at the fact that DC ruined not only my favorite superhero, but also my favorite celebrity.

Henry Cavill is the hottest man on the planet, he was a perfect choice to play Superman, and the movie was *horrible*. Absolutely horrible. The biggest letdown of my entire life, and that's coming from someone who just broke up with her ex-fiancé.

Then of course I made the mistake of telling Andy he kind of looks like the guy, and he's been doing all these weird things to stir me up. When we went shopping a few days ago at the little pop-up shop for Halloween costumes, he put on a long white wig and started talking all gruff, as if he was Geralt in *The Witcher*.

I should have known something like this was coming, but honestly, I continue to be surprised by just about everything

Andy does—not because he's inconsistent, but because I'm just not used to the care and attention he's been giving to me.

Maybe it sounds shitty to say it feels surprising to be considered important to the man I'm sleeping with, but it's the truth.

So seeing him here, wearing a costume he clearly picked out to rile me up…I have to work at not launching myself across the room at him.

"I think you're going to keep that on later," I tell him, biting on my lip and just giving in to the fact that my embarrassment is flushing bright on my cheeks.

"Oh, yeah?" he asks, his smirk morphing into something tinged with lust. "That so?"

I nod, tugging on my braid and pulling it around over my shoulder so I can play with the ends of my hair.

"After the Spooktacular?"

I nod again, even though I wish we could avoid going to the Halloween party the city hosts on Main Street every year and head back to Andy's house instead.

Downtown events are a huge deal in Cedar Point, and there's usually something going on in town on a regular basis. There are larger functions, like Summerpalooza and the Halloween Spooktacular, that shut down the main roads and bring just about everybody in to town, and then there are the smaller events, like the weekly Saturday Market and the monthly Craft Fair. Sometimes there are one-off events, too, like when the school hosted a movie night in the parking lot.

I'm not big on crowds, but I usually go to the events if I'm back in town because it's important to my family. Our ancestors having been the original founders makes us a part of town history and creates an obligation to be present and involved, at least for my parents. There's always some kind of conversation about why it's important to go.

This year, though, will be my first Spooktacular since prob-ably high school. The event is normally just a massive trick-or-treat with kids going from store to store, and then wandering through the booths set up by locals or businesses that are slightly off of Main Street, like One Stop. There are usually little stands open with snacks for sale and back when I was a kid there used to be a haunted house in the library, though obviously that part doesn't exist anymore.

Honestly, it wouldn't matter *what* they had set up tonight—my preference is hooking my fingers into Clark Kent's tie and dragging him home.

"If you keep looking at me like that, it's going to be inappro-priate for me to walk out there and pass out candy to the kids," Andy says.

I yank my eyes from where they were glued to his attire, bumbling out an awkward laugh.

"It's your own fault."

He crosses the room, wrapping me in his arms and placing a kiss against my lips that is *also* not appropriate for children.

I hum, enjoying the way it feels when he's holding me close. When he pulls back and returns to his computer, I finally decide to muster up the courage to ask him the question I came to ask.

"And you're okay with us going together?"

Andy pauses and looks over at me. "Yeah. Are you?"

I nod. "Yeah. Yes. Definitely. I just…thought you'd want another chance to decide."

His eyes track along my face in that way he has about him, the movement a reflection of the fact that he's looking for some-thing. I never know what it is, exactly, but he does this often, almost as if he's able to read my mind if he's attentive enough.

"It's only a big deal if you think it is," he says. "I doubt the fact that we've been hanging out is a secret, especially since you basically announced that we're sleeping together at Ugly Mug…"

I roll my eyes and snort at the memory from a few weeks ago.

"But if you have an issue, we can figure something out."

Andy's expression is neutral, and my guess is that most people would think he doesn't care either way. That said, it feels like I've gotten to know him pretty well over the past couple of months, and this is the face he makes when he doesn't want me to know his opinion right off the bat, when he wants me to make my own choice first.

Which is just another indicator that what I'm saying matters to him, even if he doesn't want me to see that it does.

"I'm not trying to hide our…friendship," I finally tell him. "I just wanted to make sure *you* were sure."

"And *I'm* trying to make sure *you're* sure," he replies. "So if you're sure you're sure, and I'm sure I'm sure…"

"Stop," I say, laughter in my voice.

"Only if you're sure."

I snort and shake my head. "What time should I meet you tonight?" I ask.

Today is technically a day off for me, and I really only popped over to say hi to Andy and check in about the time for setup. Which, okay, yeah, I could have just texted him, but clearly it was the better choice to come in person.

I mean, look at him.

"We're closing early and Spooktacular is supposed to start at six, so…how does 5:30 sound?"

I nod. "Sounds good."

Then he winks at me. "See you tonight, kryptonite."

"Sexy mama!"

I roll my eyes as I drop into the front seat of Abby's car and tuck my backpack in next to my feet.

"Will you stop?"

"Absolutely not!" she shouts at me, the sound ridiculously loud in the small interior of her little VW Bug. "You look amazing."

Then she reaches out and grabs the badge around my neck, taking a look at the little name tag and press pass I made for myself using the laminator in my mom's craft closet.

Abby's eyes wiggle up and down before she finally shifts her car into first, pulling us out of my parents' driveway in the direction of town.

"What's with this getup? I thought you were going to be one of the Kardashians."

I almost smile, remembering the year my entire family and I dressed up as the Kardashians for Halloween when I was a kid. That costume would have been a copout this time, an easy way to find something to wear when I had no ideas.

Dressing up as Lois Lane, however…it's genius. I love that I'll be complimenting Andy's costume.

"Andy's dressed as Superman," I tell Abby. "Just having a little fun with it."

She glances over at me with a pleased smile on her face. "I can tell you are, and having a little fun looks good on you."

I smooth out my pencil skirt, enjoying the compliment from my friend. "Thanks. It *feels* good on me."

A few minutes later, we're pulling into the parking lot behind One Stop then walking the short distance to Main Street, where the decorations are up and tables are being set out. Once I spot Andy at the far end, spreading a tablecloth over his assigned table, I quickly yank off my flats and change into the high heels I borrowed from Bellamy.

That was an interesting conversation, for sure. The look she gave me when I asked to borrow the black pair she wears out on dates made it clear I had some explaining to do.

Not that I gave in.

I might be opening up a little bit, but let's not be too hasty. I'm not trying to spill all the beans about what's going on with me and Andy, even if I *am* ready to be his date to Spooktacular.

My thoughts might not make sense to someone else, but they make sense to me, and that's enough.

Andy looks up at me as I get closer, the toothpick he was chewing on dropping from his open mouth as he gives me some serious elevator eyes.

"You're shitting me," he says, his face splitting wide.

I shake my head. "Nope."

"You are…" He trails off and makes a noise deep in his throat, something filled with appreciation, before striding over and yanking me into a kiss that declares to anyone with eyes that we're here together.

It makes me thankful that I took the time to figure out a new costume.

"She blushed like a damn lobster when she told me you were dressed like Superman's alter ego," I hear from behind me, turning slightly but not pulling away from where Andy has an arm wrapped around my waist. "And now I get the appeal. Holy crap, Marshall!"

Andy chuckles.

"You are *the* embodiment of what Henry Cavill *should* have been as Superman."

"Don't tell me you're a fan of that guy, too?"

Abby rests a hand on one hip and pops out the other one then narrows her eyes.

"Now, I *know* you're not trying to get into a debate with me about the absolutely pure deliciousness of the most attractive man in Hollywood, right?"

Andy shakes his head and muffles a laugh before adopting a serious expression. "No, ma'am."

Abby huffs and nods her head. "That's what I thought. Now if you'll excuse me, I have some important work to be doing."

She struts off, most likely in search of Rusty's booth somewhere else along the street.

We look at each other, and Andy raises an eyebrow.

"She's something else, huh?" I ask.

He nods. "I doubt anybody else could call me to task so quickly while wearing a full-bodied cow costume." He fixes his stare on me and says, "It's...*udderly* ridiculous."

I shake my head at his horrible joke, a cheesy smile on my face.

"*You're* utterly ridiculous," I say in response.

He wraps his hand around my lanyard and gently tugs me forward, planting a quick kiss on my lips, and then we get started on setting up.

We make quick work of putting together the booth for One Stop, which has a little basketball hoop for kids to shoot at and prizes to win, along with candy and a raffle for a massive basket filled with king-sized candy bars.

Once the kids start showing up and making the rounds, I end up having a lot more fun than I thought I would. I can't get over how cute some of the children are in their costumes, and it's fun to see some of my friends from high school doing the rounds with their own little ones.

It's amazing how choosing to be here on my own rather than being forced into it by my parents completely changes how I feel—although I'm sure standing at Andy's side has something to do with it.

But my two worlds collide when my parents make the rounds midway through the evening and stop at our table.

"Well look what we have here," my mother coos, clutching her hands against her chest and giving us both a sweet smile. "Aren't you two the cutest couple with your matching costumes?"

"Patty, don't embarrass them," I hear my dad mumble before giving me a wink.

Love that man.

"Oh, Mark, I'm not embarrassing anybody," my mom says, waving a hand at him as if he's an idiot for even thinking of such a preposterous idea. "Am I, honey?"

I shake my head, trying not to laugh. Sometimes my mom is a literal cartoon character.

"Mom, you remember Andy Marshall, right?"

"Remember him?" she practically shouts. "Are you kidding? He only spent about half of his childhood running in and out of our house like a little menace. How are you, Andrew?"

Andy grins, that good-natured part of him unable to do anything but be completely gracious and respectful of his elders.

"Doing well, Mrs. Mitchell. Thanks for asking."

"How's Willy doing?"

That question is from my dad, his voice dipping low as he steps closer to Andy.

"I know he's been having a hard time."

When I look over at Andy, I see he's put on that neutral expression again, the one from earlier today—the one that says he doesn't plan to reveal his thoughts just yet.

"He's doing okay. Thanks for asking."

Andy continues exchanging pleasantries with my parents while my mind bunny-trails off into the woods, trying to remember whether I've talked with Andy about how his dad is doing recently. I know we talked about it at the beginning, when he hinted that he was dealing with some family stuff, but is that really the last time I've asked about William?

I make a mental note to talk to him about it later, returning my focus to where my parents are saying goodbye and wandering off into the crowd—though my mother makes a point to run around the table and give me a good squeeze.

"You guys are so cute," she whispers in my ear before grinning at me, giving Andy a little wave, and running off to catch up with my dad.

"Sorry about that," I say. "My parents can be a lot sometimes."

Andy shakes his head. "They're great."

I turn my head and look in the direction they just went, watching as my dad slips his hand in my mom's back pocket. Thirty-nine years and five kids later, and they're still doing that cutesy stuff. It's the kind of love I think most people want when they imagine the future, and I know I was lucky to be raised by two people who are best friends.

"Yeah. They are."

We spend the evening laughing about costumes and sneaking candy from the store's stash, finally packing things up around nine along with everyone else. I help Andy take everything back to One Stop and do a quick recheck that all the doors are locked.

Then Andy startles me by pressing me up against a wall in the stockroom and dropping to his knees, shoving my pencil skirt up and slipping my panties to the side.

I grin, telling myself I should wear a skirt every day, though it falls away when he presses his mouth against me, bringing me to a quick and dirty orgasm in the middle of the stockroom.

When he's done, he pops up and presses his lips against mine, our tongues tangling so that I can taste myself.

"What was that for?" I ask as we're shifting my skirt back into place.

Andy shrugs a shoulder and gives me a wink. "Just a little fun," he says. Then he leans close as we head out toward the front. "Besides, I'll need to save my Man of Steel for once we get back to my place."

We're woken in the middle of the night by a ringing noise, and it takes me a second to realize it's Andy's cell on his nightstand.

"Hello?"

The sound of his voice, gruff with sleep next to me in bed, has me peeking an eye open—but it's when I feel his entire body tense that I know something's wrong.

"What?"

In a split second, he's out of bed, moving across the room to turn the light on, and that's when I catch a glimpse of the expression on his face.

He looks sick, almost paralyzed, his eyes wide as he looks around the room and continues to listen to whoever is on the other end of that call.

"I'll be there in ten minutes."

He chucks his phone on the bed and grabs his jeans from the ground, pulling them on without any underwear as he hops over to tug a shirt off a hanger.

"Andy," I say, my body starting to wake but my mind still struggling. "What's going on?"

He yanks a sweater over his head and glances at me for only a second before he continues grabbing everything he needs to go…somewhere.

In that one moment, I can see that something is happening that is rocking him to the very core of his being, and I'm not prepared when I hear what he tells me as he's scrambling to get out the door.

"There's been a fire."

CHAPTER SIXTEEN

Andy

When I pull my Jeep up to the line of caution tape, I barely throw it in park before I'm out the door and jogging past the fire truck to get a better picture of just what exactly has happened.

The smell of smoke in the air is thick, and I can see the orange hue in the sky as I race down Main Street where we were just a few hours ago. My steps falter when I round the corner of Mitchell Road, when I finally see it.

One Stop Shop. Engulfed in flames.

I almost can't believe it, and really it's only when I feel Briar step up next to me, slipping her arm in to loop with mine, that I actually *do* believe it.

Because when all she says is, "I'm so sorry, Andy," I know she can see it too, know it's not just a figment of my imagination.

We watch as the Cedar Point Fire Brigade battles the flames as they curl out of the broken windows of the storefront and lick up the sides of the building. The shouts of the firefighters as they move their massive hoses around to get the right angles to spray water is the only noise I can hear other than the sound of the fire itself.

All growing up, I loved the sound of a crackling fire. Bonfires were a major thing, whether it was smaller campfires on trips into the wilderness with my parents or big raging blazes on Sunday nights during summer when I was in high school.

But seeing something I love burn to ash is one of the most painful things I've ever experienced in my life, apart from losing my mother. I can tell from this moment forward, I will never feel the same about a fire ever again.

It feels like hours later that the flames finally start to die down. In that time, Briar and I don't move from our spot sitting on the back of Sheriff Perry's truck, just watching as the firefighters do an amazing job of not only putting out the fire, but also protecting the neighboring structures from lighting up as well.

At least, that's what it looks like from where I'm sitting, feeling utterly powerless because there's not a damn thing I can do to help.

"Do you want to call your dad?" Briar asks once Sheriff Perry comes over to update us on the progress. "You can always handle things with the sheriff and I can go pick him up, if you want."

With just those simple words, the reality of the situation finally lands square on my shoulders.

Somehow, I've managed to fail my dad in just about every way possible. I didn't go to school when he and my mom told me to. I've struggled to take over One Stop from him during his health decline. I can't figure out how to help him get over this depressive state he's stuck in. I've been spending less time with him because I've been focusing more on Briar.

And now?

Now I've burned his legacy…my legacy…to the ground.

"No," I finally say, sliding down off the back of the truck bed and slipping my hand from Briar's. "I'll talk to him about this later. What I really need to do is meet with Paul to figure out the extent of the damage."

There's a long pause, and I can feel her watching me even though I'm staring at the blackened exterior walls of what used to be my family's business.

"But that will take a while, right? They said you wouldn't really have any answers until later this afternoon, and it's only…" I glance back and see Briar looking at her phone. "It's only six in the morning. Let's get you something to eat. Ugly Mug is opening. We can grab that cheese scone you love, and then we can go to my parents' house. My dad dealt with a major fire when I was younger, and I bet he—"

"Briar," I say, my tone firm as I cut her off midsentence. "I don't want to do any of that, okay? Just…can you just go?"

I fish my keys out of my pocket and hold them out to her, needing her to leave so I can focus on all the shit that's about to come my way.

This is the town's only grocery store, and pretty much everything is gone, even though the structure remains. We're cash poor and struggling financially, and now we'll be wrapped up in red tape with insurance as we try to figure out how to dig ourselves out of this mess.

Having Briar here, looking so earnest and wanting to be so helpful…I don't deserve that.

I don't.

So I need her to leave.

I can see her wanting to protest, her mouth slightly open as she prepares something to say. At the last second, she nods and takes the keys from my hand.

"Call me later, okay?" She leans in and kisses my cheek then squeezes my wrist. "And don't forget that I'm here for you. We all are."

I give her a nod then spin around to look at the damage again, effectively dismissing her.

It might be rude and completely uncalled for, but all my emotions and thoughts are a jumbled mess right now. Taking care of Briar's emotions in the middle of it all is something I'm just not capable of doing.

It's nearing two in the afternoon when I finally sit down with the fire chief to get an update on what happens next.

Paul Brown has had his job for a long time. I'm pretty sure he was the chief back when I was a kid, so I know he knows what he's talking about.

Which makes it that much more difficult when he brings in Sheriff Perry to be part of the conversation.

"Based on a first look today, I'm going to launch an arson investigation," Paul tells me. "There's a spot around the back near the parking lot that looks to be the source of where the fire started, and since it wasn't near anything electrical that might have sparked something, that's cause for concern."

"You think someone did this on purpose?" I ask, a new wave of shock rippling through me.

"Well, there was a strong scent of turpentine in that back

area, which is an accelerant, and the fire moved through the building incredibly quickly. Normally, when a fire is accidental in a building of your size that has the appropriate fire safety equipment—which you had, because you passed your last inspection—the damage is much less extensive." Paul shakes his head. "But the place lit up like a torch like *that*," he says, snapping his fingers, "which makes arson a very real possibility."

I drop my head in my hands, trying to dig into the back of my mind to understand who the hell would set our building on fire.

"I have to ask, Andy."

My head flies up at the sound of Don's voice. The sheriff is a good man, but I haven't been on the receiving end of his interrogation voice since I was in high school and he caught me, Rusty and Boyd with beer behind the liquor store.

"Where were you last night?"

"At my house. With Briar."

"Ah, I heard you were seeing the Mitchells' oldest girl," Paul interjects, and I can't mistake the way he seems to be adding some extra friendliness to his tone, as if he doesn't want things to get heated.

"I'm gonna need to hear from her that you were with her to make sure you have an alibi," Sheriff Perry continues, ignoring his colleague's attempt at joviality. "She can come down to the station any time in the next forty-eight hours."

My head starts to swim. Alibi? Like I'm some kind of criminal who lit his own store on fire?

"Now, I can see on your face you're takin' offense," Paul says, leaning back in his chair and folding his hands over his stomach. "We're just doin' our jobs, Andy."

"I know, I just…" I pause, realizing this is even more serious than I thought it was going to be. "It's just a lot to take in."

He nods his head. "I understand." Then he slips a piece of paper in front of me. "This is a little flyer I had Luna put together after the last big fire. It's got all the information on what you need to do. Calling your insurance and filing a claim, what information you need, that kind of thing."

"Thanks Paul," I say, rising from my chair. "You have my number if you need anything?"

He nods. "Sure do."

Then I turn to look at Sheriff Perry. Even though I'd rather tell him he's an idiot if he thinks I would ever start that fire, I extend my hand instead.

After we shake, as I'm leaving the office, Paul calls after me. "Oh, and Andy?"

I turn to look back at him.

"Nobody will be allowed on the property until the investigation is complete, okay? I know you'll be wantin' to check it out, but I'll call you when you're clear to do so."

I let out a long breath, lift a hand in a little wave of acknowledgment, then head outside.

Because I gave my keys to Briar earlier today, I'm without a car, so I decide to try to clear my head by walking back to the house. The normally fifteen-minute drive takes me about an hour and a half to walk, and my stomach is growling by the time I finally make it back to Brooks Road.

It's that exhaustion and hunger that must make me blind to the fact that my Jeep is parked out front when I walk up the steps to my apartment. I let Quincy outside then strip my smoky clothing and get straight into the shower, scrubbing away the scent from my skin as well.

Once I've gotten dressed and eaten one of those fancy granola bars Briar has started leaving in my cabinets, I bring Quincy back inside and then trudge over to my dad's house, prepared to talk to him about what's going on, if he's even able to listen to me or hear what I'm saying.

But when I push the door open, my eyebrows about fly off my face at the sight before me.

My dad, fully dressed and sitting at the kitchen table with Briar, each of them holding a handful of playing cards, the rest of the deck out on the table between them.

"Look who it is," Briar says, reaching out and placing a hand on my dad's wrist. "It's Andy."

When my dad turns his head to look at me, he smiles. Actually smiles, for the first time in months.

"There's my boy," he says, his voice sounding a bit wobbly. "How are you doing, son?"

The emotions from the day seem to catch up with me all at once, and right there in the doorway, I choke on my words, tears welling in my eyes.

Instead of walking into the room, I step backward and out onto the front patio, closing the front door behind me to put an added barrier between myself and the two people sitting in the kitchen.

What the hell is going on?

Only another few seconds go by before I hear the door open and Briar slips out, shutting it again softly behind her.

"Hey."

I don't look at her, unsure of what I should be saying and struggling with the overwhelming feelings of shame.

Part of me is upset that she's here, insinuating herself into my family and my problems that have nothing to do with her. But that part of me is small, and I'm mortified that it exists, because I know it comes from a place that has nothing to do with Briar and everything to do with ego.

An ego that's embarrassed by the fact that she's here, seeing so many of the ways I've failed…seeing how I've not been able to take care of my dad.

But the rest of me can't believe she came here when I sent her away. By the looks of it, she hasn't gone home to change, which means she came straight here to check in on my dad right after I asked her to leave.

Has she eaten? Has she slept? Did she even think to take care of herself?

"I can tell you're not happy I'm here and…well, I just want you to know I didn't say anything to your dad, about us or the fire."

I look over to where she's standing, her back leaning against the front door and her arms crossed. It looks like a defensive posture, but I think it's less defense and more offense. And I hate that she feels the need to do that with me.

"I just said I'm your friend, since I wasn't sure he remembered me from when I was younger, and that I was here to help him today. I don't know if you know, but I used to volunteer at The Pines, and interacting with people struggling to take care of themselves is something I'm pretty comfortable with, so…it was actually pretty easy to get him to shower and dress. We've mostly just been hanging out and playing cards. I made him some breakfast and lunch, so he's pretty good until dinner."

Maybe it's ridiculous of me to pick this moment to fall in love with Briar Mitchell, but I don't know that it's really something you can choose. I think it just *happens*.

And that's what happens right now. In this moment. As I watch her try to explain herself and the entirely selfless actions she took today in the wake of an absolute disaster. Thinking of my father, thinking of me.

How can I *not* fall in love with her?

It's been coming for a while, even though I didn't want to admit it. It began as far back as that first time I was able to get her to really smile on her first day of work and has been growing and growing as we've gotten to know each other and spent more time together.

Believing I could know Briar in such an intimate way and *not* risk falling head over heels for her was my first mistake.

Pushing her away this morning was my second.

And continuing to hold on to her even though I doubt she'll ever love me back will absolutely be my third.

She stands there for a moment longer, looking a little uncertain, and that's when I realize I've just continued to stare at her without saying anything.

I move quickly across the small space between us and wrap her in my arms, wishing there was something I could do or say to convey to her just how much I appreciate her—her heart and her soul and the way she handled this situation so much better than I did.

But the only thing that comes to mind is small and not nearly enough.

"Thank you."

Then I tuck my face into the crook of her neck and breathe in the scent of her, a scent that's masked significantly by the smell of smoke and ash from the hours we spent sitting and watching what I thought was my world crumbling around me.

Now I know better.

My world wasn't dissolving into flames. It was sitting beside me, holding my hand.

A few hours later, Briar and I leave my dad's house, our fingers looped together as we walk back to my spot over the garage.

When I followed her back into the house a little while ago, my father beckoned for me to come over and play cards with them. So I did. For two hours. We rotated through all the favorites from when I was younger and played with him and Mom on camping trips.

Gin rummy.

Crazy eights.

War.

Slapjack.

It turned into quite a rousing evening of card games, and I had to regularly remind myself not to stare too much as my dad interacted with Briar, his expressions still muted but friendly, his tone quiet but present.

Ultimately, I decided not to bring up the fire to my dad. Not yet, anyway. Maybe it was a bad call. Maybe I'll regret not telling him immediately. But I sat across from him at the kitchen table, watching him manage little smiles and short responses to Briar's questions, and I just couldn't imagine ruining the few good moments I've managed to have with my dad in months. Especially when I don't have any answers about what's happening next.

The games turned into Briar telling me to sit with my dad while she made us dinner. Nothing fancy, just beans and rice and quesadillas, but I felt almost overwhelmed by her ability to maneuver the situation so gracefully.

Overwhelmed, and impressed.

Once we get back to my place, I'm just as overwhelmed by the need to show her how thankful I am.

"Can I take a shower?" she asks as we cross the threshold of my living room. "I really need to wash all this smoke smell away."

I place a kiss against her lips and squeeze her hip. "Absolutely. Mind if I join you in a minute?"

She smiles, but her eyes are tired. "Sure."

I take some time to make sure Quincy's got enough food and water, even though Briar told me she already took care of that earlier. When I finally head back to the bathroom and strip down, I find Briar standing under the water, her head tilted back and her eyes closed, just enjoying the spray of water as it sluices down her body.

She peeks over at the sound of the glass door opening.

"Let me," I say, taking the loofa from her hand.

"I can do it."

"Briar, you're exhausted. You hardly got any sleep last night and then spent the entire day thinking about anyone but yourself. Let me take care of you."

She looks at me for a moment before her head falls forward in what I decide to take as a nod, and I make quick work of lathering up the loofa with the body wash she says makes me smell delicious.

Then I take my time, rubbing it in small circles around her body, making sure to get all the smoke and dirt off her skin, pressing firm to knead her muscles as well. She moans as I swipe along her shoulder blades then over the curves of her hips and ass.

Once I've scrubbed up her back, I move around to her front and dip low to get her legs and feet, then I transition up to her stomach and across her breasts and chest.

That's when I notice the little smile on her face.

I turn her slightly under the spray so I can start rinsing her off, but once I drop the loofa, Briar grabs my hands and brings them around to the front of her body, placing them on her breasts.

When I squeeze, she hums, shifting on her feet and pushing her back against my front.

"I want your hands on me," she says, her voice quiet as she holds them against her body.

"You want me to make you come?" I ask, my voice deep from the lust that's been racing through my veins.

Her head bobs just a little bit, and I slip one hand down from her chest, across her stomach, between her thighs, relishing the little whimper that echoes off the walls when my middle finger slides between her lower lips.

I use the soap to wind her up, higher and higher, circling that nub over and over, around and around, as my other hand moves back and forth between her breasts, pinching and tugging at her hard nipples.

My cock is a pipe between us, lodged in the crevice between her ass cheeks, and I can't help it as I rock myself against her, the soap slicking my way.

"Andy," she whispers, her head back against my shoulder and her mouth close to my ear.

Suddenly, she's spun herself around in my arms and pressed her lips to mine, opening her mouth to kiss me, her tongue thrusting into my mouth with the same type of movement I wish I was using to thrust inside of her. I push her back against the wall, enjoying the friction of our bodies sliding together, and then I feel Briar lifting her leg to wrap around my hip.

I open my eyes and find her already watching me.

A beat goes by as words pass unspoken between us. A short pause as we both acknowledge the importance of this moment.

Then I hook my arm in the crook of her knee to hold her leg up as I press my dick against her and, after looking into her eyes again, push into her tight heat.

Maybe it's the emotion of the day. Maybe it's the fact that I realized I'm in love with Briar just a few hours ago. Maybe it's simple biology and my body is excited to be inside of her bare.

I don't know what *it* is, exactly, but it feels like something within my chest has broken open. Like a dam has burst forth with an overwhelming level of emotion and longing and desire I've never felt in my entire life.

As I move my hips, back and forth, pushing into the very heart of her, I know I am well and truly gone and there will never be another one out there who will fit me the way Briar does.

The echoes of our cries and pleasured groans surround us, the slapping of wet skin dominating my mind as we both tip over the edge and find that bit of bliss.

We kiss for long moments before we rinse and towel each other off, the intimacy between us feeling like a physical thing we can hold and touch.

Then we crawl into bed together, wrapped in each other's arms as we fall into a much-needed sleep.

CHAPTER SEVENTEEN

Briar

News about the fire travels fast, which is unsurprising in a town of only a few thousand people where there's only one grocery store that has now been burnt to the ground.

My parents called me about it early yesterday morning, only a few hours after I left Andy to go back to his house and get my things, and that's when my dad suggested I go check in on William Marshall.

Oh, how glad I am that I did.

He was sitting alone, in the dark, staring at a picture of his wife. I don't know how long he'd been there, but it had to have been a while.

I honestly think having someone he's not as familiar with show up at his house was probably a good thing and enough of a shock that it was easier for me to get him to follow my lead. When I said I would wait for him to shower and change so I could make him breakfast, he took that as direction and actually did it.

He didn't say much for a while, so we spent a good chunk of our time in silence apart from the moments when I decided to share something. It went against all my natural instincts to just talk to someone I hardly know about my life and town happenings, but it seemed to help him a little, since his mouth started to loosen up as more of the day went by.

I know he went through a heart attack that put him in the hospital for a while during the spring, but I didn't realize his difficulties in recovery aren't actually heart-related.

Well, actually, maybe it *is* heart-related.

William Marshall is depressed—very depressed—and I could see it the minute I got there. It makes me wonder what his doctors have been prescribing him during his recovery, and whether or not he has a therapist or psychologist to talk to about what's going on in his mind, and in his heart.

I made a mental note to talk to Andy about that, thinking he might have just felt really overwhelmed by everything and never thought to get his dad to see somebody. I can see how easy it would be to not know the signs of depression, or be able to recognize it but feel completely lost as to how to help.

As I drive around the lake, heading toward the community center, I think about my time spent with William. When I called Abby after I'd gotten him to get in the shower, she was shocked that I'd gone over there in the first place.

I tried to explain it to her, but everything I said came out wrong, as if it was all about how much I care for Andy, and that's not...I mean, yes I care about Andy. Obviously. We've grown to be very good friends and enjoy each other's company, but I went over there *because* we're friends. Not for any other reason, as Abby tried to imply.

"You're starting to walk the line," she told me. "I'm here

for you, I promise, but if you're serious about not wanting to stick around town, I think you're starting to wade in dangerous water."

Am I?

My feelings for Andy are definitely different now than they were when I was in high school, different than even how they were when I first started hooking up with him. But that's to be expected, right? A little intimacy goes a long way in developing different feelings for someone.

But that doesn't mean I feel anything...romantic. I can just have strong friendly feelings. I'm sure of it.

Besides, it was about Andy's dad, not Andy. That's what I was trying to tell Abby even though it didn't come out quite right. I need to think less about that weird phone call with my friend and more about what's up with William and how I can help him get better. Andy needs his dad, desperately—especially considering the fire—and I want to help them sort through and figure everything out.

But today isn't the day to talk to him about his dad.

Today, most of the One Stop employees are meeting with Andy in one of the unused rooms at the community center to talk about the fate of the store and what's going to happen next.

He left early this morning, kissing me softly, then telling me he needed to handle a few things and to feel free to hang around his place for as long as I wanted. Around ten, a text came through that asked me to meet with other employees about the fire.

I'm worried. For Andy, of course, but also for the town.

Losing the one grocery store will have a really big ripple effect on the entire community. There's so much to think about. Food insecurity, trips down the mountain, getting food to the elderly or young who can't manage it themselves—and that's just off the top of my head. I can't imagine there's been enough time for Andy to have fully prepared himself for a meeting like what we're about to have, and I worry that whatever conversation we're about to have is premature.

When I pull his Jeep into a parking spot outside the small building, Andy having taken his dad's 4Runner this morning, I recognize a few cars that belong to my coworkers. The building is alive with activity. I pass a sewing class for moms and kids and a yoga class for seniors before I finally make it to the Maple Room.

"Thanks for coming, Briar," Andy says as I push through the door, that same exhaustion from yesterday apparent in his eyes. "I think you're the last one that said you could come today, so let's get started."

I slip into one of the chairs and lean forward, resting my elbows on the table as my mind begins to race with questions despite the fact that he hasn't even started speaking yet.

"This morning I got a preliminary report back from Paul. It looks like the fire *was* arson, and this morning, the person responsible came forward and signed a statement at the police station."

Sitting up straight in my chair, I wait for him to share.

"It was Linden Perry."

"Don's boy?" Lois asks, as much shock in her voice as I feel in my body.

"Are you serious?" I chime in.

Andy nods. "There's still a conversation going on about whether it was arson or accidental, but that's for the police to sort out and not something we should be speculating on."

I shake my head and cup my hands over my mouth, still in

disbelief that the sheriff's youngest son would be the one responsible for something like this.

"Now, the reason you're here is because there's still a question of what's going to happen with the store."

He looks around the room, and something inside me cracks at the pain I can see in his eyes.

"A final decision hasn't been made yet, because I need to confirm with my father, but it's likely that One Stop will close. Permanently."

Protests go up around the room, Lois the most vocal of the group. Maryanne and Elvin—the two other full-time cashiers—look shocked, and some of the other employees I don't know as well are sitting with their mouths open wide. Even the small group of part-time bag boys—who managed to show up to a meeting when I think they're supposed to be in school today—seem to have things to say.

I, on the other hand, know this is a mistake and keep my mouth firmly shut.

Andy puts his hands up, an unspoken request for silence, and once the group complies, he continues.

"The reason I've asked you all to come here is so I can let you know that we will be covering your pay through the end of November as if you were working your regular hours. But at that time, you will need to find employment elsewhere, or file for unemployment through the proper channels."

I shake my head. It's a *mistake*.

Andy goes on a little bit longer, sharing some information about an anticipated timeline for insurance payouts and providing details about when to expect to hear from him again. Then, slowly, everyone trickles out from the room, disbelief still tingeing the air.

Once everyone is gone, he crosses the room, sitting backward in the chair in front of me, resting his forearms on my table.

I have things I want to say, opinions I want to give, but I keep them to myself, choosing instead to stroke my hand down his forearm.

"You okay?"

He nods but doesn't look me in the eye. "Yeah. Just…sad."

"This seems like a big decision. What made you decide…I mean, it just feels really rushed."

Andy leans back and crosses his arms, lifting one hand to rub at the stubble he hasn't shaved off in a few days. He lets out a long sigh, one that hints at a deep emotional turmoil he hasn't let me see before.

"One Stop was struggling *before*," he finally tells me. "And with the additional costs and time it will take to get it up and running again…"

He trails off, his face turning to the side to stare out the large window on the far wall. Little patches of red flush around the base of his neck, and I can see a glassy sheen take over his eyes. I can't imagine what's on his mind right now in the wake of a few very emotional days.

"I let him down, Briar," he says, his voice sounding ragged and choked, like it's painful to even speak the words out loud. "He believed in me, believed I'd be able to handle this someday, and when he needed me to step in, I let him down."

I'm out of my chair and wrapping myself around Andy in a flash, squeezing my body in to sit in his lap so we're face to face. It's not comfortable by any means, but it gives me the best ability to surround Andy with every ounce of empathy and care and support that I have.

"You didn't let him down," I say, keeping my voice firm even though there's a part of me that wants to cry *with* him. "Your dad loves you, and he's proud of you, no matter what."

I pull back and look at Andy's face, placing my hands on either side and holding him still so he has to look at me.

"But I bet he would be even *more* proud if you fight as hard as you can to save the store."

He watches me with watery eyes but doesn't say anything.

"One Stop is a Cedar Point staple. It's an important part of our town," I continue. "For generations, families have come up against tragedy and hard times, and what did they do? They fought through it, came out stronger on the other side, and I know you can do the same. I *know* it."

I think I see a spark in his eyes, but it flickers out like a candle in the wind just as quickly.

"It sounds good in theory, but I worry it will just delay the inevitable. What if the store ends up reopening then closes just a few months later? It was already struggling, and this will just add a heap of new problems."

I lick my lips and take a deep breath, gearing myself up to share the little blip of an idea that began to brew in my mind as I lay in his bed this morning.

"Let me help you," I say in response. "I don't know everything, obviously, but let me use my MBA for *something*. It has to be useful somehow, right? We can set up an office in your living room, or in my parents' guesthouse. We'll pull all the information we have and start fresh, figure out a way to make sure *when* One Stop reopens, it's even more successful than it was before."

There's a long pause as Andy's eyes track between mine, and I worry I've said the wrong thing. Maybe I should have just let him do this his way. I know in my relationship with Chad, offering to help always got me a firm talking-down-to, my ex not wanting me to upstage him in any way. I thought maybe it would be different with Andy, but now I'm not sure.

"You would do that?" he asks, his hands tightening on my waist. "You would give up your time to do something like that?"

I nod my head, hoping I'm hearing him right, hoping this is him deciding he wants to give it a try.

"Absolutely."

That flicker I thought I saw in his eyes seems to stir again, this time not put out so easily.

And then I see resolve crossing his face. Determination. His brows furrowing slightly and his chin tilting down, his watery eyes clearing.

"Okay."

"Okay?"

He nods. "Yeah. Maybe it all crumbles, but let's give it a shot."

I grin and squeeze him close, letting out a little shriek of both excitement and nerves. "Fuck the crumbles," I tell him. "This is going to be amazing."

"Mom? Dad?"

I don't hear anything, so I walk through the house and look out toward the lake, catching sight of my mom sitting on the deck and watching the sunset with a glass of wine. I slide the door open, her head turning at the sound of me coming outside.

"Briar!" my mom says, giving me a big smile. "Hey, sweet girl."

She stands from her chair and rounds the back, wrapping her arms around me in that way only my mom knows how to do, the way that makes all of life's problems fade for just a second.

Then she pulls back, her hands on each of my arms and a sympathetic look crossing her face.

"How's Andy doing? I heard about the fire and I just feel so terrible for him and Willy."

I nod. "He's taking it pretty hard."

"And Linden?" she continues, putting a hand to her chest. "I can't believe he was responsible. Margie called me just a complete mess over what happened."

Margie, Linden's mom, is my mom's best friend, so it's not surprising that my mom already knows the information I just found out a little bit ago at the meeting with Andy and the other employees.

"Did she say why he did it?"

Mom shakes her head. "No. Apparently Don won't let her get involved because she's too emotional, and he's told the department they won't be posting Linden's bail for at least a few days."

My mouth drops open in surprise. "He's going to make Linden stay in *jail*?" I ask. "I mean, I know he burned down a store, but come on—he's a kid."

"He's 19, Briar, and I guess Don wants to make sure there's no confusion or suspicion of preferential treatment or whatever. Margie's just beside herself."

"I can imagine."

Mom shakes her head then runs her fingers through her hair

and lets out a long sigh. "Well, enough about that. Take a seat, honey. Would you like some wine?"

I plop down in the Adirondack chair next to my mother's but decline the drink. "Thanks, but I'm actually here to talk to dad about something important. Is he here?"

"No, he went down to the station to talk to Don." She pauses. "Anything...*I* can help with?"

My first instinct is to tell her no. I don't like to be an imposition in general, and asking my mother for help is something that's hard to do even though she's always trying to be helpful.

But then I think about the conversation I had with Andy, how thankful I was that he decided to accept *my* help...and I wonder if asking my mom to step in might make her feel as good as it made me feel.

So I decide to give it a shot.

"Actually, I think there *is* something you can help with. If you want to."

My mom sits up perkier in her chair, her smile from when I first got here returning to her face. "Anything."

"Well...Andy's worried about the store. There are a lot of hoops that need to be jumped through to get the insurance payment, and he's not sure if there's anything business-related that's salvageable. I told him I'd do everything I can to help him, and I'm wondering if we can use the guesthouse as a makeshift office?"

"Oh my gosh, I would *love* to have you guys use the guesthouse. Please let Andy know we are behind him 100%." Then she settles into her chair and taps a finger against her lips. "I bet I can get it reorganized to fit a table and chairs in there. And Rita was just telling me the school got a bunch of new computers and they're selling off the old ones online. I could get you guys a few to use."

My mom continues to ramble for a few more minutes about all the ways she can think of to make the guesthouse into the niftiest makeshift office there ever was, and I just sit and listen to her ideas, unable to hide my smile.

It's amazing what happens when you let people in, when you give people the opportunity to help, when you stop shutting everybody down and instead start believing in them.

It really does make all the difference.

Less than twenty-four hours later, Andy and I pull up outside Guesthouse de Mitchell—or as my mom has been calling it in all her texts to me, Short Stop, which I think is the cutest nickname in the world.

"I already told you—she said she made some changes and wants us to see them before she finishes up," I tell him for at least the third time.

Andy felt concerned about the idea of my parents stepping in to help, but I quickly reminded him of my own epiphany about helpfulness, which I talked to him about in bed last night as we tried to hash out a timeline for what we want to get done.

"I just don't want them to go out of their way," he says, also for at least the third time.

I stop just outside the door to the guesthouse and turn to face him. "What did you tell me on that night we first had dinner at your house? When you told me about the small business loans my parents gave to some of the younger startups?"

Andy's shoulders drop a little bit, and I can see some of the defensiveness he's carrying around fall to the side as well.

"You told me sometimes, people just need a little help to get things going, and there's *no shame* in needing that little bit of help."

He takes a deep breath and lets it out. "Okay."

I nod then plant a kiss on his lips before turning and opening the door to the guesthouse.

And my jaw promptly drops right off of my body and my head explodes.

The guesthouse my parents have is a studio space with a little kitchen and bathroom. The last time I was in here was very briefly over the summer when I helped my mother get the place ready for my brother's girlfriend to stay for a little while. There's a bed with a beautiful quilt, lots of cute little tchotchkes on the walls, and an antique dresser with a mirror on it.

Or at least…there *was.*

The entire space has been completely emptied of all the bedroom furniture and decorations.

Instead, there is a long table against one wall with two computer stations set up. On another wall is a wooden desk with a third computer. There's also a round table next to the little kitchenette area, and a massive whiteboard on wheels.

"What do you think?" I hear from behind me, and when I turn, I see my parents standing on the small deck, smiling.

Well, my dad is smiling. My mom is positively beaming, her hands in a ball under her chin as she waits to hear our thoughts.

"Rita was able to give us a few computers, and I figured you'd be able to have the main desk for Andy then one or two other stations for you or maybe your dad? Or if you need another employee to come in and do some work. And they were about to get rid of the whiteboard, too, since they're switching to all that weird tech board stuff where you can touch the wall like it's the computer screen."

I glance at Andy, watching his reaction as he listens to my mom. He looks overwhelmed.

"The table is just something we had in storage that we used to have in the guesthouse before we switched to a larger bed. So…well, I hope it'll do the trick and be a good space to work in while you're sorting through everything."

Andy glances around for another moment then crosses the room and wraps my mother in a hug, I think startling both her and my dad.

"Thank you, Mrs. Mitchell," he says.

My mom looks at me over his shoulder and pats him on the back.

"I keep telling you to call me Patty," she says, her voice soft.

He nods but doesn't say anything else, and the honesty of this moment…a boy who lost his mother getting support and help from a mother who has cared about and loved him since he was a kid…it's a beautiful thing to see.

CHAPTER EIGHTEEN

Andy

The first few weeks after the fire go by at record speed, and some of that has to do with the woman who is busting her ass every single day to keep the momentum going for the store.

Briar has absolutely blown my mind. Not only with her work ethic—the constant joke between us being my comment to her about the handholding back on the day she first came by the store—but also the fantastic experiences she's bringing to the table from when she got her MBA.

I know that, logically, a master's in business is a big-time degree. I even said that to her a few months back when she first interviewed, but it's a completely different experience to see it in action, in person.

The things she knows about finance and marketing and business strategy…regulations and ethics and legal issues…I can barely keep it all straight, but she's leading us into the deep end without fear, like an absolute badass.

By society's standards, I should be somewhat put off by the

fact that Briar is so damn smart and independent and capable. I should feel threatened by her ability to navigate just about every single difficult moment so far with an ease and grace I could never have dreamed of. I should be wary of her critical mind.

I could not be more the opposite.

It has been so impressive watching her work. Being a part of the process. Seeing her excel and soar in so many ways.

And it just makes me fall even more in love with her.

When we first got set up in Short Stop—Patty's nickname for the guesthouse that has stuck like glue—Briar laid out some of the ideas she'd been thinking over for how to change things around at One Stop to make it more profitable. We were able to review some of the older data that was backed up on my dad's home computer, including old surveys and request forms. Apparently, the cake and floral cooler sells out almost every day, and there have been requests for years that One Stop expand the bakery options to include things like freshly made bagels and breads, as opposed to just the pre-packaged bulk items we order for the shelves.

It hadn't ever occurred to me to change anything, to do anything other than just keep trucking along with the plans my dad had for the extension. But, after seeing her notes, I was really impressed and super on board.

We got to work on a new business plan, on creating new financial and budget paperwork, on filing a new business license with the state. We connected with a local architect who was happy to help us put together some ideas for making changes to the layout to incorporate the bakery functionality and get information on the associated permits, and we started exploring alternate technology options for more updated register and stock tracking systems. With the finalized paperwork from the police and fire department, we were able to file an insurance claim that is already in the process of completing a payout, thanks to a special phone call from Paul to the insurance company.

On top of that, Briar put together a proposal that was approved by the city council for the way to handle getting groceries into the hands of residents who were suddenly finding themselves without a grocery store to shop at. I sat in the audience as she presented her idea—online orders submitted to Wellington's at the base of the mountain, which the owner had already agreed to fulfill at cost, and then picked up and delivered by the employees of One Stop who are currently out of work—and watched the faces of the council and the community.

I certainly wasn't the only one who was impressed.

We've been working almost nonstop for the past few weeks, barely getting any time together that isn't work-related.

Today, though, we're both not working at all.

Today is Thanksgiving, and thanks to the awesome program Briar set up, everyone in town who wanted to purchase a turkey and sides to eat a meal with their family was able to do so.

Including the Mitchell family.

"Thank you for having us," I say to Patty, wiping my feet on the mat and taking my jacket off as I step into the house.

Then I turn to look behind me, seeing my dad still standing at the door, not moving.

"Come on in, Willy! It has been far too long since I've seen you," Patty enthuses, walking right up to my dad and wrapping her arms around his shoulders in a tight squeeze.

I watch as my dad blinks a few times…then raises his arms and wraps them around her in return.

"You too, Patty."

My dad has been interacting a little bit with Briar over the past few weeks, though he hasn't come out of whatever place he's mentally hiding in like he did that first day. I think having her there might have been such a big shock that he tried to be friendly, but the very next day he was right back in his bed, blinds closed, staring at the TV.

Briar has been encouraging me to get him connected with a therapist or psychologist, and she's totally right. It pains me to admit that I should have seen that months ago. Knowing he's struggling with depression should have spurred me into action much sooner than when I finally made a call last week.

I was too focused on trying to get him back to normal, and not enough on how to actually help him work through all the things he's currently struggling with. I haven't told him yet that I called somebody, because I have a strong gut feeling he's going to be incredibly unhappy about it. Still, I have to do what feels right for him, even if it makes him angry.

"We brought rolls," I say as I enter the kitchen and hold up a bag I included in our most recent grocery order. "But we'll need to throw them in your microwave for a few minutes or something."

Bellamy laughs. "Give me that bag. You don't microwave rolls, Andy. You bake them."

There's quite a crew of people over at the Mitchells' for the holiday dinner. Mark and Patty, Bellamy and Briar, obviously, but also their brother Bishop, who lives just down the mountain, and the baby of the group, Busy, who goes to school down in Southern California.

"Didn't realize they'd be inviting over just *anybody*," a deep voice says from behind me.

When I spin around, I see Rusty leaning up against a counter.

"Oh, hey!" I step over and give my friend a hug, which Rusty returns with a hearty slap on the back. "Abby here, too?"

Rusty nods. "Yup. Well, she will be—ran back to the house to grab the sides she spent all morning on."

I grin. "Tell me she made slutty brownies."

"I don't like that word," Patty says, walking into the kitchen with my dad's arm looped in hers. "She should call them her strumpets or something."

Busy bursts into laughter as she mixes something in a bowl. "That is *absolutely* what she needs to start calling them. That is the best name ever."

Patty takes a minute to reintroduce her kids to my dad. I know he's friends with Mark and knows all the Mitchell kids, but I honestly don't know where his mind is at, so giving him a refresh is probably a good idea.

"No Boyd?" I ask when I don't see the oldest Mitchell sibling.

"Nah, he decided to stay east this year. Hopefully he'll be back for Christmas, though," Bishop says from his spot at the counter.

"Stop it, Bishop," Bellamy chides, slapping her brother's hand as he tries to sneak a piece of bread from the bag she just opened. "If you keep snacking you won't be hungry for dinner."

"When have I ever *not* been hungry?"

The two glare at each other for a good ten seconds before Bellamy chucks a piece of bread at him, which he catches, and then she turns away with a huff. Bishop grins and splits the roll in half, stuffing some into his mouth.

"Briar's in the guesthouse," Busy offers. "She told me to come get her when you showed up so you wouldn't know she's been working. But…" She shrugs and points at the bowl in her other hand. "Oops."

I snort a laugh and slip my jacket back on as I walk toward the sliding door. "I'll go get her."

Leaving the crowded kitchen behind, I head out across the deck and grass, through the row of trees that separates the Mitchell house from Short Stop.

Before I even make it up the stairs, I see Briar come outside, wrapped up in a thick jacket and a scarf, my 'easily cold' girl probably struggling with the recent dip in temperatures.

When she sees me, her eyes widen. "I can explain."

I laugh and shake my head, taking the final steps up to meet her at the top. "You're not in trouble, Briar, but you shouldn't be working today."

"I know," she says, twisting her fingers. "But I thought of an idea that might help with the way we're changing the addition, and I just wanted to make sure I got the whole thing down on paper. Then I got wrapped up and lost track of the time."

I can't do anything but smile, still constantly blown over by just how amazing Briar is and how dedicated she is to seeing this project succeed, then pull her in against my chest.

"Guess who came with me today."

She drops her head back so her mouth is inches from mine. "My dad."

A smile stretches across her face and her eyes go soft. "Really?"

I nod. "Uh-huh. He told me he wanted to spend time with his favorite people on Thanksgiving, and that includes you."

Briar starts nibbling at the inside of her cheek, and I stroke my thumb over the outside of her mouth, trying to soothe the nervous tick I've been seeing less and less.

"So you think he likes me?"

Squeezing her tighter, I press a kiss to her forehead. "I think he definitely likes you." I pause, keeping my mouth pressed against her skin, enjoying the way her warmth seeps through my layer of clothing to warm my skin underneath, the slight scent of that sugary vanilla lotion she recently started using before she gets into bed at night. "Not as much as *I* like you, though."

"Oh, well that's probably a good thing."

We both laugh a bit but continue to stand there, just enjoying each other's presence and warmth.

With every moment we're together, whether it's snuggled together like right now or standing out on the banks of the lake throwing rocks or sitting inside of Short Stop for hours on end working on the rebuild and reopening, it becomes harder and harder to keep my feelings to myself.

We've been on this friends-with-benefits kick for two months now, and things have felt far more serious than that for at least half that time. Is it too soon to tell her I'm in love with her? To tell her every day I get to be around her is a day that makes my life exponentially better?

I'm not sure. I've never felt this way about someone before, so it feels like normal rules don't apply.

She tilts her head back again and looks up at me, her eyes tracking between mine, and not for the first time, I wonder if she feels the same. Does she look at me and see her future? Is she overwhelmed by what she feels when I wrap her in my arms?

"Hey, lovebirds!"

I turn my head to see Abby walking through the trees, then watch with amusement as she lifts a ceramic dish into the air over her head with a flourish.

"Slutty brownies are here! And dinner's gonna start soon."

Briar giggles and gives her friend a wave. "Be right there!"

she calls out. Then she turns back to look at me. "Ready?" she asks, and I nod, linking her gloved hand with mine before we head down the stairs to follow in Abby's wake.

"That was delicious, Mrs. Mitchell," I say, draping my napkin over one knee.

"Andy," she chides. "How many times have I told you to call me Patty?"

"A lot," I answer. "But those were all before I was spending so much time with your daughter."

My response gets quite a bit of laughter from the table and an eyeroll from the woman in question.

"Briar, Briar, Briar," Bishop says, shaking his head. "Always such a rule-follower, and now she's hooking up with her boss?" He tsks, but there's a clear level of teasing behind his tone. "What has become of your moral compass?"

She narrows her eyes at her brother then picks up her uneaten roll and chucks it at him. He catches it easily and does exactly what he did earlier: splits it in half and shoves most of it in his mouth.

"You know, I'm starting to see a pattern here," I interject. "Bishop teases the girls, and then you throw food at him." I look at Bishop and give him a nod. "I'm onto your schemes."

He shrugs, chuckling good-naturedly, then bites into the other half of the roll.

"How are things coming along with the reopening?" Mark

asks, leaning against the back of his chair like a king in his throne. "I saw a crew out there a few days ago."

"Yeah, they're in the beginning stages of demolition," I tell him. "Tearing down and trashing everything that's burned and not salvageable. That way, once we start the actual construction in December, we can move quickly and hopefully get things completed before Christmas."

"Wow, that's an aggressive timeline."

I nod at Mark's accurate assessment.

"When I spoke with the construction company, I had the same reaction, but it makes sense that they'll be done with the rebuild part fairly quickly. It's not like when I was building the extension and figuring things out by myself," I joke. "These guys actually know what they're doing."

"You're not worried about snow?"

I shake my head. "Snow rarely comes before late January. We should be fine." Then I hold up my crossed fingers. "Hopefully."

Briar's dad leans forward, looking past me and over to his daughter.

"How are you liking the stuff you've been doing, B?"

She shrugs a shoulder, but I can tell in the way she tilts her head back just a bit and how her eyes light up that she's loving it.

"It's been really fun, actually. There were several courses during my degree program that I thought would be a waste, but so many things have really come in handy."

"It'll look great on your resume, too," Mark adds, smiling at his oldest daughter. "You're basically project-managing, and that will be great experience once you're ready to apply for jobs."

Talk at the table continues around me, Mark sharing a story about his own job search back in the day at one end of the table and the twins squabbling over something at the other end.

But somehow all the words around me start to sound like they're being spoken under water, muffled and diluted and thick like the teacher in *Charlie Brown*. All I can hear is that inaudible mumbling as my mind starts to work through what Mark just said.

Once you're ready to apply for jobs.

Because that's what Briar will want to do, right? What she *should* do—apply for jobs that will allow her to use her degree and get back out there into the real world.

Out of this town she's so eager to leave behind.

Twisting my fork in my hand, I flick my eyes around at all the people gathered at the table. Briar has this amazing family full of supportive and caring people; even that wasn't enough to get her to want to stick around town. What could possibly change her mind? Certainly not me. What the hell do I have to offer her besides a minimum-wage job working at a failing grocery store?

Even that fun game we were playing with each other, about the…what did she call it? The Cedar Point bucket list? My ridiculous attempt to convince her to rediscover the amazing facets of Cedar Point life? Even *that* would never have been enough to actually get her to change her mind.

I feel foolish, having dealt with my thoughts about Briar over the past few weeks. Here I am, wondering if it's the right time to tell her I love her, and she's probably just biding her time before she leaves.

When I was younger, I used to look at my parents' relationship as the guidepost for what I wanted in the future. They were best friends. They loved each other so much. Talked about everything. Fought rarely.

That's still the type of relationship I want now, the type of relationship I have started to feel like I have with Briar.

It's only been a few months, but things seem to be...progressing. We both seem to be growing and working through things, becoming a team.

Because that's what you have to be. You have to be a team. When the entire world is against you, that person is the one who is always, always, *for* you.

I can see it clearly, the two of us long-term.

With only one bump in the road.

Briar doesn't want to live in Cedar Point.

That was something my parents had. They both loved this small town, were both born and raised here and chose to stay because they wanted to raise their own kids here.

Just like I want to.

And just like Briar doesn't.

How many times has she vocalized her desire to leave? Made it clear she's looking for a bigger life that's more than this little town can provide?

Enough times for me to know it's unlikely that her perspective will ever change.

If I love her as much as I think I do, the best way I can love her is by supporting her in what she wants.

Which is to find a job somewhere else and leave this town behind.

I thought it was weird how aware I was of the moment I fell in love with Briar Mitchell, and it's just as weird to be aware of the moment when I realize it will never work.

But really, I always knew that, didn't I?

I knew she wanted to leave and I still pursued things, still allowed myself to fall in deep—deeper than I've ever fallen before. And oh what a painful fall it is when you realize there's nobody there to catch you.

Abby brings out her dessert, the slutty brownies that are apparently getting renamed strumpets, and Patty brings out apple pie and ice cream. There's animated talk at the table about the rebuild and the high school swim team and Patty's cross-stitching class at The Pines.

"They're all making funny patterns to send to their families for Christmas," she says with a laugh. "Barry is sending one to his grandson and his new wife that says 'No longer living in sin.'"

The table erupts in laughter.

"And Marsha is sending one to her newly single daughter that says 'Anything can be a dildo if you're brave enough.'"

Even I have a laugh at that one.

But there's still an underlying layer of sadness within me for the rest of the day, though I work hard to try to hide it.

Not well enough, though, because Briar corners me later in the evening when I've stepped away from the group to get some more strumpet.

"You okay?"

I look over my shoulder and find her standing in the doorway that leads from the kitchen to the dining room.

Nodding, I turn back to finish plucking a brownie out of Abby's Tupperware dish. "Yeah. Why?"

"You just seem...not you."

I shake my head. "Nah, I'm good. Just have a lot on my mind." Then I spin around to finally face her, my mouth full of chocolatey goodness. Hopefully if my mouth is full, she won't expect me to answer any more questions.

"Well, I know it probably sounds hypocritical since it's like pulling teeth getting me to talk," she says, her lips tilting up at the side, "but I'm here if you want to talk about whatever it is that's got you…distracted."

I swallow the bit of brownie and cross the kitchen, stepping up to Briar and giving her my best relaxed face. "Thanks." I kiss her on the lips and stride back into the dining room, leaving Briar and her observations and questions behind.

When we have sex later that night, it's the first time I feel distracted, the first time I have to really work to keep my attention on the beautiful woman who has her body wrapped around mine.

I'm wondering when things between us will finally come to an end. Who she'll move on with. Whether she'll be like this in bed with someone else.

I know she can tell my mind isn't here with her. Briar is incredibly observant, and I can see her concern in the way her eyes stay focused on mine as she sits astride me, instead of closing like they normally do because she's so lost in pleasure. I can feel the tension in her body struggling to let go.

We both work hard at that orgasm, and we both lie awake for hours afterward instead of drifting off, our minds focused on each other and unable to find sleep.

CHAPTER NINETEEN

Briar

"Thanks for coming," I say to Bellamy as we pass the sign that reads *Now Leaving Cedar Point.* "The idea of going alone just didn't sit right with me."

"Psht, girl, I am so here for you," my sister says as we cruise through the winding mountain roads that will lead us out of our hometown and down to Sacramento. "Besides, you know I'm always looking for an excuse to head out of town for a little bit. I love it, but a girl needs to get some McDonald's every so often, you know?"

I shake my head at my sister's fast food addiction—an unfortunate obsession to have when you live in a town that doesn't have any fast food restaurants—then lean forward to adjust my heat settings and make sure I have plenty of warm air coming my way.

Bellamy is driving me down the mountain to collect all my things from Chad's. I got a text from him last night letting me know he'd waited around for me to retrieve it long enough, and that anything I hadn't picked up by the end of the weekend would be chucked in the trash.

Such a classy guy. Thanks for the two days' notice on a holiday weekend when I'd like to spend time with my family.

I told him I'd come down on Sunday, which works out great since Bishop left early this morning to head back to school, taking Busy to the airport on his way. I just hope Chad's lack of response doesn't mean I'll show up to a burning pile of MBA textbooks in the green dumpster behind our apartment complex.

Although, in light of recent events, maybe I shouldn't joke about fires.

The drive from Cedar Point to the area of Sacramento where I used to live normally takes about an hour and a half, though I'm sure it will take a bit longer since we're dragging a trailer and going under the speed limit. We're about halfway there when I finally decide to tell my sister what's on my mind.

"I think I might move back to Cedar Point."

My sister looks over at me. "You already did that."

A small laugh falls from my mouth. Leave it to Bells to make something that feels monumental to me sound super simple. "I mean, long-term."

She looks at me then back at the road, then back at me and back at the road, before she reaches out and puts her hand against my forehead.

I smack it away, pursing my lips at her absolutely ridiculous reaction.

"Who are you and what have you done with my Cedar-Point-hating sister?" she says, giving me a dramatic look of terror.

"Okay, enough with the theatrics."

Bellamy giggles. "Sorry. I just feel so, like…I don't know,

shocked, I guess? When did you decide this?"

I nibble on my lip, still deciding how much I want to share. "It's been on my mind for a while," I say. "I've been enjoying being back home…far more than I expected. It couldn't hurt to stick around for a bit, you know?"

My sister looks at me again then gasps. "Oh my god!"

Eyes wide, I look around, worried we're about to hit a deer or fly off the side of the road.

"What!?" I shout.

"You're totally flipping in love with Andy!" she practically yells at me.

My shoulders slump, my hand coming to my chest. "Jesus, Bellamy, I thought something was seriously wrong and we were about to plummet to our deaths. Don't do that again."

"Sorry, not sorry," she says. "I won't apologize for cracking your mysterious code."

I roll my eyes and cross my arms. "That's just…ludicrous."

"It's not. You're totally smitten, and you're gonna have his *babies*," she teases, drawing the word out nice and long. "Briar Marshall sounds so great. You won't even have to change your initials."

Shaking my head, I lean my elbow against the window, wondering if sharing the move home with Bellamy was a mistake. I haven't decided officially, and now she's turning it into something it's just…not.

As much as I care about Andy, I mean…I'm not…in *love* with him. That's the opposite of what I want. Right? I'm still figuring out my shit, and moving home might possibly play a role in that very unplanned shit I need to work through.

"Hey."

I look over and see a completely different expression on my

sister's face.

Contrition.

"I'm sorry, okay? I get so excited when you talk to me about stuff and forget that you don't like to be teased. Please, tell me what you're thinking about."

Looking forward again, I weigh it in my mind, deciding my sister's apology is sufficient enough, and that I need to not be such a stick in the mud with her as well.

"I'm thinking about asking Abby to get a place together," I tell her. "She's been wanting to move out of her house for a while but can't afford it on her own, and she needs a little space from Rusty."

Bellamy snorts.

"I'll bet. That house of theirs must have a steady stream of women coming and going. That would be enough to drive me nuts."

My nose wrinkles up and I try to shove away the thought of poor Abby dealing with her brother having sex in their house. I'm pretty sure I'd die if I had to deal with something like that from Boyd *or* Bishop, or either of my sisters.

No thanks.

"Anyway, apparently Cecil and Lois have a second house on their property. Maria and her husband were using it, but they're moving out before Christmas to a place down the road that has a little more space."

Bellamy glares at me. "Lois lives on the other side of the lake. It'll take twenty minutes to get there."

I grin. "Exactly."

She snorts and shakes her head. "Gotta put as much space between us as possible, huh?"

Sighing, I look out the window. "I'm not trying to put space between me and you, Bells. I just like my independence."

Bellamy is silent next to me. I wish she could just be excited that I'm considering moving to town for a while instead of focusing on the fact that I'll be on the other side of the lake. Scratching at the back of my neck, I realize I might need to be a little more transparent with my sister than I'd planned.

"Chad pretty much controlled everything about our lives," I say, deciding to just spit it out, as quickly as possible, my eyes still focused out in the distance, to the rows of trees and bit of fog we're driving through. "I followed him after college because I was lost and didn't know what I wanted to do, and he took that as permission to be in charge of everything. I rarely did something without his okay, and once I did, things started to deteriorate."

I pause, knowing I need to word this right so she understands.

"I know it might not look like it from the outside, but I've never really been on my own. It's important for me to learn how to take care of myself—emotionally, financially, physically—and I worry I'll fall back on mom or dad or you if I live too close. Okay?"

When I finally look over at my sister, I see a single tear tracking down her cheek, and I reach out and take one of her hands in mine.

"I'm sorry he didn't treat you right," Bellamy whispers. "You deserve so much better."

I squeeze her hand. "I know I do. Logically, at least. Emotionally, I'm still figuring that part out."

We drive in silence for a little while longer, and then something occurs to me.

"The house has a dock," I tell her.

Bellamy looks over at me.

"You can jet-ski over in less than five minutes."

A smile stretches across her face. "Sounds perfect."

"What's all this?"

Abby's eyes are wide as she watches me unload my boxes from the trailer one at a time into the storage shed next to the garage. I figure it'll be easier to collect it all and put it back into the trailer to move into my own place if I keep it all down here rather than lug it up to my room.

"We went and got my stuff from Chad's," I tell her, lifting a particularly heavy box of books.

"Yay!" she shouts, clapping her hands together and bouncing up and down on her toes. "That's awesome!"

"It felt good to get it all wrapped up, but it was *not* awesome."

Abby's excitement evaporates and she crosses her arms, a bitchy look coming onto her face.

"What did he do?"

I grin, appreciating my friend's constant ability to throw down and come to my defense over pretty much anything.

"He was just a dick," I say, not wanting to get into it. "Did the whole *knew you'd be back* routine before he realized I really was there to collect all my stuff."

An aggressive scoff comes from Abby's mouth and her hip pops to the side.

"As if you would *ever* go back to him. What a shithead."

I giggle, still moving between the trailer and the shed. "Pretty much. But hey, it's over, over, over, and I'm officially done with him forever."

"Thank you, sweet baby Jesus!" she says, putting her hands in the air like she's in one of those Pentecostal churches you see in movies about the South.

She watches me for a few minutes, sweat beginning to bead on my brow as I move back and forth between the trailer and the shed, even though the temperature is getting close to freezing.

"How come you're putting everything in the shed?" she asks.

That's when I stop, thinking now is as good a time as any to ask her what she thinks about my idea.

Without responding to her question, I hold up a finger and go over to where my purse still sits in the passenger seat of Bellamy's RAV4, pulling the semi-crinkly paper out and handing it over to Abby.

I watch as she looks it over, her eyes scanning all the way down.

She lowers the piece of paper and looks at me. "This is a lease agreement."

I nod.

She keeps staring at me, and I decide to give her another minute to get it before I have to explain it to her myself.

Her eyes widen suddenly, her mouth opening into a legitimate O shape as all the pieces connect. "Oh my god!" she shouts. "Is this for you? For you to move into your own place?"

I cross my arms, realizing I should have thought through the fact that she might shout it to the rooftops when she found out, but I'll have to tell my parents sooner or later, or they'll wonder why I'm never staying at their house anymore.

"Wait," she pauses. "Where did this come from? I thought all you've ever wanted is to leave. You hate Cedar Point."

I lean back against the trailer and cross my arms, deciding to be honest with Abby about what's been on my mind.

"I don't hate Cedar Point."

She pins me with a look that says, *Bullshit.*

"Okay, I *thought* I hated Cedar Point," I clarify. "But I don't. Not really. All the time I've been spending here, all the work I've been doing…" I trail off, looking down at where I'm absentmindedly shifting around the gravel in our front drive with my shoe. "I'm still processing everything, but I think this is the right move."

"Wow," she says, her grin returning. "That's so awesome. And you're gonna move into your own place?"

"*Our* own place."

Abby's head tilts to the side. "What?"

"It's a lease for a two-bedroom," I tell her. "One for me, and one for you."

"Are you serious?" Abby asks, her hand coming to her chest and her eyes beginning to water. "Are you being seriously serious with me right now?"

I nod, smiling at my friend's sudden surge of emotion. "Yeah. You've been wanting to move out, and I've been thinking about sticking around town for a while." I shrug. "Who better to learn how to be on our own with than each other?"

Abby bursts into tears and wraps her arms around me, and I can't get the grin off my face.

She pulls back to look at me. "You're serious, right? You're actually staying? You're not going to leave again?"

"I don't know how long I'll be in town," I tell her honestly, "but it would be at least as long as we put on the lease."

"Well, problem solved," Abby says, digging into her own purse and pulling out a pen.

She holds up the paper, makes some notes on it, and shoves it back in my hand.

"It's official now. No backing out."

When I take a look at the bottom, I burst into laughter, harder than I have in a long while.

Abby signed the lease agreement, and she also wrote in her own idea about length.

Forever, it says, in all caps.

The next day, Abby and I meet with Lois to check out the little two-bedroom house that's just a few hundred yards from her own.

"The kitchen is a bit dated, but Maria said to tell you she's never had any problems with the appliances. The only big adjustment is the really small oven," Lois tells us as we wander through the living room and into the kitchen, weaving through half-packed boxes scattered everywhere.

I glance at the oven, grinning when I see one of those old tiny ones from the fifties.

"But the fridge is brand new, and the stove is gas."

"I don't know about that oven," Abby mumbles, eyeing it like it's a bear ready to attack.

I giggle. "You'll be fine."

She hums her disagreement, but we move on, stepping

247

through to check out the laundry room and the garage and pantry then back inside to check out the bedrooms.

"It's got two bedrooms, and two baths," Lois continues, espousing the virtues of her guesthouse like she's a realtor on *House Hunters*. "One room has an attached bathroom, like a master. The other bathroom has a door to both the second bedroom and the hallway so guests can use it."

Abby and I step into the larger bedroom first. "I get this one," she says. When she catches my expression, she shrugs. "What? You're gonna be at Andy's all the time anyway."

As we continue our tour of the adorable property that really would be a great first place for the two of us, I think about what she just said.

Will I be at Andy's all the time?

Letting out a long breath, I push open the closet door of the smaller bedroom, thinking it's a great size.

But also thinking about Andy…about what staying in town means for the two of us.

When we started things together, it was just supposed to be a little fun, a way to enjoy each other and still allow ourselves the other things in life that are important.

And it worked. I had fun with Andy. I had sex with Andy. I also worked on my business plan. Spent time reflecting on my relationship with Chad until I decided to finally get all my stuff. Thought through what I want from a relationship in the future. Re-evaluated how I feel about my hometown. Decided to start opening up and spend more time with my family.

Some very legitimate and real life-changing processing and reflection.

Maybe I've done what I need to do in order to move on to something new.

And by new, I mean a real relationship with Andy. Something that doesn't come with the friends-with-benefits descriptor, one that sounds a little more official.

Like...girlfriend.

I roll my eyes. Why is it that saying girlfriend and boyfriend in your late twenties sounds so stupid?

Regardless, I think maybe I need to talk to him about this, the fact that I've signed a lease. I mean, I would have talked to him about it no matter what, but I want us to discuss what it means for *us*.

I don't know exactly where his mind is at, but I figure it has to be somewhere at least *close* to mine, especially considering the way he looks at me and how entwined our lives have become.

I know I'm not imagining things. I know Andy feels more for me than just friendship and base attraction. There's something deeper there, something more important.

I can only hope he's as eager to explore it as I am.

CHAPTER TWENTY

Briar

"I understand what you're telling me, but I'm telling *you* that what we need is for everything to be delivered by the fifteenth."

I listen to the woman on the other end of the line click around on her computer like she's breaking the keys off of her keyboard before she finally speaks again.

"We can have it delivered by the fifteenth if you absorb an extra hundred-dollar fee."

I lift a fist in the air but keep my voice calm and collected.

"That would be wonderful. Just go ahead and charge the card you have on file."

Once we wrap up a few more logistical details and I finally get off the phone, I stand from my chair and raise both arms in the air.

"Thank you," I tell the empty room. "Thank you very much."

Then I plop down on the floor and starfish my arms and legs out to the sides.

I've been trying for two weeks to get new shelves installed in the rebuilt One Stop between certain dates, but every manufacturer of the shelves Andy and I have agreed on either doesn't have them in stock until after Christmas or can't get the ones they *do* have in stock delivered by the date we want. Clearly a problem, because we can't have a store without shelves for product.

Thankfully, I found a new supplier that has the exact same shelves in a different color—it's actually the same color, just with a different name—and they're going to get them here three days earlier than Andy and I needed them, giving us extra time for setup with the rest of the employees before opening.

I can't believe everything is coming together. It actually makes me want to cry when I think about it. All the hard work, the long hours, the frustration and irritation as we've faced issue after issue, after we've had to hurdle all the things that felt insurmountable in order to make this happen by the deadline we've been pushing so hard to meet.

It's been one of the most difficult, emotionally taxing experiences of my entire life.

And I've loved every minute of it.

I'm surprised, actually—not only by how much I'm enjoying the work I'm doing, but also who I'm doing it for.

Working alongside Andy to make this happen for him. For his family. For the town. I can't imagine anything better.

Today is the first day of December, and the amount of effort that has gone into rebuilding the grocery store since the day of the fire in the wee hours of the morning on the first of November is beyond insane.

We've gotten everything in the site checked for fire damage, and anything unsalvageable was removed. A construction crew is currently in the process of beginning the actual rebuild of the one wall that needed to be torn down, replacing the roof, and completely gutting and overhauling the interiors with new electrical, new insulation, new flooring, and new drywall and paint.

It started a few days ago, and I'll be honest, I wasn't sure I really believed Diego when he told me the timeline. But now, only a few days in, I'm a convert. The local crew is moving quickly and efficiently, and I can see them working longer hours and busting their asses to make this happen for us, understanding—as fellow Cedar Point residents—the significance of the need for the store to be completed.

Now, we're finalizing orders for everything that goes *inside* the grocery store. The shelving is one major component, but also glass cases, new tech for the cashier stands, and the actual food products to be put on those shelves and in those cases and sold at those stands.

God, thinking about it all gives me a head rush.

"You having fun down there?"

I turn my head and smile as Andy steps into Short Stop, fanning his jacket and taking it off as he enters the warm space.

"An absolute blast," I say, unable to hide my smile. "Is it really cold out there?"

"Have you not been outside in a while?"

I shake my head as I crawl off the floor. "Not since I got here this morning. Been on the phone with the lady from Broadwares. Guess what."

He grins. "Just tell me."

"We're getting all the shelves delivered on the fifteenth."

I thrust my arms in the air, still enjoying my celebratory moment.

Andy nods. "That's awesome. I'm not surprised."

My arms fall, my expression wiping clean when I realize he's not rejoicing with me.

"What's wrong?"

He shakes his head.

I cross the room and wrap my arms around him. "Tell me."

Andy sighs, returning my embrace, pulling me in close so my warm body is snuggled against his, which is still cool from being outside.

"My dad didn't respond well when I talked to him this morning." He squeezes me closer, his face nestling into the crook of my neck. "I knew it would be *something* like this, but I just worry."

I nod, knowing exactly what he's talking about. "It's going to be okay, Andy. You're doing the right thing. This is going to really help him."

Andy and I had a long chat a while ago about his dad, about the depression and how to handle it. He was upset at first but then finally realized that the reason it feels like too big of a problem for him to manage on his own *isn't* because he's too weak. It's because it *is* too big to handle on his own.

He's not a mental health expert. He doesn't have a full understanding of how to treat depression. And with his dad spending *months* unwilling to talk to anyone or leave his house, it's important to acknowledge that whatever is going on inside his mind is far more serious and significant than love and a 'cheer up' will fix.

So we've been discussing the benefits of getting someone else involved. Surprisingly, Andy agreed with me and contacted his insurance company to get some advice. They connected him to one of the psychologists here in town and got his dad an appointment for next week for them to visit him at home, since it would be unlikely for William to agree to go in to see someone.

"What did he do?"

"He threw a plate across the room and yelled at me. Then he started crying."

I squeeze Andy harder and rub my hands up and down his back, wishing there was something I could do but knowing all I'm capable of providing is exactly what I'm giving him. "I'm so sorry. Are you okay?"

He nods against me then pulls back and kisses my forehead. "I will be."

He drops his arms and heads over to his computer, and I watch him for a long moment before I return to mine.

Things between me and Andy have felt a little off since Thanksgiving, and I'm not sure why. It seemed like everything was going well at dinner and as we hung out and played games. Even his dad managed to spend time with all of us, though he did kind of keep to himself.

Then, before I knew it, we were back at Andy's, having sex that felt incredibly distant and nothing like what it had been, and we haven't had sex since.

It's strange to take the sexual part of our connection away, especially since it feels like such a very important component of what we have together. We're supposed to be in a friends-with-benefits relationship, right? But we're not doing any benefits stuff, and we're not really doing any friend stuff anymore either since most of our time is wrapped up in getting the store back off the ground. So really, we've turned into this couple who spends all day together at work and then doesn't have sex when we're together at night.

Although it doesn't feel fair to imply that the sex is the only important thing. I mean, yeah, it was great, and it *will* be great again once we sort through whatever this weird tension is. But the true beauty of our relationship is a different kind of intimacy, the kind that only comes when you truly know somebody at their deepest, darkest, most vulnerable parts.

That's how I feel about Andy, like we've seen each other laid bare. We've talked about some of our deepest fears and emotions and secrets, shared some of the darkest and scariest parts of our pasts. It's one of the reasons I think we should try to turn this into something more serious. He makes me feel like I can be the truest version of myself.

Even though things are off-kilter right now, I know there's something amazing there, which is why I'm so glad we're still doing little affectionate things like hugging and kissing. It says to me that a bump in the road can't get *completely* in the way of the fact that it just feels better to be close to each other.

It's funny, when I was with Chad, I never sought physical affection. Not when I was with Nick, either. But now, with Andy, I can't get enough. I want his hands on me constantly, and it doesn't even have to be sexual. I just enjoy feeling his touch, in whatever way he wants. Whether that be holding my hand, an arm around my shoulder, a hand in the back pocket of my jeans...it doesn't matter.

"My mom came by earlier," I say, my stomach protesting how long I've been working without taking a break. "She said they're making grilled cheese for lunch. Wanna go be a thief with me before we dive back into work?"

Andy grins, though that same semi-distant expression stays on his face. "Sure."

I take him by the hand and lead him outside, shrieking with laughter at the cool temperature. It's only California cool, which means it's probably not lower than 40 degrees, but that is practically freezing for a native Californian.

Sprinting through the row of trees that divides Short Stop

from the main house and then across the yard, I yank open the sliding door, still giggling. When I look at Andy, I can see whatever distance was in his eyes before is gone, replaced by flushed cheeks and bright eyes I'm probably wearing as well.

"You weren't joking about the cold," I say. "It's freezing."

He shakes his head then reaches up and slips his hand to the back of my neck.

I squeal from the feel of his cold skin, but then he's pulling my mouth toward his. This kiss, one of the first ones initiated by him in days, draws a moan from my chest. I love the way he opens his mouth and licks into mine, our lips cold but our mouths warm and wet.

"Alright, you two. Not in front of the mama."

I give Andy's mouth one final little nip, enjoying the way his eyelids are a bit heavy when I pull back, then I turn and smile at my mom.

"We're here to steal grilled cheese. You weren't supposed to be here so we could get away with it."

Her head tilts to the side and she gives me a smile that looks slightly confused.

"You're in an awfully chipper mood. Take a seat and I'll make you two lunch. That way you don't have to be little thieves."

Andy chuckles. "Thank you, Mrs. Mitchell."

Mom points a spatula at him. "Patty." Then she turns to the fridge and begins pulling out the materials she needs. "What are you kids working on today?" she asks, chucking a few different types of cheese and a package of bread out onto the counter.

"Briar's just been kicking ass, making sure we have all the supplies we need to keep things on schedule," Andy says.

I love hearing him praise me.

"Andy has been handling the in-person friendly stuff, since

I'm horrible at that."

"You are not."

I level him with a blank stare and he laughs.

"Okay, I might be better at it, but that doesn't mean you're *horrible.*"

I lift a shoulder. "Regardless, it's a lot of paperwork and phone calls."

My mom nods as she puts butter in a pan and sets it on the stovetop.

"Well, Mark and I think you're both doing a fantastic job. Don't forget we're here to help if you need anything else."

"That's very kind of you, Mrs...Patty," Andy catches himself mid-sentence when my mom spins her head around and pins him with a glare. "But honestly, Briar is doing an amazing job." He looks over at me. "I really don't know how I would have done this without you."

His words are soft, his tone serious, his eyes focused on mine. It's something I've grown to really appreciate about Andy. He's a good communicator, and he knows how to make sure I understand exactly what he means when he says things to me.

Which is why I think there's a deeper level to what he's saying, a level I'm desperate for the two of us to sit down and talk about.

"Oh, Briar!"

My head flies to the door when I hear my dad's voice.

"Hey, dad."

He walks across the room and comes up behind me, wrapping an arm around my shoulders and pulling me in for a good squeeze then dropping a kiss against my temple.

"What brings you two over today?" he asks, dropping the mail on the desk in the corner and then spinning to look at us as he leans up against the kitchen counter.

"Stealing food from your amazing wife," Andy says. "It makes me feel like I'm in high school again."

My dad laughs. "Well, I'm not surprised. I love sneaking food from Patty."

Mom snorts, though she doesn't turn away from where she's facing the stovetop. "He *thinks* he's sneaky, but he's a lot more clumsy than he used to be."

I smile, watching my dad pretend to sneakily come up behind my mom and wrap his arms around her. She pretends to be startled, throwing her spatula in the air and spinning around with her hand on her chest.

"You've proved me wrong, Mark Mitchell. You're still the same master of stealth you've always been, just like when you stole my heart."

Then my dad yanks my mom against his chest and dips her back, giving her a firm smooch I'm sure the neighbors across the lake can hear.

"Not in front of the children," Bellamy says as she hops up on the counter on the other side of Andy. "You'll scar us for life."

"Oh hush," my mom says, then she shrieks when my dad pinches her on the ass.

"I could have gone my entire life without seeing that," I say.

Bellamy snorts then lays her head down and closes her eyes. "I came down because I smelled food. My exams are coming up and I feel like I'm dying. Feed me please."

"Oh no, those sandwiches are for *us*," I say. "Go steal from your own mom."

She chuckles, though it's muffled from where her face is tucked into her arm. Then she peaks open an eye and stares at me. "Funny."

A few minutes later, my mom slides two plates across the island for me and Andy then gets to work on a new sandwich for my sister.

"Hey Briar, I wanted to tell you something interesting."

I look at my dad, my mouth full of bread and cheese, and nod.

"I was talking with Niles Orson the other day—do you remember him?"

My brows furrow and I try to think back to who he could be talking about. The name sounds familiar but my mind is drawing a blank, so I shake my head.

"He's a business owner down the mountain. Owns a bunch of real estate through the Bay Area but mostly focuses his efforts on developments."

I nod and take another bite.

"Well, he's looking for a project manager to help guide and direct some of the developments he has going on, and when I mentioned to him that you got your MBA and have been taking the lead on the One Stop rebuild, he seemed interested in meeting with you."

It feels like everything in the room stops.

I stop chewing. Mom stops cooking. Bellamy stops moving. Andy's hand freezes, his sandwich hovering in front of him. My dad just stares at me.

And my heart—it feels, for a split second, like my heart pauses.

"Well that's…great," I finally manage, unsure what else I should say in the wake of my dad trying to help me figure out what to do next when I've already been making decisions on my own.

"So you're interested?"

My dad looks at me expectantly, and the little pause in my chest turns into something more like a belt being squeezed around my lungs. Unsure how I feel, I take a second to sit up straighter and pull my shoulders back, taking as deep of a breath as I can.

"I...don't know," I finally say. "I feel pretty busy with the One Stop project."

And I'm pretty sure I'm staying here, I want to tell him, but I need to talk to Andy about it first, so I stay silent.

"Yeah, but that's going to end soon," my dad continues. "And no offense to Andy"—my dad grins at him—"but I'm pretty sure you want to do more with your degree than work at a grocery store."

"Mark!"

My mom's use of my dad's name is like a whip through the room, and I can see that my dad is startled, unsure of why he's getting a rebuke.

She's looking at him with her chin down and her eyes narrowed, then she shakes her head just once and tries to subtly point him out of the room. It's incredibly unsubtle, but that little display of pretend sneakiness earlier is a good example of how my parents operate, so I'm unsurprised that their *real* sneakiness is so blatantly obvious.

"We'll be right back," my mom says, ushering my dad through the door to the dining room.

"Yeesh, that was awkward," Bellamy says, her face smooshed against her hand and her elbow on the counter.

I look at Andy, suddenly realizing that my dad was...kind of rude. I can see the tense set of his shoulders, the agitation in his expression, the focus with which he stares at the plate in front of him.

"Hey, I'm sorry about my dad," I say, resting a hand on Andy's back. "He usually has more tact than that."

There's a long pause before he turns to look at me.

"He's right though."

My head jerks back. "What?"

"Your dad…he might not have said it in the most tactful way, but he's right." Andy's eyes search mine. "You *do* want to do more than work at a grocery store, and you *should*."

I swallow something thick in my throat, realizing this is about more than just my dad.

"I'm gonna…" Bellamy slips off her stool and points out of the room, exiting with as much grace as a baby elephant—clearly a family trait—then Andy and I are alone and staring at each other with…something between us.

"I feel like you're…I mean, do you not want my help anymore?" I ask, trying to take what he's said and frame it in a way that makes sense to my mind.

"Of course I want your help. This whole project wouldn't be where it is without you, Briar…but that doesn't mean you're going to continue to work for One Stop after it's done."

I haven't worked up the nerve to talk to Andy about what's been on my mind, or the things I've been thinking about our relationship. I'm waiting to sign the lease before I share with him that I'm moving into a place with Abby.

So, the fact that he seems eager to get me moving on to the next job feels…wrong. Not what I was expecting.

Logically, yes, my dad is right, and so is Andy. I will move on from working at One Stop at some point—but I didn't think I'd be getting a shove out the door. Especially when I've been working so hard on this plan to stick around town.

"You should talk to that guy," Andy says. "See what kind of

job he can give you."

Something uncomfortable turns over in my stomach, knowing Andy wants me to consider what my dad said. But I shouldn't be surprised, right? To Andy, all we are is friends, nothing more. That's what I told him I wanted. That's certainly all he expected.

And I haven't given him any kind of true indicator that my thoughts or opinions have changed.

So then, why does it feel like I'm losing something completely different? Something much more special and precious?

Andy rises from his seat and leans forward, pressing a kiss against my temple, before he puts his plate in the sink and heads out the door, back to Short Stop.

Back to the very temporary space we're working in for the time being, until life goes back to normal.

CHAPTER TWENTY-ONE
Andy

I'm at the half-completed construction site for One Stop when I see Mark Mitchell walking slowly through, his eyes taking in everything he can see.

Maybe it's a forewarning or some sort of subconscious thing, but I know if he's here to talk to me, it's not about the building.

It's not about construction or business things or anything city-related.

It's about Briar.

And the conversation in their kitchen from a few days ago.

The conversation that reminded me of something I've been trying desperately to ignore, with very little success.

"Hey, Andy," he says, once he's standing next to where I'm reviewing plans laid out on a table.

"Mr. Mitchell."

He chuckles, taking my outstretched hand in his and giving it a firm shake, a fatherly shake. Then he releases it, resting his hands on his hips and letting his eyes scan the completely open and empty store.

"Can't believe what it looks like in here," he says. "I've been coming into One Stop since I was a kid. Did you know it was half this size back then?"

I nod. "My dad's talked with me a little about the work that's been done over the years."

Mark crosses his arms. "It's crazy to see how it's changed. Your dad has done an awesome job with keeping it going and making it a store everyone wants to shop at."

I give him a smile. "Thanks. He'll be happy to hear you think so."

"I'm sorry if I gave you the impression that I—"

"You don't have to explain," I say, knowing I shouldn't interrupt Mark Mitchell but also not wanting him to go through the awkwardness of trying to apologize to me when he didn't do anything wrong. "I know you didn't mean anything by it. You're just looking out for Briar."

He bites the inside of his cheek, and suddenly, I can see so much of who Briar is in her dad, in the way he stands and how he gets those nervous little twitches.

"Well. I'm glad you understand," he says, crossing his arms. "Briar is…she's the one out of our brood who was always desperate to spread her wings, even more than the rest. I know you two are…involved and this whole conversation has been about more than just her job, but I also know she's got her sights set on something bigger than being a cashier."

I sigh, scrubbing my hand across my chin.

"That's why I'm not going to offer her a job when we re-open," I tell him, the decision only having been finalized in my mind earlier this morning as I looked at Briar next to me in bed.

I woke early, far earlier than normal, and spent a long while just looking at her as she slept next to me, the bit of pre-dawn light outside giving me just enough to be able to see her. For some reason, that was when it clicked for me—that wanting her in my bed every night and every morning is selfish, and the best thing I can do—the most unselfish thing I can do—is make sure she's free to find the next great thing.

Mark's head shifts, his brows rising. "Really?"

I nod. "Briar is important to me," I say, not wanting to go into too much detail with her dad.

If I ever tell someone I'm in love with Briar Mitchell, it certainly won't be her father.

"I know she wants to leave town, and I'm going to try to help her make that a reality."

"By taking her job away?"

I shrug a shoulder. "By making sure she's not wasting her time. It seems like the best way to encourage her to take the passion she currently has and apply it to something else. Something…" I trail off, looking around the store that has always brought me happiness. "Something better than here."

There's a long moment where neither of us says anything before I decide to share one last thing.

"A long time ago, Briar told me she didn't want to be stuck here her whole life," I tell Mark. "You and I might love it here, but I can't expect her to feel the same. If I don't help her move on, I'm worried *stuck* is exactly how she'll feel."

When I look over to where he's standing a few feet away, on the other side of the little table I've been using for my paperwork and coffee, I find him watching me, looking oddly pleased.

Then he bobs his head and reaches his hand out. When I take it in mine, he holds it a bit long, still watching me.

"You're a pretty great guy, Andy," he says. "And for what it's worth, I'm glad Briar has had you to talk to and rely on while she's been back."

I give him a tight smile. "I am, too."

Then he releases my hand and gives me a wave before spinning around, heading through the cavernous space, and exiting through the front.

Picking up my coffee, I hold it with both hands, enjoying the warmth seeping through the cardboard and heating my cool hands. The lower temperatures aren't normally an issue at work, but with a few windows still needing to be installed and the electrical not turned on yet, the interior of the hollowed-out One Stop feels much like the walk-in did that first day Briar and I kissed.

The construction crew is mostly finished, which is wonderful. Diego told me he anticipates being completed within the next three days, which would be two days ahead of schedule, an unheard-of milestone for a construction company in the mountains. It's not easy hauling supplies up and down those windy roads on big rigs, but the guy has been intensely dedicated to this project with an energy I've never seen before.

This morning, he asked me to look around and make notes about any small construction issues I see—nails that aren't flush with drywall, spots here and there that need putty, stuff like that—and as I wander around, making notes on my phone in one hand and holding my coffee in the other, I can't help but let my mind roam as well.

The conversation with Mark was unexpected, but I'm actually thankful it happened.

He's a good man.

A great one.

For some reason, it's important to me that he knows I'm

not trying to keep Briar hostage in a place that doesn't make her happy. I want him to know I support her going in search of the bigger and better she's always wanted in her life.

Obviously, my feelings for her complicate things. It's not every day you fall in love with someone, only to realize the most loving thing you can do is encourage them to leave you behind. But I feel like love is one of those crazy things in life you can only truly understand if you're willing to sacrifice for the happiness of another person.

It's what parents and grandparents do for their kids, the most unconditional love out there.

And it's what I'm going to do for Briar.

Sure, I think about what it might look like for me to tell her how I truly feel. I wonder if she'd be ecstatic or put off, if she'd see it as the next step in our relationship or a strong veer off course.

Eventually, though, I always set those thoughts aside.

Briar doesn't want a relationship. She's too busy trying to get over the last guy, the one who made her feel small and unimportant. I get the feeling she doesn't want to fall in love.

If only she understood that what I want is to make her feel something that's pretty much the opposite of falling. I want to help her rise and grow and bloom. Up, up, up, as far as her dreams and plans can take her.

I can see why it would feel scary. I've gotten hints and flashes of her relationship with Chad, and it seemed like a lonely place, a place where she didn't have a lot of…control.

The last thing you want to feel when you're desperate to regain that control is that you're plunging down without the ability to brace yourself.

Without knowing if anyone will be there to catch you.

"I promise. This is going to be helpful."

My dad sits in his recliner, staring off to the side, out the window. It's the first time he's looked like a man who wishes he were anywhere but sitting in that chair. I *could* consider that a win if I wasn't struggling so much with how angry he is at me.

He's furious.

His emotional state since his heart attack has mostly been sad, kind of lazy and lost. Seeing him fly off the handle at me last week when I told him I'd scheduled a meeting for him and the psychologist…I don't ever think I've seen him like that.

He doesn't say anything in response, just stares at nothing.

For the first time, I feel my own anger bubbling up, my own frustration with the fact that he's just sitting there, giving up on me.

"Dr. Dale is really nice," I say, keeping my tone even and trying to get him to give this a chance. "I went and met with her the other day, to talk to her a bit about what you've been going through and—"

"You don't know what I've been going through."

My dad's words are laced with something akin to hatred, something aimed at *me*. It sows something uncomfortable and unwanted in my stomach.

"You can't fix me, Andy," he continues. "I've been broken for a long time."

He shakes his head and stares off out the window again, the

one I opened up to let in some fresh air and natural light when I got here this morning and found him sitting in the dark, again.

"You should just leave me alone."

Suddenly, I feel overwhelmed. Full to the brim, with every emotion I've felt since the day my dad had his heart attack. Since the day I brought him home and he looked at me with dead eyes, like nothing mattered in the world anymore.

"How am I supposed to do that, huh?" I ask, my voice choked as my mind wars between feeling tired and upset and angry and bitter. "How am I supposed to leave you alone? What, just never come over here? Let you sit there in your chair until you *die*? Until you wither away and turn to dust?"

He finally looks me in the eyes, and he looks so unlike my dad that the welling in my chest finally breaks forth.

"Don't you understand that I can't lose you?" I shout at him. "Don't you get that you're all I have left? I still need you!"

I spin around, pick up the remote control off the coffee table, and chuck it across the room, enjoying the satisfaction I feel when the plastic cracks and shatters into pieces as it slams against the kitchen wall.

"I still need my dad, and you've been sitting there for months thinking I should have just left you alone?"

I shake my head, my chest heaving with the exertion of finally letting out all the emotions that have been grappling for time and attention in my mind and body. Hell, maybe *I* need to talk to someone, too.

"Something in that mind of yours is saying the only thing that matters is being with mom, telling you your life doesn't matter anymore without her here." I point at my chest. "But what about me? Do I not matter to you? Does how I feel not count for anything?"

When I look at my dad again, I can see tears falling down his face as he watches me.

"I love you, and I need you, and I will *never* just leave you alone. You're fucking *stuck* with me. Got it?"

My chest is heaving as we stare at each other across the room, the relief from having finally gotten some of that out of me indescribable. Rationally, I know this isn't entirely about my dad. Yes, the things I said are valid, but I'm also just exhausted. Emotionally taxed. Beyond spent.

I'd been handling this stuff with dad and keeping the store afloat all alone. And now, with the rebuild and Briar compounding that...it just all feels like so much.

A knock at the door cuts through the tension between us. I shake out my arms and cross the room, yanking it open to find Dr. Dale standing on the other side and Briar standing a few feet behind her with wide eyes.

"Hey, thanks for coming," I say, stepping back and waving an arm out. "Come on in."

She grins at me, though there's a bit of empathy in her eyes that lets me know she was probably more aware of that conversation than I intended.

"Sorry, I was pulling up at the same time," Briar whispers. "I'll wait out here."

I nod, leaning over and kissing her cheek before closing the door and walking across the room.

"Dr. Dale, this is my dad, William. Dad, this is Dr. Angela Dale. She's going to be chatting with you today."

My dad just stares at her in silence, so I take a few more minutes to give her a tour of the house before grabbing her a bottle of water.

"I'm going to take off so you two can talk," I say, mostly

for my dad's sake, since I already confirmed this with Dr. Dale yesterday.

"I'll be done in about an hour," she says, giving me a smile. "We can chat afterward."

I nod. "Sounds good."

Then I look at my dad, wondering if I should say anything else before I go.

I squat down next to his chair and set my hand on his.

"I'm sorry for yelling at you, I just…I mean it. I still need you. So please, you don't have to believe she can help you, but at least tell her what's going on. Please." I swallow, stand, and give him a kiss on the forehead. "If not for me, then for mom. She wouldn't want to see you like this."

Without looking at him again, I head outside.

"I was thinking we could do some kind of charity donation for Christmas," Briar says as she lies on my couch, staring at the ceiling.

She rolls onto her side and props herself up, resting her head in her hand and her elbow on the cushion.

"Like, with every purchase, customers can have the option to round up to the next dollar, and give that change to…I don't know, the nursing home or the community center or something." She grins at me. "What do you think?"

I nod my head, my eyes dropping down to where Quincy is snuggled next to my right leg, just enjoying the long strokes I'm

271

giving to her tummy.

"I think that could be a really great idea. It just gets complicated with the paperwork."

She shakes her head and rolls onto her back. "I can volunteer my time to handle that—no problem. Besides, most of the time, the paperwork is done at the time of the actual donation, and that won't be until after Christmas, so I'll have a lot of extra time."

Part of me feels like I should just let her think she'll be able to manage a charity donation in January, but I also think allowing her to continue believing she still has her job in a few weeks is unfair. It also completely flies in the face of the reason why I'm letting her go, both professionally *and* personally.

If I'm supposed to be encouraging her to find a new job somewhere else, I need to tell her sooner rather than later. I'm sure there is some kind of ethical line I'm crossing by telling her about the dissolution of her job as we both hang out in my living room, but we've already crossed just about every ethical boundary that *should* be in place between a boss and an employee, so… it doesn't seem like too big of an issue.

Which is why, instead of just agreeing with her about the donation and volunteering her hours, I tell her the truth.

"Listen, Briar…" I start, reforming the words in my mind. "I figure it's better to just talk with you about this to get it out of the way. I've decided to eliminate one of the cashier positions."

Briar sits up on the couch, confusion covering her face.

"What? When did you make *that* decision?"

"A few days ago. Part of me wanted to tell you it was the budget, but I'm just going to be honest." Taking a deep breath, I spit it out. "I'm not just eliminating *a* cashier position. I'm eliminating *your* position."

Her shoulders hunch in slightly. "Why?"

I shake my head. "Because I know you don't want to be here, and you have options to get another job."

"But I don't," she tells me. "I don't have another job."

"But you will."

"You don't know that."

"Yes, I do," I say, unwilling to let her sidestep this. "Of *course* you will. Look at what you're capable of, Briar. Look what you've done since you've been here. There are so many opportunities out there for you."

Her nostrils flare and she stands up, pacing the room. "This is about what my dad said, isn't it?"

"Partially, yes."

"Well, that's just…stupid."

"Maybe."

She stops pacing.

"But I don't think it's the wrong thing to do."

"How is it not the wrong thing to do?" she demands. "Tell me why firing me is a good choice. I've busted my ass for you. I've given all my time and energy to helping with One Stop, and you're going to get rid of me?"

"My opinion hasn't changed," I assure her. "Your help has been… It wouldn't have happened without you, but you'll be able to continue doing work like this for someone else, someone who can pay you a lot more and give you the chance to spread your wings."

Briar crosses her arms and glares at me, but I can see the signs of something I've never seen before on her face. The redness at her temples, the glassiness in her eyes…

"This is a mistake," she whispers, just as a tear tracks down her face.

A pit begins to grow in my stomach, knowing I'm the reason Briar is crying.

"You're pushing me out the door when I'm not even sure I want to go. What if I want to stay?"

"But you *don't* want to stay," I tell her through gritted teeth, knowing she wants to get the hell out of here. "You don't. Leaving Cedar Point is all you've talked about some coming back. Maybe you've gotten swept up in what's been going on between us. Maybe you're starting to think you could stick around here for a little while, but you're not going to be happy, Briar. You want something else, something I can't give you…and I love you too much to keep you from going after it."

She stands there, tears falling from her eyes, her face red and pinched and, if I'm honest, devastated.

Briar looks at me like I've just taken away everything that matters to her, and it is the worst feeling I've ever had in my entire life.

"I hate you," she whispers.

And then she grabs her bag off the floor and storms out the door.

When I finally go back to my dad's to see how the therapy meeting went, I show up right as Dr. Dale is leaving the house.

"Andy," she says, giving me a smile. "I'm glad I get to see you before I go. Do you have a second?"

I nod, swallowing down the remnants of the emotions I was

feeling just a short while ago as I watched Briar speed off down the drive in her brother's blue truck.

"Sure."

The two of us head out to her car, a little Camry parked next to my Jeep, giving her a chance to talk to me about whatever is on her mind.

"Obviously, doctor-patient privilege is a very real part of my job," she begins, "but I got permission from your father to talk to you about this."

We come to a stop next to her trunk, and she pops it open to drop her bag in the back. Then she closes it and leans back on her car, focusing her attention on me.

"Your father is struggling with depression, which we already guessed. There's a lot of self-hatred there, from years of burying things he didn't want to deal with after your mother died."

I grit my teeth and nod, wishing I could have thought to get him connected with someone sooner. Knowing he's been depressed for years, even if he hasn't shown it, stings. Makes me wish I'd paid more attention...makes me thankful that Briar cared enough to notice and say something.

"It's going to take a while for him to unpack everything, but I just wanted to let you know that...he *did* talk to me today. Not a lot, not super deep, but he talked to me." She lifts a hand and lightly pats my arm. "I just want to reassure you that there is *always* light at the end of the tunnel, okay? And you did the right thing by getting him connected with someone else."

"Thank you, Dr. Dale," I say, appreciating this bit of positive news in the wake of what felt like a very *not* positive day.

She grins, squeezes my arm, and then climbs into her car, giving me a wave before she backs up and heads down the drive.

CHAPTER TWENTY-TWO

Boyd

I stare at the computer screen, looking at job postings online that I know I'll never apply for, wondering how the hell I'm even in this position—again. I've been at this for an hour and haven't made any progress, my mind refusing to absorb any of the information and making it a big fat waste of my day.

I'm still reeling from my conversation with Andy yesterday. It shook me so hard I haven't even responded to his text messages checking in.

Bellamy came into my room a little while ago with a phone pressed to her ear.

"Yeah, she's here."

That's all she said, but I knew she was talking to Andy, knew he was being the really amazing guy who wanted to make sure I got home okay after I stormed out a crying mess.

I can't believe I cried.

That makes twice in the past few months, when I pretty much never cry. I think I can actually count on my hand the number of times I've cried in my entire life.

There was the time Nick and I broke up, when I vowed to never let a man make me cry again.

There was the time my dog Shep died.

The time I found out my dad was in remission after a long battle with cancer.

There was the *almost* crying over the summer when I tried to talk to my brother Boyd about what was going on with Chad, but I couldn't manage to get it out.

And then yesterday. Yesterday, as I allowed big fat tears to streak down my face in front of a man who decided to fire me so I'd leave town.

Because that's what happened, right? He looked me in the eyes and told me he was getting rid of my position because I need to leave town.

Pushing my laptop off my legs with a sigh, I climb out of bed and wander downstairs to find something to eat. Yesterday when I got home, I went straight to my room and didn't come out at all. Not even when my parents let me know there was leftover soup and salad if I wanted it.

So to say I'm starving is an understatement, but that doesn't mean I don't wish I'd come down at a different time when I walk into the kitchen and find Bellamy sitting at the counter, her laptop and books and pens scattered across the island.

I avert my eyes and focus my attention on crossing to the pantry to dig around for some cereal.

"Morning," Bellamy says. "How'd you sleep?"

I nod, giving my sister a smile as I set a box of Cinnamon Toast Crunch on the counter.

"Okay. You?"

Bellamy tilts her head from left to right. "I haven't been

sleeping that well, honestly." Then she reaches back and stretches out her arms and her neck. "My coursework is a lot more difficult this semester, and this fucking project is just, ugh…"

Grabbing a bowl from the cabinet and milk from the fridge, I make quick work of getting my pitiful 'meal' together.

But when I take a second to actually look at my sister, I can see the lines under her eyes and the stress on her face. She looks exhausted, in both her expression and body language, the way she's slumped over the counter and staring blankly at the screen of her laptop.

"What classes are you taking this semester?"

Bellamy looks over at me and blinks a few times.

"Uh…" She pauses and looks around, like she's trying to remember. "An auditing class, advanced financial accounting, business strategy, a leadership class, and then a general psych class I should have taken freshman year but put off."

I nod, remembering what it was like to get my bachelor's in business. The rigorousness of completing the degree in four years is extensive, and math was my least favorite component of the business courses. Looking at financial statements, economics, business math classes, and accounting…those were the things I struggled with the most.

Bellamy shocked me a few years ago when she told me she was majoring in accounting. The idea of all those numbers and tax codes and…no. Just, no. It sounds like an absolute nightmare, and to do the entire degree at home, alone, without any other students to work with in person just makes it all sound like a mess.

For me, I mean.

My sister is thriving, flexing those amazing mental muscles, just like Boyd did with his degree in computer science. But she does look exhausted right now, and instead of going back up to my room to close myself off and look for jobs, I set my bowl back on the counter and lean forward, looking at the books she has spread out.

"Which class is giving you the stress face?"

She grins at me. "Business strategy. I feel like my accounting classes make logical sense, you know? Numbers make sense. But the strategy stuff is just...it feels like a big guessing game."

I smirk, knowing exactly what she's talking about.

"Do you want some help?" I find myself offering. "I got an A in my business strategies and communication class. It's been a few years, and there's no telling whether we hit the topics you're covering, but—"

"Yes!" Bellamy says, her eyebrows rising. "Absolutely."

I nibble on the inside of my cheek and round the counter, taking a seat next to her.

"Okay then, why don't you tell me about what you're working on?"

My sister looks at me for a long moment before she turns and launches in. We spend a few hours working together to review some of the strategic concepts she's struggling with, as well as sorting through and organizing her ideas for the final presentation she has to give in real time over a video call.

I remember helping business students with things back when I was getting my MBA. It was a part of my school's curriculum to have master's students work with undergraduates, and I hated it. Being a teacher would definitely not be my vocation in any life.

But helping my sister feels different. There's a dedication I feel to helping her understand information, to backing up and saying something again in a different way to help her grasp an idea or theory she's struggling with.

By the time we wrap up, I'm feeling oddly buoyant, even though my earlier mood should have me feeling down in the dumps. I guess there's some truth to that saying about lifting others up, how helping others helps the soul.

"Thank you so much, Briar," Bellamy says as she closes her laptop. "I honestly feel like you just explained all of that in a way that makes me not feel like an idiot."

My brow furrows. "In no way are you an idiot," I tell her, incensed that she could ever believe such a thing. "You're a badass. I could never do all my coursework independently, and you make it look so easy."

She shakes her head and chuckles. "Sometimes it is. The math stuff, I mean. But not all of it."

I lift a shoulder. "Regardless of whether or not it *looks* easy," I continue, "you work your butt off. Don't think I haven't noticed your light on late into the evening. I know you're in there studying, making sure you're giving yourself the best opportunity to learn that you can."

I slide off my stool and take my bowl to the sink.

"You have a lot to be proud of, and you don't have to be perfect at everything to be proud of yourself."

There's a lull of silence from behind me before Bellamy speaks again.

"I wish you could talk to yourself like that."

My hands freeze under the warm water, covered in suds.

"That was such a great little pep talk, you know? And it totally made my day. But I feel like you're *really* hard on yourself about pretty much everything in your life."

I turn off the water and set the still soapy dish in the sink, but I don't turn around.

"You have a lot to be proud of," she continues, repeating my own words back to me. "And you don't have to be perfect to be proud of *yourself.*"

That same sticky tar in my throat from yesterday has returned, and when I rotate around to look at my sister, it grows even more, making it almost impossible to respond.

"I might be a lot younger than you, but I love you, and I'm here if you want to talk to me. I mean, I know you can talk to Boyd and Abby and Andy, but…I don't know. I'm here, too."

Maybe it's the fact that my few months spending so much time with Andy has made talking easier. Maybe it's the fact that it felt good to share that tiny piece about Chad in the car last week. Or maybe it's that I finally recognize my sister wants me to talk to her because she also wants to talk to me.

Regardless of the reason, I find myself opening my mouth.

"Andy fired me."

Then, before I can control it, I burst into tears.

Bellamy races around the island and immediately pulls me in for a hug, her embrace welcome and needed in the light of what's happened.

"He told me he loved me and then he fired me," I sob, returning Bellamy's hug and tucking my face against her shoulder.

We stand there for a long time, just rocking slowly from side to side, Bellamy rubbing soothing circles into my back and telling me everything will be okay.

Eventually, my sister and I end up in the den, sitting on the oversized couches and snuggling with pillows as I share with her all the things I've been keeping to myself, from what really happened between me and Chad to what just occurred between me and Andy, and everything else under the sun.

It's surprisingly cathartic, letting all the emotions out to

Bells, and I know it isn't just about Andy. This is a deep well of emotional stagnation, years and years of unhappiness pouring out of me, desperate for somewhere to go.

The loneliness of being in a relationship with someone who made me so incredibly unhappy.

The worthlessness of moving home and needing mom and dad to help me.

The struggle to figure out who I am and who I want to be.

And of course, without a doubt, the rollercoaster of feelings for Andy that seems to dominate my every waking moment.

"I'm just so upset and so mad at him at the same time," I say, my fingers tugging at a loose thread on the pillow in my arms. "How can he tell me he loves me too much to let me stay here? How does that make any sense?"

When I finally look at my sister, I see a softness in her eyes, her lips tipped up as she watches me.

"Because when someone loves you, they want what's best for *you*," she says. "Not what's best for them. Andy could have told you he was in love with you and tried to keep you here, but he didn't, because all you've been talking about is leaving." Bellamy shrugs her shoulder. "*Your* happiness means more to him than his own."

My entire body sags into the couch as I think that over. The entire concept feels foreign, not because I'm unfamiliar with the idea itself but because I can't remember the last time I was on the receiving end of it.

Chad's focus was always himself. All the changes I tried to make in order to make him happy—it was never enough. I lost myself somewhere along the way, and Chad never cared.

With Andy, he's doing the exact opposite. He's pushing me away because he doesn't want me to have to change for him, because he believes I'd be happiest somewhere else.

Even just a short while ago, I would have agreed with him. Over the past few weeks, though, that perspective has been shifting. Changing. Morphing into something new.

"Abby and I signed a lease yesterday morning," I tell her. "I was going to tell Andy, but I didn't get the chance."

Bellamy smiles at me. "Did you sign the lease because you want to be with Andy? Or because you want to be in Cedar Point?"

"Both," I tell her honestly. "I feel happy for the first time in a long time. Some of it is because I'm looking at life here with new eyes, but some of it is because of Andy. Honestly, it's a little hard to separate the two."

"How about this—are you in love with him?"

It takes me a while to answer, my mind scrambling to find something to say that's honest.

"I'm not sure I really know what love is supposed to look like," I admit.

Bellamy scoots closer on the couch, plucking away the pillow I've been holding in my lap and taking my hands in hers.

"Then maybe it's time for you to figure it out," she says. "Not in the context of someone like Chad, who was so clearly self-absorbed, but in the context of a man like Andy. Someone who, it seems like, very much wants you to be happy."

I nod, realizing she's right. "Yeah. Maybe it is."

We sit there in silence for a while longer, Bellamy pulling out a book from one of the shelves in the corner when she realizes that I need some time to mentally process everything. I lose track of time as I stare out the large bay windows facing the lake, thinking about...everything.

My conversation with my sister today.

The one with Andy yesterday.

All the other interactions the two of us have had.

And if I'm honest with myself—really, truly honest—I know my feelings for him are much larger than I've allowed myself to even realize.

For most of my life, I've avoided the big feelings love provokes because they felt too scary, too out of control in a life where all I wanted was to be in control.

Of something. Of *anything*.

It felt like being a Mitchell controlled my life growing up, so I left, trying to find my own independence and autonomy. Then, instead of taking the freedom I finally had and using it to figure out who I was independent of my family, I handed that control over to a man who never had my best interests at heart, who only thought of himself.

Now, everything feels like a jumbled mess. I thought coming back to Cedar Point would make me feel lost again, thought I'd go back to being that same girl I was before.

But if anything, I've felt more found here over the past few months than I ever have anywhere else.

Some of that is simply because I've grown up a little bit over the last decade. I've had life experience and handfuls of independent friends and a wonderful role model in Holly.

But a big part of it has to do with the experiences I've had with Andy over the past few months.

Andy and his charming grin and genuine heart.

The man has slowly gotten me to open up and reveal my true self. He's supported and believed in me, taken me into his arms and looked at me like I'm his entire world.

As much as this thing between us was supposed to be just two people having a little fun, I've seen those looks from him as we eat dinner, as we wander around town together, as he moves inside of me.

Andrew Marshall is in love with me.

And the *truth* is, knowing that doesn't make me feel out of control. Knowing that makes me feel safe and cared for and, of course, loved.

In a way I haven't ever felt before. In a way I never would have *allowed* myself to feel before, for fear of something horrible happening.

Because for my entire life, I've been afraid of falling in love. And yet, now that I'm fairly certain the way he makes me feel *is* love, I realize just how wrong I was.

Falling in love isn't scary when the man at the bottom has spread a net so wide there's no way he won't catch you, a net woven entirely out of what I'm realizing are the best parts of love.

Trust.

Intimacy.

Respect.

Sacrifice.

Andy has given me all of those things without me even knowing it. He's cast out a net that won't let me plunge past him, flailing and lost and alone.

In the same breath of loving me and wanting what's best for me, though, he's taken away the thing I'm so desperate for—control, of myself and my life and my future. He thinks he's doing a good thing by firing me and sending me off to the better future he thinks I can find away from him.

But he needs to let me choose that future for myself, needs to do exactly what he's been doing all along—talk to me, listen to me, support me—and then allow me to make the decisions I think are best.

Not make them for me.

Not choose for me, as if I'm a child who can't see what's best for herself.

The longer I sit on the couch, the more I think about it, the more frustrated I get.

How dare he? How *dare* he love me and then push me away?

Before I can help myself, I'm up off the couch and striding out of the room.

"Where are you going?" my sister calls after me.

Yanking a pair of keys off the table by the entry, I pull open the door and call out over my shoulder.

"To work."

CHAPTER TWENTY-THREE

Andy

When I woke up this morning, I lay in bed for a long time trying to decide if I should go over to the Mitchells' house—to Short Stop—and get to work, or if I should find a way to work somewhere else.

After the way things ended with Briar yesterday afternoon, I felt it was fair to give her a little space, especially with how emotional she was, something I've never seen from her before.

So instead of working from the little guesthouse that has become a home away from home over the past month, I went to the jobsite, deciding to stick out the cooler temperatures and work on the laptop I thankfully brought home the other day. I've been here more and more over the past week since there are an increasing number of details I need to be around to approve or decide on in real time if I want us to stay on deadline. So, it actually works out better this way.

At least that's what I'm trying to tell myself.

It's been a little tough to focus with all the noise of the construction, but I've managed to pick a corner that's out of the way and next to the power source the team is using. It's working, even though I'd much rather be sitting at my makeshift desk next to Briar, warm from the heater and from the knowledge that she's busy with her own projects just a few feet away.

But it wouldn't be fair to her to show up at her house when she's so upset. Even though I technically didn't fire her from her current job helping with the reopening, I can understand why she might not want to work with me at all anymore. Staying away, at least for a day or two, is probably a good way to give her the space she needs.

"Andy?"

When I hear my name called out, I tilt my chair back, peering around the little wall blocking my view of the full room.

My eyes widen when I see Keegan walking through the construction site, dressed for work in short jean cutoffs and a long-sleeved top that she's tied into a knot at her hip. *Mitch Bitch* stretches across her chest.

How she's not freezing to death when I'm sitting here in a thick winter coat and gloves is beyond me.

"Over here."

Her eyes catch mine as I wave her back, wondering what on earth she could possibly be doing here. We're clearly not open, that's for sure.

"Hey, you," she says, giving me that same smile she used to give me when we were in high school, the one she continued to give me after we graduated. It's a flirtatious little tilt of her lips, a flash in her eyes designed to tell me she has something I want. Keegan has looked at me like that many times over the years, and in a few of those instances, back in my late teens and early twenties, that smile was one of the reasons we ended up in bed together.

Today, though, it does absolutely nothing for me. It hasn't done anything for me in a long, long time, and definitely not in the wake of knowing what it feels like to be looked at the way Briar looks at me. With those wide eyes and that little way she nibbles on her cheek...

There isn't any comparison.

"Hi Keegan." I stand from my plastic chair and tiny work table, crossing toward her. "What can I do for you?"

She shrugs a shoulder, her eyes rising to track around the room. "I heard they're finishing up soon and just wanted to come by to see how the place is coming along."

Well, I'm glad she thinks I have time to give her a tour as we scramble to reopen a business that burned down.

"Is it true you're gonna re-open in two weeks?" she asks me.

I nod. "Yup. Should be opening just in time for everyone to get their holiday groceries. Trying to beat the snow."

She grins. "I'm so glad. It's been crazy ordering things through the online thing Wellies put together for us," she says, referencing the grocery store, Wellington's, that sits just on the outside of Tahoe National Forest at the base of the mountain.

"Briar actually put that entire system together," I tell her. "She coordinated with Wellington's to make sure nobody has to drive down there to get food. It's pretty great, right?"

Her smile falters slightly, catching that I've just taken her negative comment about the grocery-buying process and shifted it to a positive. Just another second later, her face looks exactly like it did when she first walked in.

Like a cat who wants some cream.

"Sure is. I actually just put in an order for a few bottles of wine. Any interest in coming by to have a drink?"

I've made it very clear over the years that I'm not interested in starting anything up again with Keegan. I've pussyfooted around it. I've stated it plainly. I've tried pretty much everything under the sun to get her to understand how I feel about it, but Keegan doesn't like to give up.

"I appreciate it, but I think I'll pass," I tell her, trying to keep it friendly even though I'm irritated. "I've been seeing Briar, so...I'm not exactly free."

Keegan already knows Briar and I were seeing each other. She's seen us together around town, drinking together at The Mitch, bumped into us on Halloween and a bunch of other times over the past few months. Things between Briar and I might be uncertain at the moment, but the fact that she's here, trying to make plans with me...it's not surprising, but it *is* distasteful.

Her nose scrunches up as her expression sours then she rolls her eyes and laughs. "From what *I've* heard, you're just hooking up, so what does it matter?" She steps forward and runs her hand along my jacket. "Besides, she's not sticking around anyway. It can't be anything serious, not with a girl like her."

I take a step back, letting her hand fall away.

There was a time when her forwardness was attractive, back when I was much younger and just looking for something easy. Stress-free. A good time and no strings.

Now, all I want is to string myself to Briar. All I want is the difficulty that comes along with getting her to feel comfortable opening up to me, the stress of learning her expressions and emotions. Every moment with her, even the strange, awkward, bumbling ones...every moment is good.

A girl like Briar is exactly what I'm looking for. Whether it's serious or not, difficult or not, complicated or not, I know for sure that something with Keegan *isn't*, regardless of how things with Briar and I end up.

"I need to talk to you."

The sound of Briar's voice has my neck about breaking as I turn to find her standing a few feet away, watching me and Keegan with an unreadable expression.

"Briar," I huff out, the coolness in the air enough to have my breath fogging in front of me. "Keegan was just—"

"Leaving," Briar interrupts, her attention shifting to focus solely on the woman standing next to me. "Thanks for swinging by, but Andy and I have some work things to take care of."

My attention remains on Briar, but I don't miss the devilish giggle that falls from Keegan's mouth, or the way she walks toward Briar with a sway to her hips.

"Try to take care of him all you want," Keegan says, winking at Briar then looking back at me. "He knows where to go once he gets bored with you."

Then she stalks across the open room toward the exit, waving her fingers at us both as she walks through the front door.

"God, she really hasn't changed at *all* since high school," Briar says, rolling her eyes.

I nod. "Yeah. Listen, Briar, I don't want you to think—"

But Briar waves a hand, dismissing me before I can say anything else.

"I'm not worried about Keegan, Andy. You told me you love me last night. The last thing I'm worried about is her coming in here to *take care* of you."

She makes a fake gagging noise I can't help but chuckle at.

God it feels good to see her, to laugh with her, even for just a moment. And knowing that she was able to see me here with Keegan and not worry at all...I can't help but revel in the small bit of happiness it makes me feel. That she is sure enough of me and my feelings to not let something stupid cause an unnecessary problem.

"How are you?" I ask.

"Fine," she says, her expression tense. "I'm here to talk to you about what happened yesterday."

My laugh trails off at her words, and I nod. Briar might have started things off between us as someone who struggles with hard conversations, but that's definitely not who she is anymore. She may have left my place in a storm of emotion, but I figured we would be talking at some point.

As quiet as she was when we first started spending time together, she's really come out of her shell. She tells me what she thinks, how she feels, what she wants. She's still slow and methodical about it, still cautious in her approach—she wouldn't be Briar, otherwise—but she doesn't hide from me anymore.

"I'm glad you want to talk about it," I say, tucking my hands in my jacket pocket.

"I've been thinking about everything you said."

My brows furrow, suddenly realizing that the emotion rolling off of Briar is anger. Somehow I missed that during our interaction with Keegan. Considering the fact that she left in tears yesterday, I assumed she'd be sad, or possibly even thankful. I wasn't expecting anger.

"And the only conclusion I can come to is that you, Andy Marshall, are full of shit."

My jaw drops.

"You spout all this crap about loving me too much to let me stay here," she continues, her tone snippy, her body taut with tension, "but did you ever stop to think I might love you too much to leave?"

I grit my jaw, my hands flexing and unflexing into balls of

frustration at my sides.

"Yes," I say, my tone gravelly. "I *did* think about that. I *worried* about that."

She crosses her arms and glares at me.

"I can't let you choose to live a life that won't make you happy, Briar."

"Well that's all fine and dandy, except it's not your decision to make," she spits back. "You don't get to decide what makes me happy. Whether I'm making a stupid decision or a great one. Only I get to do that. If I want to choose you, if I want to decide to live in Cedar Point for the rest of my life, loving you, being here with you, that's *my* choice, not yours."

I swallow something thick, wishing I could convince her to stop pushing this, wishing I could come up with some kind of explanation as to why this isn't the right thing.

Because hearing her say she loves me, even if it's in anger, is almost enough to make me do something selfish.

Like keep her here.

For as long as she's willing to stay.

Her shoulders fall and she tilts her head, her ire dissolving to give way for the emotions anger is so good at masking.

"I spent my whole life fighting to leave this town, desperate for something else…something that made me feel like I was in control of my own life. It was only natural to believe I wouldn't be happy coming back here, but I wasn't happy out there either. I haven't been happy anywhere." She pauses. "Until you."

I grit my teeth, knowing my resolve is beginning to buckle.

"There's no way loving me can make you happy enough that you don't regret sticking around, Briar."

"Who says I expect *you* to make me happy?" she asks, surprising me. "I'm the only one who can make me happy, Andy. I can't expect anyone—not a man, not friends, not my family—to be able to make me happy. I have to find that inside of myself. I have to find it in making meaning out of the life I live."

She steps forward, the anger in her countenance replaced with something else. Something softer, more desperate.

"When I say I wasn't happy until you, I mean it's because of what you've shown me. You've helped me see the good in this town. You've reminded me of the things that make it amazing. I finally feel like I understand what my parents mean when they talk about loving it here so much. They talk about this place like it's a friend, a family member…a living, breathing thing that ebbs and flows and changes as time goes on."

Briar reaches out and takes my hand in hers, lacing her fingers in mine.

"I've never felt about anything in my life the way I've felt about everything that's happened in the past few months, the past few weeks. Being back here was my greatest fear, because I was ashamed to come back when I wanted to leave so desperately. But being here with you, seeing the town through your eyes, and working so hard to help the people who live here… it's changed everything. For the first time in my life, I'm happy."

Then she steps into me, pressing the front of her against the front of me, and she wraps her arms around my chest, bringing me snug and close.

"You helped me fall in love, Andy Marshall. You've helped me love this town again when I never thought it was possible." She leans back slightly, looking me in the eye. "But you've also shown me that real love, between two people, looks a lot different than I thought it would. And do you want to know what it looks like?"

Unable to help myself, desperate to know what she has to

say, I nod.

"It looks like holding hands when the world is burning down," she says. "It looks like helping each other learn to appreciate something new. Talking and laughing and quiet moments that are filled with happiness."

My heart is racing in my chest at her words, at the beautiful picture she's painting of the two of us.

"It looks like pushing each other to be our best. Building each other up. Helping each other when we fall. You've given me all the pieces of love, all the things I didn't know I wanted in a relationship, and I've never been happier in my entire life."

She presses her forehead against mine.

"You act like my love for you won't be enough to keep me around." Her eyes look between mine. "But what you don't seem to understand is that I'm staying, no matter what."

She pulls away, tugging a piece of paper out of her back pocket and handing it to me.

I unfold it, my brows lowered, confused as to what she could possibly be showing me.

"What is this?" I ask, my eyes scanning across the photocopied document with a handful of signatures on it.

"A lease."

My gaze flies up, connecting with hers, not sure I heard her correctly.

"Abby and I are getting an apartment. We move in at the new year."

I look back at the paper in my hand and skip down to the bottom, to the signatures dated a few days ago. Then over to the lease terms. The length.

"A lease. For a year," I mumble, surprised, my mind instantly recalling the memory of what she said to me on the day she interviewed for her job at One Stop.

"I figure if I'm serious about being here, I need to be here, seriously. And I can't do that if I'm living with my parents."

I take a deep breath then let it out, feeling my last protests begin to bubble up.

But then I look into her eyes, and I see something there I haven't really seen before.

Certainty.

Briar is looking at me with clear eyes. She might not know exactly what she wants to do with her life, but she knows where she wants to be. And that sureness, that confidence...I've only seen it in fits and starts here and there. Never with this blazing brilliance. Never with this shoulders-back, chin-high, this-is-me kind of attitude.

And it makes me love her even more to see her so sure and certain in herself.

Just like that, any kind of protest I could conjure evaporates, leaving only an absolute gratitude that the choice she's making includes me.

"Well, if you're going to be sticking around," I say, passing the paper back to her, "I guess the least I can do is let you keep your job."

At that, her smile spreads wide.

And then she launches herself into my arms and presses her lips to mine, the cold air recalling memories of our first kiss in the walk-in.

As we stand there, in the middle of a jobsite, construction workers milling about around the corner, I know nothing has ever tasted as delicious as knowing she's mine.

CHAPTER TWENTY-FOUR

Boyd

"You excited?"

I look at my sister, unable to hide the smile that's been hovering at the edges of my lips for the past hour.

"Definitely."

Bellamy squeals, though she does it quietly, which I didn't know was a thing.

We've been in here for a while, Bellamy's bedroom apparently a better place to do hair and makeup than the bathroom, and my sister has been painstakingly helping me get ready for my first *official* date with Andy.

When she found out we had a plan to drive down the mountain to go to the movies tonight—each of us taking a much needed night off from the increasing crunch of prepping for the opening—she insisted she be the one to help me get 'all dolled up,' a phrase I've only ever heard from my mother and other women in their 50s.

"I still can't believe *you*, the person I've always thought would be in monogamous relationships until you die, actually believed a friends-with-benefits relationship was a good idea," she says, capping the mascara she's been applying for what feels like ten minutes but is probably only ten seconds.

"It just felt…easier," I offer, trying to explain to Bells what it was like to have feelings for someone for so long. "He was this guy I'd had a crush on since I was in a training bra, you know?"

She laughs.

"I couldn't help but want something physical with him, but at the same time, I just didn't think I was ready for anything more than that."

"Tilt your head back. Perfect." My sister begins applying lipstick in a bold color that we argued about for fifteen minutes before I finally agreed. "I know all about the long-term crush," she tells me, her eyes trained on where she's painting across my lips.

"Do you?" I ask, though I'm careful to keep my mouth from moving. The last thing we need is a deep burgundy smear across my cheek.

Bellamy nods as she finishes up then reaches over to grab a piece of tissue. "Blot."

"Who is it?"

She eyes me for a second then retrieves the tissue once I'm done.

"I'll tell you, but you're not allowed to laugh."

I nod. "Promise."

"It's Connor Pruitt."

I instantly make a face. "Keegan's brother?"

"I said not to laugh!"

"I didn't!"

"You made a face."

"Yeah, but I didn't *laugh*."

She glares at me. I can't be entirely sure, but I don't think she's as mad as she's pretending to be.

"Tilt your head back."

I follow her directions, staying still as she uncaps some lip gloss and smears it on. Once she's done, I rub my lips together.

"What's so great about him?" I ask. "And how long have you liked him?"

She sighs. "Forever. For as long as I can remember. I know you might not like Keegan, but Connor's great. Really. He's handsome and kind and...well, I just have always liked him, so..."

Bellamy trails off, and I realize this is one of those older sister moments I'm trying to start having with her, the ones I missed out on when she was younger because I wasn't around.

I reach out and put my hand on hers.

"If he makes you happy, that's all that matters, okay?"

She looks up at me from under her lashes, and I realize just how much she wanted my approval. It surprises me a little bit, considering the fact that we've never been that close.

It feels good, too.

"So, tell me more about him."

Bellamy becomes a sudden fount of information, overflowing with every little thing she can tell me about Connor.

She talks about him as I slip on my wool tights and pull on my dress, as she helps me zip up the back and adjusts the fancy braid she did for me. She follows me down the stairs as I collect the things I need to put in my overnight bag and get my purse ready.

"Sounds like you've been paying a lot of attention," I say, laughing and giving her a smile as I loop the strap of my bag over my shoulder.

Bellamy blushes, and then I see her nibble on the inside of her cheek. "Maybe."

"Well, he sounds great. But like I said, as long as he makes you happy, right?"

She nods.

"Thanks for all your help."

"Of course. Any time." Then she wraps her arms around me and gives me a hug. "I'm so happy for you," she says as she pulls away. "Have fun tonight."

I give her a little wave then head outside, where Andy is just stepping out of his Jeep, looking incredibly handsome in a pair of dark wash jeans and a light grey sweater.

"Hi beautiful," he says, eyeing me up and down as I walk toward him. "Look at those lips."

Once I've finally reached him, he tugs me close, his mouth inches from said lips.

"I'm supposed to knock on the door on our first date," he teases, his nose bumping mine.

"And I'm supposed to pretend you're not going to get lucky later," I retort. "But I have an overnight bag with me, so I think we can both assume it's a foregone conclusion."

He grins. "Perfect."

Then he presses his lips to mine, licking into my mouth with the confidence of a man who has learned exactly how to kiss and touch me over the past few months.

"This is supposed to be a first date!" I hear shouted from behind me. "Leave room for Jesus!"

I pull back on a giggle, which is only amplified when I see the smear of lipstick and gloss on Andy's mouth. I lift my hands and try to wipe it away, but he shakes me off, grinning and attempting to pull me in for another kiss.

"No, we have to clean you up," I insist on a laugh, my stomach still aching as I lean back and place my fingers on his face.

He finally relents, allowing me to rub along the sides of his mouth and the light bit of stubble on his chin where the dark color has smeared to.

"Hmmm," I hum.

"What?"

"That's gonna chafe my thighs later."

Andy's eyes widen, and he spins me around, marching me to the Jeep and helping me get inside. Then he climbs in on his side and starts her up, pulling back onto the road and peeling out.

"What's the hurry?" I ask, still giggling.

"I'll ask you one time, and then I won't bring it up again."

I nod, my brows furrowing.

"Do you want to see the movie and go to dinner? Or do you want to go to my place and throw a frozen pizza in the oven?"

"Why would we…"

My voice trails off as Andy glances over at me, and I see the lust in his eyes. Then I let my gaze drop down to the sizeable bulge I can see tenting his pants.

I grin, knowing exactly what I want.

"Take me home, Mr. Marshall."

Andy smiles and speeds down the road.

"Thank you so much for being here today."

Andy's voice booms out to the crowd that's standing outside

the shop early in the morning on a Saturday, huddled together and trying to keep warm in the 40-degree weather.

"As most of you know, One Stop Shop has been in my family for three generations. Opened by my grandfather in 1959 then operated by my father beginning in 1992, this grocery store has been a Cedar Point staple for over half a century. What many of you *don't* know is that after the fire just seven weeks ago, I strongly considered shutting One Stop's doors for good."

I think I hear a few gasps from the crowd, though I'm too far away to get a good read on their reaction. If it's anything like what *my* reaction was, I'd completely understand.

I'm standing just on the outside of the new sliding doors at the front entrance holding the magnetic key to unlock them as soon as Andy gives me the word. We planned this whole thing out a few days ago. He'll give the speech, they'll do the ribbon-cutting thing with Mayor Cabot, and then I'll unlock the doors. Myself and the other employees working this morning will go directly to our stations, though everything inside is all set. We've been here since four in the morning getting the final touches in place and making sure everything is ready to go, from the deli to the cashier's tills to the new floral department and new bakery.

"But it was the support of one woman that convinced me One Stop was just too important to board up. That this town was too important to let something like a fire sideline so many families. And that woman is none other than Cedar Point's own Briar Mitchell."

There's a polite smattering of applause, and I give everyone a wave but don't leave my spot. Andy reviewed his speech with me last night, and I asked him to take out the part about me, but he refused.

"It has been her long hours, creative thinking, and business savvy that has propelled us into being able to open our doors before Christmas, and One Stop will be forever grateful for the time and energy she put into making this store a better and more intentional service for the community."

I expect him to go on from there to talk about how his dad wishes he could be here today, but I stare at Andy as his speech differs from what he shared with me last night.

"While living away from Cedar Point, Briar spent years working for an amazing florist who had a significant impact on her life. It was actually Briar's idea to use the store expansion to add a bakery and a flower shop, and as a thank you for all the work she has done to improve our store for the community, the flower shop will be named The Briar Patch."

I swallow awkwardly, emotions at the beautiful gesture welling up inside my chest. It's super cheesy, but making me a permanent part of his store is absolutely the kind of thing Andy would do to show me he loves me.

He goes on to read the rest of his speech, and then Mayor Cabot says a few words before the two of them hold an obnoxiously large pair of scissors and snip a big red ribbon.

More applause echoes in the air and music plays over the speakers as Andy gives me a nod to unlock the doors.

Then I race inside and get to work.

It's an achingly long day, and of course, plenty of little things go wrong. One of the coolers starts leaking and Andy has to call in a repair guy. A toilet gets clogged. There aren't enough carts for everyone who wants to shop. We run out of pennies.

But all in all, it's a wonderful re-opening day. When I finish closing up that evening with Maryanne and Elvin, I realize all three of us have worked twelve-hour shifts, and that doesn't even include the prep time before opening. Knowing they must be exhausted, I send the two of them off and lock the front door, then stroll slowly to the back room.

It's weird being in a place that looks so much like it used to and yet is so different. The walls are a different color and the floor tiles have a different pattern. The shelves are a different size and made out of metal instead of wood.

It's the same One Stop I've been coming to since I was a kid, and yet it's not.

It feels similar to the way I feel about Cedar Point. The town is still the same, filled with the same people and some of the same businesses and scenery. But the feeling in my chest when I wander through downtown or head out on a run or drive the full loop around Lakeshore Road…it's something new.

It's the same Cedar Point I've always know, and yet it's not.

When I push through the swinging doors to the stockroom and round the corner to peek into Andy's new office, I know it isn't just the décor that makes this building feel so different. That makes this *town* feel so different.

It's also the man who works here, the man who will work and live here for the rest of his life and is proud to do so.

"Hey."

At the sound of my voice, Andy looks up at me. His eyes are tired, his hair is a mess, and his shirt is wrinkled as he slumps over some paperwork on his desk. Even so, there's no denying the way he lights up when he sees me, almost like my presence is a little bump to a dying battery.

"Everything's closed up."

He nods. "Great."

"How did you think today went?"

Andy leans back in his chair and stretches his neck, lifting his arms over his head to stretch those, too.

"Really well, actually."

"Yeah?"

He nods. "Yeah."

"That's great. I'm so glad."

We both just look at each other for a long minute, and I try to think back to what he looked like to me when I stood at this door at the end of my *first* first day, when he invited me out to drinks. I can't remember exactly, but probably a lot less tired.

"What's that smile for?" he asks.

I giggle. "Just thinking about you."

"Oh yeah?"

I nod.

He stands from his seat and crosses the office, wrapping his arms around my waist, prompting me to wrap mine around his neck.

And then he kisses me. Slow and long and deep.

It reminds me of how I felt so early on in our relationship.

Known.

Like he sees me at the heart of who I am, like he knows the little things and the big things and loves them just the same.

It makes me feel like I can fly.

And I think that's been his goal all along.

EPILOGUE

Andy

TWO AND A HALF YEARS LATER

When Boyd let me know he was back in town with his fiancée, making plans to get together was a no-brainer. We might not see each other often, but it's always good to take the time to catch up.

He brings me in for a hug and slaps me on the back when I show up at the Mitchell house, then squeezes my shoulder before inviting me in.

"Good to see you, man," I say, following him through the entry and over to the den. "It's been a while."

Boyd nods and plops down on one of the couches. "Yes it has," he agrees. "Not since you came to visit, I think."

Back when Briar and I first started dating, I told her it was important for me to call Boyd and talk to him before he found out from someone else. He was surprisingly easygoing about it, though nobody could mistake him for thrilled. Then, a few days later, he and his girlfriend showed up for Christmas as a surprise

306

to the family.

That's when we had the real *talk*, the one where he did the thing brothers have to do: threaten their sisters' boyfriends with bodily harm if they hurt her.

But ever since then, things have been fine between us. A few months ago, we took a week off during late Spring and flew out to Boston to see him and Ruby. It was a great trip, though while we were there, he prodded me on what my plans were for myself and Briar.

If it were anybody else, I would have given some vague *Oh we're just figuring things out* kind of response, but this was Boyd—one of my oldest, closest friends, and Briar's brother. If anybody would understand my perspective, it would be him.

I told him I wanted to wait at least three or four more years before proposing. Briar has been working her sexy ass off to save money so she can finally open her own bookstore, and I don't want to take away from that. If I'm honest, I love her too much to tie her down, at least not yet. She's a bird who just figured out her wings, and the best thing I can do is let her fly as high as she can go for now.

Boyd was surprised but understanding, and he hasn't brought it up again.

"So, what are your plans while you're in town?" I ask, crossing one leg over the other, resting my heel on my knee and settling my hands against my stomach. "Gonna see any old friends from—"

"Okay, I gotta be honest with you," Boyd interrupts. "You're not actually here to see me. I was just the excuse to get you here."

My brow furrows. "What?"

"You're a few minutes early. I was supposed to take you straight out back, but I brought you in here for a few minutes so

Briar could finish."

I let out a chuckle, still feeling confused. "Finish what?"

Boyd stands from the couch and waves for me to follow him. "I'll show you."

I trail after him through the house, noticing for the first time that most of the lights are off, except for something coming from outside. When Boyd pulls the sliding door open, I step out onto the deck that faces the lake, my eyes looking up at the dozens of fairy lights hanging everywhere, the entire yard washed in a muted glow.

"What's going on?" I ask, turning around to see that Boyd has closed the sliding door from the other side.

He waves and smiles then points behind me.

When I look in that direction, I see someone standing on the long dock that stretches out from the Mitchell family property.

Briar.

It's been an amazing two and a half years since she told me she was staying in Cedar Point, and life is good—no, better than good. It's extraordinary. One Stop is thriving, and so much of that is because of the things we've put in place together, things she had a huge hand in creating when it felt like everything in my world was going up in smoke. I couldn't be more thankful.

Neither could my dad. It's been a long road for him as he's been working through his depression. It took a few months of meeting with Dr. Dale before he finally got to a point where he was well enough to come back to work, and even then, it was months longer before he seemed back to his true self.

We've had some pretty wonderful and emotional conversations, the two of us, about that period of our lives and what we were each going through at the time. Ultimately, I'm just thankful I have my dad back. He still goes to therapy every week, still struggles with some of the same emotions and feelings he had before. He's learning to navigate them better, to not shove them down and pretend they don't exist.

It means he's a little less jovial than he used to be, but it also means he's learning to be the real him, not just the guy he thinks everyone wants him to be. I'd much rather have the genuine version of him, any day.

Boy does he love Briar, though. He's been talking about me marrying her for at least the past year, if not longer, since back when it was still too soon to start talking about it. Though, if I'm honest, it's something I've thought of since the day Briar told me she was staying. Even if it *is* something we'll need to wait quite a while on, it still feels good to know I'm with someone who makes me want forever.

She's been this incredible one-woman show since she decided to go all in on Cedar Point. All in on *me*. Still working full-time at One Stop, but also an active member of the small business sector of the city council, back to volunteering at The Pines, and working in a project-management capacity with some of the other small businesses in town to help them identify areas where they can improve, cut costs and build up their businesses. It's like she finally gave herself permission to go full steam ahead after the life she wants, and I can't wait to see her achieve every dream she sets her sights on.

Still feeling confused as to what's going on, I make my way toward her, crossing the plush green grass then walking along the wooden dock, finally reaching Briar at the end.

"Hey," I say, smiling at her and pulling her in for a hug. "What's going on?"

She tilts up onto her toes and presses her lips against mine then drops down and takes a step back. That's when I finally take in what she's wearing.

It's a beautiful dress, tight in the right places and showing off just a little bit of skin. And her hair is down. For as long as I've known her, Briar has been very much a hair-in-a-braid kind of woman.

"Look at your hair," I say, reaching out and taking some of the soft waves in my hand. "You look so pretty."

She smiles at me, but then she starts nibbling on that lip, cluing me in to the fact that she's nervous.

"I have something important to talk to you about," she tells me. "If that's okay with you."

I nod, concern crossing me face. "Of course."

She clears her throat and unfolds a piece of paper in her hands.

"When I first moved home almost three years ago, I was certain I would never be able to find happiness here, in Cedar Point. I'd spent years searching for it without success, and I was sure there was no way I would find it in my hometown."

She shifts on her feet and glances up at me, then looks back down at her paper.

"But you surprised me. You showed me how I could find happiness anywhere, as long as I'm happy with myself. That's who you are to me, Andy—the man who makes me want to be the best version of me. You make me want to dig deeper and climb higher and laugh louder. And I know, without a doubt, that there isn't anyone else on this earth I'd want to spend the rest of my life with."

My eyes widen as Briar suddenly kneels down in front of me and pulls out a box from who knows where. All I can focus on is the beautiful woman in front of me who is…proposing? That's what's happening, right?

"I heard the conversation you had with Boyd in Boston, and I know you want to wait a while longer. You said you don't want to clip my wings before I have a chance to use them."

Briar shakes her head, a tear falling from one eye.

"But like I just told you, being with you isn't clipping my wings. You make me feel like I can fly every day. As cliché as it sounds, you are the wind beneath my wings."

We both burst into laughter, each of us batting away tears.

"You encourage me and support me and love me in so many beautiful ways, and I would love nothing more than if you would be my husband. Andrew Marshall, will you marry me?"

I move closer and drop down to my knees in front of her, taking her face in my hands.

"Absolutely."

And then I kiss her. Deep and slow. My tongue tangling with hers, the elation soaring through me unlike anything I've ever felt in my life.

When I pull back, she takes a few seconds to pull the ring from the box then slip it on my finger.

"You won't even have to change your initials," I say, the thought popping into my mind out of nowhere.

Briar giggles, the smile never leaving her face. "Perfect. That was my master plan all along."

I kiss her again, short ones, over and over, still in disbelief.

"I can't believe you proposed to me," I say, sticking my hand out in front of me to examine the traditional gold band and feeling like it looks perfect on my finger.

"Neither can I," she replies as both of us rise to our feet. "I hope you don't mind, but we have somewhere to be."

"Where?"

She leans to the side and shouts, "He said yes!"

I spin around at the sound of loud cheering, my eyes trailing back up to the deck to find a big group of friends and family outside under the fairy lights.

"Ready to go celebrate?"

I look back at her, taking in the joy in her eyes and the way her smile lights up her face. It's a moment I never want to forget. Ever. Then I slip my hand into hers.

"I'm ready for anything with you."

For more stories from Cedar Point and the Mitchell family,
make sure to visit

WWW.JILLIANLIOTA.COM/CEDAR-POINT

jillian liota

ACKNOWLEDGEMENTS
from the author

It seems like every book is an adventure, and *The Opposite of Falling* was no less. I wrote Briar and Andy's story with a very clear beginning, middle and end in-mind (which isn't normally how I write) and I'm truly shocked at how beautifully their story unfolded.

But also like every other book I've written, this story could not have come to fruition without the amazing, supportive, helpful minds, hearts and souls of some very important people

As always, thank you first and foremost to my husband, **Danny**. It never ceases to amaze me how much you step in to keep our lives moving forward when I'm lost at my computer for days and weeks with no end in sight. Thank you for your constant, unending, undying support and love. I love you forever.

Thank you to my family: **mom** and **dad**, **Caitlin** and **Kevin**, **Jordan**, **Cheyenne** and **Mike** (and now baby **Elena**!)...the only reason I can write healthy, loving and supportive families is because of you crazy lot.

To **The Jillybeans**, the greatest reader group to ever exist, and to my ever-supportive **ARC Team**, thank you for always helping me get the word out, for getting excited about new releases, and for caring about the words I put on the page.

My girlfriends, my book club, my **Kaipii Ohana** ladies: This is the first book I've written since we've all scattered the globe, and celebrating a book release doesn't feel the same without you. I love and miss you all and hope to see you again soon.

As always, to **C. Marie**, the best editor on the planet, for not only editing this body of work but for also helping keep me on schedule, your incredible skill is much appreciated.

And to everyone who decided to pick this baby up...whether you found it in a dusty Salvation Army shelf for a dollar or you bought a signed pre-order...whether you read it in KU or bought it or borrowed it...your choice to read something I've written is such a gift. Thank you for giving my words your time.

Looking forward to seeing you all back in Cedar Point very, very soon!

<3 always,
Jillian

Have you read the first book in the Cedar Point series?
Continue to the next page to read the first two chapters of

THE TROUBLE WITH WANTING

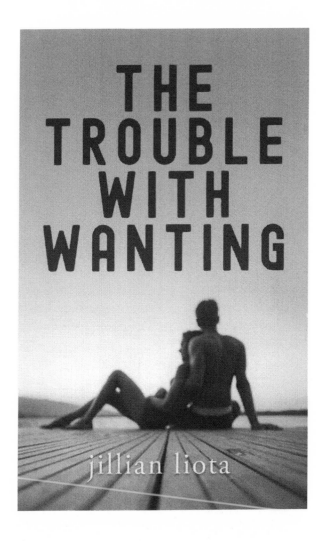

CHAPTER ONE

Boyd

"Paging Boyd Mitchell. Passenger Boyd Mitchell, please see the closest Summit attendant. Thank you."

The sound of my name over the intercom pulls my eyes from where they've been focused on my phone, my attention briefly drawn away from the work that dominates my focus at all hours.

I quickly scan the crowded seating area at Gate C21, taking in the host of cranky, agitated passengers waiting to board the flight, as if one of them might be able to confirm that I did, in fact, hear my name announced throughout the terminal.

I don't know why I do that, especially considering the fact that I'm usually traveling alone, but coming from a family as large as mine, one that is always in my business and full of a bunch of know-it-alls, I can't help but believe I'm never alone, no matter how much I wish it were so.

Grabbing my carry-on and tucking my jacket into the crook of my arm, I carefully make my way through the extended legs and belongings of my fellow travelers.

Boston Logan International Airport is always a busy place, but today it seems especially so with families and groups trying to squeeze in last-minute summer vacations before the weather on the east coast begins to turn crisp and school starts back up.

It's the reason I'm traveling today as well, even though I don't really have the time to take off from work to spend two weeks in Cedar Point.

But it's tradition, and my mother would absolutely pitch a fit if I were the one Mitchell child who bucked the tradition I had such a large hand in creating.

The last two weeks of August are *officially* Mitchell family time, and the idea that this two weeks on the calendar could belong to anyone or anything else is unjustifiable, work be damned.

It started when I left for college then continued when my sister Briar followed a year later. Originally, it was just a chance for us to catch up and reconnect with our family after long, boring summer jobs before starting school again.

My parents took that idea and cemented it into stone, turning those two weeks every summer into a non-negotiable family exclusive. Work doesn't matter. Significant others don't matter. Everything in life gets planned around those two weeks. Period.

A few times, my mom has even turned the end of August into a family reunion of sorts, inviting aunts and uncles and cousins back to the very town that grew them, our lakefront home and guesthouse turning into a glorified hostel with air mattresses galore and family members sleeping on couches.

I resent the obligation every year, wishing I were somehow brave enough to tell my mother I simply cannot take off of work this year, bold enough to tell her my employers are unwilling to be flexible.

But I don't think any of us Mitchell kids have ever had the

heart—or the balls—to break free from what's expected, or to let down my mother.

"Boyd Mitchell," I say when one of the Summit Airlines attendants finally nods me over to the counter. "I was called up just a minute ago."

Her head bobs once but her eyes never leave the screen in front of her as she types furiously. She must be writing a dissertation, because I can't imagine any airline computer program needing as much information as she's providing.

"Can I see some identification?"

I slide my driver's license forward, having already had it in my hand. The woman in front of me—Kimmy, her nametag says—takes a look at it, looks at me, and looks back at the ID before returning it.

Seems I've passed the test.

Suddenly, a wide and completely disingenuous smile covers her face. I almost want to ask her to go back to ignoring me.

"You've been upgraded to first class, Mr. Mitchell. Let me just print you up a new boarding pass and we'll get you all settled."

I usually hate flying Summit. It's the airline my job partners with, and I have to fly regularly for work. It does come with some nice perks like getting upgraded here and there, but the number of times my flight has been canceled or delayed due to mechanical issues is ridiculous.

I always wonder if I'm actually going to get to travel when I arrive at the airport, or if I'm going to be hanging out in the terminal for hours while I get booked on a new flight.

Most of my travel for work keeps me moving on short-leg flights around New England and the east coast, an hour here, two hours there, so when I'm stuffed into an economy seat, I don't stress over it. My flight to the west coast this morning, however, is an almost-7-hour doozy, so this upgrade couldn't have come at a more perfect moment. I can feel my broad shoulders and long legs silently thanking the upgrade gods for their gift.

As Kimmy makes the necessary adjustments, I turn and take another look around the gate.

City life is perfect for me. I'm an eyes down, nose to the grind kind of guy, and I don't make it a habit to pay attention to what is going on around me.

Having grown up in a small town, I know what it's like to have people paying attention to my every move at all hours of the day, and I remember what it was like to wish those eyes weren't watching and setting town tongues wagging. In Boston, if you give someone a little too much eye contact in a public space, you're likely to get a stream of foul language shouted in your face. You're supposed to keep your gaze down and stay out of other people's business.

Like I said, it's perfect for me.

But my therapist has been encouraging me to keep my head up, so I try to remind myself to take a look around a few times a day. Apparently, paying attention to the world around me will provide me with a 'new perspective.'

I don't know what she's hoping I'll find by watching a woman pick a wedgie then grab a French fry to put into her mouth, but I'm assuming there's a lesson to be learned in there somewhere.

"Hi, how are you?"

The bright voice next to me has my focus shifting down the counter to the short brunette approaching the attendant standing next to Kimmy.

This woman has her dark hair in a messy knot high on her

head and doesn't look to be wearing a lick of makeup, but damn if I'm not knocked on my ass by the most breathtaking smile I've seen in my entire life.

If only it were directed my way.

I shake my head and let out a quiet huff of laughter at myself, wondering where in the hell that thought came from. When was the last time I hoped any woman looked my way outside of a bar?

Apparently, my little laugh wasn't quiet enough, because the woman's eyes flit to mine for just a second, the tiny wrinkles next to her lids crinkling slightly as she acknowledges me. Then she turns back to talk with the woman at the desk.

"Here you are, sir."

I drag my eyes away from the brunette with the bombshell smile and look back at Kimmy. I blink once, feeling like I've missed something while I was staring, then take in the fact that she's slid my new boarding pass forward on the counter.

"Thanks." My response is quick as I retrieve the slip of paper and tuck it into my wallet.

"Absolutely. Can I do anything else for you?"

I shake my head, giving her a tight smile, and I'm turning to walk away when the brunette's words penetrate my mind.

"...never flown before and I'm a little nervous. Is there anything really important I need to know or be prepared for?"

Her voice, while upbeat and melodic, has the hint of nerves behind it, and it takes an effort to hide my smile. I don't think I've ever met an adult who has never been on a plane before. I wonder what that's like, to enter into a situation that's completely out of your control and totally unfamiliar.

Sounds horrible.

Truth be told, I also struggle with fear when it comes to flying. You can explain it to me a million different ways, but I still have trouble with the concept that something weighing close to 350 metric tons can just *float* in the air.

And yes, I know it doesn't actually float. Obviously. But that's what it feels like.

With the job I have working with startup tech companies and app developers across the Eastern Seaboard, though, saying I'm afraid of flying isn't an option. So, I've had to suck it up and rack up those frequent flier miles.

Thankfully, it has gotten easier over the years, the gripping panic as we lift off the ground easing to more of a mild anxiousness that passes as soon as I've had my first drink.

And whether I'm seated in first class or not, there is *always* a drink when I'm flying. Because whiskey just makes everything better.

I'm lucky enough to come from a family that did a lot of traveling when I was growing up. My parents wanted us to see the world and all the differences and opportunities that exist. My sweet mother, hoping to calm my troubled mind, always had a bible verse for me when we'd fly. *Blessed is the one who trusts in the Lord* or *He is a shield to those who put their trust in Him.*

I again take a seat in the gate area and stretch my long legs out in front of me, settling back in to wait until we're called to board.

I have no problem trusting in a higher being, whoever that is. I grew up in the church and believe in a greater plan, a God-like figure who loves us and wants us to have good lives and be good people.

What I *don't* trust is human ability. We are innately fallible, and technology created by fallible humans is literally designed to be imperfect. As a person who does not enjoy the state of *not* being in control, I find it difficult to put complete trust in something so precarious other than myself on this great earth.

Or, I guess, in the open air.

Thirty minutes later, I'm walking down the jet bridge, first class boarding pass clutched like a lottery ticket in my hand, when my phone starts to ring. The soft notes of the familiar ringtone echo down the corridor for a few seconds as I change my jacket from one hand to the other and dig my device out of my right front pocket.

I let out a disgruntled sigh when I see the name on the screen.

THING 1 WOULD LIKE TO FACETIME

Instead of ignoring him like I should, I swipe right and watch while the call connects, moving slowly behind the handful of other passengers boarding the plane in group one.

When the call goes from 'connecting' to 'connected,' Bishop's face appears and he gives me a big, childish smile.

"Hey, dickface."

The sound of my brother's voice booms out of my phone and fills the mostly silent walkway, my cheeks heating as I give an embarrassed wave to the elderly couple who turns to glare at me.

I quickly shuffle around to plug my headphones in, popping

one in my right ear before giving Bishop a nasty look.

"Thanks for that. It's not like I'm in public or anything."

His face morphs into that shit-eating grin that says he knows exactly what he's doing, and it makes me want to hang up on him.

"It's your own fault, Boy," he says.

"Boyd," I correct him for the millionth time since we were children, my tone firm.

I hate that obnoxious nickname. It's not even a real nickname as much as it is my brother enjoying his relentless antagonism. I've never fully understood his fascination with Boy, though, since *he's* the one who couldn't pronounce his Ds until he was ten.

"Oh. *Really?* I never knew your actual name before today. Thank you, *kind sir*, for enlightening me so that I might serve at your every request."

He bows his head, and I roll my eyes at the horrible British accent.

"What do you want?"

I step through the open plane door when the couple in front of me moves forward then stop again in the galley to wait for the people in front of me to take their seats.

The flight attendant in a purple and tan uniform gives me a big smile, and I manage one in return.

"I'm getting on the plane," I grumble, hoping he'll take that as a clue that he should get to his point, and quickly.

"Bell wants me to remind you that you promised to do the Kilroy hike with us this year. You know, since you manage to find an excuse every year not to go."

I let out a sigh, wishing I'd just put my phone in airplane mode a few minutes early.

The much-dreaded—at least by me—Kilroy hike is an over-nighter that requires lugging a massive pack into the mountains just outside our hometown. I enjoy a good run or swim and make frequent use of the gym by my house, but hiking long distances has never been my thing, something my younger siblings have never seemed to care about since they demand I go with them every year.

"It can be a new family tradition," my sister Bellamy said five years ago, excitement in her voice at the idea of all of us going together and pitching tents at the campground near the top.

It sounds like a miserable time to me, but as the only voice of dissent for most things in our family, my opinion rarely matters.

Luckily, I've always had an excuse, and it's getting to the point where I'm actually impressed by how long I've managed to get out of it.

Five years.

That's quite the record of evasion.

Last year, I had an emergency company teleconference that coincided with the date that worked for everyone. The year before that I hurt my knee playing a pickup rugby game with some friends from college. One year I even used a crazy hangover to my advantage, faking a cold that kept me bedridden, though how I was feeling after splitting a full bottle of whiskey with my friend Rusty wasn't any kind of a lie.

So.

I'll tell them whatever they want, but I'm not gonna be dragging my ass up a mountain any time soon.

"Yup. No worries."

I finally reach my row, lifting my carry-on into the overhead compartment. Picking up the pillow and blanket provided on my seat, I plop down, letting out a rush of breath as the people behind me surge past like a wave.

I love first class. Being 6'4", it is quite the squeeze to sit in economy. The extra width of an upgraded seat is wonderful for my broad shoulders, but it's the legroom that makes all the difference.

Summit Airlines seats are pretty snug in the main cabin, and I usually have to manspread my legs so I don't punch a hole through the seat in front of me. I always feel like shit as I apologize profusely to the people sitting next to me, knowing I'm not going to be able to change the fact that my legs are seriously encroaching on the tiny bit of real estate they've paid for.

Flying is bad enough, and I'm a firm believer that everyone should interact as minimally as possible. My rules of the air are as non-negotiable as this trip home at the end of every August.

Don't make small talk. Don't touch me. Don't sneeze on me. Don't ask me to move to go to the bathroom more than once. Don't set your things on my tray table. Don't hog the armrests. Don't kick my chair.

It's a give and take, and everyone has to be on board with it, which is rarely the case in economy, where the mentality is more like cattle jockeying for room to breathe.

First class, though? Everyone's in a completely different mood. Nobody is bothersome. Everyone is considerate. We get a drink and a meal and enough space for our limbs and torso. Most of the time, you're left alone instead of stuck sitting next to some overly verbose crazy person who wants to share their life story.

Having the ability to sit here in silence with my noise-canceling headphones and all the room I need for my long-ass legs on this long-ass flight?

I'm overjoyed.

No one would be able to tell by looking at my face, of course, since my default expression is the male version of resting bitch face.

What would that be called? Resting dick face?

Sure. That works.

"You get bumped to first?" Bishop's voice in my ear reminds me that I'm still on the phone with him, and I tilt the screen toward me to just in time to see him stuff a handful of Cheetos in his mouth.

"How could you tell?"

He shrugs. "There's always that weird pad behind your head when you're in first."

I turn to look and there is, in fact, a pad that rests on the seat.

When I look back at my brother, I see that he's set his phone up on a table and taken a few steps back, getting comfortable on a couch I would know anywhere. The tan walls and deep blue accents of my mom's living room are as familiar to me as the lines on my hands.

"You're already home, then?" I ask, doing a quick mental calculation of when my brother might have traveled to town.

"We got in a few days ago," he responds. The *we* can only be referring to himself and his twin sister, Bellamy.

The two of them drive each other—and the rest of us—bonkers, but I am certain there has never been a set of twins who were more of a *we* than Bishop and Bell.

"I bet Mom was thrilled you showed up early."

He doesn't catch the sarcasm in my voice.

Patty Mitchell normally loves surprises, but she's also a very planned person, and balancing those two parts of her personality can be…a challenge, to put it delicately.

So, having two of her kids show up a few days earlier than she planned—before the house is ready, *good gracious*—was probably enough to send her into some sort of tizzy.

But Bishop just shrugs, his youth reflected in that *whatever* kind of look he always seems to have on his face. It wouldn't occur to him that showing up early would aggravate our mother, because he struggles to think past his own opinion and needs.

"She seemed a little irritated at first, but she came around."

Of course she did, because her love for her kids took priority over the fact that she probably hadn't set up their rooms or stocked the fridge or any of the hundred other things she likes to do before we come home.

I might keep my nose down a lot, but that doesn't mean I don't pay attention, and I know my family, particularly my mother. That woman is nothing if not the ultimate host, even to her brood of selfish children.

Before I can say anything that might attempt to clue Bishop in on why our mom was cranky with him, a pair of green leggings stops right next to me.

"Excuse me."

I let my eyes trail up the short but toned legs, over sweet hips and lush curves before I finally meet the eyes of the woman who was standing next to me at the counter earlier.

A soft blue I've never quite seen before twinkles back at me.

"I think I'm sitting right there," she says, pointing to the empty seat next to me by the window.

"Who's that?" Bishop barks into my ear, and without another word, I close out the screen, ending the call.

"Sorry about that," I say, unbuckling my belt and standing up, moving into the aisle to let her pass by me.

"No problem." She gives me that smile again as we both settle down and buckle in.

"I'm Ruby," she says, her eyes bright and cheery, that smile looking to be permanently locked onto her face but still managing to be genuine. "I saw you earlier, at the counter, right?"

I nod but don't answer.

Part of me is kicking myself, because the gorgeous girl from the counter is sitting next to me and I should *absolutely* talk to her.

But the minute I say anything, I'm breaking one of my cardinal flying rules, which just opens the door to needless conversation I'm never in the mood for.

And yet, damn if I don't feel more than tempted to break that rule just to hear that lovely voice of hers again or have an excuse to look at her.

I waffle back and forth for a moment as I stare at the black screen of my phone. Ultimately, logic wins out, and I stay silent.

Seemingly unaware of my internal dialogue, Ruby is focused on the small bag she has in her hands. It's a backpack, I guess, made entirely out of patches. She unbuttons the top and sticks her hand inside, pulling out a green Moleskine notebook and placing it in the seatback pocket in front of her. Then she rebuttons the bag, drops it on the ground, and kicks it forward.

Rapid-fire texts from my brother begin to pop up, and a quick glance confirms he's asking about 'the hot girl' and wondering if I'm bringing someone home.

Instead of responding, I swipe it over to airplane mode and tuck it into the pocket in front of me.

My eyes scan the entering passengers, hoping to distract myself from the woman sitting next to me, but for some reason I can't seem to explain, I'm hyperaware of her. Her scent—jasmine—and the soft noises she makes as she explores her seat. Opening and closing the window. Her legs swinging slightly like a child's in a chair that's too big for them.

"What's your name?"

Her voice takes me by surprise and I look in her direction, finding her beautiful blue eyes twinkling at me, a small smile on her face.

"Boyd," I reply, my name popping out of my mouth, almost without my consent.

Since when do I give my name to the people I sit next to on planes? Since when does someone even *ask*?

Something moves in my peripheral vision, and when I look down, I see she's extended her hand.

In the first ten seconds of sitting next to me, she's broken one of my important flying rules by making unnecessary small talk even though I assumed my silence a few minutes ago would communicate that I'm not much for chatter.

And now she wants to break another rule by shaking my hand?

I look from her hand back to her eyes, finding her still wearing that same brilliant smile, before I feel compelled to place my hand in hers.

She gives it a firm squeeze, and damn if I don't feel that squeeze rush through my whole body, especially when she leans toward me just slightly.

Her voice is perky and happy and full of the qualities I typically find irritating in anyone giving me their attention.

But not today, apparently. Today, I find myself drawn in by her sweet smile and kind eyes, and I realize I'm leaning forward as well, mimicking her body language.

She lowers her voice, almost as if she's about to tell me a

secret—a secret I desperately want to know.

"Nice to meet you, Boyd."

CHAPTER TWO

Ruby

I hate everything about this tin can the second my foot crosses the threshold and I'm enclosed within the interior of the plane taking me to California.

I hate the stagnant air.

I hate the way the buckle feels pressed against my abdomen.

I hate that my roommate told me the entire flight is just everyone farting the entire time and breathing in each other's gas, so now I'm consumed with worry about breathing through my nose because the idea of inhaling particles from someone else's butt is making me want to gag.

But mostly? I hate how much I hate this.

I don't usually hate *anything*.

I'm the girl who claps for the performers on the T, even though they're in everyone's way. The girl who dances to the music in my headphones as I walk home from work. The person who looks people in the eye as I walk down the street and always has a smile.

I'm a massage therapist, for goodness sake. My whole job is to create a relaxing and peaceful environment for people and then work their bodies over so they let go of the mental worries that are causing them physical stress.

Even though I'm maintaining my composure and calm at the forefront of my mind, I can feel this tiny vein of toxic, sludgy pessimism and negativity slowly churning through my body.

I don't want to be on this stupid plane, going on a trip that was a stupid idea in the first place, to spend time with a stupid person I don't even want to see.

I let out a slightly shaky breath and tuck my hands under my thighs.

Okay, so none of that is actually true. I'm just nervous.

I've never flown before. I'm the only person I know who has never been on a plane, and that includes my neighbor Fiona's kids, who are 2 and 5 years old and have apparently flown "a skillion times" if you ask them.

It makes me feel like a bit of a crazy person, willingly buckling myself into a big metal machine that's supposed to defy gravity, but I figure millions of people do it every year and the number of times you hear about people dying in a plane crash isn't often enough to warrant hysteria.

Right?

Right.

Still, that doesn't help the fact that my stomach has decided to turn itself inside out.

I let out another breath, trying to steady my emotions and focus my mind on something soothing. I need to find a happy place, need to channel the calm I seek in my weekly yoga class and the peace of my daily meditations.

Taking in another deep breath, I remind myself that I have a reason for this trip, and I'm not going to back down from it just because I'm afraid of falling from the sky.

Fuck do I hate this.

I glance over at my seat buddy.

Boyd.

Such a strong, masculine name. It sounds like something out of a movie.

Even the way he said it, with that rich baritone striking a chord somewhere deep in my body, made him sound like he belongs on the silver screen. He could be a voiceover artist or someone who reads audiobooks. It wouldn't surprise me if I found out he was someone famous, or at least social media famous.

I mean…he's gorgeous.

It's not the kind of boyish charm I normally find attractive. It's much more serious, like he's got real-life responsibilities. The kind of guy who has an accountant and a barber and a favorite grocery store. A guy who drinks whiskey neat and smokes cigars and can fix his own dishwasher when it stops working.

A man kind of man.

As he stares at the phone in his hand and the flight attendants wander around finishing up their last checks, I allow myself a moment to study his profile.

Clean-shaven strong jaw, thick brows that slash across his face, and a prominent nose. Warm, chestnut eyes help to soften his otherwise harsh features, though even just based on the brief moment we spoke, he seems like the type of man who would *never* want to be described as *warm*.

When he stood up earlier to let me pass, I was overwhelmed by his size. He's probably an entire foot taller than I am, though that isn't very hard to do since I clock in at 5'3" at the start of the day when my spine hasn't fully compressed yet. I only get shorter from there.

I've always had a thing for tall guys. Call it genetics or hormones or some sort of subconscious, antiquated notion of wanting a big strong man to protect me, but damn if I don't have a thing for them big boys.

Tall and lanky has been my thing in the past—a common body type in the yoga world—but I can definitely get behind the more filled-out, muscular frame Boyd is carrying around.

Sure, I can pretend I was just being friendly when I introduced myself. I *do* love chatting with people I've never met before, but the truth is that I couldn't imagine anything better on a horridly long flight than chatting with the stud next to me—especially if it means I get to listen to that sexy-as-sin voice rumble my way.

I just wish he would smile or something, let that softness in his eyes translate onto his face a little bit.

He glances over at me and I realize I've been staring at him for way longer than is probably socially acceptable, so I smile and return my attention to the back of the seat in front of me, taking a deep breath through my nose and letting it out through my mouth, willing my body to calm itself.

This trip is going to be fine.

This trip is going to be fine.

This trip is going to be fine.

I click around on the little TV screen a bit, picking a few movies and marking them as favorites so I can watch them later. Fiona told me I should watch a movie the second I get on the plane so I can distract myself from takeoff, but as the plane lurches backward, away from the gate and out onto the tarmac, I let out a startled squeak. There is no way in hell my attention will be diverted.

The man sitting next to me shifts in his seat, and I settle on the thought that there *is* a way to distract myself. Boyd might be the strong, silent type, but I bet if I can find the right topic, he'll loosen up in no time.

"So, Boyd, are you from Boston, or are you connecting from somewhere else?"

He turns to look at me, and there's this little flutter in my chest when his eyes connect with mine.

It happened earlier, too, at the counter. When his gaze turned my way, it felt like I was in an elevator that suddenly dropped a foot. My stomach shot up and shoved my heart into my throat, punched a hole in my mind, and made my tongue trip over itself.

Thankfully, he doesn't seem to be aware of the way my internal organs are having seizures.

"I'm from California," is all he says. Then he returns his attention to his phone.

"Oh, cool," I say, resting my elbow on the armrest between us and plopping my chin in my hand. "Were you in Boston for business or pleasure?"

He clears his throat, taking his time before he responds.

"I originally came to Boston to go to college. I like it here, so I just never left."

"Wow," I say, impressed at that mentality of wanting to brave the world at such a young age. "How amazing are you to venture off on your own when you were just figuring things out? I don't know if I could have ever done something like that when I was eighteen. I mean, this is my first time on a plane and I'm twenty-four, so clearly the great adventurer I am not." I snicker. "So where did you go to school?"

Another pause. "MIT."

"Oh, wow!" I exclaim again, my eyebrows shooting up. "You must have a huge brain. I have a friend who's getting his PhD there and he's like, an absolute genius and a part of Mensa. So, yeah. That's amazing."

He looks like he enjoyed my compliment, but he doesn't say anything else. Maybe he's one of those men who struggles with knowing how to continue a conversation? I can help with that, definitely.

"So you graduated? What do you do now?"

He clicks his phone screen to black and lets out a sigh, resting his head against the seat and closing his eyes.

"I work with app developers, startup tech companies, stuff like that."

I nod, even though he can't see me.

"It must feel great to be doing something you're so good at. Well, I guess I'm making an assumption that you're good at it," I add, laughing at myself. "But I'm also assuming you wouldn't have a job doing it if you sucked. Is that what you always hoped to do? Is it, like, a dream come true to work in the tech field?"

His eyes open and he glances over at me then turns his attention to the screen on the seat in front of him. "Not really a dream come true, no, but it pays well."

He pushes some buttons and the screen lights up, but I'm stuck on what he said: *but it pays well.*

"Well, at least there's that," I say. "So, if you weren't doing a job just because it pays well…what would you do if you could do anything?" I ask, my voice kind of a whisper, my eyes wide with hope that he'll share with me.

I know he's technically a stranger. Well, okay, so not just technically. Literally—he is *literally* a stranger. And maybe it's weird that I'm asking such a personal question when I just met him ten minutes ago, but one of my favorite things is hearing about people's hopes and dreams, the things they want to accomplish that they worry are too big or too much for them to handle.

My roommate tells me all the time that I should be a professional encourager, although I'm not sure that's a real job. If it were? I would be so great at it. My favorite part about hearing people share their ambitions is that I can encourage them, build them up, tell them they're smart and amazing and worthy and they definitely have it in them to be and do whatever they want.

When Boyd looks back at me, I think I'm going to get that from him, this beautiful man I've just met on my very first plane ride. Maybe this will be a lifechanging moment where I can encourage him and believe in him.

"What would I do if I could do anything?" he asks, and I nod, a smile planted firmly on my face. "I'd watch a movie."

My smile drops slightly when he picks up a pair of noise-canceling headphones and plops them on his ears, turning his eyes away from mine.

"Can I get you something to drink before we depart?"

I tear my eyes away from Boyd's profile and look up at the flight attendant, who is hovering over us and waiting for a response. I glance once more at Boyd and see his eyes are glued firmly to the screen in front of him.

"Nothing for me, thanks," I say to the attendant, doing my best to give her a smile.

She looks to Boyd, who says he wants a whiskey neat—I *knew* it—and then she moves on to the next row of passengers.

I watch Boyd for a moment longer, feeling oddly wounded by his actions. Scanning back, I guess I could have paid more attention to the clues that he didn't want to talk to me instead of assuming he was hoping for a seat buddy to chat with.

Maybe I was being too nosy.

That's what my mom used to say about me, that I was a nosy parker, but she always said it with affection, like it was a part of me that I should be proud of, or at least not feel the need to apologize for.

I guess maybe some people don't see it that way.

I shift back from where I was leaning against the armrest, making sure I give Boyd his space, and stare blankly ahead, my fingers fiddling with my seatbelt.

Unable to distract myself, I pull out my notebook and flip to the next blank page, staring at it for a few minutes, willing my mind to create something for me to doodle so I can ignore the fact that I probably annoyed my seat neighbor.

I hate when I'm annoying.

It's the one thing I really do hate, for the most part. I'm a person who can stand up for herself, a person who has a drawer full of confidence and plenty of sass and happiness to spill over onto the floor in most instances.

But the last thing I want to be is annoying. A nuisance.

And this Boyd guy...the last thing I want is to make him uncomfortable, or for him to be upset with me. If I'm gonna sit next to him for the next seven hours, I should apologize or something.

I tap his shoulder lightly. When he doesn't react, I tap it again, a bit more firmly.

He takes his headphones off and looks at me.

"Sorry."

I want to slap my hand over my mouth as soon as I say the word, mostly because I shouted it at him and now several people are looking at us.

I lean forward and lower my voice.

"I'm sorry if what I said was nosy. I'm just…one of those people. You know? My mom always said I never met someone who wasn't a friend, probably because I talk their ear off and they don't get a choice whether they're my friend or not, but"—I shrug—"anyway, just…sorry if I did or said something that bothered you."

The silence between us is deafening, and all I can hear are the sounds of people shifting around in their seats and the airplane engine revving up then revving down again.

Is revving down a thing? I'm not sure, but that's what it sounds like.

He just stares at me, his jaw clenching and unclenching. Then he lets out a sigh and tucks his headphones into the pocket in front of him.

"Aeronautics," he finally says, his rich voice expanding and filling all the empty space around me, making my heart flutter wildly in its cage.

"Huh?"

"If I could have done anything, I'd have gone to school for aeronautics. My dream was to be a pilot, or at least someone who works for an airline, maybe streamlining services or finding new ways to advance the technology that improves flight." He shrugs. "But I'm afraid of flying, so my dad told me to major in something else."

I'm stunned silent, which doesn't happen to me often.

I thought maybe I'd get a polite nod from him in a best-case scenario, a glare and a grouchy retort in the worst case.

But he just spoke several sentences in a row to me. I wasn't expecting him to suddenly word-vomit and share his actual dream, and the sound of his voice has my heart moving just a bit faster, causing my tongue to trip over itself again.

When the silence stretches for a beat too long, I finally manage to spit something out.

"But you're flying today," I say. "Does that mean you've overcome your fear? Maybe you could go back for aeronautics now?"

He scrunches up his nose a little bit and shakes his head, accepting his drink and a napkin from the flight attendant.

"I'm just as afraid of flying today as I was when I was a kid. I understand lift and propulsion and engines and all the stuff you're supposed to understand when it comes to how an airplane flies." He shakes his head again. "It still doesn't sit well with me."

I laugh. "Oh thank *god*." And then I keep laughing.

He gives me a questioning look.

"I'm just thankful that other people are afraid too, that I'm not some sort of freak who is completely irrational. It's what everyone I know made me feel like before I left for this trip, and let me tell you—implying someone is stupid for being afraid doesn't ever take away their fear."

I didn't appreciate the people who tried to make me feel like I was an idiot for being afraid. Fear is fear, and shaming someone does nothing but make you an asshole.

"You're definitely not a freak, and you're not alone in being afraid," Boyd says. "Most people are afraid of flying to some degree. It's all about the unknown. That's what most fear is. My mom has always said fear is just rooted in a lack of understanding."

I play his words over again in my mind, letting them percolate. The idea has merit, but I don't think that's what drives my fear.

He must see my disagreement on my face. "You don't agree?"

I shake my head.

"I mean, I think what your mom said is true to some degree, but I don't think fear is caused by a lack of understanding. We feel fear because of love."

The face he makes when I say it has me laughing.

"That is…one of the strangest things I've ever heard," he says, lifting the tumbler of whiskey to his mouth to take a sip.

"Why? Is it so implausible to believe we are afraid because we have something to lose?"

He looks like he's about to refute my opinion but pauses, and I can tell by his expression that he's mulling it over.

"Sure, it sounds ridiculous when I use a word like *love*, but look at you—you *just* told me you understand how planes work yet you're still afraid. If you're afraid to fly, it's probably less about not understanding how flying works and more about not wanting to die, right?"

He's silent, so I barrel on.

"And why don't you want to die? Because you love your life, or your kids or your spouse, or your job or your church or whatever else that matters. That fear builds because you imagine what life would be like without you for your family, or the things you would miss out on with the ones you *love*."

He's quiet for a moment. I've never seen someone so clearly working a thought over in his mind, his brows pressed together until they're almost one long caterpillar.

I assume he's gearing up to disagree with me, but what he says is a surprise.

"Let's say I agree with you—how would you explain that a lot of people are *not* afraid of flying?" Then he smirks. "A lack of love?" he tacks on, sarcasm in his voice.

I shake my head with a smile. "It's not a *lack* of *love*. It's about the *existence* of *logic*. Think about it this way: Some people believe there isn't a reason to be afraid because of data or science or whatever other argument that exists about safety. Other people ignore legitimate reasons to be afraid and choose not to be because they've accepted that death is inevitable and sometimes weird things happen."

He nods, his lips pursed, and I think I've won the argument—although I don't think we were in an actual argument as much as we were just debating something. My mom says there isn't a difference, but there totally is.

"So which one are you?" he asks, leaning closer.

"What do you mean?"

He grins. "Are you afraid because of love? Or are you afraid because you lack logic?"

I burst into laughter, enjoying the look of surprise on his face, his eyes wide and his own grin growing.

"Definitely both," I reply, enjoying the rumble of laughter that slips out of his own mouth, the two of us laughing together.

It's a good feeling.

"Sorry for rambling," I say, giving him another smile. "It's way too early in the morning to be debating something so highbrow. So, how 'bout them Sox, huh?"

Boyd looks at me with a twinkle in his eyes, a kind of friendly charm I wasn't expecting from him, regardless of how well we got on with our chat.

What I wouldn't give to look at that kind of handsome joy every day for the rest of my life.

A stupid thought, sure, but still true.

"I bet you ten dollars you can't name a single player on the team this year."

I narrow my eyes, trying to hide my smile as I shake my head. "I'm not a gambling girl."

"You'd gamble if you knew you were probably going to win." His response is as quick as lightning. "People only choose not to gamble when they're afraid they'll lose."

"That is so not true." I giggle. "Some of us poor folk don't gamble because we can't take the risk. Not all of us are first class aficionados with money to throw around willy-nilly."

"Nobody says *willy-nilly* anymore."

I snort. "Clearly that's false, because I just did."

He bites his lip and shakes his head, and I can't help the little thing that keeps bouncing around in my chest.

We like him, it tells me. *We like him a lot.*

Is this flirting? We are definitely flirting, right? I hope so, because it has been far too long since I've enjoyed a good flirt sesh with someone as handsome as Boyd.

That's a lie.

I've *never* flirted with someone as handsome as Boyd. He is in a league of his own.

Before I can say anything else, the plane lurches forward, and it feels like my stomach is going to fall out of my body.

My eyes slam shut and my throat closes up, my hands gripping the armrests for dear life as the plane barrels down the runway, all the good feelings from my talk with Boyd rushing out of me with a surreal quickness.

It's going to be okay.

It's going to be okay.

It's going to be okay.

I'm like that for who knows how long before I feel a hand on top of mine, the warmth and roughness surprising me enough that my eyes fly open, taking in the man sitting next to me.

He lifts my hand and twists his fingers in mine, the sensation robbing me of my voice—and maybe my sanity.

For the rest of my life, I'll remember exactly what he says to me. Not just the words, but the soothing tone of his voice and the earnest caring in his eyes, so surprising from someone I was expecting to ignore me for the entire flight.

"It's okay to be afraid," he says. "I can't take that feeling away from you, but I can hold your hand until it's over so you know you're not alone."

RUBY AND BOYD'S LOVE STORY CONTINUES IN

THE TROUBLE WITH WANTING

AVAILABLE ON AMAZON AND KINDLE UNLIMITED

ABOUT THE AUTHOR
jillian liota

Jillian Liota is a southern California native currently living in Kailua, Hawaii. She is married to her best friend, has a three-legged pup with endless energy, and acts as a servant to two very temperamental cats. When she isn't writing, she is traveling, reading a good book, or watching Harry Potter.

Always.

To connect with Jillian:

Join her **Reader Group**
Sign up for her **Newsletter**
Rate her on **Goodreads**
Visit her on **Facebook**

Check out her **Website**
Send her an **Email**
Stalk her on **Instagram**
Add her on **Amazon**

jillian liota

ADDITIONAL TITLES

from jillian

THE KEEPER SERIES
the keeper
keep away

LIKE YOU SERIES
like you mean it
like you want it

HERMOSA BEACH SERIES
promise me nothing
be your anything
give my everything

THE CEDAR POINT SERIES
the trouble with wanting

all titles available on amazon and kindle unlimited